Apart from Love
Panda Books

Chi Li, born in Hubei Province in 1957, is the founder of the "Neo-realistic Group" and is one of the most popular writers in China today. She has worked as a nurse and an editor of a literary magazine before taking up writing as a fulltime occupation. A national award winner, she has written a great number of stories, many of which have a growing foreign readership.

Apart from Love

Chi Li

Panda Books

First Edition 2005

ISBN 7-119-03663-7

© Foreign Languages Press, Beijing, China, 2005

Published by Foreign Languages Press

24 Baiwanzhuang Road, Beijing 100037, China

Website: http://www.flp.com.cn

E-mail Address: info@flp.com.cn

sales@flp.com.cn

Distributed by China International Book Trading Corporation

35 Chegongzhuang Xilu, Beijing 100044, China

P.O. Box 399, Beijing, China

Printed in the People's Republic of China

CONTENTS

CONTENTS

Editors' Note

WHEN the Cultural Revolution came to an end in 1976, especially after 1978 when China adopted the policy of reform and opening to the outside world, one tidal wave of creative writing after another has washed over the face of Chinese literature. Chinese women writers have added their indelible inscriptions to this New Age Literature. Their works present a good cross-section of life in China. Among these writers are Shen Rong, Wang Anyi, Zhang Jie, Cheng Naishan, Tie Ning, Lu Xing'er, Chi Li, Zhang Xin, Fang Fang, Chi Zijian, and Bi Shumin, to name only a few.

The late 1970s and the early 1980s was a period of literary renaissance, thanks to the relaxed political climate and growing democracy in China. Many women writers emerged, dealing with all kinds of subject matters and attracting widespread attention. The school of "wound literature" took shape, which mainly focuses on people's lives during and after the Cultural Revolution. Shen Rong's "At Middle Age" raises the problems of middle-aged professionals, who enter the new age with marks left on them by the Cultural Revolution and who have to divide their time between career and family and more often than not neglect

one or the other. Cheng Naishan, perceptive, objective, pene-
trating, and compassionate, captivates her readers with stories
about the lives and loves, the destinies and the emotional entan-
glements of the industrial and business families of China's
metropolis, a class which has weathered political vicissitudes before and during the Cultural Revolution. "The Blue House," her
representative work, is one such story describing the turmoil going through the Gu family, the former steel giant in Shanghai
who owned the Blue House.

Women writers were truthful spokesmen for the youth who
suffered during the Cultural Revolution. Problems of the young
people of the time were frankly dealt with, such as their disrupted education; lack of interesting employment; the difficulties
met with by boys and girls sent from town to the countryside;
the low incomes and overcrowding which threaten to break up
young couples' marriages; their mental confusion after the turbulent years in which traditions were thrown overboard and bu-
reaucracy, nepotism and corruption were rampant. Zhang Jie's
"Love Must Not Be Forgotten" had aroused considerable interest
as well as much controversy. Boldly unconventional, idealistic
and intensely romantic, the story sheds interesting light on the
changes in the attitude to love in socialist China, still strongly
influenced by feudal ideas about marriage at the time.

While reform was still dawning on the Chinese horizon,
Zhang Jie captured the historic social changes of this mood of
reform in her important novel, "Leaden Wings." First published
in 1981 and an instant bestseller, the story has as its central
theme the modernization of industry. The publication of this
book aroused further controversy. Exposing various abuses and
man-made obstacles to modernization, it came under fire for

"attacking socialism." But many readers welcomed it as painting a truthful picture of modern Chinese society of the time.

In the mid-1980s, seeking out and examining the roots of Chinese culture became the dominant trend, hence the term "root literature." Leading this trend was Wang Anyi's novella "Xiaobao Village," which dissects the rights and wrongs of traditional moral values by portraying what happens behind closed doors in a tiny village that is generally extolled as a paragon of humanity and justice. The author's rich choice of language and her profound grasp of the cultural life and nature of people in a small village, places "Xiaobao Village" on a par with Ah Cheng's "The Chess Master" and Han Shaogong's "Father."

Wang Anyi, who represents the writers whose formal education was disrupted by the Cultural Revolution knows from first-hand experience the problems of young people who have returned from communes to the cities. In her stories, a sense of humanism appears. She is not one simply to condemn or write off the 10 years of her generation lost because of the Cultural Revolution. In her creative world, authentic human feelings live through the traumatic days of the Cultural Revolution. They are perpetuated along with—perhaps in tandem with—the old class relations, with all their old prejudices, suspicions, and tolerances, too. Wang Anyi analyzes China with an imagination that seems nourished by both pre-revolutionary and post-revolutionary culture. Her stories are alive with such tensions and contrasts. Her stories "Lapse of Time" and "The Destination" have won literary prizes in China.

In the late 1980s, Neo-realism came in vogue in Chinese fiction, of which Chi Li, author of "Trials and Tribulations," and Fang Fang, who wrote "Landscape," are both hailed as founding members.

Chi Li is an active writer on the Chinese literary scene. Her stories, like the above-mentioned "Trials and Tribulations" and "Apart from Love," mostly focus on the female world, their love and marriage, though her attitude has nothing to do with feminism. The detailed and earthy descriptions conjure up a vivid picture of life in the late 1980s.

Fang Fang began by writing humorous stories, which are full of caustic and witty remarks. She then turned to stories about magic in which her characters summon up wind and rain like spirits. But she later changed her style again. She is sort of unpredictable, constantly surprising readers and critics because she does not confine herself to a certain style. One of the most popular female writers in present-day China, she is best known for her stories about urban life, with characters ranging from intellectuals to laborers. Her "Landscape" depicts the relationships between an illiterate docker and his nine children, and the hardships they endure in a raw struggle to survive.

During the transitional 1990s, New Age Literature came to an end. The transformation of social and economic patterns in China has given rise to multiple literary patterns with writers of various pursuits locked in a keenly contested competition. The principle of literature has changed from serving life to serving man's existence, and from presenting people's aspirations for life and the historical destiny of collectives to depicting ordinary people's existence in this world. Works by women writers started to describe the petty vexations of people working to earn and survive in the mundane world. Neo-realism, first appearing in the late 1980s and represented by Chi Li and Fang Fang, has developed to a new height. Chi Li's relatively recent stories, "To and Fro" and "Life Show," have presented a vivid, realistic picture of the life of women in the fast-changing Chinese society. Bi Shumin, a doctor-turned woman writer, focuses on specific social and e-conomic phenomena, revealing the contradictions in modern so-ciety and the true nature of man in the face of the social and e-conomic reforms in China. But her works don't just stop there. Her novella "An Appointment with Death" and full-length novel *The Red Prescription* aim for a broader philosophical meaning beyond the superficial implications of subjects like hospice care, life and death, drug use and rehabilitation.

Today, China's relaxed political climate and growing democ-racy have resulted in more truthful writing and a wider range of themes. Love, social injustice, the value of the individual, hu-manism and other subjects formerly taboo are being fearlessly tackled by women writers—often with an unabashed display of emotion.

As editors, we hope that this series of women writers' works, compiled and published by Foreign Languages Press, will open a door to the world of Chinese women writers and to the everyday life of ordinary Chinese, for our readers who are interested in Chinese literature and China as well.

Apart from Love

SCALPELS apart, it was sport that fascinated Zhuang Jianfei most. Although he was always a loser no matter what ball games he might play, he was great at being a spectator, and such an expert that he corrected the misjudgment of a firstrate international referee or point out the inexperience of a coach.

He had been watching sporting events ever since he was in his mother's womb. Back then it was merely his mother's courtesy towards his father, but he seemed to have benefited from this antenatal education. The past thirty years had convinced him that he and sport had some kind of special relationship. A sports field was invariably the scene of bustling activity, full of vigour and vitality, free from polished deception or affectation; full of strength and beauty and fierce competition. Here the wisdom of fighting was pooled without the commonplaces of life. It was the distillation of life itself. Could a man really be called a man if he was not crazy about sport?

So before today, it was beyond Zhuang Jianfei's wildest thoughts that he would miss the Uber Cup women's badminton final and the Thomas Cup men's. He simply had to watch an international-level final if a Chinese team was involved. The whole surgical department and then the entire hospital had learned about this passion of his over the six years he had worked here. The department head avoided putting him on night duty if there was an important sports event that evening. Just like this time.

Mr Zeng was a doctor-in-charge, known as the second scalpel in the surgical department. He was in his early fifties with clear fair skin and good taste in clothes. In recent years his heart had been playing up so he had given up watching games despite his habitual craving. He was now forced to place all his hopes on explanations and outcome. He thought China's sport announcer Song Shixiong's voice was too sharp, he was too passsionate and the words he used were often inappropriate. Zhuang Jianfei, then, had become his ideal guide. It so happened that afterwards Zhuang loved to ponder over a match with somebody. And so young and old had formed a perfect team. Before leaving work today, Dr Zeng waited for Zhuang Jianfei at the bottom of the stairs. "See you tomorrow, Dr Zhuang," he said. Zhuang Jianfei replied with their mutual understanding, "Yes, tomorrow."

If it hadn't been for the Uber Cup final that evening, they would not have bothered to say anything. As colleagues who saw each other every day, they might at most have said "Hi".

As usual, Zhuang Jianfei's wife Ji Ling had their dinner ready. What was different was that Zhuang Jianfei did not pace around the dinner table rolling up his sleeves and commenting: "Hey, great food!" He kept looking at the clock.

Before they finished the meal, the game began. Putting down his bowl, Zhuang Jianfei seated himself in front of the TV set in the lounge.

The final was between China and Korea. As everyone knew, this small country Korea, in just a few years, had sprung into the sports world like a hungry tiger down from a mountain, as if wishing to swallow the whole world. This game would be a bloody battle.

The first women's singles player for the Chinese team was Li Lingwei. She looked somewhat sluggish. The announcer explained that this queen of the world badminton circles had just suffered from several days of high fever. Patting the back of his chair, Zhuang Jianfei all of a sudden broke into a sweat. Sure enough, Li Lingwei lost the first set. "Too bad!" Zhuang Jianfei shouted at the screen. The team doctor must have sneaked into his position through a back door, a fellow who was interested only in going abroad and gaining some foreign currency. How come he could not even cure a high fever? He should have given her an infusion of sylvite. How could she get the strength otherwise?

Fortunately Li Lingwei kept up appearances after all. She won the second and the third sets and gained one precious point for China.

Zhuang Jianfei wiped his sweat with his hand and welcomed the second women's singles player Han Aiping with warm applause. He sensed a redoubled feeling of empathy towards all players from Hubei Province as if he was related by blood. Great! Han Aiping was tough and well seasoned. She beat a small young Korean girl with a sure hand in almost no time. Since she had won the first and the second sets, there was no need to play the third.

China's third women's singles player was the new talent Gu

Jiaming, A little girl from Hubei again. Zhuang Jianfei could not help feeling inspired with enthusiasm.

Before Gu Jiaming entered the court, Zhuang Jianfei's wife Ji Ling without any warning stepped squarely in front of the screen.

"I bet you Gu Jiaming will win!"

She did not move aside.

"What's the matter with you?"

Zhuang Jianfei did not realize until this moment that his wife looked extremely serious. He hoped that nothing would go wrong, particularly at a time like this. With a hopeful smile to head off a disaster, he said,

"Come on! Sit here and watch the game with me. My mother always does with my father."

"I am not your mother," said Ji Ling.

Zhuang Jianfei found it impossible to go on smiling.

"Well. The third round of singles has started."

Turning her head away, Ji Ling stood there firm and erect.

Zhuang Jianfei demanded, "Please step aside."

Ji Ling just turned her head in another direction.

"Ji Ling, I request you step aside!"

"Great!" the announcer exclaimed in high excitement behind Ji Ling.

Ji Ling gave a smile and swayed a bit. The TV went off with a crackle.

"What are you doing!" Zhuang Jianfei jumped up.

"Turning off the TV."

"Who asked you to?"

"No need for me to ask anybody for approval."

"You really are being unreasonable!"

"Who's unreasonable? If you just try to remember, you'll real-ize that you have looked at nothing but the clock ever since you entered this house. I haven't said anything. I've been working in the kitchen all the time. I've been waiting for you to ask me."

"Ask you what?"

Zhuang Jianfei quickly searched his memory. There seemed nothing to ask. All was normal. He continued: "I don't remem-ber needing to ask anything. If so, please remind me. Now quickly turn the TV on."

Shaking her head sadly, Ji Ling closed her eyes. When she opened them again they were brimming with tears. "No! I won't!" she shouted at him, her voice full of grievance.

Zhuang Jianfei seized her arm and tried to drag her aside while Ji Ling, struggling to hold her ground, kicked him.

The TV was now turned on. Gu Jiaming smashed a beautiful killing smash. The announcer exclaimed again, "Wonderful!"

Ji Ling rushed at the TV and pressed the button with all her strength. Zhuang Jianfei followed and clasped her around her chest. Ji Ling scratched her husband with her sharp varnished nails. In an instant, she had won. She had occupied the TV set, her hair dishevelled like a lion. She was crying: "Well! You've come to blows! You've hit me, Zhuang Jianfei, you son of a whore!"

Staggering back a few steps in astonishment, Zhuang Jianfei stared at his wife as if she were some apparition. This was cer-tainly not the Ji Ling he had been in love with for two years and married to for half a year. His Ji Ling was the studious pure sweetheart from whose mouth no dirty words had been ever heard. At this awkward moment, he even felt like laughing. The magical change made him feel cheated. But who had cheated him? Who had ever cheated him?

Beating her chest with fists, Ji Ling continued to yell tearfully: "Hit me. Hit me here if you have the guts! Go on, beat me to death. You are a damned cowardly bastard if you don't dare!"

Zhuang Jianfei had gripped a cup in his hand.

This cup was part of a high-quality imported coffee set, jade green in colour with an exotic design. The past came clearly into view. It had been the day just before their wedding. Braving heavy rain, the two of them ran around all over the three towns of Wuhan in search of a coffee set to their liking. They were disappointed and tired as they dragged their way into a shop to take a breather. It happened to be a newly opened wholesale store and up there on the shelf this translucent jade green coffee set sparkled with lustre. Both of them spontaneously uttered "Oh" and pointing, said, "Let's get it!"

They bought it. Each cup cost 8.99 yuan. Neither of them hesitated or minded about the high price.

Ever since then the coffee set had been cherished.

Zhuang Jianfei raised the cup and smashed it against the floor. Amidst the sound of breaking, to his great satisfaction, he heard Ji Ling's voice shrieking sharper than broken glass:

"Ah! You son of a bitch!"

The Bank of China was a lofty Western-style building made of huge blocks of rock. Zhuang Jianfei climbed to the top of its stairs this June evening. He sat down heavily and finished five ice lollies at one go. After having re-evaluated his marriage, he cool-headedly discovered the basic reason why he had wanted to get married. That was: sex.

Zhuang Jianfei was born into an intellectual family. His father was an expert in critical interpretation of ancient Chinese texts and his mother a professor of contemporary literature in a Chinese department. His parents were both career-minded. When Zhuang Jianfei was still a little boy they both made contributions in their respective fields. Zhuang Jianfei grew up, as a Chinese would say, amid seas of knowledge and mountains of books. He was gifted, intelligent and fond of book learning. He was at the top of his class and grade all the way from primary school to university. His shortcoming was well concealed: he was always trying to do something beyond the bounds of propriety, hiding away from the eyes of others.

He experienced a special kind of pleasure from his genitals when he was still in his infancy. Nobody prompted him. He learned it all by himself. Just before he left primary school, he learned from *A Handbook for Barefoot Doctors* that there was a disgusting name for this thing: masturbation. So for a while he stopped his underground activities. However, puberty soon overwhelmed him with the momentum of an avalanche. Late at night, shutting himself in his small room, he visualized to his heart's content the pretty girls whom he wouldn't deign to look at during the day and satisfied himself wantonly. In the daytime he was the son of a professor, a good student, followed with interest and praised everywhere. He found favour in the eyes of many a girl student yet treated them indifferently one and all. He didn't allow them to visit him at home in order to gain his parents' trust.

His mother would have been so distressed that she might have preferred to die if she had got to know about it.

Zhuang Jianfei's method was foolproof. Foolproof for many

long years. Anyone who thinks that men who masturbate are invariably effeminate or have narrowing amorous eyes is really fooled. The difference between a gentleman and a hooligan is just that the former hopes to get married after masturbation while the latter goes as far as rape or promiscuity. Zhuang Jianfei was a gentleman. His desire was to get married.

In theory, getting married does not simply mean securing a sleeping partner. Of course Zhuang Jianfei was clear about this. Marriage means setting up a family, finding a lifelong companion and creating a stable social unit. Based on such sensible considerations, Zhuang Jianfei restrained his yearning for the other sex, suffering hunger and thirst until the age of twenty-nine and a half years old when he married Ji Ling.

It seemed now that attaining such a mature age did guarantee reliable judgment in dealing with such matters. The problem was that he was in that hungry state where a person ceases to be choosy about his food.

Why did he have to do it by stealth? Why should he have suffered the hunger and the thirst? He felt a grudge but did not know against whom.

Sitting on the top step of the Bank of China eating ice lollies, Zhuang Jianfei stared at the street in a trance. He thought of Mei Ying with mixed feelings.

Mei Ying was a surgeon in another Wuhan hospital. She was the type of woman with a full figure and graceful bearing. Her body sent out messages that she was within sight but not within reach. At an ordinary small academic meeting, Zhuang Jianfei and Mei Ying sat next to each other. For the whole afternoon, Zhuang Jianfei got an indistinct whiff of savoury milk that came from underneath the flimsy summer wear of the seat next to him. Usually she would have smelt of disinfectant. She put on a pair of gold-rimmed glasses when taking notes, which she otherwise took off and placed on the folding table. In the middle of the meeting, Mei Ying accidentally knocked her glasses off the table. Zhuang Jianfei did not let the glasses land on the floor but caught them nimbly as if fishing out the moon from the bottom of the sea.

Only then did Mei Ying cast her eyes at Zhuang Jianfei. "Thanks," said she. "Presbyopic glasses," she added.

On hearing "presbyopic glasses", Zhuang Jianfei could not help laughing. He joked, "Must be a souvenir from your grandmother."

Mei Ying laughed too.

After a while, Mei Ying said in a low voice, "My name is Mei Ying."

"My name is Zhuang Jianfei."

They laughed together, finding it funny to introduce each other in such a serious way.

The meeting came an end and everyone else dispersed. Only these two hesitated. They had talked very congenially and had just come to the point where they would like to have continued. So they went together to a restaurant for dinner.

Even though it had been already over three years now, Zhuang Jianfei could still accurately recall the details of that meal.

Walking ahead of him, Mei Ying led the way directly into a private room on the second floor of Lotus Sichuan Restaurant. In a poised and an easy manner, she sat down and briskly yet courteously gave her order to the waiter, as the mistress of the house would to her servant: "Just some ordinary dishes. Diced

chicken with red chili, saute pork liver, shredded beef with special hot sauce and a big bowl of vegetable soup."

Zhuang Jianfei inwardly gasped in admiration and felt
ashamed of his inferiority. He had been contented to enjoy a
good family upbringing. Now it dawned upon him that he was
totally ignorant about food. He was captivated by Mei Ying's
demeanour.

After the dinner, their hearts as well as their stomachs were
hot. As they strolled along a small path in an unknown park,
Mei Ying showed Zhuang Jianfei a way forward in his career.

"You shouldn't be doing abdominal cavity surgery. In Wuhan
that's Qiu Fazu's territory. He once studied in Germany and has
a German wife backing him up. No matter how beautifully you
may flourish your scalpel, you'll never outstrip him in reputation. Kept down by him for a decade or two, and you'll be a loser for life. Do what you can at once and transfer to thoracic
cavity surgery. There are famous experts in this area too, but
you are young and full of energy, your eyes and hands are quick,
and you've got a strong wrist. There's no doubt you can do better than them. I think you've the potential to take advantage of
rapidly developing new techniques and thoracic cavity surgery is
particularly popular right now. You will get a good head start in
this field."

When he thought of all the experts all over the country in this
branch of the profession, Zhuang Jianfei, green as he was, naturally felt sceptical.

"Can I do it?"

"Yes!"

Mei Ying gently thumped his solid arm with her fist. "I won't
be wrong in my prediction. You are a ... hard to come by."

Later Zhuang Jianfei gave Mei Ying's suggestion serious thought and decided to accept. Soon after he had changed his academic field, he was unexpectedly involved in rather complicated surgery for a ductus arteriosus. Still more unexpected was his miraculous success in the operation. It was a sensation throughout the hospital and many people looked at him with new eyes.

Zhuang Jianfei went secretly to Mei Ying's home. In her homely night gown with her hair tied up, Mei Ying was radiant with happiness. On the table was a celebratory meal. As soon as the door was closed behind him, Zhuang Jianfei embraced her feverishly. Nestling close to him, Mei Ying caressed his newly shaven bluish stubble and asked what he would like to drink, wine or spirits.

Zhuang Jianfei answered, "I'll just drink you!"

When Mei Ying's body was laid in front of him, however, he appeared clumsy and shy for this was his first attempt.

Mei Ying laughed. "I am more than willing to help you. I mean it!" she said.

Zhuang Jianfei had always been a brilliant pupil. Within that single short night, he not only completed his apprenticeship, but even showed the possibility of surpassing his master. At dawn, Mei Ying surrendered. She shed tears in the dim light behind the dark curtains.

"Why were you not here when I was young?"

Zhuang Jianfei came the next night. No words this time: just action. The scope reached beyond the limits of the bed. The battlefield was extended to the floor, the chairs—everywhere. Before he took his leave, Zhuang Jianfei declared, "I'll marry you!"

Mei Ying looked down.

"My son is doing an M.A. in America, and my husband is lecturing there. They'll be back in just six months."

"I don't care. I'll marry you!"

"I'm already forty-five, old enough to be your mother."

"I don't care about your age!"

"But I ... long for their return every day."

Zhuang Jianfei felt prickles running down his spine.

"Is that true?"

"Yes."

"Such being the case, why do you...? It's because I don't have enough strength, isn't it?" Zhuang Jianfei said in a strangled voice. "Not strong enough to separate you, right?"

"Wrong. I also long for a grandchild day and night. That you can't possibly give me."

Gazing at him, Mei Ying started again: "It's my fault. Don't come any more." She walked over to him, bringing with her that savoury milk smell. "You will understand one day, my child."

Child. That was what she called him. Her manner and tone were exactly those of an old granny who has experienced many of life's vicissitudes.

But Ji Ling. She was born and bred in Flowery Building Street in Wuhan. In her own words when there was an argument with a customer: "You're right. I'm a real petty Hankou girl."

Every Wuhanese knew Hankou's Flowery Building Street. The street had once seen women in heavy makeup and the joy of "spring" in songs and dances. In the past it had been sign of Hankou's prosperity. Now the vermillion railings were faded and the young women had aged. Moss grew everywhere in the deep narrow lanes between the tile-roofed houses. In all four seasons, wet or dry, a shabby atmosphere pervaded the street, shamelessly betraying its air of coquettishness.

Yet Ji Ling's mother had said over and over again to her five daughters: "I've never been a whore."

Ji Ling's mother was a sloppy woman who had become old and fat. She was fond of playing poker all alone in the central room, door wide open, a cigarette dangling from the side of her flabby lips and the ash dropping bit by bit down the greasy front of her clothes. She didn't care. But the moment a situation arose, she could swiftly change her appearance into one that was astute, capable and spotless. She knew well the ways of the world so she had equipped herself with several different appearances. Of her five daughters, it was Ji Ling that she doted on most. For it was Ji Ling, she felt, who most took after her.

"Nonsense!" Ji Ling denied this assertion, much annoyed. Her mother just chuckled.

Ji Ling's father's ancestors had lived in Flowery Building Street for generations. However anyone else might regard the street was their business; her father took it as an honour. He often put on airs and indiscriminately kicked aside the farmers' vegetable baskets which sat in the way. "You yokels," he said in a derogatory tone. Not even many of the Central Government leaders could stand their yokelish origins being revealed. But Ji Ling's father was a city dweller. His ancestors had lived in this big city for generations. At the age of thirteen he had gone to work as an apprentice in the Fragrant Teashop. The tea had given him a pale, greenish look and thin, weak fingers and an artful mouth. It was artful in two ways: sampling tea and chatting.

He was a person who could be incredibly loquacious with whoever came his way. All five daughters were disgusted with their
father. They openly referred to him as "Stick Insect" without
saying it to his face. Quite a few of his daughters' boyfriends
had broken away because the father glued himself to them, re-
lating anecdotes of Flowery Building Street and the art of
savouring tea.

The mother would often lead four of the daughters in verbal
battles against the father. Ji Ling never got involved. She just
gave her father a disappointed glance. More than anyone else in
the family, she made her father feel nervous.

Ji Ling was a fine woman.

She did well in her studies at school. But at the university entrance examinations she suffered some setbacks. She failed
twice. Her mother then tried to force her father to retire so that
Ji Ling could take his job. But Ji Ling said, "No. I'll try and
find a job on my own." For this reason the father felt deeply
grateful to his youngest daughter.

Unlike other girls in Flowery Building Street, Ji Ling's style in
dressing was simple but tasteful. She did not perm her hair or
wear eye shadow. At most she would slightly touch up her eyebrows and wear pale pink lipstick. In her light-coloured blouse
and a dark skirt, she looked just like a quiet, pretty university
student.

Soon after, she started to make friends in society and got a job
as an assistant in a wholesale wine and spirits store. A few
months later, she transferred to an office as a typist. It was a
tiring job. After six months, a friend's uncle arranged for her to
work in a fairly large Xinhua Bookstore in the centre of town.

A Xinhua Bookstore was a civilized and clean place filled with knowledge, and a government institution, what's more. To obtain this position was not easy and Ji Ling was satisfied. All by herself, she had changed jobs several times without causing any disturbances. She was very proud that all these changes were made without her paying any substantial costs or arousing any slanderous gossip. Her parents were proud, too, and so were the neighbours in Flowery Building Street.

"Look at the Jis' youngest daughter. She is from our Flowery Building Street," they would say.

And so Ji Ling's social status rose considerably.

With a job secured, the next step was to look for a partner in marriage.

Ji Ling's four elder sisters had all tried to do it on their own for a while and two of them had even become pregnant. But despite tears and quarrels none had succeeded. In the end, all the matches were done through go-betweens. Of the four brothers-in-law, the first was a shoe-shop assistant, the second a worker in a soy-sauce factory, the third a railway signalsman and the fourth a self-employed labourer who was forever losing money in business, what business Ji Ling did not know. With a flick-knife in his belt, he looked like a frightened stray cur. Ji Ling would not so much as look at them. Seeing that her mother and elder sisters were ready to interfere with her marriage, she warned, "Mind your own business. I'll do it myself."

"The other four used to talk the same farting nonsense!" said her mother.

"I'm not them."

"Then let's wait and see." Shuffling her playing cards noisily, her mother continued: "My dear, as I told you before, you are a girl from Flowery Building Street. However smart a frog can

never jump higher than two metres. It's all my fault. I was tak-
en in. I didn't know I had married into Flowery Building Street
until the red veil was lifted from my head."

Raising his eyebrows, the father took a sip of tea.

"Well then, I'll reason it out with you. You say you were
cheated, but the go-between...."

Ji Ling shouted, "Not again! Nobody will think you dumb if
you don't quarrel!"

Fourth sister happened to be there and cut in, "Oh, since
when has this home of a whore produced a responsible young
mistress?"

"My fourth girl, I tell you: your mother has never been a
whore!"

The family was just like that! It was shameful!

Ji Ling just had to break away from this family at all costs!
Her own home would be a modern, civilized one, beautiful,
neat and clean, like those in foreign movies. She would stand
firm in her ambition.

After eliminating six boyfriends, Ji Ling more or less decided
to choose Guo Jin.

Guo Jin's father was a cadre in the municipal Party committee
office; his mother was a doctor. Their native place was in Zhejiang. Men from south China have fair skin, are good at cooking
and do not flaunt their masculinity. Guo Jin himself worked in
the electronic band of the municipal song and dance troupe. His
drawback was his height, only 1.63 metres, the same as Ji
Ling's. But Ji Ling usually wore high heels, so he was shorter
than her most of the time. Ji Ling felt that she would regret it
all her life once she agreed to bind herself to Guo Jin in mar-

riage. She would have to wear flat-heeled shoes for ever.

It is remarkable that opportunity always beckons you unawares at a crucial moment. On the last of the three days she had asked Guo Jin to wait for her formal answer to his proposal, she had bumped into Zhuang Jianfei. Under the oriental cherry trees at Wuhan University, her little handbag fell to the ground and out dropped *Girl Dora's Story* by Freud. Other things that fell onto the book included cherry blossoms wrapped in a handkerchief, some loose coins and a tube of Fragrant Sea brand perfume. The Fragrant Sea had broken and the smell enveloped Ji Ling and Zhuang Jianfei for a long time.

Like many sensitive girls, Ji Ling possessed the instinct to grab an opportunity even before she knew it to be one. As Zhuang Jianfei was retrieving the book and the handkerchief, Ji Ling felt sure that, simply from the look of his hands, this was the best choice she could possibly make in her life. She was forever observing people's hands. From her observation of the hands of her family members, of her classmates and friends, of her customers and of traders in the markets, she drew this conclusion: The hands of those from wealthy families are plump and fair with small fingers which often turn up at the ends; people from intellectual families and who are intellectuals themselves have slender fingers and beautifully shaped hands; the hands of everyone else look rough, stupid, short or sturdy with an infinite variety of peculiarities. Zhuang Jianfei's hands were typical of an intellectual from an intellectual family. Her guess later proved to be correct.

The boy named Guo Jin was heartbroken. He had been sure that she would say "yes".

Zhuang Jianfei wanted to buy a set of books by Freud which

was not available on the market. Ji Ling got them for him. After this purchase, their contact continued. Out of courtesy and self-respect, Zhuang Jianfei did not inquire about Ji Ling's family situation and address until long after. Ji Ling considered herself lucky. Almost all her previous boyfriends asked her this question the first time they met: "Where do you live?" Ji Ling would randomly name a street. When she had to give an explanation later she would slyly argue: "It was because I didn't want you to go and visit me at home after knowing each other for such a short time. It might create a bad impression."

Ji Ling did not need to play this trick on Zhuang Jianfei. He let her take the initiative. Yet Ji Ling tried to keep steady. She did not lay her cards on the table until a year later when their friendship had deepened.

That was spring the following year. On the green lawn in the middle of the Eastern Lake Park. Ji Ling said all of a sudden, "Jianfei, let's stop seeing each other from now on."

Her sorrow was totally out of harmony with the view of green hills and water around them on that warm and sunny day.

"What are you joking about?"

"Why do you think I'm joking?" Ji Ling clasped her knees.

"I live in Flowery Building Street in Hankou. My mother is a housewife, my father a petty official and all my four elder sisters and their husbands are very ordinary people."

The surgeon who wielded a scalpel daily naturally maintained his composure but inwardly he was greatly agitated. He had guessed at Ji Ling's family origins. He believed that at least it could not be as low as common townsfolk. Judging her from all aspects, her origins were probably so far out of the ordinary that all this time she had kept silent about them. Only a true princess would conceal her genealogy. He had deliberately allowed her to involve him in this game. In the end there'd be something to delight him.

But now Zhuang Jianfei could not feel any delight.

"Then what makes you think my family origins are different from yours?"

As soon as he said these words, Zhuang Jianfei felt that he had injured Ji Ling's self-esteem. What this girl needed now was warmth, promises, a solemn pledge of love. If it had not been Ji Ling but Wang Luo who worked in the same hospital as he, or any of the other girls, no doubt they would have stood up, given him a sideways look and walked off.

Ji Ling did not walk away. She sat on the lawn in the same position and answered readily: "Your hands. They show me that you are from an intellectual family." Raising her small hands, Ji Ling moved them around a couple of times like a pop song star.

"My hands are not so good as yours. I have always had a sense of inferiority about my family. They are poor, vulgar, lacking in knowledge and education. Besides, Flowery Building Street is notorious. I don't want to be looked down upon."

Zhuang Jianfei was impressed by her lack of sophistication and purity. Comparing his hands with Ji Ling's, he could not help feeling laughing.

"You are like a little witch."

"Then let me tell your fortune by your hand."

Her fingers scrawled in his palm, her face under his nose. This face was glowing and plump, suffused with a layer of golden fine hair in the sunlight. Zhuang Jianfei decided that he would choose her regardless of her family background.

Zhuang Jianfei compared Ji Ling and Wang Luo. Wang Luo

was from a highly educated family and had once trained in piano and dance and could still recite parts of *Romeo and Juliet*. It was really funny recalling Zhuang Jianfei's love affair with her. Working in the same hospital, they would see each other every day, but each day she would write several letters. In one of them she lamented that he had not accepted the hint she had dropped when they were in the lift. It was conveyed in the expression in her eyes. Another time she phoned him and all she said were three words: "Waiting for you." Later she blamed Zhuang Jianfei for making her wait in vain for forty minutes by the flower terrace. Wang Luo disdained to talk about household matters or the main daily necessities such as fuel, rice, oil and salt. What she liked to discuss were music, poetry, current affairs and major social issues. However, she did not have the courage to face reality. She had many freckles on her face, and she resented people mentioning them. One cold day, Zhuang Jianfei accompanied her to a department store to buy face cream. He proposed: "Get a box of Baiqueling." Wang Luo immediately lost heart and the next moment she was running away. Feeling like a fool, Zhuang Jiangfei chased her along the street.

In comparison, Zhuang Jianfei felt Ji Ling was more natural and lovable. What was more, Ji Ling was much plumper. That was very important.

One morning, in mid-spring, Zhuang Jianfei suddenly appeared at the gate of Ji Ling's home.

It was a Sunday, the only day of the week on which Ji Ling's mother gave up playing cards. She had her daughters, sons-in-law and grandchildren visiting her. She washed herself, did her hair and dressed in clean clothes. It was a fine day. For the first

time in the family history, the daughters, prompted by a sudden
impulse, had decided to give the place a general cleaning. A
new, semi-automatic washing machine was carried out to the
lane and attached to the tap outside the gate. Ji Ling's father
had a special interest in new commodities. He went so far as to
put aside his teacup and stay beside the washing machine to study
its various functions.

That was a good day in the life of the Jis. Zhuang Jianfei happened to come along, picking his way through the small lanes on
his motorbike.

For a moment Ji Ling was dumbstruck. Her face flushed and
she became all flustered.

However, her discomposure was unnecessary. Her mother and
elder sisters were all slick and smooth. They instantly knew everything from Ji Ling and Zhuang Jianfei's expressions. Without
talking to him or asking about it, they worked out Zhuang
Jianfei's social class. In a soft voice they invited the guest to be
seated, offered him tea, rushed out to buy food and drink, and
instructed their young children to call him "Uncle".

Ji Ling's mother's kindly face was all smiles. She called all her
sons-in-law "my child". She did not talk much to Zhuang Jianfei
nor leave him out in the cold. She treated him in an unusually
warm way and made sure that he felt at home.

The way Ji Ling's father behaved surprised everyone. Completely out of character, he did not grab hold of the guest and
indiscriminatingly relate anecdotes about Flowery Building
Street. Instead, he pretended to be engrossed in the washing
machine, just saying in the end, "Look, Xiao Zhuang. How can
they call this automatic if you have to wring out the wet clothes
before spin-drying them?"

Zhuang Jianfei thought the little old man was rather amusing.
Lunch was typical Flowery Building Street fare: plentiful,
strong in taste, rich in oil and bright in colour. One course after
the other arrived on the table. Even serving chopsticks were
used at the feast. The way they used them was so natural and
skilful that it seemed that the family's good habits of hygiene
were long-standing. Everyone helped Zhuang Jianfei with the
serving chopsticks and he was inundated in a huge pile of delica-
cies.

Afterwards the mother questioned Ji Ling. She told her all
about Zhuang Jianfei and of course about his family: his home
was in a house on Luojia Hill by the East Lake with wooden
floors and heating. His parents were both senior intellectuals.
He had a younger sister who had graduated from university and
was working in a scientific research department.

"Then it means that he is the only son of the family. Excellent!" Drawing deeply on her cigarette and slowly breathing out
the smoke, her mother continued: "An eligible match. Perfect
beyond words. Be sure you get hold of him!"

Zhuang Jianfei was already ensnared. He had prepared for
the worst when he paid his visit to Ji Ling's family. Who would
have thought that everything turned out to be just the opposite
of what he'd imagined? Ji Ling had been too pessimistic about
her own family.

Above all was the strong human touch which made up for the
regret hidden deep in his heart: his own mother was a rigid
woman. He had never lacked material necessities. What he did
lack was his mother's laughter, the kind of expression in Ji
Ling's mother's eyes that showed her concern that he ate his fill.
He thought a mother's love should be a spoiling, doting, unrea-

sonable one. But his mother would never be unreasonable.
Zhuang Jianfei came to an understanding: a woman better not
be too knowledgeable, clear-headed or methodical. Being just
like a cloud, hazy and soft, would be good enough.

He suddenly realized why nowadays able businesswomen, female postgraduates and the like were never chosen as partners in
marriage, while pretty, gentle, virtuous girls were in short supply.

Indulging in this theory, Zhuang Jianfei felt extremely cheerful. From his expression Ji Ling drew a definite conclusion: he
was bound to marry her.

Ji Ling won. She had succeeded in another significant step in
life. All she needed to do now was to wait for Zhuang Jianfei's
invitation to meet his parents.

Ji Ling waited patiently. She did not appear to be overanx-
ious. When she was together with Zhuang Jianfei, her dress became more and more informal, and sometimes she exposed a lot
of her body.

They had gone beyond the limits of embracing, kissing and
caressing. But she resolutely refused his further demands. "No.
It's not time yet. No!"

After suffering several times, Zhuang Jianfei said to Ji Ling
one day, "My family has invited you to visit us this Sunday."

The day had finally come.

Ji Ling's whole family had had quite a lot of discussion about
it. Should she take along a present? How should she address
Jianfei's parents? What should she wear? What should she say?
Should she volunteer to wash up after the meal? What would be
the right amount to eat? No one in the family had ever visited a

professor's home. Out of self-respect, Ji Ling did not ask Jianfei for advice.

Never mind whether Ji Ling was ready or not, Sunday duly arrived.

She put on a brownish-red wool dress. The design was unique and it was beautifully made, and was not available in any shop in the streets. It had been hastily made by their neighbours, the Bais, a couple of old tailors, so old that they looked like a pair of dried shrimps. They had been master tailors at the former "Number One" clothes shop that only made bespoke clothes for the foreign madams and young ladies living in the concession area. They had stopped trading years ago. This time they made an exception for Ji Ling for this important event in her life. Ji Ling's hair was done by another neighbour who came to offer help of his own accord. He was the youngest yet the most popular hairdresser at the "Hong Kong" hairdresser's. Earlier, he had asked someone to go to Ji Ling's home as a matchmaker for him. Now he had relinquished his resentment and his virtue had won. The whole of Flowery Building Street busied itself for Ji Ling.

The problem of what present to take along remained unsolved. Although Jianfei had come empty-handed on his first visit, it was excusable, for he had done so without his parents' knowledge. But Ji Ling had been invited by his parents. She would be accused of being ill-bred if she did the same. But if she gave a present that was worth a lot they might get the impression that the girl was of humble birth and manipulating.

The sound of Jianfei motorcycle came closer and closer. Ji Ling was still trying to work out a solution. Her mother puffed anxiously at her cigarette.

"In my opinion, just take a tin of good tea." Ji Ling's father suddenly spoke up from a dark corner, and handed over a tin of tea leaves. Undoubtedly the intelligence and wisdom he displayed concerning Ji Ling's marriage affairs was the peak of his existence. It was estimable that a man could know and correct his shortcomings as he grew old.

Ji Ling's mother laughed. "You old bastard! The sun has risen in the west."

Holding the treasured tea, wearing her new dress and cheeks aglow, Ji Ling sat on the back of Jianfei's motorcycle, her arm around his waist. Her black, sweet-smelling hair looked like a sail of victory.

The two young people floated in high spirits all the way.

However, they soon met with a setback.

Jianfei's family gave Ji Ling a tepid reception. During her four hours' visit, she spent half the time alone on the sofa in the lounge leafing through magazines, the other half at the dinner table where no one spoke to her. Jianfei generally was not good at smiling. To ease the embarrassing situation he said with a faint smile on his lips something about popular social science books. Jianfei's mother uttered only a few words: "Help yourself. Don't stand on ceremony." "Take a seat." "What will you drink?" His father hemmed and hawed but did not say anything much. From time to time he stared at Ji Ling from behind his spectacles. The question of washing up or not was non-existent for all the chores in the kitchen were done by a silent middle-aged help. Even she took no notice of Ji Ling. The tin of precious tea was put to one side. No one thanked Ji Ling's parents for it. After the meal they moved to the lounge. Ji Ling thought at least they would chat with her for a while and ask about her age, education, work and so forth. But they showed no desire to do so. It was time for a nap. They made it clear that they were ready to see their guest off.

Tears sprang up in Ji Ling's eyes as soon as she stepped out of the small house.

Jianfei patted Ji Ling apologetically on the shoulder. "You must not take it to heart. They're like that all the time."

He saw Ji Ling down the hill. Looking back at the small building surrounded by green pines, she felt a keen hatred taking root in her heart. She did not pour out her grievances to him, not a single word. But the seeds of revenge were planted inside her.

It made Jianfei's heart ache to see Ji Ling's pitiful look. He would have felt indignant even if Ji Ling had had nothing to do with him. He went back home in a rage and flung his helmet onto the lounge floor. The noise woke his mother from her nap.

"What's the matter with you?" she frowned.

Upon hearing this insincere enquiry, Jianfei kicked the helmet across the room and knocked over a small ornament. The noise brought out the whole family.

His mother was forced to state her view: "She is not suitable for you. She's poorly educated. And her prim and vulgar manner suggest her petty origins."

Jianya asked her brother to calm down. She said, "Brother, you know that we are not good at entertaining guests. We can't be sociable even if the visitor is a central government leader. You know that we have our pride as intellectuals."

"But Ji Ling is a member of our family, not a guest."

His mother asked: "When did this become a fact?"

"Now. Soon."

"Brother, Mum's right. Ji Ling is a bit too petty. Judging by her clothes and appearance, she's obviously no intellectual."

Jianfei retorted, "You understand nothing but intellectuals." He turned to his father.

"This is a purely personal matter. I will not have a hand in it," said his father.

"But she will become your daughter-in-law."

His father looked distracted for a moment.

"Quite honestly, I don't think she's as good as Wang Luo."

Jianfei walked around the room and smiled bitterly. "Strange. No one thinks about what's best for me. To put it bluntly, you're all thinking about yourselves and cannot accept a girl of a low family status."

"Nonsense!" His mother was livid. She slammed her book shut.

Jianfei aimed a violent kick at his helmet, which struck Jianya's instep and made it bleed.

For the first time, noise of destruction swept through the Zhuang household. It was followed by a three to one sharp dispute.

Ji Ling was sobbing. "Jianfei, I feel really bad about it. I'm sorry."

"It's not you who should feel sorry."

"Let's break off our relationship."

"Break off? Why?"

"For you. For me. And for our parents. It's all right if I am not happy. My origins are humble anyway. But I cannot bear to see you unhappy. You should enjoy everything."

"Ji Ling! You are kind!"

Oh, Ji Ling, girl from Flowery Building Street, you were expected to hate those who stood in your way, to curse them, to swear at them. But you acted just like a young noblewoman. Who could despise you!

Ji Ling observed what was going on in Jianfei's mind. "How can I hate your parents? It's they who gave birth to you and brought you up."

Jianfei's eyes brimmed with tears.

"I've got to go now. Let's leave it at that. Let's part, never to meet again."

Ji Ling unfastened the pearl necklace and placed it in the palm of his hand. Jianfei held her closely in his arms together with the necklace and vowed: "We'll get married right now! No one can stop us!"

However, getting married was even harder.

Before Zhuang Jianfei had a steady girlfriend, his parents had decided that their son's wedding chamber would be the biggest room in the house. But now that Jianfei was so obsessed with marrying Ji Ling, it went without saying that he lost this privilege.

Fortunately, the hospital authorities valued their qualified personnel, encouraged freedom in choosing one's spouse and rewarded those who married at a mature age. Jianfei was allocated a dormitory room. While silently decorating the tiny matchbox-like room, Jianfei and Ji Ling felt unspeakably miserable.

Then they suddenly heard that a doctor in the surgical department was leaving for Canada. Jianfei went to the hospital director's home that very night to recount his difficulties. Luckily he obtained the doctor's one-room flat.

To get married they needed money. According to common

practice in Wuhan, as much as ten thousand yuan was the absolute minimum. But their joint savings came to less than two thousand. Under the covetous glares of the four elder daughters, Ji Ling's parents declared that they would be fair—Ji Ling would get the same dowry as the others. Nevertheless, they secretly sewed eight hundred yuan inside the soft silk quilt made for her and sent a message to Jianfei that if his side held a big wedding, they would not let people laugh at them. But Jianfei's parents remained silent.

Hua Rufen was the head of the hospital director's office. She admired Jianfei and was fond of him. Seeing him in such a predicament, she naturally sympathized with him. She had been a prize student of Jianfei's mother and they had continued to keep in touch with each other. Jianya brought over a deposit slip of just one thousand yuan only after Hua Rufen had acted as mediator. Jianfei felt like tearing up the receipt in his sister's face. However he found it hard to act heroically. It was a shame that his poor situation did not enable him to show a strong will. He was choked with hatred against God knows whom, and his neck flushed crimson.

After alternate bouts of joys and sufferings within that half year, Jianfei and Ji Ling both became thinner. When they finally lay down legally in the same bed, they could not refrain from caressing the other's prominent cheekbones and then in tears threw themselves into each other's arms.

After all their trials and hardships, family life was calm for six months until just now when the calmness was suddenly ruptured again. This time the conflict occurred between the couple themselves, something which had many new implications. After pondering for several hours on the steps outside the Bank of China, Jianfei realized that his marriage was not unusual. Once you uncovered all the layers of wrappings, a marriage revealed itself to be a produce of sexual desire plus human work. He believed that this was also the case with many others.

He could console himself that he was not a man who was confused and irresponsible. He was formed by the times in which he lived. There was no escape.

Anyway his marriage was not that bad. In every respect Ji Ling was a rather good wife. She looked after him with meticulous care. She was fascinated by his talents and his successes in his career.

Knowing that Ji Ling was a girl from Flowery Building Street, one should not wonder where her dirty words came from. A naive, impetuous lad when he left home several hours ago, Jianfei had grown into a mature man by the time he returned home. He pushed open the bedroom door.

"Hello. Is my baby still angry?" he said.

The wardrobe was wide open, and so were the drawers. The bed was a mess. All Ji Ling's clothes and cosmetics had disappeared.

She had threatened before to go back to her parents' home each time she felt wronged. Jianfei had not held out a white flag and she had not dared to act rashly. Now Jianfei showed good will but she had left.

At lunch time the next day, Dr Zeng found Jianfei in the canteen.

"How was it?" he asked expectantly.

"Let's put it off until after lunch."

Jianfei grimaced as if he had toothache. There were too many people around. Before he had not cared how many were around when he talked about sport events.

Jianfei quickly finished his lunch, and followed by Dr Zeng, went to the on-duty office. He reclined on the edge of the bed and for a long time said nothing. He didn't want to get his family farce mixed up with his work, but he didn't want to tell a lie either. Anyway, it would be really difficult for him to think up a lie. Who'd believe that Jianfei had not watched the sports event because of a headache?

"Is it a surprise?" Dr Zeng found Jianfei didn't look his usual self and got excited himself. "It must be an unexpected result! Did Korea win? Ah, they must have! Was Li Lingwei defeated? But she is the queen of the world badminton court!" He quickly stroked the grey hair at his temples, then with one hand shakily poured out some water to wash down some medicine while pressing the other against his heart. He babbled on about how fortunately he hadn't watched yesterday evening, otherwise he certainly would have died in front of the TV; that he had purposely left his transistor radio behind when he went to practise shadow-boxing this morning to avoid listening to the news, for he was afraid he'd faint by the lake in the park. Man has premonitions, he asserted. His premonition had saved his life. But how could the Chinese team have possibly lost?

Dr Zeng talked rapidly, not allowing the other to put in a word. Finally he turned to Jianfei.

"It's got to be admitted that this will be regretted for ever. However, Dr Zhuang, nothing is worth harming one's health. You didn't eat much at lunch today."

Jianfei could not keep silent anymore. He told him: "I didn't watch the game."

Dr Zeng looked wooden for a minute; his face turned rather red. "That's impossible!"

"It's true. I didn't watch the whole way through." Jianfei told the truth before Dr Zeng's questioning, sorrowful eyes. "My wife quarrelled with me. She turned off the TV."

"Just because of that!" Dr Zeng heaved a long sigh. "It's you who've ruined the Uber Cup final. Is there any hope for tonight's Thomas Cup?"

"Not much," Jianfei answered honestly.

"Why not?"

His wife had run away, but he said, "She's gone to her parents' home."

"Run away?"

No matter how hard he tried to save his face, the truth was laid bare with one remark. Jianfei forced a smile: "I have to go and see her."

"You should have gone to see her last night if you wanted to watch tonight's Thomas Cup. Dr Zhuang, you've made a mess of things. It's not unusual for a young couple to quarrel, but you've got to understand this point: quarrel only in bed."

With his broad experience Dr Zeng tried to help Jianfei through the aftermath.

"Go and sort things out this afternoon. You've got a major operation to do tomorrow. Don't let emotional upsets come too close to an operation. Anyway, you ought to watch the Thomas Cup tonight. Don't let a trifling quarrel between husband and wife affect your watching an international game."

"I have no excuse to take time off."

"You don't need an excuse. Hasn't your anger caused a

toothache?"

Jianfei did feel some pain, but it wasn't toothache.

"Dr Zeng, please keep it—"

"A secret. Hurry up. The time hasn't come for you to remind me of anything."

"Thanks."

I should have asked for advice earlier, Jianfei thought to himself. It seems that many people have had similar experiences. Dr Zeng, for example, is in perfect harmony with his wife. With this analogy in mind, Jianfei felt that his difficulties would be soon solved.

The Jis' gate was wide open. Ji Ling's mother lay slumped on a rattan chair which was on the point of collapse. The fat woman was dozing off, her hair dishevelled, the cigarette ash falling bit by bit onto the greasy front of her garment and finally, following a complicated route, down onto the floor.

It was the first time Jianfei realized that his mother-in-law was so ugly. He even felt embarrassed. Hesitating for a while, he decided not to disturb her and headed for the attic. Before getting married, Ji Ling had lived up there. Her little bed was still kept for her after she got married.

"She's not here."

Jianfei was startled. He turned round. His mother-in-law had opened her blood-shot eyes.

"Where is she? Her work unit said she'd asked for sick leave."

"Who are you talking to? You should say 'Hello' even if you're talking to a dog."

After struggling with himself for quite a while, Jianfei gritted his teeth and responded, "Mum, I'm looking for Ji Ling."

"Didn't I marry her off to you?"

His mother-in-law spat out her cigarette butt with a "pooh". Hands pressed against her hips, she stood up unsteadily, fetched another cigarette and lit up. A little girl in the neighbourhood heard them and came over to watch Jianfei. As his mother-in-law stood up, her playing cards slid down from the chair. The little girl hurried over and picked them up agilely from a half kneeling position, put them back onto the chair and then returned to the doorway from where she watched Jianfei with interest.

"Didn't I marry my daughter to you?"

Those who suit their actions to the time of day are wise, Jianfei said to himself.

"Sorry. We just had a bit of a quarrel and she left home. I've come to fetch her back."

"Sorry? What sort of creature are you with all those airs and graces? Don't be priggish in front of your old lady. My daughter suffered all sorts of bullying and humiliation in her husband's family and now the bastard has beaten her out!"

"I didn't beat her. We only pulled each other about a bit."

"Of course you won't admit beating her because that violates the law. But doesn't dragging somebody about mean beating them?"

The little girl giggled. His mother-in-law did not care at all but Jianfei did not want to debate matters concerning his wife and himself in another's presence.

"I'd like to see Ji Ling. I want her to go back with me."

His mother-in-law laughed sarcastically, which made her fat quiver all over.

"You really live up to your intellectual family status with those strange and refined words of yours. It makes me feel embarrassed to refuse. As it is, you can only blame our family who never bother about what others hope for." She laughed again.

Jianfei felt agitated and hot all over.

Not long before she had kept calling him "my child", inquiring after his well-being and showing concern that he would not suffer hunger, thirst or wrong from her daughter. How could she change so easily today? So a loving mother is not always loving—Jianfei learned this common truth from this profoundly awkward situation. He fell silent with misery.

"You want Ji Ling back. OK. But on one condition."

"Go on."

"Let me ask you. How has Ji Ling behaved in your home?"

Just mind your own business, you good-for-nothing! —It would have given him great satisfaction to answer back but the consequences would be disastrous. Instead he replied: "She's done well."

His mother-in-law patted her lap, which crackled loudly.

"You've said it. She's done well. She gets your meals ready. She warms up the quilt for you. She has never ever given you a cold look, debased her sister-in-law or cursed her parents-in-law. Nor has she committed adultery or given birth to an illegitimate child! Go and ask whether there is another daughter-in-law in the whole of Flowery Building Street more virtuous than my daughter. Your parents are so damned snobbish, sending her away with a mere thousand yuan. Up till now they've taken no notice of us, the parents of their daughter-in-law. You are even worse, beating her and smashing cups all over the place, not giving her a thought. Let's put it to the neighbours and see who's in the right. I warn you, if you want this case settled, get your parents round here. We'll sort it out in front of everyone. Since ancient times, people have raised their heads to marry off a daughter and bowed their heads to welcome a new daughter-in-law. What evil did I do in my previous existence that such a good daughter of mine should be made suffer like this!"

She wanted his parents to come. If his mother were present to see her son's mother-in-law with her own eyes, it would not be strange if her blood pressure shot up. It was a farce. He didn't know how to cope.

He called up to the attic: "Ji Ling, can't you come downstairs for a while?"

He called once more, really angry by now.

"What are you doing this for?" he shouted.

Up in the attic was perfect silence.

The little girl had collected a crowd of children of assorted ages. They were all watching him with interest.

His mother-in-law suddenly stopped talking. She dozed off a-gain. She had achieved her goal and was now showing him the door. She was no fool. In fact she was pretty astute. Although she looked sleepy, the deterrent force was there in her. If Jian-fei tried to go up to the attic, the earth would shake, no doubt about it.

Brought up on a university campus, it was only now that Jian-fei realized that Flowery Building Street really deserved its repu-tation. In this place nothing was impossible, nothing was sur-prising. Once he understood this Jianfei had no alternative but to sullenly call off the battle.

Sleeping alone in a double bed for the first time, Jianfei was sure that he would feel lonely. So before going to bed, he made an exception by drinking two small glasses of wine and found a dull hypnotizing book on some specialized theory. One person in a double bed was actually incredibly comfortable. He was not drunk and he didn't read. Nothing was necessary. Spreading out his arms and legs and relaxing his whole body on the bed, he was so comfortable that he even began to feel it was a little unfair on Ji Ling.

Things got complicated the next morning.

The moment he opened his eyes, a problem arose. What to eat? Everything had been done by his mother or childminder when he was a child, by the canteen and friends when a bachelor, and by Ji Ling after they had got married. Ji Ling's breakfasts had been always well-prepared and appetizing.

Doctors hate restaurants. Disease finds its way in through the mouth, and the restaurant is a source of evil which kept the doctor busy all day long. In his temporarily wifeless state, Jianfei was forced to enter a restaurant he absolutely loathed. After waiting in a long queue his turn came but he could not find any food coupons in his pockets. He blushed and asked: "Can I manage without food coupons?"

The assistant said scornfully, "We're state-run. Go to a private place. Next!"

Jianfei was squeezed out at once, and so was his appetite.

The whole morning everyone was busy with shift relief and ward rounds. In his superior manner, Dr Zeng treated Jianfei as a mere junior doctor. No one mentioned the problems with his wife. Jianfei rested assured that all was well here. He gradually settled down to his work and felt better. Yet before going to the operating theatre, his sleeves rolled up and scrubbing his hands with disinfectant, Dr Zeng said, "Can you do it?"

A most irritating question for a confident young surgeon with high ambitions.

"It's not that serious yet," replied Jianfei.

With sterilized arms raised, Dr Zeng stared at Jianfei from over the large gauze mask over his mouth and nose, like a robot from outer space who does not trust the human race.

Jianfei didn't like confronting him this way. He added: "I slept very well last night, never better."

The operation lasted five hours. The doctors estimated that it would need three hours at most but Jianfei had taken five. Normally it was nothing. Dr Zeng had been assisting him at the table and he understood clearly that the operation required that amount of time. Towards the end, however, Jianfei felt uneasy. He had lost his quickness and dexterity. How would others regard this time? He couldn't let a trifling family affair ruin his professional reputation!

Once these distracting thoughts arose, his hands began to shake. The final suture was not nearly as beautifully neat as his previous ones. The others probably could not tell the difference, but Dr Zeng had sharp discerning eyes.

His vest and shorts were wet with sweat by the time the operation was over. He felt particularly tired. In the presence of everyone, Dr Zeng declared that Zhuang Jianfei had accumulated three days of leave and suggested: "It's time you took them." Jianfei felt there was a sting in his words.

The canteen had forgotten to save food for the operating staff. Bowls of hard cold rice and some gherkins were all that was left.

It was already twilight when Jianfei got home after a ten minute motorbike ride. His stomach was rumbling. He searched high and low for something to eat. There was only a handful of crumbs in the biscuit tin. They usually just bought small quantities of biscuits to keep them fresh, so they got eaten up pretty quickly. It went without saying that Ji Ling was responsible for buying things. She loved window shopping, and was an experienced buyer, too.

There were noodles but not enough for even one bowl. There was a big container of rice but no vegetables. Jianfei was surprised to see a square cotton bag in the rice. He opened it to smell and found that inside was Chinese prickly ash. It prevented weevils. He had learned this in *A Hundred Thousand Whys* in his early youth. But while he had laid aside and neglected this knowledge, Ji Ling had put it into practice, she had applied all her knowledge to maintain their home. How could one complain about such a wife?

He ate two bowls of dumpling soup at a privately-run place. The dumplings were mostly dough without meat stuffing. He was even more tired after a shower but had to force himself to do some washing. On turning on the light he discovered a layer of dust all over the furniture. Rummaging through drawers and chests, he failed to find any food coupons. What would he eat tomorrow morning? It was true that without a wife a home was not a home.

Hua Rufen came to visit him. She explained that she urgently needed to see him but didn't dare to contact him at the hospital at this crucial and sensitive moment. Jianfei wondered what special situation could affect the hospital at this moment.

Hua Rufen spoke in a low voice: "The U.S. visitors quota has been granted!"

Long ago, the hospital authorities had briefed the surgical department on people who might be allowed to go to the United

States to learn about heart transplant operations. This news had caused excitement in the department for quite some time. Gradually, the issue had been forgotten. Now, it had been brought up again. There would be bumps and bruises among the contending members of the surgical department staff.

"Exactly," Hua Rufen agreed. "Many intellectuals are philistines. They don't really want to acquire advanced skills. The United States is just an Ali Baba's cave for them."

A doctor in the acupuncture department who had been disparaged in the hospital went to the United States and earned fifty thousand yuan in a year. It sounded like Ali Baba's cave.

"How come you see it like that too?"

Hua Rufen wore her hair short in an old-fashioned style. She sat on one corner of the sofa with her knees pressed together, holding a worn black bag in her arms. Both her hair style and her rigorous posture reminded Jianfei of his mother.

"Do you also plan to get a fridge and a colour TV?"

"Most of all I want to see a heart transplant operation."

"That's good. You are the most promising member of the surgical department. By the way, I heard that you're having problems with your wife?"

"Does that matter?"

"Certainly. Unmarried people and those who do not have good relations with their spouses will not be considered."

"Why?"

"Because they're afraid that such people won't return if allowed out."

"That's a joke."

"No, it's not. There've been precedents. Are you having difficulties with each other?"

"Yes. She's run away to her parents'."

Only now did Hua Rufen raise her eyes to look around the room. "Have you told anybody?" she asked.

"Yes, Dr Zeng."

"You are naive! Anyone will stab another in the back out of self-interest. Dr Zeng, he—You are so naive!"

"Will Dr Zeng stab me in the back?"

"You'd better make it up with your wife as soon as possible. Within three days you two must show up together and smiling in the hospital. It'll do even if it's for only a few minutes."

"But her mother's terms are too harsh."

"Agree to them all."

"But this—"

"A great person should be magnanimous. Accept them all. Do as I say!"

So saying, Hua Rufen got up to take her leave. She was afraid that someone she knew might see her here. Before opening the door, she again urged Jianfei to get things done within three days. She thought the chance was simply too important for him to miss, the chance of a lifetime to inspect heart transplant operations. Zhuang Jianfei's future success would hang on it. She said, "We should do things with a clear conscience and let those who are really good go abroad, for the sake of the country and the people, as well as the career of the individual."

Jianfei tossed about in bed the whole night.

In the patient records room, Zhuang Jianfei met Wang Luo. The white work gown fitted her beautifully. The white hat touching her eyebrows set off her graceful nose and freckles. She flashed a smile at Jianfei as if she was bestowing on him a reward.

She had sensed that Jianfei had been about to break off with her, and had quickly indicated that she wanted to break with him before he made his intentions clear. Jianfei had agreed. So their affair had come to an end but together they had a secret. They both had a tacit understanding of this. When they came across each other they still nodded like ordinary colleagues or greeted each other on holidays.

There were rows of tall bookcases in the inner part of the records room. Standing there, gravely dignified, Wang Luo asked in a tone like a Bodhisattva's: "Dr Zhuang, do you need me to go and talk your wife round?"

Jianfei gasped: "How did you get to know?"

"Many people know and so do I. The news has gone from the surgical department to the department of internal medicine."

"Who did such a thing?"

"Don't be a fussy woman and try to find out who did it." Wang Luo hit the nail on the head: "Everyone has the right to compete for the opportunity of going to the United States."

"It's contemptible!"

Wang Luo chuckled. "In the age of competition, that's by no means a derogatory term. Contemptible means are perhaps employed to achieve a noble goal."

This kind of abstruse philosophical conversation was a game Wang Luo was good at. She had always disdained to talk about trivial things and took delight in big issues like this. But Jianfei was in no mood to enjoy her words. He hastily gave up the search for a particular medical record and started to leave, pretending he had located and read through the record.

"Thank you for reminding me."

"Don't worry. I just want to help you talk your wife round."

"There is no need. She has just gone back to her mother's place to take a few days' rest."

"A woman best understands a woman."

"You're right there, Wang Luo."

"It's better to address a colleague as Dr So-and-So." Standing behind Jianfei, she continued in a soft voice: "I want to tell your wife that watching an international badminton game is a pretty refined sort of recreation. I also want to let her know the saying: 'The wolf wins when the shepherds quarrel'."

The records room supervisor, who sat like a statue at her desk fiddling with cards every day, year after year, was bending behind a bookshelf in the front row to eavesdrop on their conversation. Jianfei hurried out and bumped into her. The haggard-looking woman panicked, having failed to dash back in time to her desk. She knocked against a shelf and in a flash bags of records fell to the floor with a crash and the dust accumulated on them over the years fouled the air.

"I'm sorry," Jianfei said without turning round.

"He's certainly some gentleman!" Wang Luo remarked to the woman caustically.

Hua Rufen was right: someone was stabbing him in the back. He was a man, and would not allow himself to be so easily butchered!

Ji Ling's parents had hidden her at their home like a princess. Severe morning sickness made her wan and sallow. The more she suffered, the more she hated Jianfei. Confined to bed for days, she had brooded over the whole matter and had decided to seize on this opportunity to make Jianfei and his parents understand what she was really like.

General principles were widely known. Ji Ling was simply too good at using formulas in an argument. But at this stage it was not the time to pretend to be compliant or accommodating, nor to stress love only. She was still young. She had still over half her life ahead of her. Since she had married into the Zhuang family, first, the Zhuangs must accept her and take her seriously; second, Jianfei must take her seriously.

At present the situation was just the opposite: the Zhuangs had neither accepted her nor taken her seriously.

They had just given her one thousand yuan for her marrying into their family. That was the disgrace of a lifetime for her. Yet Jianfei had been reluctant to tear the receipt up. If it were her, she would have torn it into pieces without the slightest hesitation. Money is not vulgar. Sometimes it is the expression of a person's value. Her fourth sister married beneath her to a self-employed labourer who always lost money in his business and for that marriage her husband's family had given her ten thousand yuan. Three years ago ten grand had been a large sum. Her mother-in-law wrapped the receipt in red paper and personally pressed it into her palm. This detail was still talked about with general approval in Flowery Building Street.

It was significant that up till now the Zhuangs had not paid a visit to their daughter-in-law's parents. Other people were watching closely, making wild guesses. To win credit for oneself, that was what everyone was trying to do. While it was their right to ignore their daughter-in-law, they had no right to despise the elders.

Zhuang Jianfei had not taken her seriously, either. In the past six months of their married life, she had seen clearly all that was between them. Jianfei didn't ignore her or look down on her. It was simply that he didn't understand what a husband's duties were nor did he know how to love his wife dearly.

Only six months and they already had a daily routine.

After getting up in the morning, Ji Ling hurried to make breakfast which they ate in haste. After breakfast they went their separate ways to work.

"I'm going."

"Is the door locked?"

"Yes."

They both spent their lunch time at their respective work units.

After work Ji Ling went directly to the market. When she got home she hurried to prepare dinner. When dinner was ready, she busied herself cleaning the room and so on. As he entered, Jianfei said, "I'm starving." Then the young couple started to eat dinner. Occasionally there was praise: "This meal is delicious."

In the evening, if there was a sports programme on TV, Jianfei was engrossed in watching it. If not, Ji Ling watched alone, knitting at the same time, while Jianfei read in the bedroom.

When it was past ten o'clock, one of them would suggest: "Let's go to bed," and they went to bed.

They had sexual intercourse every other day, accurate as a clock. Zhuang Jianfei had formed the pattern without asking Ji Ling's opinion. He showed a great variety of skills in bed. Whenever Ji Ling could not understand tacitly, he would remark that he thought girls from Flowery Building Street were good at "having fun". It turned out not to deserve its reputation. Then he would give a strange laugh. If Ji Ling responded: "But I'm not a whore," he would laugh even louder.

Ji Ling was not totally unworthy of her origins. She was not the type of insincere prig who said that she loathed affairs in bed, nor did she lack in imagination and creativity. But still she couldn't keep up with Jianfei. It made her feel suspicious. She had a colleague nearly forty years old called Sister Zhang. They were the best of friends despite their difference in age. Ji Ling once confided her misgivings to Sister Zhang.

Sister Zhang enlightened Ji Ling: "Don't you understand? Your husband has slept with a dissolute older woman."

Many times in the middle of their enjoyment of a beautiful night, Ji Ling would cross-examine Jianfei. Each time he became evasive. Later, when Ji Ling was together with him again, she felt estranged.

They had not taken any serious contraceptive measures after they got married. Every month Ji Ling paid close attention to her menstruation. Before they got married, Jianfei was rather attentive. He would call as soon as it was the date.

"Has it come yet?"

"Yes, it has." Ji Ling would say in public.

If her answer was "No", Jianfei became highly sensitive and nervous: "Why not?" And he would urge her, "Keep watching!"

At these words Ji Ling could not hold back the smile surging from the bottom of her heart.

Since getting married, however, Jianfei's interest had obviously waned. It was ten days past the normal date for this month but he did not show the slightest awareness. Another ten days passed and Ji Ling was almost sure that she was pregnant.

The early morning of the day on which they quarrelled, Ji Ling was in a good mood. She wanted to give Jianfei a happy

surprise. She had kept some morning urine to take to the hospital for a test. She had deliberately placed a small bottle near the
toilet paper. Being a physician as well as a surgeon, Jianfei
would understand. He was in the toilet for quite a while. When
he came out, he said beaming, "It's a lucky day today. I'll enjoy
myself this evening when I get back."

As soon as he got home that evening he looked at the clock
and said, "Live transmission starts at six fifty."

So from morning to night he'd been over the moon just because of the women's badminton game for the Uber Cup.

How could Ji Ling vent her spleen but by swearing at him?
Jianfei had never uttered a dirty word. The whole Zhuang family used cultured language. This made Ji Ling's swearing take on
another function, that was, of revenge. Anyway, according to
the law, Ji Ling was now a member of the Zhuang family. So,
the Zhuangs, therefore, were no longer so refined and elegant.

All those matters were far, far away from what Ji Ling had
projected for her life.

She had planned to get a job to her liking, to work well, to be
agreeable to her boss and colleagues and to try to get more
bonus.

She had planned to find a husband of high social status, to
give and receive love, to have a son and lead a conjugal life together.

She had planned to take turns visiting their parents on holidays and Sundays, to get on well with them and to enjoy family
happiness.

That was all! Simple and practical. To achieve her ambition,
she was willing to take on the full load of housework. And in

fact she had done so. But Jianfei had not taken her seriously.

This time, if Jianfei didn't act in accordance with her terms, she would divorce him. On hearing the word "divorce," her mother turned on her.

"Nonsense, damn you. Divorce is not a thing to be mentioned casually!"

Ji Ling didn't regard divorce as seriously as her mother did. No matter what other people said, no matter how they tried to persuade her, she would not change her mind. She could not cherish a man who didn't take her seriously, whether he was royalty or millionaire overseas. A girl who had grown up in Flowery Building Street, she had found food and clothing by herself since childhood. She had listened to former prostitutes talking about the past, to elder brothers and sisters talking about the "cultural revolution" and their experiences working in the countryside; she had seen all kinds of movies, ancient and modern, Chinese and foreign; she had observed the latest fashions and new ideas. She had a prolific knowledge of life!

Her mother was tough and experienced in coping with Jianfei. Behind his back, however, she put in innumerable good words for him and tried to persuade her to go back to her home. She argued that by marrying Jianfei Ji Ling had indeed climbed up the social ladder. One should be content with one's lot. It's wrong to crave the crown of a foreign empire once you've become emperor of China. There's an old saying that a good woman does not marry twice.

Sister Zhang was the only person Ji Ling could consult and trust in. She was not only Ji Ling's bosom friend but also chairperson of the Trade Union and women's representative of the Xinhua Bookstore. She had handled many disputes between cou-

ples and always said that where men were concerned an ace
should be kept in hand. So they had kept Ji Ling's pregnancy secret in order to deal the Zhuangs a heavy blow at a critical moment.

It was decided that next time Jianfei came, Ji Ling would meet
him personally. If his behaviour was not acceptable, Sister
Zhang would accompany Ji Ling to see the authorities at
Jianfei's hospital and ask for a divorce in the name of the organization. Sister Zhang would prepare a letter of introduction.

Ji Ling now waited for Jianfei to come.

Zhuang Jianfei came again. This time both his parents-in-law
were in the central room. His mother-in-law was still wearing
the same greasy outfit, playing cards, a cigarette dangling from
her lips. His father-in-law was huddled up in a small bamboo
chair like a shrimp, holding his teacup in both hands and looking dumb.

"You're both home," Jianfei greeted them.

Nobody responded.

"I've come to see Ji Ling."

Nobody responded.

"If Ji Ling doesn't come out today I'll stay."

His mother-in-law opened her mouth: "You know the conditions for Ji Ling's return."

"I still think it better that affairs between husband and wife
do not affect their parents."

"We are already affected," his father-in-law said. "Frankly,
your parents think too highly of themselves. Look around Flowery Building Street. It has the biggest and oldest jeweller's in the
whole municipal city, Sijimei Steamed Dumpling Restaurant

which is well-known home and abroad, the customs clock tower, the concession area, Wang Yuxia Food Store..."

His words were cut short by Ji Ling's appearance.

She stood on the dark, narrow stairs, in a knitted sleeping gown, her hair touching her shoulders. On her feet she had a pair of bright red shiny slippers. Jianfei felt as if he had seen a star.

Ji Ling addressed him coldly: "Come up."

As soon as he was upstairs, Jianfei wanted to embrace her but she dodged away. "You've come to solve the problem," she said.

"That's right," Jianfei affirmed with a double-edged remark. "I have many problems."

He caught hold of her and without much ado kissed her several times and fell with her in his arms onto the bed. He whispered fervently: "Let me solve this problem quickly."

Ji Ling didn't want to end all her troubles this way. What was more, Jianfei was being too fierce and she was afraid that the foetus wouldn't stand it.

"I'm sick!" she protested.

She shouted a few more times as she grappled and struggled with him. But he won't listen. He was burning hot as if running a high fever and was pressing her so hard that she felt dizzy. There was nothing for it but to butt him with her knee.

Just a gentle blow but Jianfei shrivelled up and rolled to one side, his hands covering the sore spot.

He moaned silently, gritting his teeth as he endured the shooting pain. He was just about able to tolerate the pain in his lower regions but the pain in his heart grew immensely. No one had ever refused him. Moreover he was her husband. He had the right. What grounds had she for doing so? Not allowing him to watch TV! Cursing him! Running away from him! Forcing him to come again and again to beg for pity! And insulting him in such a way!

Ji Ling sat on the wooden chest in front of the window, not showing the slightest trace of apology.

Straightening up, Jianfei roared in a strangled voice: "Come back home!"

"I didn't do it on purpose."

But she had. Only Jianfei was in a position to know the nature of such an act. It was deliberate and malicious.

"You come back home with me!"

"It's not the right time for us to discuss this matter."

"It has nothing to do with the time, be it right or wrong. You are my wife and you should come back to my home."

"Hey, your home."

"It's your home too."

"My parents have told you the terms on which I'll go back. I'll do what they want me to."

"I repeat. This is our private affair."

"But I am your parents' daughter-in-law."

"Impossible! I tell you. It's impossible to get my parents to come here."

Ji Ling's face was even colder. "Then go away."

"I give you two days to come back home. Otherwise you'll regret it!"

"Then let's wait and see," Ji Ling said resolutely.

Zhuang Jianfei rode along aimlessly. He had not expected that things would end up such a mess. They had quarrelled before.

As long as he took the initiative to be intimate, especially in bed, all their problems could be solved readily. He could not understand why his old ways had not worked this time.

He felt a strong urge to visit a friend, have a drink and a talk about the matter to find out what the others would think.

Who should he visit? He had his classmates when he was at university and a gang of bachelor friends when he was single. As time flew by, they had all got married. After marriage, friends automatically drifted apart. It was as if each had formed a unit, a cell with a woman, and friends had become unnecessary. You voluntarily discarded them, so when you were in need who did you turn to?

He passed by a grey residential area that he remembered was called "Oasis". One of his university classmates lived here. He clearly remembered the building where his friend lived because he had noticed some graffiti when he had attended the friend's wedding two years ago: there was a concrete electricity pole just opposite the balcony of the wedding chamber on the third floor and exactly at that height were the shocking words in flaming-red paint—so-and-so raped so-and-so.

As he paused on his motorbike beneath the row of characters, he looked at the balcony on the third floor. He remembered everything except the guy's name. He smiled ironically and was about to leave when suddenly someone called from above:

"Isn't that Zhuang Jianfei?"

The moment he heard his name called, he remembered who it was.

"Lu Zhilao." He waved at him.

Because of his connection with his father-in-law, Lu Zhilao lived in a two-bedroom flat. His father-in-law was in charge of supplies and marketing at a large steel plant. The position was not high but had plenty of potential.

The rooms were decorated with wallpaper like one of the better grade hotels. Lu Zhilao wore sideburns and a shirt in a bold floral pattern. The ends of the shirt were tied together to expose his chest with its curly hair which was less than a foreigner's but more than that of most Chinese. There was a gold chain around his neck and a gold ring on his finger. The cigarette he offered Jianfei was a U.S. "Hilton". He welcomed Jianfei with special warmth. They used to attack each other viciously in their university days to show that they were on good terms.

"Have you given up medicine for business?" asked Jianfei.

"No. I do business in my spare time."

"It looks as if you've made a fortune."

"A fortune is out of the question. But I can afford meat for each meal. How about you?"

"Still poor as a scholar. How can I be mentioned in the same breath as this golden image?"

Lu Zhilao laughed magnanimously. "It is not a bad thing to have lots of money. Let me tell you about a deal. Profits guaranteed. As a former classmate, I'd like to see you become rich, too."

"I'm afraid—"

"Don't speak evasively. I'm very obliging. I'll only charge an information fee."

But for the moment Jianfei's anxieties were his domestic problems. What he needed most was stability and unity. Lu Zhilao chattered on about promoting the sale of Japanese infrared alarms, boasting in the most fantastic terms as if banknotes could float down like snowflakes.

"All you have to do is open your purse to catch the money."

Jianfei was not interested in this illusion of getting rich quick. He had come to discuss practical domestic matters and the husband-wife relationship.

"Is your wife fine?"

Lu Zhilao could not follow his sudden change of topic and nodded his head hastily.

Jianfei explained: "I mean is your relationship good?"

"Have you heard something?"

"No, I'm just asking."

"What a fellow you are! Everything is OK with me."

"Have you got a child?"

"Good Heavens! How come you're fussing like a woman? Why have a child? I'll leave it until I've earned enough money and enjoyed myself while I'm young. Don't you realize how poor we Chinese are?"

"I do. But I'm fond of children."

"I'm not interested yet." Lu Zhilao cut the topic short. He took up a carton of "Hilton" and threw it at Jianfei, announcing that the Japanese infrared alarms business had already begun. Jianfei could not work out why his former classmate was treating him so generously. Then Lu Zhilao said, "I have a little favour to ask you."

"I hope I'm able to help."

Jianfei had taken flight from his parent-in-law's home and was trying to get help from his friends but in the end it was he who was being asked to help.

"For you, it's as easy as lifting a finger." Lu Zhilao snapped his fingers. A young girl came out from the inner room. Obviously this was not the lady of the house.

"Thanks!" The girl smiled at Jianfei.

Jianfei felt embarrassed.

"Help this girl get rid of her problem secretly. Three months already." Lu Zhilao sounded happy and relaxed.

Jianfei didn't want to do such a thing, nor did he have the energy to arrange for an underground deal like this. But he had promised.

As he saw Jianfei off downstairs, Lu Zhilao told him that Sun Zheng lived in the building right opposite his.

Sun Zheng was also Zhuang Jianfei's former university classmate who had shared the same dormitory with him, sleeping in the bunk bed below his for five years. Sun Zheng was the sort of person who wore glasses and buttons up his shirt collar and cuffs, earnest in everything he did.

Jianfei had an impulse to drop in on him. Sun Zheng wouldn't grab him and ask him to do an abortion for a stranger.

As expected, Sun Zheng behaved dutifully. His wife had gone to work and he stayed at home to look after their child while revising an article to contribute to a journal. His daughter was just two years old and tied him up like a snake. After being frightened of Jianfei for a minute, the baby girl started to pester him. She kept wanting him to throw her up in the air. So Sun Zheng got the chance to talk. He talked seriously about his living and working conditions.

He told Jianfei that he shared a two-room flat with another family. His room was 13.5 square metres and the other was 14, which was really unfair, especially when the other one had a better view. If you got a room with a better view, you should get a smaller room. How could one person have both advantages? But there was nothing he could do about it. Lots had been drawn when these rooms were distributed so it only proved that his lot was no good.

The lounge was for the common use of the two families. "Jianfei," he said, "normally we should be talking in the lounge. It's strange that neither family receives its guests there. So now it's piled up with coal briquets and odds and ends. The wife of the other family is a shrew and the husband a miser who is always trying to use more electricity and water but pays less for both. What's worse is their ten year-old son who acts like a hooligan. He's always taking peeks at our daughter when she wees. Whenever there is a chance, the boy lures her outside." It was ironic that people spoke of the families as living together like this united household. If anyone said to him when they came in: oh, you're living in a united-household flat, he was sure to fly into a rage. "Jianfei, you understand me," he said.

Before Jianfei had time to utter a word, Sun Zheng continued. He told him that they were all skunks in the medical magazine office where he worked. None of the staff members except him knew about medical science. Before transferring there, they had all been accountants, kindergarten teachers, warehousemen and the like. However, they had the impudence to try to push him out. As he helplessly watched those didactic, exhortatory magazines come out one after another he felt deeply ashamed.

Then he talked about rising prices, the tight family budget, how tiresome and difficult it was to bring up a child, and so on.

"How is your relationship with your wife?" Jianfei asked.

"That is a question worth discussing," Sun Zheng said. "Social scientists hold different views on this." He expounded the theories of social scientists. Like a diligent student who has not quite put his finger on the right spot, he gave a long reply without coming to the point.

"What about your own marriage?" Jianfei asked again.

Sun Zheng gave a hollow laugh. "Why ask about me? My marriage is not bad."

Jianfei said, "My marriage isn't bad either—"

"Then that's good." Obviously Sun Zheng was just going through the motions of talking to him. His little daughter Beibei wanted a drink so he went to get some water for her. He was so serious that the process of pouring out some water was excessively slow. First he sterilized a glass with hot water, then a spoon. He went outside to tip out the used water. He set the glass down firmly in the centre of the table lest it be knocked off. And then he searched out the Essence of Honeysuckle amongst a row of medicine bottles... Beibei stared at him with anxious eyes all the while, smacking her lips greedily.

All of a sudden, Jianfei noticed that Sun Zheng had turned into a little old man with lots of wrinkles on his forehead and a pale face, all thin and weak. Jianfei sensibly decided to take his leave. While he bustled about, Sun Zheng suddenly asked: "What brings you here?"

The serious man had totally reversed the order of things. He had been worn down by being meticulous.

Friends, my friends! Riding along the asphalt road in melancholy mood, Jianfei was bitterly disappointed by his peers.

Just before dinner, Jianfei rushed to Mei Ying's home.

Mei Ying was cooking in the kitchen. When he arrived she nearly dropped the slice in her hand.

"I was just passing by and was struck by a sudden urge to ask your advice on a small professional problem."

Mei Ying's husband laughed loudly: "You're welcome. I like unexpected visitors." He was a big man with an open manner. He was chopping some spring onions, garlic and the like.

Their son was in the lounge room teaching a delicate, pretty girl to play piano. It looked as if they were sweethearts. The old couple were cooking for the young couple. Everyone looked happy and the place was permeated with an atmosphere of good cheer.

The girl gave Jianfei a drink and asked him for his comments on the hands of a pianist and those of a surgeon. He replied that a pianist's hands were constructive and a surgeon's destructive. The whole family laughed.

Mei Ying's husband took the slice from her so that she could go and talk to Jianfei. Jianfei apologized to him.

Mei Ying understood the implication of the word but she didn't betray anything.

In the study Jianfei told her in one breath about his awkward predicament. Mei Ying immediately made three essential suggestions:

First, learning about heart transplant operations in the United States was a major step in his career in thoracic cavity surgery. He had to get ahead, whatever the cost.

Second, sex was not the only connection between male and female. A husband and wife had many other duties. No doubt Jianfei had not adequately understood these. Ji Ling must have hidden reasons. Jianfei should try to move her with love.

Third, Jianfei's parents would have to intervene personally to settle the matter. People were equal. If you despised others then some day you'd get into trouble.

Jianfei felt that he now had a clear understanding of the whole matter. After all, that was what Mei Ying was like, mature and rich in experience. Several years had passed and only now did Jianfei realize why she had refused to marry him, though she had been madly infatuated with him. Her husband, her son and daughter-in-law were all outstanding people. In the ocean of people, outstanding figures were scarce, yet Mei Ying had three, and she would never abandon them. Life involved far, far more than sex between male and female—she was absolutely right! A wise woman indeed! With an impulse to kiss her surging inside him, Jianfei just held out his hand to her as a friend. Mei Ying shook it and gave him an understanding smile. During this short mutual gaze, they had together crossed dangerous rapids. Jianfei had become mature. What he wanted now was not a lover but a good teacher and a helpful friend. Mei Ying deserved the name of both.

After another long sleepless night, smoking and pacing around, Jianfei finally made up his mind to see his parents. Meanwhile, Ji Ling took resolute action.

Accompanied by Sister Zhang, Ji Ling went to where Jianfei worked. They went straightaway to the president's office. Sister Zhang had arranged that they should go straight there for if they went to an office at a lower level, their visit might make so much of an impact if people tried to restrain them or make peace.

They were received by Hua Rufen whose face lit up with pleasure the moment she saw Ji Ling.

"Good. Good that you've come. I knew you would but didn't expect you so soon. This is excellent!"

Both Ji Ling and Sister Zhang were so confused that neither of them knew how to respond.

Hua Rufen continued in a jocular tone: "You young couple should stroll around the hospital hand in hand."

While Hua Rufen poured out something for them to drink, Sister Zhang whispered in Ji Ling's ear: "The guilty party has filed the suit. You'd better complain and cry tears. Real tears."

Hua Rufen handed them a glass of water. "Have you seen Jianfei?" she asked.

"No," Ji Ling answered.

"Then let me call the surgical department to ask him to come and see you."

"That's not necessary," said Ji Ling.

Hua Rufen sensed something odd in the atmosphere.

"Is anything the matter?"

Ji Ling licked her pale lips. Sister Zhang held her by the shoulder.

"I have come to seek help from the hospital authorities. I want to divorce Zhuang Jianfei."

Sister Zhang presented a letter of introduction: "I am here on behalf of Ji Ling's work unit. We did an investigation and found that she has been maltreated at home, mainly emotionally. I hope that we are able to cooperate with each other."

Hua Rufen could not believe her ears.

"You want a divorce?" she asked in disbelief.

Although Jianfei had been mentally prepared, his preparations only amounted to a fight on paper. He could not hold back the strong feeling of humiliation the moment he entered his parents' home. The tribulations he had suffered before and after getting married appeared before his eyes. Ji Ling's parents were unpresentable, yet their home was their daughter's rear base, her sanctuary. They were ready at all times to spread their wings to protect their child. Jianfei envied Ji Ling in this respect. His own parents were highly educated. Their feelings ought to be much richer than those of ordinary people. But, for whatever reason, these erudite people of humanities had become estranged from the human race.

Jianfei had tried to show his parents that his marriage was a happy one. Unfortunately, just six months later, he was forced to go and ask them for help. Everyone else thought that this was the only want to solve the problem. On his way he cited many examples in modern or ancient times, to convince himself that a man must stoop to compromise for the greater good. For instance, Han Xin of the Western Han Dynasty stooped to accept the humiliation of going through someone's legs and Gou Jian of the Spring and Autumn Period slept on brushwood and tasted gall after being defeated, and so on. It sounded childish. Yet he was serious.

From his own bitter experience, Jianfei now realized that marriage did indeed temper a man.

From his early youth through to his university days, he had tried to work out why many middle-aged men were so smooth and sly when conducting themselves socially, and why they were able to endure humiliation. But all his efforts had been in vain. Now he understood that it was marriage that had a large part to play. Very rarely was some noted personage a bachelor. On the contrary, many outstanding figures experienced more than one marriage. Viewed from a certain angle, marriage could be regarded as a school of life. Mei Ying was an excellent graduate.

She had repeatedly stressed that sex was not the only relation between male and female partners. Those words were really worth their weight in gold.

Unexpectedly, Jianfei's parents set their work aside and emerged from their study to meet their son in the lounge. Jianfei felt somewhat encouraged. It seemed that his parents had begun to treat their married son as an adult, no longer taking no notice of him as before.

"Ji Ling has left home," he said.

His parents and younger sister were shocked. They all stared at him, waiting for more revelations. Jianfei noticed that in a twinkling his mother became composed. Her composure was followed by a trace of a sneer in her expression. He did not feel like saying any more but his mother waved a finger at him: "Go on."

Jianfei sketchily related what had happened, keeping back the condition for Ji Ling's return home. He wanted to see first how they would react.

His sister Jianya's attitude was the fiercest. "That's just what you'd expect from those awful little towngirls in Hankou who run away to their parents' homes whenever anything happens. Ji Ling has already gone up in the world simply by the favour you've done her of marrying her! Just ignore her for a few days and she'll quietly come back home."

"Jianya, you act like a little child."

"Brother, how come you are so weak-willed? What is Jing Ling—nothing more than a girl from Flowery Building Street."

"Don't talk like that. She is your sister-in-law!"

"But ... but she has betrayed you!"

Her words set Jianfei laughing. Ji Ling had not betrayed him.

She had just run away from home.

His father's brow was furrowed. He was worried. "You mean your wife has run away?"

"Yes."

"Why did she do so?"

"It seems there is no substantial reason."

"Why didn't she listen to you?"

"I don't know."

"She should understand that you married out of your own free will."

Jianfei nodded his head.

"It is outrageous for her to do this!"

"It is rather."

"Which body is in charge of matters of this kind? What about the law?"

Jianfei did not know whether to laugh or to cry. "I don't think there is any law about this, dad."

"All right, all right." His mother, who had been silent so far, now opened her mouth. "Jianfei, how shall I put it. The fact has proved that it was you who were wrong, not us."

Jianfei had a faint sensation that the tip of his heart was quivering at these words, which made him particularly uncomfortable.

His mother modulated her tone when speaking, putting on a demeanour she knew was attractive to students. Looking her son in the eye, she asserted, "I know your disposition very well. Ever since you were a child you have tried to keep all your sorrows to yourself. I thought you'd pretend to be happy even though you weren't. So what surprises me is not Ji Ling's running away but your coming back home to tell us about your troubles. Perhaps your purpose is not just to vent your grievances and to get sympathy from your father and sister. Their bookish sympathy can't satisfy your needs—" Her words became more and more caustic:

"If you want us to do anything for you, you'd better come straight to the point."

"No! I don't want you to do anything for me," responded Jianfei.

In fact, so long as Ji Ling and he were husband and wife, his parents were relatives of Ji Ling's parents by marriage. And his parents should go and visit their relatives. Even some of the emperors had lowly relatives. Jianfei felt that the quivering at the tip of his heart had become an ache.

"Dad, I'm going."

Then he turned to Jianya and waved to her.

His mother said, "We are not saying we won't help you."

Courteously, Jianfei inclined slightly towards his mother: "Thanks. But that won't be necessary."

The telephone rang. Jianya said, "Hang on brother. Perhaps this call is for you."

Jianfei also had a strong premonition: the call had something to do with him.

Jianya looked shocked when she answered and hurriedly called her mother over.

The call was endless. Just as Jianfei was about to leave, his mother hung up.

"She wants to get divorced," she told Jianfei.

"Ji Ling?"

"Who else would it be but her?" Jianya cut in. "The call was from Aunt Hua. They are all set to take action."

His mother asked his father to call his institute for a car. Then she turned to Jianfei: "I hope that you can go to study in the United States. Don't be swayed by personal feelings. Don't try to save a little only to lose a lot. No matter how strong your vanity is, I will help you all the same."

Marriage is not private. It belongs to all those around you. You cannot possibly act independently and take the initiative in your own hands. You cannot afford to be negligent. Even if you do not interfere in other people's affairs, they'll interfere in yours. Marriage does not mean only sex, it is far from that. A wife is not merely a partner for sex, either. She is a partner for life. To lead a life, you have to shoulder responsibilities as a husband, pay attention to your wife's changing moods, show her loving care, accommodate yourself to her and be prepared to bear the scrutiny of others. You should stumble along with her to your destiny, each supporting the other.

Of all those people around him, Jianfei felt that Mei Ying was wise. She once said, "You will understand one day, child." Now he understood.

The conflict had arisen suddenly and was resolved thus.

Jianfei's parents hurried by car to Flowery Building Street. They stopped over at Wang Yuxia Food Store on their way to buy a bag of colourful cakes. Upon arrival they handed the present to Ji Ling's parents the moment they saw them: "We were so busy before and had to postpone our visit until this late moment."

Naturally those words were from Jianfei's mother to Ji Ling's mother, who was surrounded by neighbours who had gathered to watch the event. The words more than adequately saved her face. So she smiled cordially and received her guests with immense zeal. She gave instructions right away that the table be set with wine and a meal prepared, and drew on her personal savings hidden in her inner pocket to entertain her daughter's parents-in-law.

Ji Ling's mother had experienced various aspects of life through a couple of dynastic changes and was expert at adapting herself to changing conditions. She had been notified of the visit when the car stopped to ask the way. Slipping inside her room, in the twinkling of an eye she had put on an entirely new look. Jianfei's mother had never expected that a Flowery Building Street housewife could look so neat and creditable. She felt somehow consoled.

Sister Zhang had been discussing a divorce with Ji Ling's mother. Seeing that the wind had changed, she naturally wanted to do a good deed in bringing the couple together. She led Jianfei to a corner of the lane and had a long talk with him, scolding Ji Ling for getting into a temper over trifling things and Jianfei for his being too careless with her.

When he heard that Ji Ling was pregnant, Jianfei felt a surge of emotion within him. He stayed with his parents through the dinner until at long last it was over. As soon as his parents got into the car, he got on his motorbike and flew at a fantastic speed to Sister Zhang's place.

Ji Ling cried the moment she saw Jianfei. Sister Zhang had told her everything. Ji Ling was full of regret. She was almost dehydrated from constant vomiting. It was inappropriate for her to meet her parents-in-law, so she had been lying down at Sister Zhang's home waiting for Jianfei.

"What did you eat the past few days?" asked Ji Ling.

"Just made do with snacks." Jianfei answered.

Ji Ling howled with sorrow again. Jianfei apologized to the new life, gently pressing his hand on Ji Ling's belly.

"My son, your father begs your pardon."

"It's a daughter." Ji Ling smiled through tears.

They leaned against each other, and at great length put the respective parts together to bring out the complete story. One moment they blamed each other and the next moment contended to examine their own faults. They cried, laughed, expressed jealousy and looked forward to their future—filled with every kind of emotions.

It was late before they knew it. Sister Zhang had bought food home and invited them to stay for dinner, which they declined. Jianfei said, "Let's go home."

"Let's," Ji Ling agreed.

"Divorce" had become a joke. Jianfei had finally solved all the problems satisfactorily. He believed that from now on he had experience.

Only Jianya still took the incident to heart and treated Ji Ling tepidly. She wrote in her diary: "Brother's wife doesn't love him. He is to be pitied." She herself, however, already over thirty years old, was still searching for a husband after her heart. In her opinion, there were no real men in contemporary China. But contemporary China did not tolerate single women. So she added in her diary: "I am also to be pitied."

Translated by Ma Aiying and John McLaren

Trials and Tribulations

MORNING began in the middle of the night.

In the murkiness of the small hours came a resounding thump, followed by a bloodcurdling wail. Yin Jiahou woke with his heart pounding, his body stiff with fright, and for a moment thought he was having a nightmare. By the time he realized that his son had fallen out of bed, his wife had already scrambled down from the bed in her bare feet and in a quavering voice was calling his name. Mother and son bumped into one another in the dark and knocked over several household articles as they stumbled about in the narrow, overcrowded space.

His first, instinctive reaction should have been to turn on the light, he knew. When something happens in a household at night, the father must remain calm and collected. But he couldn't find the pullcord! Panting, he spread his arms wide and groped blindly across the wall. "The light!" his wife spat through clenched teeth, then began to sob. In a burst of agitation, Yin Jiahou jumped up, put one foot on the bedside table and grasped the pullcord near where it joined the switch at the top of the wall. One mighty pull and the light was on, but the pullcord came away in his hand. Flinging it aside in irritation,

Yin Jiahou anxiously called out to his son: "Leilei!"

Choking with sobs, his beady little black eyes open wide and round as saucers, Leilei stood and stared at his father as if at some stranger. Yin Jiahou spread out his arms and asked uncertainly, "Are you all right? Leilei, it's me, your father!"

"Ass!" his wife hissed, and elbowed him aside.

"I'm bleeding," said the boy suddenly.

Leilei's leg had a scrape on it, from which blood was oozing. When they saw the blood, Mother and Father stared at it, dumbstruck. Yin Jiahou was the first to emerge from shock and fetch iodine, cotton swabs and disinfectant powder from a drawer, while his wife stood there as if frozen, tears welling up in her wide-open eyes. As he deftly bandaged the boy's leg, Yin Jiahou woke up completely, and as he did so his feelings of guilt gradually subsided. It was he, and no one else, who was stopping the flow of his son's blood. Using his foot to push aside all objects knocked over in the commotion, Yin Jiahou cleared a little space on the floor in front of the bed and set his son down in the middle of it. "There," he said, ruffling the boy's hair. "Now let's go to sleep, hm?"

"Oh, no you don't. Leilei has to have a wash first," his wife interposed. Her tone was one of firm resolve.

"If you wash him, he'll be all awake and excited; then how will he get back to sleep?" Yin Jiahou protested weakly.

"He woke up when he hit the floor!" his wife retorted, and started off on a long harangue: "Just go out and have a look around, and see if there is one single worker who has worked for seventeen years without receiving housing. You call this dump a place fit for humans? It's a pigsty, a doghouse! And I'm the one who managed to get hold of it at all! If you're a man, if you

want a wife and child, you've got to have a place to put them!
But you're such a fool you just take everything they dish out,
without so much as a fart in protest! What kind of a man is
that?"

Yin Jiahou hung his head and felt his shame burn in his chest.
He sat on the edge of the bed, his eyes fixed in a blank stare.

But what connection was there between their living quarters
and the boy's falling out of bed? His wife was just taking advantage of this excuse to let off steam. During their courtship, Yin
Jiahou had been as qualified as any of the other workers to receive a housing assignment, and back then he had actually told
her they would be able to get a place soon after they got married. Having boasted so recklessly, he now had no choice but to
submit whenever it pleased his wife to heap scorn on him. Actually, in the beginning it had only been because the factory director had promised him that he had dared to guarantee her a
house. Now his wife could run him down whenever she liked,
but he certainly couldn't do the same to the factory director.

Yin Jiahou waited for an opportunity: only his son would be
able to shut off this flood of words. As his wife was taking a
breath, he quickly cut in, "Leilei, my boy, tell Papa how you
fell out of bed."

"I was going to piss," the boy said.

"Say 'pee', Leilei, not 'piss'," his mother interjected.
"Aren't you supposed to call me when you want to pee?"

"Today I wanted to go by myself."

"Just look at that!" his mother exclaimed triumphantly, her
eyes blazing. "He's just four! Only four years old! Who else has
a four-year-old that smart?"

"That's right!" Raising his head, Yin Jiahou tried to conceal his satisfaction. Not every husband has the skill to calm the wind and waves of his wife's temper so successfully. "Our Leilei's really something!" he added.

"Ah, my boy!" His wife was obviously tickled.

Turning his rosy-cheeked little face up at them, Leilei chirped, "Papa, it's your turn to take me on your monthly pass today, isn't it?"

"Today?" Yin Jiahou suddenly realized it was ten to four in the morning. "That's right," he answered, "but it won't be time to get up for an hour yet. So back in the steamer with you, little dumpling."

"What does that mean, Papa—'back in the steamer'?" Leilei asked.

"That's what we say when you go back to sleep after having woken up," his father answered.

"When you go to sleep in the afternoon after having woken up in the morning, is that called going back in the steamer, too?"

Yin Jiahou laughed. Only when talking with his son could he laugh so unself-consciously. His son was his harbour of refuge. "I suppose you could call it that," he answered.

"The nurse at the kindergarten called it noonday nap. She's wrong," said the little boy.

"No, she's not," said his father. "Leilei, look at you; you're all wide awake from washing your face."

"He was wide awake when he fell!" his wife snapped, her tone still bellicose.

Yin Jiahou had no stomach for a major confrontation at this hour. He had the whole day ahead of him, and he'd need her help in all kinds of ways before it ended. "Right," he offered soothingly, "it was the fall. But let's not worry about that now;

we've got to get some sleep!"

His wife sat motionless until Yin Jiahou had lain down, then exclaimed in martyred tones, "Sleep! How's a body supposed to sleep with this light blazing away?"

Having just about arrived at the end of his tether, Yin Jiahou was preparing an equally ugly retort when he remembered it was he who had broken the pullcord. He swallowed once, set his jaw and climbed resignedly out of bed.

In the very instant the light went out, the screwdriver in Yin Jiahou's hand flashed, sending a thought racing through his brain. He didn't dare look down at his wife; he was too terrified by what had occurred to him.

As his eyes adjusted, he discovered it was not so dark after all. The light of dawn was already shining through the curtains, and buses were rumbling by in the street. Yin Jiahou had a distinct vision of his home as a beam upon which he and his wife stood and struggled to keep their balance. You may have got out of bed first to comfort the boy, but I was the one who bandaged his scratch. I'll repair the pullcord I broke, and you can preen yourself over the housing you acquired for us. All of a sudden Yin Jiahou felt terribly aggrieved. Screwing up his courage, he looked again at the screwdriver in his hand. The sky grew light, and Yin Jiahou felt as if he had had a dream about his family but couldn't for the life of him remember what the dream was about.

In the end he got up late.

His shift started at eight a. m., and he had to catch the six-fifty ferry if he didn't want to be late. To get to the ferry he had to take the bus for four stops, with a ten-minute walk at either end. And what if the traffic wasn't running smoothly? What if the traffic was running smoothly, but he couldn't elbow his way on to the crowded bus? If he didn't have his son with him, of course, he could always force his way on the bus, but today it was his turn to take the boy. After yawning briefly Yin Jiahou began to dress himself with lightning speed, at the same time prodding his son gently with his foot. "Leilei! Leilei! Quick, get up!"

His wife pulled the towelling blanket over her face and mumbled through it, "Must you make so much noise?"

"I'm going to be late," Yin Jiahou replied anxiously. "Leilei won't wake up." His wife didn't move. As a last resort, he scooped up his son with one arm and said, "Hey! Wake up! Now!"

"Ow! You're hurting me," the boy complained.

"Leilei, you mustn't sleep anymore. Papa's going to be late, and he still has to heat up your milk," Yin Jiahou said in desperation.

The common washroom had two sinks shared by ten families. Morning was the worst time; everyone had to queue up to wash his face and brush his teeth. At a single glance Yin Jiahou could see there were five or six people ahead of him—if he went to the latrine now, he would get back just in time for his turn at the sink. He addressed the woman in front of him: "Jin, I'm leaving my washbasin here behind you. I'll be right back." Miss Jin nodded expressionlessly and hooked her foot around the rim of the basin, preparing to brag it forward.

The latrine was full as well; four old men squatted over the four holes, each smoking a cigarette, eyes lidded in meditation. Yin Jiahou's breath was becoming increasingly audible as he ex-

pelled it through his nostrils. "What's the matter, Yin? Can't
hold it?" one of the them cackled.

Yin Jiahou forced himself to grunt politely in acknowledgment
but kept his attention on a remnant of cobweb which hung across
the brickwork window. The old man chuckled again: "When
you get old, everything takes more time. There's nothing for it
but to squat here until I can produce something. After all, one
has to get in the habit of going at the same time every day.
You're certainly obliging, doing your business at home when you
could do it on company time at the factory."

Rot! Yin Jiahou ached to burst out, but didn't for fear of of-
fending his neighbour, which would have done no good at all.
Practically at the limit of endurance, Yin Jiahou hunched over
anxiously and made to leave. Just as he reached the door, he
heard the rustling of paper behind him, and his legs practically
gave way.

Back in the washroom, Yin Jiahou's washbasin was just in
front of the sink, but the person behind him in line had stepped
over it and was brushing her teeth. Throwing caution to the
winds, he elbowed her aside and began to wash his face and
brush his teeth; by now, he didn't have time to be polite. The
woman he had pushed aside, her mouth full of toothpaste, shot
him a look and said loudly as he left the washroom, "Now
there's low breeding for you!"

Yin Jiahou heard the cutting remark, but hoped his wife
hadn't. If she had, she was sure to let fly at the woman, as if
she was roundly cursing Yin rather than merely making a snide
remark.

Unfortunately, the boy had fallen asleep again.

"Leilei! Leilei!" Yin called out and slapped the boy on his

bottom while lighting the paraffin stove for his milk.

"Papa, don't hit me. I just want to sleep a little bit longer."

"You can't. Papa's going to be late."

"What's so bad about that? Papa, please. Just now I was bleeding a lot."

"OK, you sleep. Papa will carry you," Yin Jiahou said hoarsely.

Flipping aside the towelling blanket, his wife sat up, her eyes a deep red. "Come on, Leilei, Mama'll get out your new clothes for you. Your sailor suit. You can sling your submachine gun over your shoulder, and you'll be just like a sailor on a ship."

The boy perked up: "With ribbons hanging from the cap?"

"Of course."

Yin Jiahou shot his wife a grateful glance, but she paid him no attention. While she saw to the child, Yin Jiahou poured the milk into a vacuum flask, found his monthly pass, his wallet, his cigarettes, his keys and his copy of *Thunder Shakes the Land*, a *kungfu* novel by Liang Yusheng. Stuffing a roll of lemon cream biscuits in Yin Jiahou's shoulder bag, his wife admonished him as always, "Now, Leilei has to eat a few biscuits before drinking his milk. He mustn't drink milk on an empty stomach." Catching hold of the handbag again, she shoved in an apple, saying, "Eat it after lunch." Finally she stuffed in a handkerchief.

Afraid she would come up with still more items, Yin Jiahou quickly scooped up the boy and said, "Let's go, sailor. Our warship's weighing anchor."

"Bye, Mama," said the boy.

"Bye, Leilei," said his mother.

Leilei waved his little hand, and his mother waved back.

Without once turning back, Yin Jiahou strode resolutely into the seething flow of humanity on the street. He knew as well as if he had eyes in the back of his head that a woman with her clothes thrown over her shoulders, her bare heels squashing down the backs of her shoes and her hair done up in a way that looked like a crow's nest, was standing forlornly in front of a window in the tumbled-down row of old houses. She was watching father and son as they walked away. This was his wife. Are you sorry that your wife isn't a bit prettier? But think: in the whole world there is only her to see you off and wait for your return.

Today they had good luck: just as Yin Jiahou and his son arrived at the bus stop, a bus pulled up.

The bus was as jerky and clumsy as an old cow, and you could hear it roaring and screeching a mile off. It pulled up at the stop and came to a halt easily enough, but it was so packed with people the doors couldn't open. For a little while the people inside and outside the bus worked together—the former, who wanted to get on, kicking. Yin Jiahou pulled his shoulder bag round in front of him and hugged both it and his son tight. Darting back and forth like a boxer in the ring, he looked for the best door to get in by and for the weakest link in the human chain separating him from the bus.

A ticket-seller stuck her head out the window of the bus and yelled, "The doors are broken. They're broken! Broken!"

The bus started off again amidst a storm of vile language directed at the ticket-seller. The curses had not yet died down when the bus suddenly screeched to a halt and all the doors opened with resounding thumps. Passengers wearing crafty smiles, as if they had taken part in some secret plot, swarmed off the bus, while the waiting crowd, suddenly realizing they had been deceived, rushed toward the bus with a threatening roar. Yin Jiahou, however, who was an old hand at bus riding, had seen through the bus-driver's trickery from the beginning, and had kept pace by trotting alongside. On the bus, a man with a fat face was smiling mockingly at Yin Jiahou. Puckering his lips, the man screwed up his face as if he were calling the pigs. Keeping his eyes fixed steadily on the face, Yin Jiahou allowed all the anger and hurt he felt to gather and swell up in his breast. Having made sure the man would exit by the middle door of the bus, Yin Jiahou waited at that door. Good! Afraid of being squeezed, Fatface was alighting last, as slowly and carefully as if the bus were his private limousine. From one side, Yin Jiahou caught hold of the handle on the inside of the door and leapt onto the bus with one stride, pushing Fatface heavily against the door with his back and then twisting his body. Fatface began to moan, but the waiting passengers pulled him aside impatiently, sending him spinning onto the pavement. Yin Jiahou heaved a deep, contented sigh.

Leaving behind everything in the world outside the bus, Yin Jiahou raised his head and prepared to deal with everything on the bus. Although no one offered a seat to him with his child in his arms, they did move a bit to give him a place to stand, which in itself was not bad. With one hand he held the overhead bar and with the other his son as he listlessly observed the passing scence through the bus window. The sky was growing lighter minute by minute, and the rosy hue of dawn tinged a row of shops. Every morning and every evening he passed these same shops. Without knowing exactly why, Yin Jiahou felt fed up, tired of the worry that constantly dogged his tracks. Right now he merely hoped that the bus would arrive soon at the riverside without breaking down.

His son's hopes were far more numerous.

"Papa, put me down."

"It's too stuffy down there," said Yin.

"No, it's not. I'll get the monthly pass and show it to the auntie when she comes round to check."

The surrounding passengers all praised the child's intelligence which made him all the more insistent and Yin Jiahou had no choice but to set him down. When the bus rounded a sharp corner, however, several young women came plummeting towards them. Yin Jiahou bent quickly over his son to shield him and tried to fend off the falling bodies by pushing backwards with his hands. One of the women shrieked, "Help! A pervert!" Puzzled, Yin Jiahou turned and asked, "What did *I* do to you?" Someone answered for her, "You felt her leg."

The passengers loved this. Everyone burst out laughing. The woman let fly a stream of abuse, directing it pointblank at Yin Jiahou so that a spray of saliva landed on the back of his neck. When he saw how prettily she was made up, the fist he had clenched relaxed. But what the father had restrained himself from doing, the son went ahead and did: reaching through Yin Jiahou's legs, Leilei began to pummel the woman with his tiny fists, muttering, "C'mon, let's fight! Fight!"

"Leilei!" Yin Jiahou scolded, and quickly scooped up the boy, but not before he had suffered a kick. Leilei let out a roar half of pain and half of anger, his hair standing on end and his ears wagging back and forth. Throwing himself across Yin Jiahou's shoulder, he gave the young woman a crisp blow on the ears. All eyes were fixed on the unfolding spectacle as the woman first stared in shock, then suddenly began to whimper.

Father and son alighted from the bus in triumph. Leilei, over-joyed, strutted about with his chest stuck out a mile and his little rear end wagging in self-satisfaction. But Yin Jiahou's head drooped; somehow he couldn't share in his son's elation.

Being on the ferry was practically the same as being at the factory; all the passengers were Yin's fellow workers.

"Oh-ho, so it's your turn to deliver the little thing again," boomed a convivial voice.

"Mm-hm," grunted Yin.

Naturally someone offered them a seat, but the boy would not sit still; people kept on calling him over to play with them. One pretty woman worker, having just married, showed a particular interest in children, and Leilei liked her a lot. When he spotted her, he immediately went over and cuddled up to her. "Mr Yin," she called, "leave Leilei to me. I'll feed him his milk."

Yin passed her his shoulder bag, then dusted off his hands and stretched his shoulders backwards a few times to relax them. It was the first time he'd had a breather all morning.

"Your little youngster's certainly got an eye for the ladies," somebody remarked.

"Mm," responded Yin.

"Come on, make a foursome with us."

"Nope. I only watch cards, I don't play," said Yin.

A cigarette came flipping through the air. Yin caught it ex-pertly, stuck it in his mouth and lit it. With two brief toots of its whistle, the ferry left the landing-stage awash in its wake.

Foursomes of card-players quickly formed, the players all pulling out newspapers or magazines or pulling off one shoe to pad their bottoms, and instantly the deck was covered with little circles of players. Yin Jiahou squatted at the spot where three circles adjoined, observing all three games. By the time he'd smoked half his cigarette, nothing interesting had happened, so he rose and left. There'd been a time when Yin Jiahou had been an absolute fiend for cards; that was before he turned twenty-five. He'd been quite a cardshark; in fact, he got so good he never lost and came to think himself invincible. One morning, however, on this same ferry deck, he lost to a couple of in-significant-looking types. After that, he suddenly felt card-playing lacked the slightest bit of interest. So what if one won? So what if one lost? He'd never played again. Sometimes he kib-itzed a bit, long enough to see that the players were completely in the dark and would end up tricked by Lady Luck no matter how hard they tried. When he saw how the more they were tricked, the more obsessed they became, shouting till their faces were red and the veins stood out on their necks, Yin Jiahou sud-denly and acutely felt how meaningless it all was. Back then he must have looked as idiotic as they. Ah! he sighed inwardly. How this old world treats us!

Leilei's milk and biscuits had made their way into his stomach without ado, and now he was sitting placidly on a folding stool no bigger than your palm, listening to the pretty woman worker tell stories. When Yin Jiahou approached, the boy looked right through him. As Yin Jiahou regarded Leilei coolly for a few mo-ments, a vague heartache welled up in his chest and enveloped him like the smoke he exhaled.

Yin tossed a number of cigarettes to the people around him in return for the one he'd caught when he came on board. If you smoked someone else's, you had to give some away in return;

otherwise you kept feeling you owed somebody something. A real man had to be big-hearted. As he tossed the cigarettes, he affected a casual, careless expression; his manner was magnanimous, his movements fluid and untrammelled. At this moment he was content, and often he felt this contentment only while riding the ferry. Off the boat—at the factory, at home, on the bus—everything was so much more complicated than this reciprocation of cigarettes, so much stranger, that he often couldn't work out whether he owed or was owed. Whenever he felt confused on this point, he tried to tell himself to forget about who owed whom: it was too small and calculating, too confining.

The Yangtse River was in flood; waves chased each other over its vast surface. The ferry was moving downstream, and Yin had a strong sensation of the boat slicing through the waves, propelled by the wind. The sun slowly rose ahead of the boat as a flock of pure white river gulls chased the spume tossed up in the boat's wake, their movement in flight precise and pleasing. This was morning on the Yangtse River, of which millions dreamed, but the passengers on the boat were indifferent, having seen it so many times. Yin Jiahou leaned against the rail, smoking his cigarette, his spirit as empty as the river was vast. Ever since he had stopped playing cards and become a husband and father, he liked to lean over the rail of the ferry, blowing smoke out over the river. Gradually his heart became as heavy as if the entire weight of the tremendous river were pressing on it.

Xiao Bai squeezed his way over to bum a smoke off Yin. Bai was a secretary in the factory offices, a sallow-faced, angry young man, scornful of the world and its ways, who harboured literary ambitions.

"Shit!" Bai began emphatically. "Your trousers are split to hell, man. And in a good place. Looks like your crotch wants a place in the sun."

Looking down, Yin saw that his trousers were indeed split, and that the white piping of his underwear was showing through. They hadn't been split this morning when he'd put them on; his wife wouldn't have let them pass inspection if they had been. It must have happened in the fracas on the bus.

"It's from getting pushed on the bus. Nothing for it now," said Yin. "But it doesn't matter. Where this split is, if a man sees it, it doesn't matter, while the women won't dare look there."

"I love it. You have such a vivid way with language," said Bai admiringly.

Engineer Jia, who was leaning off to one side reading the newspaper, smiled conspiratorially, neatly folded his newspaper, tucked it into his bag and sidled over.

"Yin, not only is what you say interesting; it is also rather scientific."

"Here, Jia, have a smoke."

"No, thanks. I've given up."

"Again?" Bai mocked.

"This time for real," said Jia. Pulling out his newspaper and spreading it flat, he showed them an article in the middle of the crease which warned that not only did cigarettes contain tar, nicotine and other carcinogens, they were also radioactive. A pack a day for a year was equivalent to two hundred and fifty X-rays.

Carefully refolding the newspaper, Engineer Jia declared solemnly, "A man must have strength and spirit. Just look at our national women's volleyball team. They've won the world championship four times in a row!"

Feeling suddenly ashamed of himself, Yin Jiahou took a deep and forceful drag on his cigarette, then hid his face in the cloud of blue smoke.

"What's so great about winning four championships?" retorted Bai. "All you need for those physical kinds of things is brawn. But look at Cao Xueqin.* He lived in a rat-infested old grass hut, ate nothing but rice gruel and pickled vegetables, and worked ten years to produce the undying classic *A Dream of Red Mansions*."

"Aw, bullshit!" someone interrupted rudely. "You go on and on about mental versus physical, but the truth is that if someone's born with enough intelligence he can become great even by just playing a game. Look at Liu Dahua, the international chess master. What title sounds better than 'international master', I ask you?"

The discussion was rapidly gaining participants.

"A good-sounding title isn't worth a fart! Just look at Zhou Jihong. A chit of a girl, but one somersault into the water and she gets a gold medal, a three-bedroom flat and thousands of yuan in prize money."

Still puffing away at his cigarette, Yin Jiahou felt more depressed than ever. His restless, angry heart swelled with indignation, heaving like the waves on the river. Everyone was human. We are all human!

Bai, feisty to the end, was ferociously disputing the arguments of the others, his face flushed: "Money-grubbers! Only litera-

---

* Cao Xueqin (?-1763), Qing-dynasty author.

ture offers real satisfaction. Poets. Poetry. How can material
enjoyment compare with spiritual? Some poems make you want
to laugh and cry—now *that's* what's interesting in life. One
young poet wrote a poem, a poem with only one word, and it's
amazing! Listen: it's called 'Life', and it goes: 'Net'. How's
that? Fantastic, eh? Which of you doesn't live in a net?"

A momentary hush fell. Everyone looked blankly, humour-
lessly at one another. Suddenly Yin Jiahou felt his palms grow
hot, and a strange excitement took hold of him. "I have a response to that one," he said abruptly. "The title is the same,
and my poem also has only one word—"

All eyes were now on him. "—Dream," he said decisively.

A roar of approval went up. Everyone liked Yin Jiahou's
"dream". Several literary enthusiasts, Bai at their head, clustered around Yin and began to quiz him on his views of modern
poetry.

With a sudden hoarse roar, the ferry whistle drowned out all
other sounds. Tracing a graceful arc on the river's surface, the
ferry came to rest against the landing-stage. Yin Jiahou laughed
and snapped his fingers resoundingly. No one on this earth was
loftier than anyone else, and Yin Jiahou was not of a lower order than anyone else. Who could tell what might befall in the
days to come?

His son trotted towards him with the bandage wound round his
little leg, holding his toy submachine gun and uttering fierce
war-cries. Yin Jiahou thought to himself how brave the boy
looked. Who was to say this child might not someday become a
general?

Life was, after all, full of hope and promise. Such a fine,
clear May morning!

They flowed ashore with the human tide. It was time to find a little something to eat. Since they had made their ferry, they now had enough time to stop for breakfast.

The restaurant where they ate was located very conveniently: it was a food stall next to the road. Two stoves made from old oil drums were situated one on each side of the shack, blue flames leaping high out of their tops. One stove was being used to fry dough sticks, whole rolling rafts of them, from which a fragrant, oily smoke arose which burned one's throat slightly. The other stove was topped by an enormous wok half full of seething yellow water with an even yellower layer of foam on top. This was for boiling noodles, single servings of which were passed through the water in a bamboo strainer, lifted out, lightly shaken and dumped into a bowl. When soy sauce, sesame oil, sesame paste, monosodium glutamate, pepper and a little chopped onion were added, you had a bowl of so-called hot "dry" noodles, a Wuhan speciality. Yin Jiahou had eaten them for breakfast ever since he was little. For twenty cents you could fill yourself—what other big city could provide such a hearty meal for so little money? He had never so much as dreamed of eating anything else.

The ticket-seller counter was under a willow tree next to the shack. The ticket-seller had put on a light coat of makeup, but her clothes were spatted with grease spots. A little blackboard was hung on the tree with a grandiloquent announcement scrawled on it: HEY! Cold noodles are here! HO!

Cold noodles were actually "dry" noodles that had not been swirled in the boiling wok. Yin Jiahou decided to buy dough sticks and cold noodles, as the latter could be slurped up more quickly than the hot "dry" noodles.

Both father and son moved speedly and decisively, well-trained as they were by experience. Yin squeezed his way into the group clustered around the ticket-seller, while his son raced over and got in line for hot noodles. Noting that there was a long queue for dough sticks, Leilei set down his gun as a place-saver in the hot noodle queue and ran over to queue for dough sticks.

In the end they didn't have to wait at all for their dough sticks. Yin Jiahou patted his son's head approvingly, which made Leilei proud as a peacock. But when the boy saw that his father had bought tickets not for hot noodles but for cool, he sagged like a blighted plant and plodded over to pick up his gun. The people in the queue for hot noodles had not paid the least attention to this placemarker; several of them had already stepped around it. When Leilei discovered this, he aimed the submachine gun at them and swept them with a rapid volley, adding sound effects.

"Leilei!" Yin Jiahou shouted in shocked reproof.

In less than three minutes breakfast was over. Everyone ate at the side of the road, leaving their bowls and chopsticks wherever they happened to be when they finished. Yin Jiahou did the same, setting down his bowl, giving Leilei a little push and then setting off. Holding a fried dough stick between his thumb and forefinger, the boy munched as he walked along, smacking his lips. It was delicious. Meanwhile, Yin Jiahou thought to himself: this kid is really cruel! He took up his gun so casually and mowed down all those people! What would become of such a boy? And who could he have inherited this it? Yin Jiahou certainly wasn't that fierce, and his wife was only fierce in one specific area: her mouth. What was he to do with the child? He reminded himself it was high time to pay attention to Leilei's education. No longer could they afford to muddle along! Immediately his back hunched a little, as if a weight had been placed on his shoulders.

After they boarded the bus that would take them to the factory, Yin Jiahou struck up a conversation with his son.

"Leilei, when we get home tonight, don't upset your mother by telling her we ate cool noodles."

"It wasn't 'we'. It was you."

"Right. It was me, then. To be a good boy you've got to learn how to be considerate of others."

"Pa, why will Mama be upset?"

"Because Mama doesn't like us to use the bowls and chopsticks at the restaurant. They have germs on them."

"Germs that make your tummy hurt?"

"Yes."

"Then why didn't you do like Mama said?"

He had underestimated this four-year-old. The old explanations were for toddlers; they wouldn't work anymore.

"Yes, you're right. We shouldn't have eaten the noodles. But if we want to eat breakfast at home, Papa has to get up when it's still dark out and light the coal stove. Just in order to eat a bowl of noodles, I have to lose sleep and waste a lot of coal. If we want to eat breakfast at the factory canteen, we're always too late, and they're out of food. And if we bring our bowls and chopsticks, it's even harder to squeeze our way on to the bus. So there's nothing for it but to eat at the food-stall. Luckily, Papa's been eating cool noodles since he was little. I'm used to it, and I can fight off those germs. But if you're in bad health, you absolutely must not eat the food there."

"OK. I know."

The boy was quite satisfied with Yin's honest answer. That's right, thought Yin to himself. It takes just this kind of skill and patience. He was just about to launch into a discussion of why it was not good to shoot at people with the toy gun when the little boy spoke first: "So when we get home tonight, I should go straight to Mama and tell her: 'Papa didn't eat cold noodles to-day.' Is that right?"

Yin Jiahou shook his head, not knowing whether to laugh or groan, and reflected that he hadn't even resolved these questions for himself. If he were to tell the boy that he must not lie under any circumstances, then how was Leilei to deal with the many situation in life which demanded the concealment of the truth?

Having dropped Leilei at the factory kindergarten, Yin set off at a run for the workshop.

Much time had been wasted at the kindergarten. The nurses there heartily disliked such "temporary residents" as Leilei and grumbled that today's beds, towels and cups were already ac-counted for, and lunch and cake already planned; now they'd have to start all over and make a new plan, but they'd already bought today's food, and there was just enough. How were they to make room for all these "temporary residents" that had showed up? "Not enough gruel for all the monks," so what did he want them to do? What a hassle! And so forth.

Yin Jiahou simpered as he explained his situation, terrified that the nurses would maltreat his son.

When the bell rang for the start of the shift, Yin Jiahou had just stepped through the main door of the workshop. The old man who noted latecomers and absentees was seated there, his finger pointing to Yin Jiahou's name on the name-list, his lips mumbling something as he watched Yin approach.

This man had suffered some brain damage in an industrial accident, impairing his reason, but that only made him all the more immovable and impartial in his new job. Also, everyone at the factory believed him endowed with an almost supernatural ability to estimate the correct time.

Yin Jiahou's eyes met those of the old man, and Yin flashed him a shallow, obsequious smile to which the old man did not betray the slightest reaction. Yin could only hurry past. Returning his gaze from the back of the retreating Yin Jiahou to the book, the old man lowered his head and carefully wrote the number 1.5. The workshop was so vast that to arrive at his team's section from the main door would actually take a minute and a half. Yin Jiahou was marked late again.

He was not an ordinary operator in just any old factory. He was a modern operator who had had a year of theoretical study and another year of rigorous training under a Japanese specialist, and he worked in a modern sheet steel factory on an imported Japanese machine.

Steel ingots the size of the prefabricated cement blocks used in building arrived at their factory and within ten minutes were pressed between rollers into sheet steel as thin as paper, which was then rolled up tight, tied and stacked into piles. Yin Jiahou's job was to roll up the sheet steel and tie it up.

His control panel was in a glassed-in room which was painted a creamy yellow. The sloping face of the panel was covered with all kinds of switches, lights and knobs, beneath which were directions for use, all in Japanese. A colour television monitor displayed progress at each stage of the rolling process. The workshop was as tall and spacious as a cathedral, the atmosphere just

as solemn. Not a single worker was to be seen busying himself a-
long the whole production line, and the quality of the sheet steel
was monitored and automatically adjusted by radioelectric sen-
sors. Totally automatic, no need to go and sweat blood and tears
on the floor; what more could a worker ask?

When the factory had been built in the seventies, it had been
made commensurate with advanced world standards. Now, in
the eighties, it was still the only one of its kind in China. All
kinds of people came in droves to tour it, from foreigners to mi-
nority nationalities, from primary school students to leaders
from Party Central. If it weren't for the various other problems
that got mixed up in his work, Yin Jiahou would have been perfectly satisfied with his job, and proud of it, too.

Yin had a classmate from middle school who worked in a
steelworks not far from his own factory and who could never
wear a white shirt. In fact, whatever he wore was stained a
filthy orange at the collar and cuffs by the end of the day; no
detergent could wash those stains clean. This classmate had
written a will requesting he be dressed in a snow-white shirt for
his own funeral, and had sent the will to the Minister of Metal-
lurgy. For this he had been punished by the administration. Yin
Jiahou, on the other hand, scarcely had a single shirt that wasn't
white; they all looked smart with any jacket. Whenever he felt
particularly dejected, Yin Jiahou forced himself to remember his
classmate and console himself by comparing their present jobs.

This was exactly what he was doing at the moment.

Glancing at his white cuffs, he reassured himself of the supe-
riority of his job and turned a deaf ear to what everyone around
him was saying.

He had been standing steadfastly at his control panel doing his job, watching as the sheet steel came flying like a fiery dragon into his station, only to end up curled into a well-behaved roll, bound and carted off .... but then the factory heads decided to hold a meeting of the whole workshop to elect bonus recipients. When at the end of May, after several meetings, April's bonus had still not been assigned, the factory leaders decided that the workers' enthusiasm for production was being seriously affected.

The workshop supervisor had looked fidgety at the beginning of the meeting. Now he was a million miles off track, going on and on about the completely irrelevant topic of family planning.

Someone gave the person in front of him a little push in the small of the back; this was the signal for the person in front to perk up and pay close attention to the workshop supervisor. When the signal was passed to Yin Jiahou, he suddenly noticed how strained the atmosphere had become.

What if something ... unexpected happened? Yin Jiahou thought, alarmed.

Finally the workshop supervisor turned to the topic of bonuses, catching everyone off guard, and at last let slip a scrap of real information: the factory office had issued a regulation stipulating clearly that it was forbidden to use the "merry-go-round" system to assign bonuses. If it was discovered this system was being used, not only would the bonuses be taken away; fines would be levied as well—this time for real!

Suddenly Yin Jiahou seemed to have lost his bearings, and he felt a sort of sour lump congeal around his heart. But he quickly regained his composure.

The word "merry-go-round" was in fact taboo in this context; it had never once been heard on the workshop floor. In the sev-

eral years since unequal bonuses had been introduced as a regula-
tory measure to combat the "egalitarianism" of the past, everyone had silently agreed to use the "merry-go-round" system as a
matter of course. First, second and third prize went to different
recipients each month until everyone had received them, whereupon the cycle began again. All the workers got along fine, so
there was nothing embarrassing about this system. The workshop leaders closed their eyes to the practice, and everything
went smooth as silk. The workshop had even been designated a
"model work unit of spiritual civilization".

Everything had been so perfect; whence today's bolt from the
blue?

The eyes of his co-workers kept roving back and forth across
Yin Jiahou; the workshop supervisor was watching him, too.
This month it was supposed to be his turn to receive first prize.

The first prize bonus was thirty yuan. Yin Jiahou and his wife
had long ago planned how they were going to spend it: they
were going to buy their son a battery-powered toy, then go out
to Banks' for a Western-style meal. "Let's squander a little, enjoy ourselves for once," he told his wife. And she had replied
smilingly that she'd often wondered what Western cuisine tasted
like but had never dared hope to eat at Banks', seeing as how
there was never any money to spare at the end of the month.

A few days ago his wife had asked, "Have they given out the
bonuses yet?"

"Soon," he had replied.

"First prize, huh?"

"That's right!" he had answered. "It's mine for sure this
time."

Unwillingly recalling his wife's rare smile that time, he reflected on the bitter truth she so often asserted: there's no free lunch! He stared blankly for quite some time at his snowy-white cuffs, then popped the joints in his fingers one by one.

The leader of the second work team edged over to Yin Jiahou. They were in the same situation. "Hey! Yin!" he said. "A good man will always end up bullied; a good horse will always end up broken."

"Oh, come off it," Yin muttered irritably.

"Someone must have written a letter to the factory director telling him what was happening," said the team leader. "A lot of sons of bitches seem to enjoy doing that lately. We may be shift heads, you and I, but I'll be damned if we get any more bonuses no matter how hard we work. It's damned unfair! If we're going to get the short end of the stick, it should at least be for a good reason."

"Stop whining," said Yin.

"Let's wait and see who they choose to win the bonuses," said the second work team leader. "If the choices are absolutely ridiculous, I'm going to write a letter to the Party Disciplinary Committee of the company and dump this bellyful of bile."

Yin Jiahou elected not to answer.

If before the bonuses were awarded Yin Jiahou had been trusting to his luck, when the results were announced he could only despair. He had thought to himself that even if they didn't go by the "merry-go-round", April's first-prize bonus should still be his. The whole workshop had been overhauled in April, and he'd been at the factory day and night, working like a horse. Nobody had worked as hard as he; everyone knew that. But determined to ward off disaster, they went to the opposite extreme and gave him only third prize: a bonus of five yuan.

They even went so far as to read out the attendance records. Affecting a resigned expression, the workshop supervisor announced who had skipped work, who had been ill, who had been absent for personal reasons, and who had been tardy—but he neglected to say how many minutes late they had arrived. When someone pointed this out, the supervisor waved his hand and said airily, "That's not important. You know the timekeeper's not quite right in the head." So Yin Jiahou received another stab in the back. If the supervisor had announced that someone was a minute and a half late, he would have been laughed off the podium, and that would have been the end of that, but if he just said someone was late, that was a different kettle of fish. Yin Jiahou had arrived late that very morning, this was a great salve to the consciences of many who voted for him to receive only third prize.

When the supervisor called on Yin Jiahou by name to ask if he had anything to add, Yin opened his mouth to speak, but then was suddenly struck dumb.

What could he say?

That morning on the ferry when he had blurted out his one-word poem about life, he had been inspired and witty, right on top of things. In an earnest conversation with Bai, he had exalted the unaffected romanticism of classical authors and decried today's artificiality and affection, leaving Bai miserable but absolutely unable to answer back. Only four hours had passed since then, but Yin Jiahou's confidence had completely given way to self-abasement.

He stood up and mumbled something so unclear even he couldn't hear what it was, then sat down again.

Thinking he heard someone stifle a giggle, Yin felt the nape of his neck flush as red as pig's blood. The truth was he didn't give a damn about the amount of money, but they all thought he—look at this! A grown man reduced to such a state, all because of five yuan! Five lousy yuan. It was enough to split one's sides. Feeling all his anger and frustration well up inside, Yin Jiahou thought of jumping up and letting out a great big laugh or saying something witty and funny. He thought of it, but he was completely unable to do so. The scarlet blush swiftly spread upwards.

Finally his apprentice came to the rescue.

Yali suddenly stood up, deliberately knocking over a drinking glass on the table, and spat out, "This is the limit!"

Seeing that all eyes were now on her, Yali blew the hair out of her eyes with a "poof" and said petulantly, "Why in the world are we going on and on about a bonus of a few lousy yuan? Thirty yuan, huh! Even if it were three hundred, so what? Just open your eyes and see who's worked more and who's worked less, and decide! As long as you have a clear idea, you won't be doing anyone any wrong."

"Yali!" the workshop supervisor said sternly.

"What? Have I said something wrong?" she answered defiantly. "Everyone seems to have been blinded by the glitter of gold."

The room shook with laughter, though there wasn't anything to laugh about. Yali joined innocently in the laughter, then said, "Mister supervisor, sir, it's already lunchtime."

"OK. The meeting is closed," said the supervisor, who was smiling too.

Yali and Yin Jiahou walked side by side. She reached over and flicked a bit of dirt off his back.

"Time for lunch," said Yin.

"Yep. Let's go," she agreed.

A number of white clouds floated in the blue May sky. The oleanders by the road were in full bloom. Master and apprentice walked lightly forward into the spring breeze, each carrying a lunch box. Yin Jiahou sensed clearly the presence beside him of this fresh, fragrant, bouncing young face and found himself wishing the way to the canteen were somewhat longer.

"You know, Yin," Yali began, "once, in our class—this was during my time at the technical school—they were choosing 'three-merit' students. Almost everyone voted for me, but the class committee knocked me off the list during their deliberations. Each of the 'three-merit' students received a brand-new aluminium saucepan as a prize. All of them used their new pots to eat out of, and on their way to the canteen they would beat on them so everyone could hear them clang. It made me so angry! So do you know what I did?"

"You cried."

"Cried? Hah, no way! I bought a saucepan just like theirs and beat on it till it rang louder than anybody's."

Yin Jiahou smiled in acknowledgment of her attempt to reassure him. Although her story was not much of a comfort, lacking as it did the least bearing on the present situation, still he appreciated her efforts.

"Right. What's so great about being a 'three-merit' student? You're strong-willed all right."

Yali giggled, redoubling her charm. Her face shone like the sun as she said, "Having a best friend is enough in life."

Yin's heart skipped a beat, but his expression betrayed nothing. Skipping forward two steps, Yali jumped up and plucked a pink oleander, blew on it once and threw it with all her might into the air. She was as sprightly and innocent as a fawn, but at the same time the prancings and twistings of her lithe young body seemed filled with compassion for him.

"I don't want to become a full-fledged worker, Yin. I want to be your apprentice forever."

"Come on. Every apprentice becomes a worker eventually."

"Oh, no they don't. I *want* to stay with you," she insisted, suddenly sounding much older, her steps suddenly heavier. Yin Jiahou's heart had ceased to pound; he remained calm and steady now as all his premonitions and suspicions of days past came true before his eyes.

In the pained, gravelly voice so often used by women, Yali said quietly, "There's nothing else I can do. I've thought it all through. I won't make any demands, ever. Will you let me?"

"No," Yin Jiahou answered. "Yali, you're too young..."

"Don't tell me how *I* am," she shot back.

"You don't yet understand—"

"Don't talk about me, I said! Talk about yourself! Tell me: you don't really like me, do you?"

"Nonsense! It's not that I don't like you."

"Then why won't you agree?"

"Yali, don't you understand? You've seen my family."

"What do they matter? I live in a world completely different from theirs. I will make no demands on you. You can't live like that—it's nothing but deadening, senseless drudgery."

Yin Jiahou's ears were ringing. As the sound grew louder and louder, scenes from his dull, meaningless family life spun before his eyes, and all the little frustrations he usually banished from his thoughts now came floating into view. Wouldn't it be a fine thing to have a mistress—this is what men say secretly to themselves. He turned and gazed steadily at Yali, and she met his eyes with the limpid pools that were her own. Suddenly Yin Jiahou was conscious of his own filthiness. "Yali," he said hoarsely, "what have you been saying? I don't seem to have heard any of it clearly; I'm all preoccupied with that business about bonuses."

Yali came to a halt, lifted her chin and looked directly at Yin Jiahou. Glittering teardrops welled up from her deep-set eyes.

Someone was walking up behind them—a group of workers, beating on their bowls as they strode along.

"Let's go," Yin Jiahou said anxiously. "Someone's coming."

Yali did not budge. The tears would not stop.

"Well, I'm off, then," said Yin.

When the group of workers had passed, Yin looked back to find that Yali was still standing there, a lone figure in the sunlight at the edge of the road. Yin Jiahou knew that if he walked back to her, he would only manage to further snarl the entanglement of emotions they were caught in; if he kept going, however, Yali's self-esteem would suffer a heavy blow. He gazed at her distant figure, unsure whether to keep going or turn back. He would be the first to admit that his wife and Yali could not be mentioned in the same breath; Yali was a woman way above par. He also acknowledged that his willingness to work overtime had not been unconnected with her presence. However, he could not agree to her proposal. The reasons against it were too many and too compelling.

Yin Jiahou turned and ran towards the canteen. But he realized clearly that the affair was not over.

There were ten service windows in the canteen, with equally
long lines in front of each. Yin chose a line at random.
The leader of the second work team squeezed his way free
from the crowd at the window, his full bowl held high, and
stopped in front of Yin Jiahou. Yin thought he was about to say
something about the bonuses: he had also received third prize,
but instead of putting up an argument he had stood up and said
that as team leader it was his duty to work harder and that even
third prize was too much for what he'd actually done. If he really is so very clever, thought Yin, he won't even bring up the
matter of the bonuses. But in case he does, I've got a good ri-
poste waiting as a special gift for him.

"Oh, no, I couldn't do that, sweetie," fluttered the second
team leader in a voice amazingly like Yali's.

"Did I hear you let off a fart?" snapped Yin Jiahou. The response he had prepared turned out to be useful in this case as
well.

Nothing had gone right that morning, and now the lean pork
strips with pickled mustard tuber were sold out. All that was left
was fat pork sauteed with this or stewed with that at sixty cents
a serving, horrible-tasting and expensive. Yin bought fried cabbage and hot radish strips and paid fifteen cents.

The canteen was a hubbub of bobbing heads. People who
hadn't got the dish they wanted grumbled and snarled a bit, but
apart from this there was only the sound of smacking and chewing. Yin Jiahou squatted on the floor, cradling his lunch box,
and began to scoff his food down like everyone else. He wasn't
about to let a lousy third prize bonus spoil his lunch. But when
he'd eaten half his food, suddenly among the leaves of fried cabbage appeared a tender, plump, bright green worm. He choked

and stared at the worm, and the saliva that signals nausea began
to flow into his mouth. Nothing had gone right that day, god-
damit! He could stand no more.

Flipping the worm into a rice bowl, he marched off to look
for the canteen manager. He found him in the small dining room
entertaining guests, half of them Chinese, half Japanese. Asking the manager to step outside, Yin invited him to taste the
fried cabbage his cooks had prepared. Glancing expressionlessly
at the worm in the bowl and then back at Yin Jiahou, the manager waved one of the cooks over and said, "Give this man another serving of cabbage and rice." Having delivered this order
with the air of one dismissing a beggar, he slipped back into the
small dining room. The young cook, who had not understood a
word of the manager's thick Zhejiang accent, widened his eyes
at Yin Jiahou, shrugged his shoulders like a foreigner and said in
mock English, "Haluo?"

Yin Jiahou had been polite enough to call the manager out of
the dining room, seeing as how there were Japanese present. As
the proverb admonished, the family linen must not be hung out
in public. But now Yin was determined to show the manager he
meant business. Storming into the small dining room, he seized
the manager's arm in a vice-like grip, pulled him into a corner
and dumped the rest of his lunch into the large pocket in the bib
of the manager's white apron.

Leilei was in detention.

All the children, big and small, in the kindergarten were napping in their cots, while Leilei sat locked in the cage of a rocket-
ship toy in the playroom, shaking its iron bars ineffectually. As
soon as he caught sight of Yin Jiahou, he cried, "Pa!" and began to cry.

Hearing Leilei's wails, a young woman came running in from the other room and cooed with thinly veiled sarcasm, "Oh, so we do know how to cry after all?"

"Of course he knows how to cry," said Yin Jiahou.

Whirling around at the sound of his voice, the nurse stood rooted to the spot with embarrassment. She was quite young and was wearing a fashionable thin woollen dress. Her bearing and her lovely eyes startled Yin Jiahou: this woman looked astonishingly like someone he had stored deep in his heart for all these years, a melancholy of painful regret, an unutterable subconscious dejection. It was precisely this hidden melancholy that had caused him to become so reticent, withdrawn and uncaring about everything, including his wife.

"I'm sorry," said the nurse. "Your boy was being naughty when he should have been napping, mowing down all his little friends with his submachine gun from under the coverlet. I really didn't have the time to deal with him, so..."

Even her voice and manner of speaking were like the other's. Yin Jiahou felt as if his heart were about to leap from his throat; his blood rushed through his veins. Smiling with inordinate warmth, he tried his best not to look at her, turning instead to his son. Yin decided he must be gentle yet firm, like a handsome model father of the silver screen. "Leilei," he began in a serious voice, "did you shoot at your little classmates?"

"Yes..."

"Do you know how I am going to punish you?"

Leilei, who had never seen his father look so grim, shook his head timorously.

"Do you know you did wrong?"

"Yes, I know."

"Fine. Now tell the nurse that you know and say you're sorry."

"Nurse, I was wrong to shoot my classmates. I'm sorry."

The young woman interposed quickly, "OK, OK. He's just a child," and lifted him out of the cage.

The tears had stopped halfway down Leilei's cheeks. And his bandage had come loose and got stuck on his heel. Assuming an expression of fathomless paternal tenderness, Yin Jiahou ruffled Leilei's hair, wiped away his tears and refastened his bandage.

"Leilei, it's tiring to come all this way on the bus, isn't it?"

"Yes," said Leilei.

"Just imagine how tired Papa gets having to carry you along," continued Yin.

"Mm-hmm," murmured Leilei contritely.

"Now if you'll be good and obey the nurse, Papa can go have a rest. Otherwise, Papa will be exhausted, and he'll get sick."

"Papa."

"All right. Now off to bed for your nap. You can undress yourself."

"Pa, come and pick me up as early as you can."

"Okay."

Leilei walked straight into the room with the cots, removed his clothes, climbed into bed and slipped beneath the covers.

"You're such a good father!" the young woman exclaimed.

This made Yin Jiahou ashamed for putting on such an act. Usually he would have hauled Leilei off and smacked him on the rear. Had he been acting for her? He wasn't willing to admit it to himself.

Yin Jiahou and the nurse stood awkwardly there in the playroom until he suddenly realized he no longer had any reason to remain, whereupon he said, "I'm sorry he's caused you so much trouble by being naughty."

"Oh, no," she protested. "It's all in a day's work. I—"

"You what?" Yin asked kindly. "Go ahead, tell me."

Flustered, the woman smiled and demurred, "It's nothing, really."

A sudden fantasy struck Yin with the force of a thunderbolt. Unable to suppress a surge of emotion, he asked, "What's your name?"

"Xiao Xiaofen."

This calmed him down quickly. Her name bore not the least resemblance to the one engraved long ago on his heart. But oh, how alike they looked! He found himself wanting to stick around just a little longer. "What were you about to say?" he asked.

Surprised, she glanced at him, cocked her head, stuck out a pink tongue and licked her lips. "I'm one of those 'youths waiting for employment'," she began. "I like working here at this kindergarten. I was hired on trial two months ago, but right away the older nurses started saying bad things about me to the administrators, trying to get the factory to fire me. I'd like to ask you not to tell anyone what happened today, for fear it'll go down as another black mark against me."

"Of course I won't say anything," said Yin Jiahou kindly. "It was all because Leilei is so naughty."

"Oh, thank you!"

Lowering her head, the young woman blinked rapidly, staining her eyelashes with droplets of tears. A sharp pain gripped Yin Jiahou's heart: why were her mannerisms so exactly like the other?

"Xiaofen, the head of the administrative department is an old schoolmate of mine; if I can put in a word with him on your behalf, everything will be all right. If anybody should be fired, it's those old biddies."

The nurse lifted a face radiant with happy surprise and stepped nearer to Yin. "Oh, could you?" she asked breathlessly. The fresh, full lips blooming like petals right below his eyes caused Yin Jiahou to step involuntarily nearer the girl. His ears rang deafeningly as a feverish idea swelled like a balloon in his brain. He could clearly see the lips slowly rising to meet his, but when the nurse closed her eyes tightly, it was as if he had received a sharp slap that jolted him awake. Before she even had a chance to open her eyes, Yin Jiahou had fled the kindergarten.

The road was deserted, the factory buildings silent. Yin ran a long way without stopping. In a broken-down warehouse, with no one else around, he stood and gasped for breath, calling one name over and over. Gradually he calmed down, wiped the tears from his eyes with a finger, and let out a long, self-mocking sigh. He had regained equilibrium.

It was time to go to the food store to attend to some business.

Incredible as it may seem, Yin Jiahou and his wife were born in the same year and month on the very same day, and their respective fathers were too. The tenth of the following month was the two "ancients"—that was what his wife called them—birthday. They were going to be fifty-nine, but according to traditional reckoning this was the year to celebrate their grand sixtieth.

Yin Jiahou couldn't remember anyone ever holding a birthday party in his honour; in fact, he'd never so much as toasted the

occasion himself. Ordinary people had begun celebrating birthdays only in the last few years, and the old ones had managed to
profit from this new custom. Five years ago had been Yin's
twenty-ninth, or thirtieth by traditional reckoning. His wife
had gone on for days about it: "Thirty's a big birthday. We'll
have to have a little celebration," she kept saying. When the
day arrived, however, she forgot all about it. Her younger sister
was to meet a prospective boyfriend that day, and Yin's wife
had gone along at her invitation. When he came back from
work, Yin's wife told him excitedly, "He thought it was me! He
kept on talking to me instead of her!" Finding it rather pleasing
that she should be mistaken for an unmarried woman, he let the
subject of their birthday drop entirely, and soon he forgot about
it himself.

He had consulted with his wife about what sort of present they
should buy for the ancients. Sixty was a very important birthday, so it wouldn't do to buy something insignificant; on the
other hand, they couldn't afford an expensive gift. Since that
excluded things to wear and things to play with, they decided to
buy things to drink—alcohol.

They discussed what sort of liquor to buy. China's ten most
famous spirits almost never appeared in stores, and their efforts
to obtain some through various connections had failed, so they
had no choice but to lower their sights and look for something
second-rate. They mustn't choose expensive liquor in a plain
package, his wife asserted; the ancients wouldn't be able to tell
how much it cost and might end up thinking they'd been slight-
ed. On the other hand, cheap liquor in a fancy package would
be too much like putting one over on them and would make her
and Yin feel guilty. They should also watch out for liquor whose

price and packaging seemed all right but which came from some
little village they'd never heard of; it might be fake. Husband
and wife had been discussing the matter for two weeks and had
still not bought the liquor.

At one time the little food store in the factory had gained
quite a reputation. People from all three boroughs of Wuhan
came here to buy liquor and cigarettes. At that time there had
still been quite a few Japanese experts working here, as the factory had just been built, and the store had been stocked especially for them with alcohol and tobacco of superior quality. After
the experts returned to Japan, however, the store's business had
gone downhill. Despite this, once in a while good things still left
in the warehouse turned up in the store.

Recently Yin Jiahou had been visiting the store every day during the noon break.

"Hi," said Yin to the man behind the counter, whom he knew
pretty well. Yin passed him a cigarette.

"Hi."

"Got anything?"

"Nope. Turned the warehouse upside down. There's no
hope."

"How about black market stuff?"

"What are you looking for?"

"Good stuff, naturally."

"How about some Maotai?"

"Fantastic!"

"How much do you want? Pay in advance. Four yuan eighty
for fifty grammes."

Yin Jiahou took some time to answer, staring blankly at the
shop assistant as he made some rapid calculations: half a kilo

would cost forty-eight yuan, and he'd have to buy a kilo, ninety-six yuan, an entire month's salary including bonus. Milk and fruit prices were up again, but his son had to have both every day, as well as eggs and lean pork. If another event requiring the presentation of a gift popped up, such as the wedding or funeral of a friend or co-worker, he'd have to cough up even more money or risk losing face.

Blinking his eyes once for emphasis, Yin Jiahou said, "The price of this liquor of yours is enough to put a person in a cold sweat."

"Oh, come on, what's so bad about it? It's been that price all along, although they keep saying it's going to go up. C'mon, we can make a deal: I'll be happy to make the money and you'll be happy to spend so much on the old guys. Don't be such an unfilial son and son-in-law."

"Oh, I'm filial, all right," Yin Jiahou protested. "It's just that while the spirit is willing, the wallet is weak."

Laughing at his own joke, Yin beat a retreat from the shop.

If the two old men knew what careful calculations he was having to make, it would spoil their taste even for Maotai. He decided that when his own sixtieth birthday rolled around, he would make sure to tell his son that a simple present, in line with his son's financial situation, would be plenty.

Yali was waiting for him where the tracks angled across the road.

Pretending he had forgotten something at the store, Yin Jiahou felt his pockets up and down, turned and started to walk off.

"I've got a letter for you," called Yali.

Yin Jiahou had no choice but to turn back and stop his play-acting. He almost never got letters; usually the arrival of a letter meant something had happened to one of his relatives.

The letter had been sent from the local train station; Yin couldn't remember that any of his relatives worked there. Opening it, he glanced at the signature: "Your Fellow 'Educated Youth', Jiang Nanxia". Yin heaved a sigh of relief.

"Nothing's wrong, is it?" asked Yali.

"No," answered Yin, suddenly remembering Xiao Xiaofen and his own buried melancholy. He realized that his heart would always belong to the woman he had lost; only she could truly spark his passion. Apart from her, he could deal coolly with any woman.

"Yali," he said, "when I tell you what I really think, you will understand. You're intelligent, civilized, young, active and beautiful. I really enjoy being with you. I even choose to work overtime—"

"I don't need you to tell me all that!" Yali interrupted stubbornly. "It may very well be what you think, but it's not at all what I think!" She turned and stalked off, head held high, proud, cold and aggrieved.

Fearing what the others might think, Yin Jiahou refrained from following her into the workshop.

Jiang Nanxia had been a short, shy, silent young man with sparkling eyes. Where had he been assigned to work? Yin Jiahou couldn't remember. The letter said:

"I am passing through Wuhan on my way elsewhere and have one free day. I heard someone mention your name, and it e-voked all sorts of emotions. I wanted to call on you, but I don't have enough time.

"Jiahou, do you remember that place? How the first night we slept in a shack on the threshing ground with all the piles of freshly harvested cotton covered with fat little pink bollworms? The poor and lower-middle peasants had given us a chamberpot to use, telling us we must under no circumstances pee on the cotton. All of us fought to be the first to try out the chamberpot, and then you said the rim had cut your foreskin. We all practically split our sides laughing, and in all the pushing and shoving the pot ended up broken on the ground.

"Do you remember that rainy day? It was raining buckets at noontime, and we were singing and strumming and playing the harmonica in our shack. Those girls from the 'educated youth' on the Sixth Brigade came, and we served them all the vegetables we had. For the next few days all we had to eat was leftover rice reheated in salt water.

"Nie Ling was so beautiful, especially her eyes. We were all insanely jealous that she liked you so much. Why did you split up in the end? I still don't understand.

"Then there was that little yellow cat that used to follow us to the private plot and meet us after work every day at the entrance to the lane. When it got pregnant, we wanted to see it have kittens, but it ran away. Too bad!

"My wife was never sent to the countryside as an 'educated youth'; she says it was just her good luck, but I think it was her bad luck. The girls who were sent down acquired a certain character, a character that seemed to make them more beautiful as women. Was your wife sent down? I think both you and I prefer women with that character; it's a sort of secret of our generation.

"Jiahou, both you and I are now well over thirty. I've already begun to go bald on top; I have a seven-year-old daughter, and I suppose I'm all right financially. But life is so full of problems. My relationship with my wife is nothing special, and I feel like I've wasted myself.

"I am now a cadre at departmental level. I've joined the Party and earned a university degree, so by any standards I should be content and glad with what I've accomplished. But I can't laugh now as freely and heartily as we did in the countryside. My wife has found a thousand different faults with me and is filing for divorce.

"So is everything all right with you? You used to be so young and handsome, generous and warm-hearted, and you loved to dance and sing; I bet you're doing much better than I.

"I saw Nie Ling in Beijing last year. She was still unwilling to explain why she and you broke up. She also has a child several years old, but she herself looks quite young..."

Yin Jiahou read the letter twice, the first time skimming it quickly, the second time reading slowly and carefully, and when he had finished he crumpled it in his palm. Sitting down with his back to a poplar, he turned his face to the sun and shut his eyes. Through his eyelids he saw rainbow-coloured spots and leaves. Before him was the asphalt road, behind that the great grey hulks of the factory buildings, and behind them lay fields. Yin Jiahou lay down in the grass in the little grove where he was and let the myriad strands of his thought float freely. Nie Ling, Nie Ling, that name he never dared use lightly, Jiang Nanxia tossed about as casually as you please. Everything welled up from the depths... All the moods in the May breeze, wistfulness, regret, anger and sorrow, floated past Yin's ears, and his face twitched slightly, making him look like he was alternately laughing and weeping.

A white cloud paused in its passage across the sky, its shadow chilling Yin's forehead. Thinking it might be a person standing there blocking the sun, he quickly opened his eyes. There among the green leaves, white clouds and blue sky, he buried his deep regret and pain once more at the bottom of his heart. After this, his memories became bright and lively.

He'd entered the iron and steel company. When he was sent to Beijing to study and work with the Japanese experts, he'd slaved to learn Japanese so he could remain competitive in his job. He'd looked for a girlfriend, found one, got engaged, married. When his parents were ill in hospital, he'd gone every day to look after them. When his elder brother and younger sister argued and complained the whole day long, he'd held a household meeting and stabilized the situation. Inflation, wage adjustment, the change from black-and-white to colour television sets and the disappearance of single-tub washing machines in favour of models with an additional spinner tub—he had been witness to all these social phenomena, and had been called upon to deal with each one. When he'd been able to solve a problem, it didn't seem to make him all that happy; when he hadn't been able to, it was an even bigger pain. For instance, he had still not replaced their old black-and-white television, and for this Leilei looked down on him somewhat. The boy was always going on about how so-and-so's father had just bought such-and-such a colour TV with computer control. In an effort to retain his son's esteem, Yin Jiahou was saving as much as he could for the colour set.

The dreams of youth are always heavily coloured with idealism, but this had somehow evaporated as soon as he reached adulthood. Yin Jiahou followed the herd in his hopes and concerns. He worried about whether or not China's soccer team would qualify for the World Cup competition, worried about the Sino-Vietnamese border conflict, worried about the prospects for curing cancer with "biological guided missiles", worried about how much matches cost per box. He had hardly ever wondered whether he should sigh over the lost dreams of his youth. The only thing he knew clearly was that he was an ordinary man living off the wages of his labour. He had no time to let his fancy run wild. The days passed so quickly, week after week flashing past. When his wife had become pregnant, he had hardly even got enough nappies together when the baby was born.

His wife was ... well, nothing special. Nobody is perfect. Memories belong to the past; the bitter present can only be chewed and swallowed. Yin Jiahou wanted badly to write to Jiang Nanxia and send a few thoughts of his own, perhaps comfort this friend of his youth who was now facing divorce. But where was he to send it?

Jiang Nanxia, best wishes to you! You didn't forget an old friend; you rescued him from the evil mood he'd fallen into over a lousy third-prize bonus.

Jumping up with a single bound, Yin Jiahou drew a deep breath and let it out; then he set off toward the workshop.

Comparing himself with Jiang Nanxia, Yin felt his own life was normal and natural, his marriage stable, his energy limitless, his outlook excellent; he was able to face and deal with reality. His self-confidence immediately redoubled itself.

The afternoon was not bad. Especially the way it started. A

group of visitors came to see the factory. Nobody knew who they were or where they were from, and nobody cared. Everyone just kept on working as if the group weren't there; they'd seen a thousand groups like it.

As the lonely little herd of visitors caught sight now and then of the workers, they must have wondered why the workers were not curious about them.

The workshop supervisor came zooming out of the depths of the workshop on a shiny blue bicycle, glanced over the visiting group, and turned and shot off again with a single push of his foot, not bothering to dismount. He went straight to Yin Jiahou's work station to tell Yin to operate the controls himself, freeing Yali to go and play guide to the visitors. Yin Jiahou, however, was already at the controls. Had the supervisor really thought that the affair of the bonuses had got Yin into such a temper that he would refuse to man his work station? That must be why he had come to look around. Well, he was wrong!

Arresting the supervisor's attention with a cold stare, Yin told him wordlessly but unequivocally: you're wrong.

As long as one person understood his feeling—especially if that person was the one most important to him in the whole workshop—he was content. Suffering the injustice of the bonuses was not important; what was important was whether anyone knew you had suffered an injustice.

The visiting group strolled about for an hour or more, while Yin Jiahou stood erect and steady at the controls; he was pleased to work alone and undisturbed for so long. His team co-workers owed him a little tenderness after that meeting, and all of them were watching him carefully, waiting for the opportunity to give it to him.

When she'd finished with the group, Yali came up to take
over from Yin Jiahou. Neither of them spoke; they worked with
a deep mutual understanding. Only Yin Jiahou could sense that
Yali was depressed, but he decided to keep silent about it.

"Aha! You're trapped now, Yin," cackled Mrs Ha, the shop
steward, as she leaned against the door-frame, blocking the entire opening. She waved a handful of crinkled memoranda at
him. "You're the last one left, you stinker. Out with the money. Two yuan. Sign here."

Handing over two yuan, Yin scrawled his name on one of the
wrinkled papers.

Mrs Ha turned and bustled off, but as soon as Yin turned
around she bustled right back again and rested her bulk once
more against the door-frame. "I'm getting old," she sighed.
"High time the reforms reached my quarter and I was retired.
Yin, I forgot to tell you what the money was for: Su Xin, the
old maid of the whole workshop, has got married! Everyone's
chipping in to give her a present."

"Oh, I know," said Yin. In fact he had never heard the name
Su Xin. He asked the people next to him, "Who's Su Xin?"

"I heard she was just hired."

"Just hired, and she's already 'the old maid of the whole
workshop'?"

Everyone laughed, but Mrs Ha broke in with her trumpet-like
voice: "Yin, I seem to remember there was something else I was
supposed to tell you."

"Fire away." Yin was dreadfully thirsty but had to go to the
toilet at the same time.

"I've forgotten." Mrs Ha stared at him vacantly.

"Well, then forget it," said Yin.

"No, I can't. I seem to remember it was something very important." Mrs Ha laced and unlaced her fingers fretfully, then finally spread her hands and said resignedly, "I just can't remember. But you mustn't blame me. I'm getting old. OK, you stinkers, I can't be blamed; you're my witnesses." And she scurried off, the hint of a crafty smile on her face.

The second team leader walked over, took Yin's arm and told him quietly that the factory office was trying to block their bid to take the entrance exams for the television university. The parent company had not issued any regulations forbidding them to take the exam; it was just that the factory did not want to let them out of its grasp, as they had been trained by Japanese specialists.

"Let's go to the factory offices and find out what the scoop is. You can ask Bai; he's a friend of yours." The second team leader was trying to infect Yin Jiahou with his own indignation.

"I'm not going to go," said Yin.

"Then let's write a letter to the disciplinary committee of the parent company and rat on the factory office."

"I wouldn't know how to write such a thing," replied Yin.

"Then I'll write it, and you can sign it."

"No, I won't."

"You want to be a factory worker all your life?" the team leader asked incredulously.

"Yes!" retorted Yin.

"Nowadays there are all sorts of sons of whores who seem to enjoy writing letters,"—hadn't the second team leader said that this very morning? Should Yin remind him? He decided to drop it.

The team leader left in a huff. Just as Yin was crossing the threshold to leave, the telephone rang, and the person who answered said, "Wait, it's for you."

Snatching the receiver, Yin barked into it, "Yeah, what do you want?" He really had to go to the toilet.

It was the factory director, calling from his office. Yin Jiahou sucked in his breath; he'd been very rude just now. This factory director was an intellectual who'd recently been installed in line with the general programme of economic reform. Yin knew that intellectuals were sensitive; it wouldn't do to give a bad impression.

Quickly borrowing someone's bicycle, Yin practically flew to the factory offices. Arriving, he bumped into Bai, who had just emerged from the building with a grim expression on his face. "Keep a stiff upper lip!" hissed Bai in passing.

This oblique, spy novel-type warning threw Yin off balance, and he began to get butterflies in his stomach.

The director asked Yin what he thought of Japanese people.

Thought of . . . Japanese . . . people? Yin's mind went blank. It had been seven years since the Japanese specialists had gone home, and nothing now was left of whatever impressions they might have given him. And what had Bai meant by "keep a stiff upper lip"? He strained to remember what he had thought of Koichiro back then. He had been Koichiro's apprentice.

"Japanese people . . . are hard-working; they can stand up to adversity . . . First, they fear not hardship; second, they fear not—" Yin caught his breath sharply. He had almost let slip a quotation from Chairman Mao. He slowed down and carefully weighing each word went on: "They are able to work in strict accordance with scientific principles and are scrupulous in their work to the last detail. They have the enterprising spirit typified by the saying—" He suddenly realized that what he was about to say bore not the least relation to Japan and the Japanese, but he plunged on regardless, "The Yellow River or bust!"

"So you think pretty highly of the Japanese, eh?" asked the factory director.

"Well, maybe not all Japanese, and not every aspect... I'm just talking about their work."

"Of course you know about the Japanese war of aggression against China?"

"Of course. The Japanese devils—" Yin stopped in his tracks. What was the factory director driving at, anyway? He disliked the idea of being toyed with, even by the factory director. Surely he had not been called off the workshop floor so urgently just to come here and be made to tread on thin ice? Seven years ago a worker had been punished for perpetrating terrorist activities against the specialists; some time ago a ministerial-level cadre had been dismissed for visiting the Yasukuni Shrine in Japan. These were questions of international relations, questions of race; how could he be suspected of involvement?

Pushing his chair away, Yin said, "Mr director, sir, if you've got something to say I wish you'd just say it. Otherwise I think I should get back to work."

"Come on, Yin, don't be in such a hurry," the director said soothingly. "I'm trying to be open and above board. Here it is: do you think that our importation of advanced equipment from Japan and our friendly relations with the Japanese represent a second Japanese invasion of China?"

"Of course not."

"All right, then why hasn't a group been organized to give a

party for the Japanese visitors? Next Wednesday a Japanese
youth delegation is coming to our factory. It's been two weeks
since the task of organization was delegated to the workers' u-
nion, but not only haven't you done anything, I understand you
have been saying to the young people things like, 'We're not going to be mannikins for their friendship party', 'Start a second
War of Resistance', 'The *qipao* is a thousand times more beautiful than the business suit', and so forth. What's the big idea?"

Yin Jiahou suddenly saw the light. Someone had framed him,
and framed him so well that even the factory director believed
it!

"Bullshit! Lies, all of it!" He'd kept the lid on his anger long
enough! Yin wasn't going to worry what sort of impression he
gave the director now; he needed to reestablish his innocence
and dignity. Those sons of bitches, he cursed. He hadn't received any notice from the workers' union. Two weeks ago his
grandmother had died, and he'd taken two days off to see to the
funeral. A few days after he returned to work, his mother's
blood pressure shot up because of the grief over her mother's
death, and he had used two of his vacation days to take her to
hospital. From the way Bai had crept past him just now, Yin
concluded he might be the one who started the trouble; he was
always hanging about with students from this or that university
and had long ago set forth his opinion that Japanese goods
should be boycotted. Or maybe it had been Mrs Ha. Right!
She'd only been pretending to have forgotten what she was supposed to tell him. Her husband had died in the war against
Japan, and she had always been hostile toward Japanese. Maybe
both she and Bai had connived to trip Yin up. He himself felt no
enmity towards the Japanese; in fact, he still had occasional

correspondence with Koichiro, sending him cards at the New Year and so forth.

The factory director smiled at Yin Jiahou's self-defence: he believed Yin and chivalrously begged his pardon. "Well, if that's the case, it's high time you got started with the organizing!" Brooking no protest, the director called the union chairman into his office and handed Yin over to him.

"Don't have each workshop plan independently," the director instructed. "I'll bring Yin here temporarily to work in the union office so he can devote himself exclusively to this assignment. If anything goes wrong when the delegation comes, you two will be held responsible."

The union chairman was a demobbed soldier. After receiving the director's orders, he dragged Yin to the union office and proceeded to lay down the law: it was going to be such-and-such and thus-and-so. Yin Jiahou made a few feeble protestations, but the union chairman rumbled right over them with the martial inevitability of a tank, not paying Yin the slightest attention, and adding in for good measure a few pontifications of universal import among the orders.

The upshot was that Yin Jiahou was expected to organize, within one week, a welcoming committee of forty young men and women, the men between 1.7 and 1.8 metres in height, the women around 1.65 metres, all of medium build and acceptable looks—if they were really good-looking, so much the better—and have made for each a Western-style woollen suit. Then he must teach them some basic Japanese, enough to greet the guests and engage in simple conversation; also, they should be familiar with everyday Japanese etiquette. Finally, all of them must know how to dance.

Yin Jiahou's scalp had gone numb. "Mr Chairman," he said.
"You get this straight: I can't do it!"

"Of course you can do it," the chairman replied blandly.
"You're an expert on Japan." Quickly finding a free table and
chair for Yin Jiahou, he sat him down and placed a stack of reg-
istration forms with pictures on them in front of him. "Yin," he
said, "you must appreciate the Party's trust in you. Our back is
to the wall. It's going to be an uphill battle. You must deal with
everyone by using administrative power. All right, let's get
down to work!"

At knocking-off time Yin ran into Bai, who said, "I heard all
about it. I'm truly resentful on your behalf. It was as if they
were examining a prospective diplomat to Japan. They're so
slavish, sucking up to the Japanese."

Yin Jiahou glared fiercely at Bai and gave a thin, cold laugh.
Jumping up, Bai protested, "Come on, surely you don't suspect
me ... me! Look, we may have different viewpoints, but if I
were the type who went around stabbing people in the back,
would I write those things I write? Huh?"

Bai felt truly hurt. In his mind, a writer's moral fibre was
necessarily identical with that expressed in his works. Although
not a writer himself, Yin knew enough to commit no such error
of judgment. Patting Bai apologetically on the shoulder, Yin
said, "I'm sorry."

At this moment, a bevy of tall and slender women strolled by,
each with a different type of bag slung over her shoulder. Calling friendly greetings to Bai, they then turned to revile Yin:

"Traitor!"

"We'll never be your friendship mannikins!"

"We're anti-Japanese!"

Frowning, Yin Jiahou said nothing. After the women passed, he turned to count them. There were fifteen or sixteen, almost all of them just the right height. Suddenly he realized how difficult this job was going to be.

It was a very tiring afternoon. He'd stood at his control panel for more than an hour, then got all worked up in the director's office and been sent to slave at the union office. He'd called an emergency meeting of all the shop stewards, found an office to serve as a classroom, gone to a shop to buy material for the suits, contacted the tailoring factory, claimed funds at the accounting office and looked upstairs and down for the factory director, who was always nowhere to be found when one needed his signature on something.

He hadn't found a single opportunity to bring up the issue of the television university entrance exam; as for the five yuan third prize bonus, he'd swallowed his anger and accepted it.

He'd given two yuan's worth of "best wishes" to the old maid who'd only just been hired, one yuan for famine relief in Africa, and when the "Save the Panda" committee had come round for donations, he had thought a moment, then stuffed two yuan into the box with the little weeping panda on the front. The Youth leaguers taking donations had twittered and hopped about like sparrows in an ecstasy, praising Yin Jiahou as the number one donor in the whole factory and as number one saviour of national treasures. Even the factory director had only given fifty cents.

The five yuan were merely part of a circulating current; they flowed through Yin's hands and then flowed away again. All of them had gone to good causes, completely cancelling out the shame of receiving third prize. Yali, knowing exactly what Yin was thinking, said, "Smart move, Master Yin! Perfect way to deal with it all!" Yin could not help thinking wistfully how wonderful it would be to have a wife who understood him so well. Even the slightest bit of common ground could mean so much. Who knew what his wife would think of his disposal of the five yuan? Again he glanced at Yali in spite of himself and immediately regretted it, for she had read the look in his eyes.

When he arrived at the kindergarten to pick up Leilei, Yin was afraid the boy would blame him for being late and was apprehensive about the possibility of finding himself alone again with Xiao Xiaofen. As it turned out, his son did not ask why he was late, and Xiao Xiaofen was safely sequestered in the midst of a gaggle of nurses. Everything was fine. Still deeply uneasy, however, about his loss of self-control that noontime in front of Xiao Xiaofen, Yin picked up his son and fled with averted eyes.

Rivers of vehicles and an ocean of humanity flooded the streets. Leilei ran ahead, darting in and out among people's legs. Heart in mouth, Yin Jiahou chased clumsily after him, calling Leilei's name sharply. His son was cast in the same mould as himself; he was the continuation of Yin's very life. Yin must not let him run off like this—he might get hit by a car; neither must he let him walk too long, lest his little legs get tired. Yin Jiahou was still all keyed up; he felt more like he had merely switched jobs than got off work.

Father and son rejoined the homeward rush-hour flow, Yin with the bag slung over his shoulder, Leilei with his toy submachine gun. In the morning they had set out with all their provisions; now they were returning with an empty sack. Yin's face was covered with dust, and his stubble had grown noticeably. His son's little sailor shirt was speckled with food stains, his bandage was frayed and trailing, and he was filthy from top to toe. The bus was jammed, as always. Having squeezed his way on with Leilei, Yin felt his stomach begin to growl. He was dreadfully hungry.

On the bus, a little girl sitting with her mother pointed to Leilei and piped, "Ma, that's the new boy in our class. His name is Yin Lei." She began to call at the top of her lungs: "Yin Lei! Yin Lei!"

Leilei, cock-a-hoop, said proudly to his father, "That's Xinxin!"

The two youngsters, delighted to meet on a crowded bus full of adults, began to call noisily back and forth, trumpeting their pleasure. Yin Jiahou and the girl's mother smiled and nodded at each other.

The mother stood and let Leilei share the seat with her daughter, then squeezed over next to Yin Jiahou.

"Xinxin is very naughty—a real tomboy!"

"My son's probably even worse."

"Raising kids is certainly no picnic."

"You're right there. What a pain!"

With their children as a ready topic, the two parents fell to chatting like old friends, though a minute before they hadn't known each other in the slightest. They talked about how sweet and lovable children were and what hard work it was to take care of them, sighed over the swift passage of time, commiserated about the inadequacy of the kindergarten and the torture of getting the kids back and forth, waxed indignant over the sheer difficulty of everything all the time. When the little girl's mother heard that Yin lived in Hankou and that he had to cross the river, and what's more had to take a bus on top of that, she

sucked in her breath in shock and said, "It's like commuting to
another country. How perfectly awful!"

"Well, luckily I'm used to it," said Yin.

"My house is right near the last stop on the bus route. If you
ever need to, you can send Yin Lei to my house for the night."

"Oh, thank you so much!"

"Really, there's no need to be so polite. Anything for the
children's benefit," she said generously.

"Wonderful," said Yin.

Yin noticed how mother-hennish he'd become, how sensitive
to and appreciative of sympathy and kindness. He'd been both
tired and hungry, squeezed to the limits of endurance in the
crowded bus; as soon as this woman expressed her sympathy and
struck up a conversation, he'd felt immediately soothed. Now
they had come to the end of the line without his even realizing
it. He certainly never used to be this way. He used to be a thoroughly manly, stalwart, neatly groomed young man who would
never casually strike up a conversation with a woman and for
whom compassion was something neither freely given nor easily
accepted. Now he clearly saw the change in himself but was unable to decide whether it was a change for the better or for the
worse.

Climbing the dike next to the river, Yin felt as if the dark
purple clouds of evening were weighing on his head. He heaved
a long sigh, as if to dispel his heaviness of spirit.

The ferry now moved against the current.

The trip upstream took more than twice as long as the trip
down; the wait was hard to endure. The sun dimmed now as it
fell into the west, and the river breeze became chiller with each

gust. For some reason, whereas in the morning all the people he knew well at the factory always seemed to find themselves on the same boat, in the evening most of the passengers' faces were those of strangers. Moreover, they were all blank, weary, beaten down. As always, there was a rush for the benches, which filled up with the speed of lightning, after which the deck also filled with patch after patch of sitting people. Yin Jiahou never rushed for the seats, for the crowd on the ferry was even more frightening than the ones on the buses: as soon as the metal barrier swung open with a clang, they rushed forward like a sea swallowing a mountain. Anyone unlucky enough to get knocked over in the midst of that had little chance of getting up again.

Yin Jiahou and his son sat on one side of the deck up towards the prow—not a bad spot; it was out of the wind. Yin used his shoulder bag to pad his bottom, while Leilei nestled between his legs, padded by a thick layer of rough brown paper, a handkerchief and a canvas union suit. The submachine gun hung on a hook overhead, swinging rhythmically with the swaying of the boat. It occurred to Yin that he could, after all, read for awhile. He fished out his copy of Liang Yusheng's *Thunder Shakes the Land*. Just when he had opened it, Leilei piped up, "What about me, pa?"

Passing his son a volume entitled *Fox Stories*, Yin said, "You can just look at it by yourself, all right? I've been through that book with you hundreds of times."

Yin had not yet read a single page when Leilei began to yell in chorus with the nearby woman vendor, "Melon seeds! Melon seeds! Five-spice melon seeds!" annoying those around them who were trying to take naps.

"What're you up to, Leilei?"

"I'm thirsty," his son replied.

"Well, for that you'll have to wait till we get home," said Yin.

"Or I could have an ice-cream bar."

Taking the hint, Yin bought the boy a Neapolitan ice-cream bar, then buried his nose in the book again. Leilei proceeded to eat only the vanilla stripe of his ice-cream bar; the chocolate stripe he mashed in the nose of a smaller boy who had been watching Leilei, fascinated, as he ate the bar. The boy ran wailing for his mama. Ah, what a pain children were! They never gave one a moment's peace! They were not always lovable little things. By no means! Yin stared wearily at the boy.

A woman with a loud, grating voice came lunging through the knots of people on the deck, her little son in tow, and addressed herself shrilly to Yin Jiahou: "Some little brat's been bullying my boy, but his father hasn't done anything about it. Is his father dead or what?"

Yin, who had been planning to apologize, was suddenly relieved of the urge. Hugging his son to his chest, he closed his eyes and began to rock back and forth.

"Shame on you!" shrieked the woman. "Riffraff!"

A moment's silence. Then "Riffraff!" again. After waiting again in silence for a response, the woman stormed off, muttering curses. Poking his head up out of his father's embrace, Leilei asked, "Is riffraff a bad thing to call somebody, pa?"

"Yes, it is. You must never call anyone that."

"What does riffraff mean?"

"It's a bad name you call somebody."

"But what does it really mean?"

Such a thoughtful, inquisitive child! Yin resolved to answer his questions as best he could. But try as he might, he could think of no way to explain the meaning of the word. So he said, "When you're older you'll understand."

"Does that mean you're going to tell me when I'm older?"

"No, you'll just understand," said Yin lamely, and thought to himself: my child, you will have to deal with all of life, including the ugly and the evil."

"Ohhh..."

The child's sigh moved Yin Jiahou, and a great wave of tenderness swept over him.

"Excuse me, sir," Leilei was saying politely and naturally to a man blocking his way. "Excuse me, please. I need to get by."

"Where are you going, Leilei?" asked Yin.

"I've got to pee," said Leilei, and added, with an air of maturity, "You just stay there. You don't have to come with me."

The boy stood at the rail and peed into the Yangtse River, then carefully did up his trousers before turning round and marching confidently back to where his father sat. What a wellbred child his son was! Yin marvelled. Yin's mother had always recalled what a filthy little ape Yin used to be, rolling about all day in the rubbish heap at the end of the alley without a stitch of clothing on. How far his son's generation had progressed beyond his own! As surely as each wave on the mighty Yangtse River pushed another before it, the future would be rainbow-bright.

He put away the novel. It's tiring, very tiring, thought Yin, but I'll keep on taking it. For the boy's sake.

As the sky dimmed yet further, the cries of the vendors on the boat grew softer, making the roar of the engines on the deck below seem especially loud. The boy lay across Yin's leg, asleep.

Unable to find anything with which to cover his son, Yin could only spread his palms over the boy's little stomach.

The darkened ferry full of sleepy people slowly chugged its way upstream. Endless were the coal-black banks stretching along the riverside, countless the tired faces on the boat. Yin had to exert a tremendous effort to keep his eyes, which were already reddened, from closing. He struggled against sleep, yawning again and again. His eyes, which looked more like those of a dead fish than a human as he propped them open by sheer dint of will, kept streaming with sleepy tears. He recalled the day's events in an effort to fight off sleep, thought of Yali and Xiao Xiaofen, remembered Jiang Nanxia's letter. Finally, without his realizing it, his head drooped forward, his two hands slid to the deck, and he began to snore. There they lay, father and son, one snoring heavily and the other lightly, one sound rising as the other fell.

Coloured lights seemingly strung in space outlined the majestic form of the Yangtse River Bridge in the distance, and now lights twinkled on both sides of the river as well. The Qingchuan Hotel towered at the river's edge, its upper half an inky silhouette, a few lights scattered across its lower floors. Those who had fallen asleep earliest on the ferry now awoke, stretched and remarked, "That Qingchuan Hotel is practically empty!"

Suddenly among the mass of heads on the deck there appeared a great ball of wild, tangled hair. This belonged to a crazy woman who appeared on the ferry every day at this time. She let out a great whoop, then announced, "The end of the world is at hand! Wake up! Wake up!"

Yin Jiahou awoke with a start and quickly covered his son's belly with his warm hand. Damn it! Why'd he gone and fallen asleep? The boy might have caught a chill! He'd had all kinds of dreams in just this short time, but now that he awoke they all flew away, leaving only a bitter taste in his mouth. In the moment he was jolted awake, he felt a stab of regret for leaving the dreams behind, but very quickly his mind cleared. Hearing the madwoman's ravings, he knew they must be approaching the pier.

"Leilei, we're there. We're there."

"Papa," said Leilei sleepily.

"Hey! We're there."

"That crazy lady's singing."

"Come on, stand up. Put on your gun."

"Does the crazy lady have to buy a ticket to ride the ferry?"

"Come on and *wake up*. What're you mumbling about?"

Suddenly the whistle blasted, making them both jump. Then they laughed: funny that people should be frightened by the ferry they rode every day.

The passengers all stood up, yawning, muttering obscenities. Someone tugged at Yin Jiahou from behind. He turned to find an old beggarman, who plumped down on his knees before them and bowed to them again and again. Yin Jiahou hesitated, then dug out a coin and gave it to his son. Delighted, Leilei proudly dropped the coin into the old man's chipped bowl. This was more fun than any game!

Yin Jiahou, however, was unsure what sort of attitude he should adopt towards the old man. Yesterday's evening paper had reported that a young woman somewhere in the north had made ten thousand yuan in one year by begging. Yin worried that his son might someday ask him about this problem.

"Pa, is it right for that old man to ask for other people's money?"

Someday was right now: his son was already asking the question. If Yin said it was right, his son might take the old man as a positive example. If he said it was wrong, then why was he giving the man money? It suddenly occurred to Yin Jiahou that he was always trapped in dilemmas like this one. He couldn't even deal with this four-year-old child! After a moment's thought, he explained seriously, "This is a very complicated social question. You're very young, so how are you to understand it?"

Fortunately, the boy asked no more but chirped up sprightly, "Pa, I'm as hungry as a wolf!"

The pontoon landing-stage had been lengthened again, compelling the passengers to cross to the bank from way out in the river. The evening rush-hour commuters traversed the landing-stage in trepidation, sliding their feet gingerly along, swaying to and fro, so long it seemed, no end in sight, and the spring wind over the river was chilly.

Why didn't they dredge the river? Why didn't they find some way to speed up the ferryboat? Why was it that people who lived on this side of the river should have to commute to the other side to work? Why didn't the factory have a boarding kindergarten? Why did every awful thing at the factory come down on his head? Why couldn't he deal decisively with his relationship with Yali? Why were marriage and love two completely different things? Yin Jiahou truly wished he were a child, with a wise and responsible father to answer all his questions.

They were home!

The fire in the coal stove was burning brightly, the oil sizzling in the wok. The fragrance of frying meat and scallions hit them full in the face as they entered the messy little house. Warm steam hissed merrily from the valve of the pressure cooker. "Mama!" cried the little boy, and ran to his mother's embrace. Yin Jiahou threw off the shoulder bag, kicked off his shoes and collapsed on the bed. His wife handed him a cup of hot water to drink and threw a damp flannel on to his face. Yin lay immobile, breathing in the flannel's healthy smell of sun and soap. Was there any more pleasurable time than this? His home! His wife! Even if she was worn and pale, even if she loved to pick fights! At this moment, visions of love under a romantic moon, yearnings for the sublime union of souls—such things were a million miles away from the mind of this hungry, weary man.

Yin's wife helped Leilei squirm his way into a fresh red-and-white-striped T-shirt and changed the bandage on his scrape, transforming him magically back into a bright-eyed, bushy-tailed, apple-cheeked little boy. Yin Jiahou let himself sink into the sweetness of the homely atmosphere.

On the table were a dish of braised beancurd and a bowl of meatball soup; there were also one dish each of glistening green cabbage and translucent orange five-spice carrot strips. The boy had a dish of lean steamed meat with egg all to himself. This was enough and plenty!

"Come on now, eat up!" Yin's wife said cheerily. She had said this at every meal since their marriage, and he never tired of hearing her. Her wifely attentiveness in this instance made up for many deficiencies.

"Vegetables are getting very expensive," she remarked as she watched them eat. "Cabbages are sixty cents a kilo."

"Sixty cents?" he echoed.

"Extra-lean meat is five yuan sixty, no haggling, but for Leilei's sake I gritted my teeth and bought a quarter kilo."

"Good Lord!" he exclaimed.

"Not counting the cost of the coal and condiments, we spent three yuan thirty on this meal alone."

"So expensive!"

"They're drinking our blood!" she said.

"Damn right," he agreed.

Discussion of the price of food was an indispensable item on the evening menu; it was also how husband and wife resumed communication after not having seen each other all day.

When Yin Jiahou and his son had eaten their fill, his wife dumped the rest of the soup and food into her own bowl, pulled her stool a bit further from the table, spread a garishly coloured women's magazine across her knees and began to read as she ate.

Now the pleasant interlude was over: time for Yin to do the washing-up. He had always felt that reading while eating was a bad habit, particularly reprehensible in a wife and mother. But his wife always protested, "I got into the habit when I was still young. Are you trying to take away the one little vice I allow myself?" So Yin Jiahou was forced to take on the duty of washing up. Fortunately, all of the people who washed dishes in the common washroom in the evenings were men, which made the prospect much easier to accept.

The men used their bit of washing-time to talk about recent developments in sports, current events and other important news; these few minutes were the foundation of whatever friendship the men in this row of houses shared. Today the news Yin Jiahou heard during the washing-up was bad—very bad.

"Well, pals, looks like they're going to tear this place down," said one of the men.

"What?" asked someone incredulously.

"So where are we supposed to live?"

"What do they care about that? If you belong to the organization that owns the place, they'll arrange something for you. If you don't you can scram."

"Is this *true*?"

"They announced it at a workers' union general meeting at our work unit, and they'll be sending someone here soon to give notice."

Several voices burst out at once: "This is unfair!" All of them belonged to men who, like Yin, were living here in borrowed housing. "This really *is* unfair," Yin blurted out in spite of himself.

Crestfallen, Yin fell silent thinking about this new development, this Damocles' sword hanging over all their heads. This was not good, not good at all.

Having brought back the clean dishes Yin immediately took up the mop, then made ready to wash the clothes Leilei had changed out of. He worked ceaselessly, bustling back and forth in an effort to avoid letting slip to his wife the news about the house. Tonight she would have to get up and go and work the night shift, so she had to get to bed early. He thought he should suffer the burden of the bad news alone for a while.

"Hey, you should get to bed," he said.

"Uh-huh." His wife still had her nose buried in the magazine on her lap. Leilei turned on the television set and was soon absorbed in a show called *The Flower Fairy*.

"Hey! Come on, it's your bedtime," Yin repeated insistently.

His wife stood up slowly. "Right, right. I've just finished the article. It was about relations between husband and wife. You should look at it too."

"Okay, I will. But you should get to bed."

Walking over and giving Leilei a kiss, she remarked, "It said mostly that husbands and wives should be completely honest with each other, that hiding things, even tiny, insignificant things, can lead to terrible emotional scarring."

"Right," agreed Yin.

Finally she started getting ready for bed, removing her outer garments. Kissing the boy again, she said, "Leilei, didn't anything special happen today that you'd like to tell Mama about?"

Instantaneously conscious of the danger of this conversation between mother and son, Yin nevertheless realized it was too late to put a stop to it.

"Oh, that's right, mama," said Leilei. "Papa didn't eat cold noodles at the stall today."

Her smile changed instantly to a glower. "What is wrong with you? How many times do I have to tell you how much hepatitis there is around nowadays? You must not use the bowls and chopsticks at those places!"

"Okay, Okay. From now on I'll be careful."

"'From now on, from now on'," she mimicked. "Don't you try to pull the wool over my eyes! Hey. Did you go visit that man today?"

"Man?" Yin faltered. "What man?"

"Look at you! 'What man?'" Yin's wife, anger now in full spate, plopped down on the edge of the bed, crossed her legs, and snapped, "The head of the housing committee at your factory, you dope! After a lot of asking around I finally found out

what sort of things he likes. And then—remember? —we a-
greed we'd spend the money to buy him a little gift, right? But
we thought first you'd better go make friends with him, right?"

It was true. This was a very important matter for their family. If there was any possibility of them being assigned housing,
they could hold off buying the colour TV. How could he have
forgotten so easily?

"Damn!" he swore, rapping the side of his skull with his fist.
"I'll go for sure tomorrow." The matter of housing had now acquired a burning urgency; he would have to do even the things
he didn't want to.

Seeing Yin Jiahou so acquiescent, his wife could think of
nothing more to say, so she merely sat and glared at him.

"What about the liquor?"

"Maotai's going for ninety-six yuan the kilo on the black market."

"Well, forget that. I'll try to find someone else. Have the
bonuses been distributed?"

"No, not yet," he lied. Her article had been wrong, he
thought. If husband and wife really were completely truthful
with each other, the emotional scarring would be even more serious. "From what I've seen at the factory," he continued, "it
looks like they're going to crack down on the merry-go-round
bonus distribution system. We might see some changes." Good,
he thought. Lay down a little padding for the eventual hard
landing. There's no way we're ever going to have that Western-
style meal now, my good wife, so now you're prepared, right?
Don't go bragging to the ladies at work saying your husband's
going to take you and your son out to a Western restaurant.

Rubbing below her eyes, his wife sighed and said, "Blessings

never come in pairs, and disasters never come singly. There's
something I was going to wait till tomorrow to tell you, to let
you rest easy tonight. But..." She heaved another sigh. "My
aunt called long distance today."

"The one in Hebei?"

"She said her third son is coming to Wuhan for a pleasure
trip. He's already set out; he'll arrive tomorrow afternoon."

"You mean the one with the tumour on his leg?"

"Yes. Probably the tumour isn't looking too good. His mother
tries her best to make him happy..."

"And he's staying here," said Yin grimly.

"Naturally. We live in the centre of town. It's easy to get
around."

Yin Jiahou was at a loss for words. No wonder he had noticed
something different about the room when he had got back this
evening, something he hadn't put his finger on right away. Now
he saw: a large sheet of organdy was hanging all bunched up on
a wire next to the wall at the head of the bed. Tomorrow
evening it would be spread out as a curtain to screen their double
bed from the folding bed, upon which would be sleeping their
twenty-year-old cousin. "Great," remarked Yin sarcastically,
dusting off the hanging cloth. He wanted to laugh and break up
the gloom that was settling over them, but his nose began to
tickle and he sneezed instead. As his wife climbed into bed, Yin
turned down the volume on the TV set and went to wash clothes
in the washroom.

Wash the clothes. Hang them up. Go back and turn off the
TV. Carry the boy, who has fallen asleep in the chair, over to
the folding bed and try to get his clothes off without waking him

up. Line up a row of chairs next to the folding bed in order to avoid a repeat of last night's debacle. Then lightly, quietly, slowly—don't wake the wife. Yin Jiahou grunted with the effort of taking such care, and a light sweat glazed his forehead.

When Yin finally got to bed, the hands of the clock stood at 11:36.

Leaning against the headboard, he took a deep drag on his cigarette and felt his joints and muscles loosen with tiny creaks as he relaxed. A strange numbness floated out from the spaces in the loosened joints, and Yin sank into a murky void.

Only the desk lamp gave off a foggy glow.

As he exhaled smoke into the dusk of the lamplight, his problems came rolling back through his mind, making him restless and confused. His eyes were swimming, and his body felt heavy, so heavy he could not roll over or even move at all. He was exhausted, worn out. What a bitter trial life was! He slid into self-pity. How bitter it was!

His wife lay flat on her back, snoring softly. Yin cast a sideways glance at her face, which seemed to have changed somehow, becoming smooth, white, beautiful. Her face became Yali's, then Xiaofen's. A wave of heat swept through Yin's chest, and he thought, can't a man's fancy run a little wild now and then? This one little thought, this tiny spark, caused a ball of fire to leap up in his heart and sent his blood racing like a wild steed through his veins.

His thoughts secretly pinned on Yali and Xiaofen, Yin crudely patted his wife's cheek. Opening her eyes a fraction, she muttered, "I'm sleepy."

"Your bloody cousin is coming to stay tomorrow!" he hissed in

an angry whisper. "And he'll be sleeping in this room!" Furious-
ly he struck a match and lit another cigarette, then flung the
matchbox to the floor.

Plucking the cigarette from between his lips, his wife said
with unwonted tenderness, "All right. I won't sleep, then. I
wouldn't be able to sleep very long anyway." She yawned several
times, wriggled her limbs, and began apathetically to unbutton
her nightclothes.

Quickly laying his hand on hers, Yin gazed into her rough-
skinned face and said, "Forget it. Go ahead and go to sleep."

"No, there's only half an hour to go. I'm afraid of sleeping
too long."

"Don't worry," he said gently. "I'll wake you up when the
time comes."

"Jiahou! Oh, Jiahou, you're so good to me..."

His smile betrayed just a hint of irony, but he was at peace,
like a beach from which the tide has ebbed.

Suddenly his wife's eyes grew moist, and she began to weep
softly: "I haven't had the heart to tell you, but they're going to
tear this place down. They've already served notice..."

"Mm-hmm. I already knew it too," said Yin reassuringly.
"I'll think of some kind of solution tomorrow if it kills me!"

"Don't get too worked up," she said. "It's not as if there were
no alternatives. I've asked around. There's a private place for
rent, fifteen square metres, fifty yuan a month not including
water and power. I know we won't be able to go out to eat
Western-style food... The funny thing is we were just like little
kids, so greedy, just dying to go..."

Quickly switching off the desk lamp, Yin Jiahou took advantage of the darkness to wipe away the tears that had welled from

his eyes. Squeezing his wife's hand, he said, "Go to sleep. Let tomorrow take care of its own problems. Everything'll be all right."

Wife of mine, I'm going to get you that Western meal. This Sunday. Somehow. Yin did not speak the words, for fear he might not be able to manage it after all. He could not control every last aspect of his life. But he would do his damnedest!

How could Yali ever understand that he and his wife were inseparable? The wife of an ordinary man should be just this crude, just this sharp-tongued, without the least pretension. As a husband, he had his regrets, but so what?

Yin Jiahou crushed out his cigarette and snuggled under the coverlet. In the moment before he fell asleep, the word he had spoken that morning on the ferry flashed in his memory: "Dream." He had a vision of himself floating above his own recumbent body and saying to it: everything you are experiencing is a dream. You are having a long, long dream, and when you wake up you will find that everything is actually not this way. With supreme faith in his own words, Yin Jiahou fell peacefully asleep.

Translated by Stephen Fleming

Sunrise

IN Wuhan, winter is the season of marriage.

On this, the first day of the lunar new year, it was as if every family in Wuhan were holding weddings. Dusk being the optimum travel time for the procession, traffic on the Yangtse River Bridge had already been jammed forty minutes by the multitude of wedding parties. A policeman was busy waving back cars, cigarettes and wedding candy being tossed out like flying locusts. Face drawn and cursing loudly, he announced that he would shout one, two, three; after that, if everyone continued to ignore his orders and scramble ahead, exercising the powers vested in him by law, he would take all those big colour TV sets and refrigerators currently blocking traffic and haul them off into the river. Shouting, "One ... two ... three!" he bolted over to where a group of men and women, all dressed in red and green, still pushed and shoved as before. Taking a VCR and an electric rice-cooker from the two opposing wedding parties, he tossed them into the Yangtse. Only then did traffic return to normal.

Zhao Shengtian and Li Xiaolan's families both lived in Wuchang. The newly-established family was also to reside in Wuchang. Actually, it wasn't necessary that the procession cross the river on the crowded bridge, but their troubles were only just beginning. Because the traffic on the bridge was blocked, the Yuemachang bridge approach was also jammed. Things got so bad at the Yuemachang approach that Zhao Shengtian became violent and ended up getting a front tooth knocked out. This day, remembered as the day the respectful groom lost his front tooth, was one that would live on forever in memory—and infamy. Yet the bride, Li Xiaolan, who was wearing the wedding dress he bought for her at eight hundred yuan, said, "Zhao Shengtian, I never knew you were such a scatterbrained bastard!" Now since when has a bride behaved like that?!

They didn't sleep together that night. Li Xiaolan said Zhao's whole body reeked of blood and dirt, like some mangy dog after a vicious fight. Zhao replied unceremoniously that Li Xiaolan was a "little whore". If not for the fact that before all of this they had already had sex, the wasted wedding night would surely have left them a lifetime of regret.

From the outset, Zhao Shengtian and Li Xiaolan thought that, since the wedding was so extravagant, there was no need to follow the customary practice of leading the wedding procession to her house.

Zhao Shengcai was adamant, however. "No way!" he said.

Zhao Shengcai was Zhao Shengtian's oldest brother. The Zhao family's old man sat off one side, smoking one after another the foreign cigarettes given to him by his oldest son. The oldest son, just like a father, decided marriage matters for members of the family.

Eight years before, Zhao Shengcai had resigned his job as butcher at the meat processing plant and headed south to the coastal special economic zones to do business. Fate surely had called upon this semiliterate, elementary school graduate to strike out on his own. Today he resided in Shenzhen, and apart from a garden, Western-style house, and a car, he even had a smart little female secretary. From the time he got rich, every time he returned to Wuhan he solemnly behaved like the head of the family. If he said no way, the second, third and fourth brothers, fifth sister and parents would of course say no way. Zhao Shengcai said, "Little brother's wedding should be the best that Wuhan has to offer." This touched upon the issue of pride. He wanted to make them all see, the neighbours, those dog bastards over at the meat processing plant, and the little bitch woman teacher who had abandoned him. Just let them see!

So Zhao Shengtian and Li Xiaolan couldn't have control of their own wedding. However unhappy this fact made them, though, as soon as they thought about how it wasn't coming out of their own pockets, they realized that not joining the procession would be a waste.

At present, in the city of Wuhan, the most popular, most fashionable means of transporting wedding parties is via the "mamu taxi", or the three-wheeled carts pedalled by macho Chinese men. Small cars had been popular for a while, but were quickly outmoded by the "mamu taxis", because sedans can't show off the expensive contents of the wedding—and Wuhan people like to show off.

Twenty "mamu taxis" were hired out by Zhao Shengtian's wedding party; six transported people, fourteen carried wedding gifts. The previous night, passing through small alleys, they had moved all the things to Li Xiaolan's home. On New Year's afternoon they met and escorted Li Xiaolan from her home. Refrigerator, TV, VCR, stereo, fully automatic washing machine, stainless steel kitchen utensils, air purifier, and eight sets of high-quality satin embroidered quilts combined to form a pile the size of a small mountain. Suspended high atop a bamboo pole was a residence gas permit. The twenty "mamu taxis" were wreathed in flowers, dripping with red silk. The route of the procession began at the old site of the Central Peasant Movement Institute, then went on to Liberation Street, taking Pengliuyang Road to Yuemachang, then turning into Shouyi Road and finally returning to Liberation Street. Travelling in a straight line, they could have done the trip in ten minutes.

The fight started thus: because of the traffic jam, two wedding parties were squeezed together on the Yuemachang bridge approach. The other wedding party only had eight "mamu taxis". Their bride, however, was much prettier than Li Xiaolan. Needless to say, the two parties thus despised each other. Among the drivers on the Yuemachang approach were several irrepressibly lonely cab drivers who, desirous to join in the fun, began saying things just to stir up trouble. Soon a whole street full of rednecks shouted and laughed together.

"Dog-fucking cabbies!" Zhao Shengtian cursed.

Li Xiaolan said, "You might as well swear at yourself. You're so spineless, always listening to your elder brother, that shameless show-off."

"You're the shameless show-off; you don't even know when to shut that stinking mouth of yours!"

"Why, you mother-fucking...!"

Li Xiaolan tried to jump out, but some bridesmaids pulled her back, kicking and screaming, onto the cart. Zhao Shengtian's eyes were wildly scanning the scene, looking for an excuse to

start a fight. He didn't expect that his old problem would flare
up again on this, the day of his wedding. Just then, a brides-
maid from the other party spat on one of his cart's wheels. Happily, he went into action. He jumped down from the groom's
seat, and with legs apart and arms akimbo, pointed at the spit-
tle, saying, "Whoever's dog took this shit, you'd better come
out and clean it up, cause if you don't, I'm gonna drag you out
and make you lick it clean."

A big, tall youth got up from beside the bride and walked
over.

"Hey buddy, what do you say you and me take this over there
and give it a go?"

Zhao Shengtian cracked a slight smile.

Like old pros, onlookers immediately spilled over to the side,
making an instant arena out of the area facing the red building
of the First Navigation of the 1911 Revolution. The pair of
bridegrooms, under the gaze of Dr Sun Yat-sen's imposing
bronze statue, then started to fight. Circling each other like
tigers would their prey, the two launched a simultaneous attack.
Zhao Shengtian went straight for the other guy's crotch, his opponent targeted Zhao's face. Raising his head slightly so as to
avoid the punch, Zhao ended up taking it on the chin and losing
a front tooth, his mouth filling with blood. Zhao's opponent,
however, crumpled in pain to the ground, writhing about,
hands covering his groin. Someone excitedly gave the youth a
count to ten; not only did the boy stay down for the count, but
he even started to cry. Zhao Shengtian was victorious! When he
thought about that guy having to wait at least a week before being able to sleep with his pretty bride again, Zhao became eu-
phoric. He was just turning to go when he heard the bride crying

from the other side, "Someone please get my brother to the hospital! Take care of my brother first!"

Brother! Zhao Shengtian immediately went numb from the waist up, his face blank. "Zhao Shengtian!" Li Xiaolan called out, "I never thought you could be such a scatter brained bastard!" Usually the two of them called each other "Little Zhao" and "Little Li". Only on extremely rare occasions did they say the other's full name.

Li Xiaolan was not some fragile, foolish little thing whose heart could be bought with gold and jewels. She felt as if she'd been cheated.

Now if this was how the couple started things off, how could it possibly go from there?

2

Big brother Zhao Shengcai did indeed resemble a rich man: he patted his bulging belly, laughed robustly and, amidst laughter, honestly admitted his mistake.

"I didn't know Wuhan was still so fucking uncivilized," he said.

To make up for things, he suggested that the newlyweds go on a honeymoon trip by plane, and he would be responsible for all expenses.

"After all, there are fewer chances for people to fight in a plane than in a 'mamu taxi'." With these words, Zhao Shengcai finally got Li Xiaolan to laugh.

The young couple made up. Neither of them had ever taken an aeroplane, and both really wanted to. Why not? Someone else was paying for it—it would be a waste to pass up the opportunity. Gesticulating excitedly, they discussed the travel destinations. They agreed that if the one-day trip from Wuhan to Hong Kong was on offer, they'd do that.

Zhao Shengtian said, "How about Beijing?"

"I've already been to Beijing. Might as well go to Shanghai."

Zhao Shengtian thought of Shanghai as a business city, without anything much in the way of scenery. Shanghai people also catered to foreigners and had no reservations about bullying natives. They'd be better-off going to Suzhou and Hangzhou.

Li Xiaolan thought Jiuzhaigou was preferable.

"But why would you want to visit a mountain valley in winter? Let's just stick to cities."

So the young couple crawled around on a map of China, searching here and there, at last choosing the mountain city of Chongqing. There, they could see mountains, stroll through the city and eat hotpot.

They bought the tickets to Chongqing. In great excitement they got their luggage together, said goodbye to family and friends, and went to the airport waitingroom to await their plane. In life—heaven only knows why—when it rains, it pours. They had another mishap.

Fog in Chongqing caused the flight to be delayed, and Zhao Shengtian and Li Xiaolan wasted the day waiting. On the second day, they went again to the airport, but again it was fog. After waiting and waiting, Li Xiaolan said to Zhao Shengtian,

"I don't feel too good."

"Try and be patient."

After a bit, Li Xiaolan said, "I'm a little nauseous."

Zhao Shengtian didn't understand her meaning. He was thinking, sure, all this waiting would make anyone nauseous.

Suddenly, Li Xiaolan stood up and, covering her mouth, ran

into the bathroom. From inside the women's toilet suddenly
came an awful retching sound. Zhao Shengtian ran back and
forth between the luggage and the bathroom. To him, Li
Xiaolan's moans sounded like the pathetic cries of a small dog
being beaten. For the first time he totally panicked.

Among the passengers was a middle-aged woman who bravely
volunteered herself as a doctor. Zhao Shengtian bowed before
her, saying repeatedly, "Thank you."

Li Xiaolan very quickly stopped vomiting. After quite some
time, the middle-aged woman walked out with Li Xiaolan, supporting her arm. Li Xiaolan's face was all flushed, completely
unlike a sick person. Zhao Shengtian went over and asked sympathetically, "Doctor, is she really sick? What's the matter with
her? Does she need to go to the hospital?"

The middle-aged woman's lightly spoken words hit Zhao
Shengtian like a thunderclap: "She doesn't need to go to the hospital, but she does need to go home. She should rest a few days
in bed. She's pregnant."

Pregnant! Zhao Shengtian was tongue-tied; his face flushed
all over. Li Xiaolan was pregnant!

The middle-aged woman said, "Don't be embarrassed. Congratulations to you both!"

Zhao Shengtian forgot to say thank you, so Li Xiaolan said it.
She was thinking much more clearly than Zhao Shengtian.

The beautiful plan to take a plane ride and honeymoon trip
thus came to a premature end, all because of Li Xiaolan's pregnancy. The young couple were extremely depressed.

This child's arrival was truly inopportune.

Today's youth have their early married lives all planned out.
Most don't want to casually have a baby just like that. Zhao

Shengtian and Li Xiaolan had decided to have a child after two years of marriage. First they would enjoy two years of newlywed life, at the same time, scraping together some savings for later.

It was precisely on the birth-control measures that they had muffed it up. Zhao Shengtian was totally unwilling to use a condom, reason being that once he put on the thing, he felt like a rubber man. Li Xiaolan was totally unwilling to use the pill, because it gave her headaches and irregular periods. When they lived together prior to marriage they were always worried about being found out, so neither was it a good idea to go the hospital to have an IUD inserted. They thus had no choice but to adopt the "safe rhythm" method. But evidently, the "safe rhythm" method wasn't all that safe after all. What to do?

What could they do? If they had the child, who would take care of it? When maternity leave was over, who could look after the kid? Zhao's mother had already announced that she would absolutely not act as an amah anymore. She had already raised six children. Add to that the six she had brought up for others. Two sixes make twelve, altogether a dozen. If she held another child her arms would start to shake. She was sick of it. For the next few years she would do just two things, play mahjong and make meals for her old man.

Li Xiaolan's parents were high-ranking cadres. Neither had retired; both were full of long-standing airs. At the sight of their grandchild they would limit themselves to a nod of the head and a slight smile, at the very most taking the child's small hand and saying, "Mmn. Not bad."

If they hired a nanny, an even greater hardship would follow—where would they find one? Where would they find a good one? With their one-room living place already completely full, where would the nanny live? Where would the money to support her come from?

Zhao Shengtian's monthly salary was seventy yuan, Li Xiaolan's sixty-four yuan. When you put all the subsidies and bonuses together, the combined income didn't even amount to a hundred and eighty yuan! Depending on his brother and parents to give them the expensive wedding had already been asking e- nough. Their parents had guided them to the shore. They were now adults. If they went home again to eat, it would be called "stealing meals". Zhao Shengtian was a person who dearly val- ued face.

So what should they do about this children thing? The bank- book that they added bits to and removed bunches from now showed only twenty-six yuan.

Zhao Shengtian and Li Xiaolan snuggled up together, talking away into the small hours of the morning. In the heat of this sudden attack, they had become kindred spirits. Zhao Shengtian stroked his wife's cheeks, and she, in turn, caressed her hus- band repeatedly. Like two cats nearly frozen to death, they clung to one another, sharing the heat from one another's bod- ies.

"What do you say we should do?"

"What do you think?"

"I think ... I don't know. You're the man, what you say goes."

"Then tomorrow I'll take you to the hospital."

"OK."

"But you mustn't be afraid of the pain, you know."

"OK."

Li Xiaolan very obediently agreed.

As if carefully steering clear of submerged rocks, they had avoided the term "abortion".

3

The gynaecological ward had a room with the sign "Abortion Room" hanging on the door. Women sat in a row on a long bench running alongside the doorway; their men were either at the windows, or walking around in the hallways and stairwells.

The nurse guarding the "Abortion Room" door and calling out people's numbers was a strangely-shaped, fat, middle-aged woman. She sat perfectly calm, staring contemptuously at the two worlds presented before her; the oblivious-to-pain, self-satisfied male world and the frightened, endangered female world. She knew what they were going through. One was about to enter hell, one was calm and safe. Who could save this despicable human race?

Li Xiaolan's number came up.

"Excuse me, does it hurt much?" Li Xiaolan asked, extremely nervous.

The fat nurse replied in a clear, warm voice, "A little. Clench your teeth and it will pass. That's just how it is, girl. In life you've got to learn how to clench your teeth." She then showed her how to clench her teeth, the flesh on her cheeks quivering as she did so. Li Xiaolan laughed, revealing her grey teeth. The nurse said, "Tetracycline teeth, same as my daughter. That bad luck generation of children born in the sixties got the evils of history inscribed on their teeth. No need to feel yourself inferior, though; just look at this dog of a guy over here—look at how he grovels beneath your skirt."

The fat nurse accurately pointed out Zhao Shengtian from among the group of men. All the men and women had a laugh.

Li Xiaolan chuckled. A young girl's lively expression once again returned to her face. She went in, completely relaxed.

There was a moment such that Zhao Shengtian felt a slight shiver rise up from the very soles of his feet. He had been moved. His whole body was shivering because he had been moved.

How many years had it been since something had touched him? Over ten years? No. Even longer. What was there to be touched by? The first page of his memory was hunger, the second, fighting. The three years at the beginning of the sixties were a period of natural disasters. His parents had to raise six kids and four old people. The six children would fight over a mouthful of rice or half a steamed bun. Later, it was quarrelling at school. Under the veil of night at the Golden Crane Pavilion Theatre doorway, he would fight with girls for movie tickets. Teachers punished him for his tricks and naughty ways; he, in turn, punished the teachers, "struggling" against the "traitorous elements" among fellow students and teachers until the time he graduated from the technical school. After he started working, not only did the situation not take a turn for the better, but society became even more complicated. Products didn't sell well. Efficiency was poor, and the relations between Party secretary and factory leader were strained. Nobody worked hard, nobody was responsible to anyone else.

Not even big brother Zhao Shengcai's generosity could move him. That was because Zhao Shengcai owed him too much. From the time they were small Shengcai had bullied and humiliated him, forcing him to drink his piss, stealing the small savings Shengtian had starved himself to put aside. Thus when

Shengcai said Shengtian's wedding was a matter of honour, Shengcai was paying for his own honour.

Was his father worth being moved by? Father used to come home carrying small articles of public property under his clothes such as wipecloths, brooms, soap, toilet paper, cups, abacuses... He handled any bad behaviour by the five older children toward the little one by turning a blind eye. If he had a cigarette to smoke and liquor to drink he thought he was in heaven.

Zhao's mother was hate incarnate. She called all her sons little bastards, and her daughter a "stinking maid". She completely mixed up all the childrens' birthdays. She was always saying how she'd rather be dead, and how her hips ached.

To Zhao Shengtian, deep-felt emotion was but an empty page. He was used to laughing a lot; even standing-up straight posed a problem for him. He was always standing with one leg bent, his whole body rocking, eyes staring blankly out into the world.

The hospital was a place only rarely visited by Zhao Shengtian. The few times that he had been, he was left with terrible impressions. How could it be that he had been touched by a hospital? He himself couldn't fathom it.

Li Xiaolan was a very squeamish girl; even when she got a shot she would scream bloody murder. From the time of the previous afternoon's decision to have the abortion, all the way until this morning, her eyes had been like an open faucet. She went weak in the knees as soon as they entered the hospital. Zhao Shengtian exhorted her, exhausting all possible mild methods, but it was of no use. If the hospital had been just a little further away, and he had lost his patience, he probably would have had to spank her and shout a bit.

Still, the fat nurse had coaxed Li Xiaolan. So cleverly and kindly she had coaxed her. The fat nurse's job was to watch the door and call out numbers; no one was going to give her a bonus because she did this extra job. Here was someone working hard, someone being considerate to others! Truly, Zhao Shengtian never imagined that, outside the abortion room of a hospital gynaecological ward, he would be moved.

"Hello! Young man, are you alive? Go and make your phone calls!" The fat nurse reminded him in a loud voice, her tone very abrasive.

"OK."

Zhao Shengtian replied super-politely, moreover bowing slightly to express his gratitude. He knew the fat nurse wasn't angry with him, particularly, but was censuring instead the entire male world. He could completely accept this. He was happy at having learned to be magnanimous.

Zhao Shengtian and Li Xiaolan had discussed the phone call the previous day.

The first call was to inform the Zhao family. Zhao Shengtian's sister Zhao Shengzhu was an elementary school teacher, at present teaching. Zhao Shengtian said that there was emergency involving family at the hospital and he would get Teacher Zhao. Arriving all panicky, Zhao Shengzhu grabbed the receiver, asking who was sick.

Zhao Shengtian told her the situation.

"God! How can this be? I must go and tell Mother!"

"I'll leave it to you, then."

"Mother is definitely going to disagree. Since when do you abort on the first pregnancy?"

"Nothing we can do. It's already done."

"You bastard!" In her temper, Zhao Shengzhu lost all concern for decorum. "How can you listen to that little monster? Of course she doesn't want kids—she couldn't handle them."

"I didn't listen to her, she listened to me."

"Oh please, give me a break. I'm going right away to tell Mother."

"Go ahead."

Zhao Shengtian's second call was to his mother-in-law. Li Xiaolan said she hoped her mother would come to take care of her for a few days.

Mrs Li deserved her title of high-ranking cadre; not waiting for her son-in-law to finish, she interrupted, "Little Zhao, first I want you to put down the phone and stop that procedure immediately."

"I'm afraid it's too late."

"What does 'you're afraid' mean?"

Zhao Shengtian turned his head to look at the "Abortion Room". A few more had already gone in, and no men were running inside to stop things.

"It's just too late."

"That's simply nonsense!"

Zhao Shengtian was left speechless.

"But you've only been married ten days!"

"Yeah."

"Aren't you the least afraid that her being pregnant more than fifty days won't look so good?"

Zhao Shengtian was even more speechless. He was definitely not going to cross his mother-in-law; of this he was quite certain.

"Mama, Xiaolan said she hoped you could come to see her."

"Of course I will. I miss my daughter. As for you, I have a hope—I hope that you won't seduce Xiaolan into doing anymore improper things."

"OK," he said. That was pretty funny, he thought—they were already married—what more improper things could they do?

"Take good care of Xiaolan. Make some chicken broth for her."

"OK."

"Make sure that if you don't want children for the time being you take the proper measures; if you do want them, try your best to have them. You are a male comrade, you should be responsible. If something like this happens again, I won't be so polite."

"OK."

4

A female doctor wearing a dull blue surgical cap entered the "Abortion Room" and said, "Give me them." She wanted Xiaolan's records.

Li Xiaolan handed them over, giving her a large desk calendar along with them. This kind of high-quality print, large desk calendar was a rare sight in Wuhan. It was a wedding gift given to them by Zhao Shengcai's secretary. With New Year just passed and Spring Festival close at hand, this was a fairly appropriate gift.

The doctor cast a careful glance at Li Xiaolan. "Are you single?"

"No." Li Xiaolan's face went red. "I'm scared of the pain...

please be gentle. "

"Oh," the doctor said. "Don't be nervous, I'll be as gentle as possible. "

Li Xiaolan went over to the curtain on the other side of the room to be examined. The room was very large, with internal heating. The examination beds were arranged in a row. Several women sat on top of them with legs spread and faces pointing upward, receiving examination. Two young male interns were administering the procedure.

The doctor instructed Li Xiaolan to remove one leg of her pants, then began fumbling around with the medical instruments. Li Xiaolan pulled off her pants with hesitation; she felt her muscles begin to stiffen again. She experienced a twinge of regret.

"Remove your panties, too," the doctor ordered tersely, a vaginal speculum glinting in his hand.

Li Xiaolan took a breath of air thick with the smell of medicine, and looked askance at the interns. The doctor said, "An '80s girl still so feudal? Take them off. Quickly now. "

This '80s girl Li Xiaolan was not feudal, not in the least. She had started dating at sixteen, and since then had seen and broken up with not a few boys. She had met Zhao Shengtian in a dance hall, hugging and kissing him on their date the following day. She didn't have the slightest notion of family seniority and respect. This daughter of a high-ranking cadre family wanted to marry into a normal household. Summers, swimming in the East Lake, she bounced about sexily in her bikini. She dared to contradict her parents and bosses. She could honestly admit to anyone that her school grades were poor, and that she couldn't get into college. This honest, carefree air was precisely what attracted Zhao Shengtian. She was so free and easy in fact, that Zhao Shengtian privately took her to be a foolish, easy-to-dupe little thing. After marriage, however, she had already clearly demonstrated that she wasn't so foolish.

No one had ever called Li Xiaolan feudal. This doctor was something of an inventor. You're wrong, Li Xiaolan silently told her, quietly removing her panties.

If she wasn't having an abortion, she would have obeyed the doctor's every word. This had nothing to do with being "feudal". A girl should have her mystery, and the right to preserve that mystery. Her fragility too—only as long as she possesses this can she be lovable. The scary thing about the gynaecologist and his apparatus was that they could unfeelingly obliterate a girl's mystery and fragility. This was precisely what Li Xiaolan feared. She felt that it wasn't a man making a girl a woman, but instead, the gynaecological ward.

As the vaginal speculum entered the flesh of Li Xiaolan's body, tears flowed from the corners of her eyes.

"Does it hurt?" asked the doctor.

Li Xiaolan nodded her head. It was not that it hurt, it was just hard to accept; she had been broken.

Her fragility and mystery had been destroyed, tossed into a pail under the bed along with all the other dirty instruments, unable ever to be brought back. Li Xiaolan saw the interns come over. She knew that she had no right to restrain them. Silently, her eyes, devoid of hope, faced the ceiling; she felt sickened.

The doctor felt her uterus. "Don't move. All women have to pass through this sooner or later."

Women are supposed to pass through this. Women? So the body makes the woman? Li Xiaolan mulled over these words, then experienced sudden enlightenment. So she was a woman and not a girl? A real woman had to go through this. They all had to open their legs, and remove their panties. It didn't matter who it was, it was the same for the entire human race. Because a new life starts from here, the sun also rises from here, without exception. Li Xiaolan didn't need to be so nervous, afraid, nauseated, and tearful—it was all unnecessary!

Li Xiaolan's head was all sweaty, her whole body limp and weak. The doctor said, "Examination's over, you can relax."

The doctor told Li Xiaolan she didn't need to put on her pants. "We'll do it here."

"Do what?"

"What did you come here for?"

"Oh." Li Xiaolan's mind was off in some distant daydream. In a completely serious, determined tone, she told the doctor, "I'm not doing it. I want the child. It just moved."

The doctor smiled, "That was my finger."

"But it will be moving before long."

"Of course. And the eight months will go by in a twinkling, and it will just pop out into the world, crying and screaming."

Li Xiaolan savoured the image of the baby coming out screaming and crying after eight months. With her colour restored to its natural peach-red, walking with a mother's steady gait, she exited the abortion room. In the face of all the problems in the world surrounding it, that child, like a bamboo shoot after a spring rain, was busy fighting its way out. How bad could things be for us out here, anyway?

When Zhao Shengtian saw Li Xiaolan, he seemed somewhat unsure that it was really her. He went to support her, but she brushed him away.

"No need," she said, laughing.

"You didn't do it?"

"You're pretty smart. I decided not to go through with it."

"What a brilliant decision!"

Zhao Shengtian's moment of exultation was like removing a huge load. He pulled Li Xiaolan over to the notice board to read "The origin of birth" and "One is better". He said he had read it through three times. Each time he became more interested, thinking that perhaps they should keep the child and try raising it. Sooner or later they were going to have one.

Li Xiaolan pointed at a bean-size foetus. "It's that big."

"Is it really alive?"

"That's pretty obvious."

"Yes!"

Zhao Shengtian and Li Xiaolan left the hospital in high spirits. All the way home they talked excitedly. This day was the best they'd had in a long, long time. They had learned an important lesson in human life—something many people never understand even to their dying day.

5

Everything tends to be easier said than done. Before now, Zhao Shengtian and Li Xiaolan hadn't the opportunity to understand this principle.

From the time they went home from the hospital, Li Xiaolan's reaction to her pregnancy became more and more acute. Her mother called frequently, encouraging her daughter to eat.

"Xiaolan, if you throw up, keep eating. Treat food just as if it's medicine. Treat pregnancy like a war."

Li Xiaolan began in earnest to treat food like medicine. With eyes closed, brows furrowed, and a glass of water in hand, she lifted her head, swallowed a mouthful, and immediately washed it down with the water. In no time, however, she tossed it back up. But finally when she began to vomit less, her feelings of nausea got worse. The smell of cigarette smoke, cooking oil, gas exhaust, makeup, pages in books—the whole lot made her sick. Smelling them disgusted her to the point that she could actually feel the acid flowing in her stomach. She lost all appetite. At the library where she worked, walking home from work, and at home she all got nauseous.

Zhao Shengtian hoped that Li Xiaolan would have the same craving for strange dishes as other expectant women, such as bean-sprouts stir-fried in vinegar, or salted mangoes. People in Zhao Shengtian's factory were from all walks of life. They all gave Zhao Shengtian and Li Xiaolan the green light. Whatever they wanted, they needed only ask. Li Xiaolan said she didn't want any of these things, that neither sour nor hot dishes caught her fancy. Zhao Shengtian was just about to give up when Li Xiaolan suddenly had a craving for the preserved beancurd made by Zhao's mother. That was the dish they had eaten back when they were dating some three years before. Pregnant women are strange like that; they can't stand to even hear the names of things they don't want to eat, but as soon as they want to eat something, they yearn for it uncontrollably.

Under the veil of night, Zhao Shengtian hurried home. The old lady was at the mahjong table, in the heat of battle.

"I forget. Haven't made it in a few years," she said, her eyes never leaving the table.

Zhao Shengtian scattered all the mahjong tiles with a sweep of his hand. "Do I have to beg you for it?"

The old lady was so angry, she slapped the table. "Will you look at this—this is what comes of raising a son! Little bastard! There's a knife in the kitchen. Go get it and put it to your old lady's throat and then see if she'll do it! Has that girl of yours behaved like a wife yet, has she ever offered her parents-in-law so much as a sip of tea? Or is momma supposed to wait on her? Ittybitty cadre's stinkin' little girl thinks she's holierthanthou, like she's some precious jewel. Well, tell her for me, there's nothing highranking about her in Grandma's eyes!"

Her partners all leapt in, whooping it up for the old lady.

"Get out!" Zhao Shengtian shouted at them. "If you don't move now, I'll have the police come and arrest you all for gambling."

The old lady screamed. Zhao Shengtian's father, fifth sister and her husband all came in from the next room to join in the fray, which soon became a chaotic pushing and shoving match.

Zhao Shengtian returned home sporting a face full of scratches. Li Xiaolan cried when she saw him. Through the tears she went on about how, from the time she was dating him until she was three months pregnant, no one from the Zhao family had been to call on her. Gushing tears of hurt mixed with mucus on her face. Zhao Shengtian pleaded with her not to be like this, that it was bad for the child, and nearly went so far as to kowtow before her. Li Xiaolan once again began cursing Zhao Shengtian, calling him a good-for-nothing, unable even to get his wife some preserved beancurd to eat.

Li Xiaolan slept until early morning then suddenly she awoke. She rocked Zhao Shengtian awake, asking, "Do you know what it's like to have no appetite?"

"I know."

"No!" Li Xiaolan cried out. "You don't know! Men cannot know! I want to jump off the top of some building!"

Zhao Shengtian was thinking: yeah—and I'm jumping, too! "What kind of a life is this?!" he muttered in disgust.

Li Xiaolan was beset by difficulties at home and at work.

Before she got pregnant, she had been a somewhat famous character in the municipal library system. The district library relied on her to handle numerous affairs. Making use of her delicate, graceful carriage, fashionable attire and sweet little baby face, she secured numerous difficult-to-obtain books. It was already two years since she'd been moved from the information room to the office, where she did public relations work. She had earned the affection of her bosses; most times, no one dared say anything if she arrived late to work or went home early.

When news of her pregnancy spread around, initially there was no change in her situation. After a time, however, she was transferred back to the information room "out of concern for her health." An eighteen-year-old girl named Ye Ye from the Loan Desk came in the office to replace her. Whenever she came across Ye Ye, no matter where it was, Li Xiaolan would come up close and mutter, "Little whore." Ye Ye went in private to see Zhao Shengtian, explaining graphically and piteously her plight. Zhao made an apology to her before he agreed to gradually guide Li Xiaolan through all of this; pregnancy, after all, was a special circumstance.

The Guide to Pregnancy pointed out that pregnant women should, above all, maintain a cheerful disposition. Zhao Shengtian underlined this in red ink. Whenever Li Xiaolan was agitated or annoyed, or feeling like calling Ye Ye "a little whore", she would look at this line. The first time it had a calming effect, but later on it wore off. She threw it away, saying, "Fuck this cheerful disposition shit!"

Li Xiaolan had become as thin as a garlic shoot. Large, brown pregnancy freckles appeared on her cheeks. Her belly was swollen like that of a malnourished child. The girl who once wore her fluffy hair in fine little curls now dragged her feet when she walked, like an African famine victim.

By comparison, Zhao Shengtian was experiencing some luck. The factory leader appointed him assistant team leader of the technology reform team, having him make improvements to the design component of an electronic software programme. Zhao Shengtian had always shown a fondness for problem solving. He spent a month on it, and saw a true breakthrough. He and the engineers saved the factory more than one hundred thousand yuan. The factory then gave him a bonus of more than three hundred yuan. They suddenly discovered this Zhao Shengtian wasn't a blockhead cowboy anymore. Of course, someone mentioned that he was about to be a daddy; the factory sent this trustworthy daddy-to-be out on important business, which again, he handled quite well. Zhao Shengtian finally felt useful; only now did he realize how meaningful feeling useful could be.

Being so busy at home and in the factory, Zhao Shengtian thought he would get really thin. But instead he got fat. Furthermore, this lean, young guy had begun to develop broad shoulders. His complexion was better than ever before. He knew that this was not a good time for him to get fat, so, in order to comfort his wife, he did the household chores as carefully and sympathetically as possible. In a tone of total longing for the unborn child he read aloud from the *Complete Child Growth and Development*, describing monthly foetal progress during pregnancy.

Zhao Shengtian put his all into it. As far as husbands of pregnant woman go, his behaviour was excellent. But Li Xiaolan would still find excuses to blow up at him.

She said, "I want an abortion. You?"

"Don't talk nonsense."

"I can't stand it anymore. Do I still look human to you? It's too painful!"

"I can feel your pain—it's also my child. We pass through the difficulties together."

"You're in the fucking pink of health, all fat and big-eared— what difficulties are you passing through with me? Zhao Shengtian, you scatterbrained bastard, stomach all full of poison. You're not going to cheat me with your sweet-talking anymore. I'm not going to be pregnant for you—no way!"

"Li Xiaolan, sober up! What are you screaming about?"

"I want to scream. I want the whole world to hear how the wife is going through a painful pregnancy, and how the man just fucking enjoys himself—"

"Li Xiaolan, if you keep this up, I'll leave."

"Get out then! You beast!... dog!"

As Zhao Shengtian went out, Li Xiaolan pushed on the door with all her might, causing it to lock with a crash. Many neighbours came out, standing in small groups in the corridor. Afraid someone would try to offer either consolation or advice, he put his head down and ran out of the building.

Zhao Shengtian slept in his workshop that night. He decided that once the child was born, he would divorce Li Xiaolan.

6

In the morning, Zhao Shengtian rinsed his mouth out with some strong tea. Not brushing his teeth was something he was unused to. All the way until noon he felt as if he had bad breath. After work, he didn't want to return home, nor did he feel like eating. He bought a pack of gum on the street. Chewing and strolling around, he looked like a bored bachelor.

"Hey, Zhao Shengtian!"

Zhao Shengtian saw a smartly-dressed female in a long skirt floating towards him. It was as if some young lady straight out of one of Qiong Yao's novels had arrived. Not until she got closer did he realize it was Hong Lili. They had dated for a time, touching lips but nothing much beyond that. They hadn't even made it to the love and marriage stage, when Hong Lili met some Hong Kong businessman in the Hankou Xuangong Hotel and left without ever looking back.

"Hello Miss, has someone abandoned you?"

"Enough of that, Shengtian." As soon as she spoke, Hong Lili no longer resembled the person in Qiong Yao's book.

Hong Lili coquettishly invited Zhao Shengtian to sit with her a bit. So Zhao Shengtian said, "Let's sit, then." Hong Lili put her hand on Zhao's arm, and Zhao Shengtian made no effort to shake it off. Thinking of Li Xiaolan, he said to Hong Lili, "You are my angel of vengeance."

"What does that mean?"

"Nothing."

"Just like you always were. Too clever."

They sat for more than half an hour in the teahouse. The name of the establishment was "Evil Designs". Afterwards Zhao

Shengtian thought that their going into the "Evil Designs" tea-house couldn't have been more appropriate.

As soon as they had found a seat, Hong Lili put a More cigarette in her mouth. Zhao Shengtian's action of reaching for his cigarettes had by this time become ingrained. The pack of Red Double Happiness in his pocket was, however, in the cigarette world, a low-class, middle-tar brand. He couldn't embarrass himself.

"Shengtian, how come you're not smoking?"

"I quit."

Hong Lili squinted her eyes and laughed. She took a drag on her cigarette, held it in briefly, then opening a crack in her red lips; allowed the light smoke to coil upwards. Her two pupils flashed, piercing Zhao Shengtian. Zhao Shengtian was thinking: so—the abandoned woman gets sentimental.

"Go with me to Hainan, eight hundred yuan a month."

"What did you say?"

"Eight hundred a month. Go to Hainan."

"And if I say no?"

"Nine hundred."

"No."

"One thousand, plus bonus, living expenses included. Quit haggling—this is top pay for bodyguards in that area."

Clever! Bodyguard! So it's a bodyguard she wants!

"Who are you asking me to protect?"

"Me. I need you!" Hong Lili grabbed hold of Zhao Shengtian's hand on the table, the diamond ring on her finger sparkling in all directions. "Shengtian, I need you. It's too risky for a single woman doing business. With your smarts and daring, and your fists, the world won't scare me anymore. Listen to me, I've been back in Wuhan for many days now and I know all about your situation. I even know that you haven't quit smoking. Maybe you're just hiding a pack of cheap ones and you can't bring yourself to take them out." Hong Lili gestured at the attendant. The attendant brought over a pack of Kent. Hong Lili said, "Smoke them, it's on me. Don't worry so much about your wife and child. Broaden your horizons a little. Poverty is a very scary thing."

This wasn't bull, it was a fact. Hong Lili was obviously rich and a thousand yuan monthly salary was quite alluring. Zhao Shengtian felt a little dizzy at the prospect. Long ago he had wanted to take off to the coast, but would always lose his nerve just when it was time to go. With graduate students and even people with PhDs out there on the street pushing snack carts, what was a technical school graduate, an electric company worker, going to do? But this opportunity had come so suddenly. According to what Hong Lili said, he would sign a three-year contract, work there three years, then return to Wuhan. It would be just like doing three years of military service. Afterwards, he would return with thirty thousand yuan.

Zhao Shengtian said, "Tell me about your situation."

"It's good."

"What business are you in?"

"Construction materials."

"Geez! So Miss Hong Lili is selling steel reinforced concrete, paint and mosaic!"

Hong Lili's silky-smooth, arching eyebrows furrowed.

"Enough, Zhao Shengtian. I'll put it to you straight. Today we'll end things here, but tomorrow when we talk you had better understand the rules—don't be asking the boss about private matters and business. You're only a bodyguard."

A wind suddenly blew the cigarette smoke screen away. Zhao Shengtian's face got hot. He hoped that his neck wasn't getting red. He waited for Hong Lili to finish, then took a deep drag on his cigarette, and blew the smoke right in her powdered face. As Hong Lili coughed and spluttered, he made a whistling sound through rounded lips.

"Sorry, but I can't leave my dear wife and child and dear old raggedy Wuhan. Moreover, I'll be damned if I go and protect a fucking loose woman!"

Zhao Shengtian stood up ferociously. "Bill," he shouted.

In his pocket was the one hundred yuan salary he had just been paid. He removed a fifty yuan note and threw it on the table. The attendant followed behind him saying there was change, but he just said, "Consider it your tip," never looking back. "Just for once let us poor folks beat those fucking rich!"

Hong Lili watched in silence as Zhao Shengtian left the tea-house and swaggered off down the street, disappearing in the brilliant sunshine. In her anger she threw an ashtray. Figuring that he had already left Hong Lili's line of sight, Zhao Sheng-tian could no longer wear the look of a carefree playboy. Angri-ly, he gulped breath after breath of air, mumbling various un-pleasantries. He headed home in great strides. Then, standing at the door, he remembered the previous night's argument. Could he just go in?

The night Zhao Shengtian left, Li Xiaolan had cooled down pretty soon afterwards. After settling down, she felt some re-gret. She washed her face, combed her hair, tidied up the mess made during their argument, and waited for her husband to re-turn. She realized that she had said some stupid things. But only through these stupid words, shouting, and crying, however, could she calm herself down. Pregnancy makes people act crazily. This fact should have been included in *The Guide to Pregnancy*.

Just as Li Xiaolan was about to fall asleep, someone lightly pushed against her. She awoke startled, but there was no one in the room. She was certain, however, that she wasn't mistaken. Someone had indeed pushed against her belly. Could it be the foetus? Instantly, Li Xiaolan lost all interest in sleeping. In a half-sitting position, she observed her belly, taking small, quiet breaths. A long, long time passed, when suddenly, the inside of her tummy again expanded, followed by a big kick. A small bump rose on the skin on her belly, then disappeared. The foetus had moved! It was definitely the baby moving! Li Xiaolan felt her eyes getting all hot, then her heart getting all hot. It wasn't tears—the heat was flowing from the eyes down into her heart, and from the heart down into her womb, flowing towards the little creature dancing around down there. She had communicated with her child! Perhaps no one would believe it if she told them. Such things had never been mentioned in books about pregnant women, but this feeling in Li Xiaolan was so real—it was as if the heat she felt was a pair of eyes pointed inward, allowing her to actually see her child.

Motherly love bloomed in Li Xiaolan as she entered the fourth month of her pregnancy.

Early the next morning, when she got up, Li Xiaolan was the picture of radiance. Her mood was clear as the blue sky. She wanted to laugh and sing. The feeling of nausea disappeared without a trace. The thought of the ripe red tomatoes and little green cabbages now on sale in town made her feel good.

She changed her clothes and cut off some stray strands of long hair. She then went out, called in to her unit to say she was taking a day off, and bought some hairtail fish that her husband loved to eat, and fresh vegetables. As she did the household chores, she was thinking that if Zhao Shengtian was angry and not coming home, she'd go over to the factory to find him. The previous night's argument had already passed far away. She had been so childish and stupid then, unable to stand even the slightest thing going wrong—that just wasn't going to do.

The food was all prepared. Working hours were over. But Zhao Shengtian still hadn't returned. Li Xiaolan went to meet him.

Zhao Shengtian was standing in his own doorway, hesitating to go any further, when Li Xiaolan, sparkling and fresh as new, came laughing home.

"You're back," she said gently, in the pacifying manner of a Japanese woman.

Zhao Shengtian's throat contracted; he barely managed to choke out a couple of sounds. He had been thrown into utter confusion by woman's mercurial nature.

7

Time flies when you're having fun.

During the fifth month, Zhao Shengtian, flipping through the book, read aloud, "The foetus' hair has begun to grow, the heart is developing well, and it can be heard in the mother's tummy."

With that, he placed an empty textile factory bamboo spindle on Li Xiaolan's tummy; indeed something was "bom-bom-bom,

bom-bom" beating inside.

During the sixth month he read, "All the heart valves are developed, giving the foetus the ability to breathe."

During the seventh month, he read, "Little hairs have grown on the skin, which is all in folds. A small amount of fat also exists beneath the skin. If the baby is born at this time, it can cry and swallow, but its ability to make a living is weak."

Li Xiaolan said, "Don't you mean its 'ability to survive'?"

Zhao Shengtian said, "Nope. 'Make a living'. Says right here."

"Oh," said Li Xiaolan, going about her work.

Suddenly Li Xiaolan came to resemble a mother. Zhao Shengtian, however, was a little out at sea.

Li Xiaolan could now eat, sleep and do work. She had put on nearly twenty pounds in weight. Her belly grew bigger by the day, making it difficult to breathe above and causing the veins below to swell. Her feet were bloated so that she had to wear Zhao Shengtian's flip-flops. Any man with the slightest imagination can understand the hardship of a pregnant woman. Zhao Shengtian, moreover, was more than willing to do things like buying vegetables or doing the washing for his wife, yet who would have thought Li Xiaolan didn't want his help. She treated housework as a form of exercise. Those who had been through it all had said that the more you walk and work, the easier it is to give birth. Li Xiaolan's life now had but one purpose: her unborn child.

Zhao Shengtian totally admired his wife's willpower. Because he didn't carry the foetus in his own body, he experienced a feeling of separation, always forgetting that there were three persons in their family. He often felt a little ashamed because of this, wishing frequently that he could do something for his wife. In the end all he could do was compliment her and read to her, reporting on the foetus' progress.

The conversations during this period became a little strange, labyrinthian.

"Shengtian, do you want a boy or a girl?"

"Whatever."

"How can you say whatever! I mean really."

"But it doesn't matter what I say."

"I mean, do you like boys or girls."

"Really, anything's fine."

"'Anything's fine' means boys."

"OK, a boy."

"Exactly. Men all want boys so they can brag about them outside—'yup—that's my boy!'"

Or it was discussing the matter of choosing a name.

"Shengtian, what's a good boy's name?"

"Shengtian, what's a good girl's name?"

"Do you think that a single-character or double-character name is better?"

Zhao Shengtian didn't know how to deal with her many questions. Having no experience, he simply didn't know what to say.

The Zhao family wanted a boy with all their heart. They saw Li Xiaolan's belly gradually arching to a point, and took it to be the shape of a boy. Old Lady Zhao made some preserved bean-curd and had Zhao Shengzhu send it over. She also made some boy's clothing. Zhao Shengcai wrote a letter, saying that he had recently asked a very famous fortune-teller to give the Zhao family's fortune. As for Shengcai, he would not enjoy both riches and children. The path to fortune had cut off the path to children. The second, third and fourth brothers were also destined to go through life without children. But the Zhao family line was not to be cut off. After all, in every ten thousand acres there's bound to be a green sprout. If this wasn't a reference to Shengtian, what was? As long as Shengtian had a son, Zhao Shengcai pledged to put ten thousand yuan toward his feeding and raising. Already there was a price on the baby's head.

Zhao Shengtian felt as if the whole Zhao family was acting out some scene in a play. He felt he would not get involved.

Li Xiaolan simply had too many things to do. Not in the least bit did she resemble Zhao Shengtian's muddle-headedness. She clearly knew what to do, and moreover, did it systematically.

She cleared out all their old cotton clothes, ripped them up one by one, and washed them. She then hung them to dry in the sun, allowing the ultraviolet rays to sterilize them before finally cutting them up into diapers.

She bought a big pile of nylon yarn and knitted seven or eight sets of baby clothes.

At work, Zhao Shengtian received a pair of white cotton gloves every month. Li Xiaolan collected them all, even making her husband ask his fellow workers for theirs. She tore up pair after pair, and knitted them into little T-shirts and shorts.

"Nylon is easier to wash than wool, and can be used for the outside. Cotton fibres are light and warm and don't irritate the skin, so they are more suitable for the baby's skin," Li Xiaolan expertly told Zhao Shengtian.

The Guide to Pregnancy and *The Complete Child Growth and*

Development contained no such details. Where had Li Xiaolan learned these things? And how did she know the measurements of her unborn child? Even if the above skills were learned from other mothers, there were other things that nonetheless stood as proof of Li Xiaolan's practicality and creativity.

Li Xiaolan bought a dozen rubber teats. Ten had holes poked through by red-hot needles. She explained that they would be used to feed the child fruit juice. The smallest hole was for the first month; the baby would gradually move to the larger holes over time. Two more teats had slits, made by what appeared to be a pair of a small scissors, to be used for feeding the infant medicine.

"The child won't get sick," Li Xiaolan said. "The more medicine I prepare for him, the less he will get sick. You know how the saying goes, an ounce of prevention beats a pound of cure."

Zhao Shengtian wanted to tell her that "an ounce of prevention" meant that actually eating and not just preparing the medicine prevented disease, but then, seeing how tired and short of breath she was from toting around her swollen belly, he couldn't bear to correct her.

As soon as the baby arrives, it will eat, drink, shit and piss. All kinds of preparations are necessary. Li Xiaolan went out everyday, returning home carrying bags of every size, including Hibiscus brand toilet paper, Guangkou plastic disposable diapers—she even brought home some colourful bells. Zhao Shengtian suspected that it was too early for the baby to use toys; moreover, the relatives and good friends would be sure to send a load of toys later on—maybe even some of the same things. But Li Xiaolan asserted that people sending gifts had to first consider whether or not the thing was good enough to send. Who sends cheap things like coloured bells? The set of bells wasn't for the baby to play with. It was to be suspended above the cradle for the baby to look at and listen to. Once the baby was born, it should be made to experience a brightly coloured, beautiful-sounding world.

Zhao Shengtian could only watch with amazement at how, of all things, pregnancy could most change a woman. The irresponsible, fragile Li Xiaolan had now become a person who knew how to live frugally. This was something Zhao Shengtian had longed for but never experienced.

Usually it was Zhao Shengtian who would read aloud the *Guide to Pregnancy* and *Complete Child Growth and Development*. After a few months, the number of readings became innumerable as stars in the sky. The one, however, who truly remembered the contents was Li Xiaolan.

Beginning from the eighth month, Li Xiaolan wiped and washed her nipples in warm, soapy water, afterwards applying a layer of fragrant facial cream to prevent cracking during the breast-feeding period. Her girlish little lotus-pod breasts grew big and round as loaves of bread. When her nipples began to sink inward, every night, as soon as she had time, she would pull them out. For the final two months, Li Xiaolan made Zhao Shengtian add a military-style cot to the room. Once when Zhao Shengtian tried to crawl on to their bed in the middle of the night, Li Xiaolan immediately switched on the light, taking the *Guide to Pregnancy* out from under her pillow. She asked Zhao Shengtian to read page fifteen, paragraph five.

Zhao Shengtian read aloud, "During the first three months and last two months of the pregnancy, to guard against miscarriage, sexual intercourse is prohibited."

Li Xiaolan only now really discovered that she quite enjoyed the book and excelled at absorbing and implementing ideas quickly. If she went to high school now, she could certainly pass the university entrance exams. She truly regretted not studying hard before. People often say that it's too late for regrets; now she could taste just what a bitter pill it was. Indeed there was no way she could return to high school.

8

Pre-delivery time arrived, filling everybody with nervous excitement.

Zhao Shengtian's boss at the factory gave him a few days vacation. "Go home and have your kid," he told Zhao.

The first night, Li Xiaolan bled a little, only reddening her panties, nothing else. Husband and wife deliberated for some time but still couldn't figure out if this was a sign that the baby was coming or not. Zhao Shengtian slept poorly all night, afraid that Li Xiaolan's condition would suddenly change. As a result, he got the short end of the stick, for Li Xiaolan slept peacefully all night. Early the next day she complained that her tummy hurt a little. Zhao Shengtian flipped through the book, but it didn't mention anything about pain, only something called "uterine contractions".

"Xiao Li, are you having uterine contractions?"

"All I know is it hurts a little."

"Is it the kind of pain that means you're about to give birth?"

"I don't know. It's a pain that weighs on you, like ordinary exhaustion."

Like ordinary exhaustion? So she's not about to give birth?

The young couple couldn't say for sure if the baby was about to come, or what signs would mark the beginning of childbirth. All they could do was sit about uneasily, pacing up and down the floors of their small, fifteen-square-metre home, waiting for the big moment to arrive.

That morning Fifth Brother-in-law was instructed to pay a visit. Fourth Sister-in-law even stopped in on her way to work to have a look, saying in a strange manner, "Hope you give birth soon to a precious son." Fifth Sister came during her students' lunch hour. Just as they were about to eat lunch, Zhao's mother came. The old lady acted as if she had a terrible memory, rubbing Li Xiaolan's shoulders like any good mother would. "Has your belly dropped yet?"

Exercising extreme self-restraint, Li Xiaolan said, "I don't know."

Li Xiaolan's mother also arrived. She said that she had excused herself from a meeting to come. Already that morning Li Xiaolan's father had twice phoned. Li Xiaolan's older sister also called long-distance from Guangzhou to ask if she'd had the child yet.

"Mother, how do you know you're ready?" Li Xiaolan asked.

"Silly girl. Your stomach hurts."

Old Lady Zhao broke in. "It depends on whether the belly has dropped or not. I remember that the baby comes shortly after it falls." She laughed.

Mrs Li expertly told her daughter: "She's walking about when it 'enters the basin'. You've already 'entered'; it's common for first time pregnancies to last as many as three days after 'entering', before the baby is born."

Zhao Shengtian and Li Xiaolan glanced at each other; they

were now even more confused than before.

After work, Zhao Shengzhu and Fourth Sister-in-law arrived. The room, suddenly filled with people, was ripe for disaster.

Zhao Shengtian and Li Xiaolan borrowed a few bowls from their neighbours and they all went to the unit's cafeteria to eat. Every serving typically contained a bowl of rice and one sweet and sour rib. There wasn't any liquor to drink, so everyone wondered how Old Lady Zhao managed to get drunk. She said she just couldn't concentrate on her mahjong game earlier today, she simply had to see what her son's child looked like. If it was a male grandchild she figured that she could call it even with this life of hers. When Mrs Li heard this her face turned frigid. Zhao Shengzhu hurriedly led her mother away, Fourth Sister-in-law went to talk to Mrs Li.

"Don't be angry, that's just the way the old lady is. Don't even think about it. The year I had my daughter she was unhappy, I had to curse her twice before she let up. However disappointing having a daughter is, it's no reason to despise someone. Xiao Li looks like she's got a son in there, anyway."

Later, Mrs Li warned her daughter, "Your fourth sister-in-law is a cool customer. If you really do have a son, she'll be a real shit to you."

"Who cares what they think."

Where did all these things come from? As if you didn't have enough troubles already!

Everybody waited anxiously the whole day; Li Xiaolan, however, was completely calm. In the evening, the young couple both felt tired, so went to bed early. After a while, Li Xiaolan woke up in pain, but it went away quickly. She thought it had been brought on by the day's exhaustive activity, and thereupon went back to sleep. When she woke up again with even more pain, the situation was already urgent; her waters had broken long before.

Zhao Shengtian never expected so much water—where did it all come from? Where was the baby? Li Xiaolan drew herself upon the soaked bedsheet, sobbing with pain and fright. She didn't know what was going on; she was scared senseless.

Zhao Shengtian, after all, was the male; frantic as he was, he still decided to take her to hospital immediately.

The Guide to Pregnancy says that having childbirth, like most things, is easily settled when conditions are ripe. There is no need for the birthing mother to be nervous. The uterus undergoes rhythmic contractions, the child comes out. The tendency of scientific books to print the good and omit the bad made Li Xiaolan extremely angry. She had no mental preparation, so when the pain hit, it seemed all that much more fierce. Even though she had heard people say that childbirth hurt, she never imagined she would be in such immense pain.

"Kill me!" she cried out hoarsely from the delivery room.

None of her female needs were being attended to. Were there any women present at all? Where was their sense of shame? All those now entering the delivery room were just birthing machines. The nurses who had seen it all before were deaf to the pitiful cries of "it hurts" and "I don't want to have it." They wore the professional countenance of skilled technicians handling each and every birthing machine. Strip off their pants, flex their pelvis, feel the uterus, shave off the pubic hair . . . all of these just added to the pain.

"I beg you . . . kill me now!"

Li Xiaolan heard her own changed voice charging through the

air. She felt as if her insides were being torn from her. She floated in her own sweat. She had ripped open the pillow by her head with all her clutching. She didn't really want to die, but at this moment she would have rather let death solve everything.

A nurse stuffed a piece of sanitary cotton cloth in her mouth, saying, "What are you shouting about! If you're afraid of pain, then don't go around sleeping with men."

Keep it up. Suit yourselves.

The pain was a boundless bitter sea. Li Xiaolan was being tossed among peaks and troughs in alternating waves of deep water and hot fire. There was no way to lessen wave after wave of increasingly intense pain, no way to escape; even if you wanted to defect, there was no stopping this punishment. There was no choice but to tough it out. Oh, the woman's hell!

Twelve hours of pain were engraved on Li Xiaolan's face. She lost and regained consciousness several times, each time waking herself up. At the moment death was truly near, she would again outrun it. "No!" she cried out, "the child, I want it!"

At the point of complete uteral contraction, Li Xiaolan was sent to the delivery room. The doctor looked experienced, and she gave Li Xiaolan a slight smile. "OK, let's start having the baby."

Li Xiaolan understood that the last difficult pass had arrived. She grabbed the handles, and pressed her feet against the delivery bed.

"Strong! Just like defecating—push down!" the doctor said.

"No strength left ..."

"That's no good! You must push!"

Think about it. Here, relaxing is not allowed. Being out of strength isn't acceptable, either. You must push, using everything you've got. As long as you're alive, you must squeeze out every bit of your life energy!

"I really don't have any strength left, doctor."

At this crucial moment the doctor shouted out, "The child's head is out! Hurry, a little push is all you need."

Child! Child! Child! For it, she eked out the very last of her strength.

The child was out!

Li Xiaolan suddenly felt a kind of lightness that defied description. Before her eyes appeared a fat little ball of pink. It was such a cute little baby, hands and feet all waving, crying, "Wa! Wa!"

"What a beautiful daughter!" the delivering doctor marvelled.

"Thank you!" Li Xiaolan's gratitude came from her deepest heart. Doctor, are you aware that before this she had never expressed heartfelt thanks to anyone?

Painlessness was such a happy feeling! Gaily opening her eyes, Li Xiaolan discovered she was being slowly wheeled out of the delivery room. The sunlight in the corridor was brilliant and beautiful, the good light of morning. Just then, a name popped out: Zhaoyang ("the morning sun"). Shining on her, warming her, rescuing her from the bitter seas, Zhaoyang was the first one to greet the new mother. My Zhaoyang.

Li Xiaolan and her husband had flipped exhaustively through an edition of the *Xinhua Dictionary*, picking out ten single-character names, ten double-character names, ten girl's names and ten boy's names. But here, in the twinkling of an eye, all forty names lost their meaning. For the first time in twelve hours, Li Xiaolan thought about Zhao Shengtian. She hoped he would approve of, and take a liking to, this name.

A nurse pushed open the glass door. Immediately, several men stood up.

"Zhao Shengtian."

"That's me." Zhao Shengtian's heart was beating wildly.

"Your wife has given birth."

"Is everything—all right?"

"Everything's fine."

Zhao Shengtian sighed, flexing his shoulders like a hero.

"What did she have?"

"An extremely beautiful little bag of gold."

"Really extremely beautiful?"

"Really."

The other men got up and hooted a few times, then sat back down. Laughing, Zhao Shengtian began dancing about, mirthfully.

Zhao Shengtian had waited here the entire night. The screams of Li Xiaolan and the other delivering mothers had deeply moved and educated him. Several times he tried to rush in, only to be restrained by the nurse. He wanted to go help his wife. Putting himself in her shoes, he thought that most men definitely could not take this kind of intense pain. Women were not to be taken lightly; the birth of mankind did not come easily!

For Zhao Shengtian, the twelve hours had gone very slowly. In a scattered, confused manner he thought of many things. He scared himself, thinking of all the premature deformed children he had seen before. Thinking of women dying in childbirth scared him even more. Please protect us! he prayed to himself. Never having believed in anything, he didn't even know who he was asking to protect him. He thought of his own mother, who had truly given of her own flesh and blood for him. Feeling super guilty about boorishly ruining her game of mahjong, he decided never again to treat her like that. He thought about how he had never given up a seat on the bus to pregnant women or to those holding babies—what a clueless jerk he had been! He even thought back to his school days, bullying his schoolmate Cao Xiaobing; chasing and attacking him, calling out, "Shame, shame, shame, Cao Xiaobing's Mama cried and cried when she had a baby." If this wasn't utterly childish and ridiculous behaviour, what was? If, after this, you chance upon Cao Xiaobing, remember to be sure to apologize to him.

9

Old Lady Zhao hurried to the hospital early that morning. When she heard the news that it was a baby girl, she almost collapsed. Fifth Sister and Fourth Sister-in-law, one on each side, couldn't even hold her up. Her buttocks sank down on to the stairs by the gynaecology ward door, her two hands busily wiping away tears. Zhao Shengtian really didn't understand what all this concern with maintaining the family line was about. The old lady had five boys and one girl; that she only kept her daughter by her side to live with her, clearly indicated she had a soft spot for girls; still, she forbade her son to have one.

People going up and down the stairs glanced down at the sad old lady. Zhao Shengtian picked her up by the arm, saying, "Let's go, don't be disgraced here."

Zhao Shengtian's act of lifting his mother astonished all three women; this kid had really smartened up.

Fourth Sister-in-law voluntarily brought a can of chicken soup into the recovery room. To Li Xiaolan this was like warmth in

the dead of winter; she had doubled her kindness and passed on
the greetings of the eldest, second and third sisters, saying they
would be over to see her before long. The sisters-in-law became
something of an allied army.

Li Xiaolan's mom called to ask if mother and child were all
right. "Good. Actually, girls are better," she said.

Zhao Shengtian thought to himself, "But I didn't say that girls
were bad."

Mrs Li asked if Li Xiaolan had things to eat. Zhao Shengtian
had by this time learned some of the tactics of maturity. He
replied, "Yes. My mother sent her some chicken soup." Mrs Li
was satisfied. Having a boy didn't matter to her; she was interested in how the Zhao family reacted to the baby girl. What era
were they all living in, anyway—still frowning on females like
that?

Most infant wards don't allow the fathers inside. Zhao Shengtian didn't care about this, though. As far as his generation was
concerned, unless it was marked "restricted area", or there was
a guard checking IDs at the door, he'd use any means at his disposal to get inside. Zhao Shengtian bought a bag of expensive
candies, went to the door of infant ward and got through in only
two attempts.

There were more than sixty babies in the ward, all wrapped in
swaddling clothes of the same colour. The nurse joked with
Zhao Shengtian:

"No glancing at the namecards. Look for the one you think is
the prettiest."

Zhao Shengtian went just a few steps, stopping by the side of
a small crib. The hair on this baby was the deepest black, its
skin the most powdery white, the lines of its eyelids so very

clear, its little red lips so full. Even more important was the feeling of familiarity Zhao Shengtian had toward this delicate little face.

"It's her," he said with certainty.

He was face to face with his newborn daughter. She weighed eight pounds and was fifty centimetres long. Without the slightest birthmark she was flawless as true jade. He had actually produced this miracle! He tried lightly stroking the baby's face with his finger; the infant immediately reacted, her eyelids, thin as cicada wings, moved.

"She laughed!" he said softly.

The nurse reminded him from one side, "She can't laugh, she was born only three hours ago."

Zhao Shengtian bent over and kissed his daughter, touching her fine warm skin. The big guy's eyes that had never before cried now moistened. Because the nurse was there, however, Zhao Shengtian immediately blinked away the tears. He was a daddy! This tender little thing with the beautiful eyes is my daughter. I have kissed her already. Everything is real and tangible. During Li Xiaolan's ten months of pregnancy, no matter what he did for the foetus, no matter what conclusive evidence was written in the black and white print of the *Guide to Pregnancy*, Zhao Shengtian always had this funny feeling. Of his every good deed, some might say it was fatherly love, though it was really nothing more than humanity. He had given Li Xiaolan moral support. From here on in it was different. He now saw his daughter with his own eyes. He wanted to hold her to him tightly and hug and kiss her, he wanted to take her little hand and walk with her in the park, he wanted to teach her to swim and ride a bike, wanted her urine to soak his pants' leg, wanted to hear her chuckling little laugh and hear her call "Daddy! Daddy!" My little treasure.

The nurse pushed a reluctant Zhao Shengtian out of the infant ward. Looking back, he said goodbye to his daughter. Goodbye, my little treasure, after three days we'll go home together, and never live apart again. You really are a beautiful little treasure!

For Zhao Shengtian and Li Xiaolan it was like meeting again after a long ordeal. The friendship and emotion between husband and wife had increased several folds. He fed her, she whispered in his ear. Openly holding hands in the recovery room, the two gazed fixedly at one another.

"Little Li, you really are something! Such a tiny body giving birth to an eight pound baby. And such a pretty one!"

"I feel I've rather let you down, not giving you a son."

"What do I want with a son? She is perfect."

"I'm so happy you don't discriminate against girls."

"Too bad we can only have one."

"One was about all I could handle."

"I really wish a string of beautiful children could follow."

"Go have them yourself then."

Smiling, the young couple spoke tender words to one another. This kind of atmosphere, however, didn't mean that their quarrelling days were thus gone forever. It wasn't long, in fact, before conflict arose once again.

"Little Zhao. What about calling our daughter Zhaoyang?"

Li Xiaolan described the significance behind the name Zhaoyang, but after listening through, Zhao Shengtian remained unmoved.

"But I think Beibei is better. She really is a little treasure!"

"There are Beibeis all over the place. How boring."

"There's also many people out there called Zhaoyang. A classmate of mine at the technical school was named Wang Zhaoyang. Plus, Zhao Zhaoyang is hard to pronounce."

"Only the hard-to-pronounce ones make a deep impression. Then again, we could call her Li Zhaoyang."

"No. She's surnamed Zhao. So you don't think she's truly a little treasure?"

"Even if she is a little treasure, there's no need to call her Beibei."

"You are so tiring!"

Li Xiaolan turned her head away, refusing to eat any more chicken soup. Zhao Shengtian paid no attention to her. Some other patients in the ward advised him, saying that male comrades should be more generous. Besides, names are just markers; whatever you call her, she's still a person. Moreover, nursing mothers shouldn't get upset, for it can affect milk production. The thought of no milk scared Zhao Shengtian. If there was no milk, what would his daughter eat?

"OK. We'll call her Zhao Zhaoyang."

The next morning Li Xiaolan told the examining doctor that her breasts were swollen and sore.

The doctor said, "The milk has come. Squeeze. Your husband is strong, let him squeeze."

In front of everybody, Zhao Shengtian drew back in embarrassment.

"Squeeze them," Li Xiaolan said. She was so open about everything. She'd already been through it all—sex, marriage and birth. Zhao Shengtian tried for some time but couldn't get any milk to come out. Li Xiaolan tried to help out, but to no avail.

They never thought that there would be so many new lessons to
learn in life.

The doctor came over and opened her shirt. Taking her
breasts in his hands he kneaded them lightly and gently, then
gave them a fierce squeeze. The pain caused Li Xiaolan to take
in a big gulp of air, but the milk came spurting out! With no
time to dodge, Zhao Shengtian got a faceful of milk. One of the
other patients pointed out that Zhao Shengtian should quickly
suck on her nipples. Suck them dry in place of the infant, because the more you drink the more there is. If the milk isn't
drunk and is allowed to collect inside, the mammary glands will
become inflamed.

Li Xiaolan said, "Go ahead."

It didn't matter how thick Zhao Shengtian's "face" was, he
still couldn't help being shy. No matter what, he wasn't about
to, in front of everyone else, lie on Li Xiaolan's breast and suck
her milk. What do you mean, what is all the fuss about? Where
did Li Xiaolan's fearlessness come from? A bit later Li Xiaolan
responded with a sentence that was her life experience talking.

"After childbirth, what is there left for a woman to fear?"

Zhao Shengtian took care of his wife in the hospital for three
days, profoundly aware of his personal shallowness. There were
too many things he didn't understand. There were so many mir-
acles in the world. His daughter, who had only been in the
world one day, knew to hold the nipple in her mouth and how to
suck; once the baby reached her breast, Li Xiaolan's nipples automatically squirted forth milk—Zhao Shengtian thought all a-
long that the milk flowed out, never imagining that it squirted.
No wonder that in Western oil paintings, stars shot out of the
Holy Mother's breasts. The painter had explained that this was

the origin of the Milky Way. How he and his buddies laughed when they saw the exhibit, saying that son-of-bitch painter could really exaggerate. Young people shouldn't be so wildly arrogant!

Daughter, daddy is ready to begin studying life together with you.

10

According to Wuhan custom, women should nurse their babies in their mother-in-law's home. The day they were to leave the hospital, Zhao Shengzhu showed up. She said mama's back pains had started up again, and that they had just hired a carpenter to make some furniture, so wouldn't it better if mother and daughter first went to a dormitory and work out something else later? Li Xiaolan gave her a frosty look. She didn't even look Zhao Shengzhu in the eye. Zhao Shengzhu sensed all was not well and changed the subject to the baby. Adding a few words of praise for Zhaoyang, she left.

Zhao Shengtian got his wife and daughter home in a pedicab.

From the time that he stepped through the door of his home, Zhao Shengtian never again considered himself a lucky person. In the past he consistently had his meals and washing done for him. His flip-flops would be right there, all ready for him to step into. Now he must take care of two people, moreover two people who required special care.

He changed the bedsheet and quilt, first making his wife lie down, then put a light comforter next to his wife and laid his daughter down. He couldn't remember where anything was. In the end, Li Xiaolan had to give him directions.

"Take a cloth diaper from the second drawer in the big

chest."

Zhao Shengtian took out a diaper.

"Take a small pillow from the small chest at the head of the bed, first drawer."

Zhao Shengtian took out the small pillow.

Just as he busied about, they heard a little chuckle come from inside Zhaoyang's swaddling clothes; the baby had defecated.

Taking a pile of single-layer diapers from the first drawer in the middle chest, he found the little towel specially used for the baby, opened up the swaddling clothes and changed ... no good. She was too dirty. First wash her buttocks, because it's easy for baby girls to get infections. But there was no hot water in the thermos. Put everything down to go and boil some water. Meanwhile, back over there, the baby was crying, her dirtied skin exposed. Go back over to cover her—you don't want her to get chilled. Zhao Shengtian ran around in confused circles. Li Xiaolan wanted to help him, but as soon as she left the bed, she covered her forehead and grabbed hold of the bedpost; she had lost considerable weight. All of a sudden, she had shed several tens of pounds. Her head dizzy, she walked unsteadily. Blood came gushing out from her lower body, making a brilliant large blotch of blood on her pyjama bottoms. "Lie down! I'll get it!" Zhao Shengtian instructed.

Zhao Shengtian awkwardly washed his daughter's buttocks, changed her diaper and wrapped her in her baby clothes. He held the eight-pound little ball of flesh ever so carefully, fearing he might injure her, or that she'd slip through and fall on the floor. In his nervousness, he broke into a sweat all over. After less than a minute, the swaddling clothes came loose.

"You need to learn how to wrap her," Li Xiaolan said. "I'll

learn too."

The things they needed to learn were far more than they ever imagined.

Mother and daughter changed out of their soiled things, creating a pile of dirty clothes. There was a dirty bedsheet, quilt-cover and pants, soiled diapers, cotton diapers, and blood-stained panties. Zhao Shengtian had to learn to distinguish them all, and to use different methods of washing them. The diapers, for example, required the use of a brush; after washing them once they must be run under boiling water. For blood stains it was necessary to soak them slowly for about ten minutes in cool water, then rub them between your hands. He buried himself in the task of washing clothes such that he forgot even to prepare meals. Nursing mothers, however, can't go without food. Li Xiaolan ate five meals a day, mostly soup broth. Apart from learning how to kill chicken and scale fish and prepare them, Zhao Shengtian found that mastering the timing of everything also required great knowledge.

Statements regarding nursing mothers in the *Women's Health Protection Manual* and popular opinion seriously contradicted each other.

The *Manual* said that because of energy consumption during the course of parturition, the system's resilience became lowered. Moreover, because she now had the additional task of feeding and raising the new life, appropriate care and rest for the mother during nursing were extremely important.

Popular opinion differed considerably. In short, it was held that nursing mothers should stay in bed thirty to thirty-five days. Thirty days for a "little" period, forty-five for a "big" one. During the time from pregnancy through delivery, the mother's strength is completely sapped, her "vital energy" drastically depleted. If she doesn't take care and becomes ill during the nursing period, no medicine can ever cure her and she'll be an invalid for the rest of this life.

Zhao Shengtian and Li Xiaolan analyzed both schools. They thought that the former was too abstract and that the latter painted too alarming a picture. They worked out that if they stayed somewhere in the middle, they couldn't go wrong. Thus, Li Xiaolan's major task for the coming month was to suckle her baby and recuperate. Zhao Shengtian would do all the housework. Being a daddy really wasn't all that easy.

Upon becoming a father, Zhao Shengtian of course felt duty-bound to care for the younger generation. But the older generation also came charging at him. No matter how busy, as head of the household, he must still welcome all guests.

Li Xiaolan's parents came to see their grandchild. They sent over two live chickens, ten pounds of ribs, and a big bag of things for baby's daily use. Zhao Shengtian thanked his in-laws profusely from the bottom of his heart, but hoped nonetheless that they wouldn't stay long. There were many things waiting for him to attend to.

Mr and Mrs Li looked again and again at their soundly sleeping grandchild.

"Mmn. Not bad."

Mrs Li said, "Xiao Zhao, your father said you've been looking after your child well."

Zhao Shengtian poured two cups of tea and put them in his in-law's hands, replying: "Yup, not bad."

"Lanlan, how many times do you eat each day?"

Li Xiaolan said, lying on the bed, "Five."

"What do you eat?"

"C'mon, what's with all these questions? You two aren't even willing to take care of me, so what are you asking me for?"

Mr Li said, "Xiao Zhao, look how Lanlan speaks to her mother."

Li Xiaolan said, "That's just how I am. Go and talk with Xiao Zhao." With that she turned over and went to sleep.

Mr and Mrs Li had Zhao Shengtian tell them how Li Xiaolan's five meals were arranged and offered many suggestions.

Mr Li raised some imminent concerns. How can a man with no experience take care of his nursing wife? After a few days when Zhao Shengtian goes back to work what will his wife and daughter do? After Li Xiaolan's maternity leave is spent, who will take care of Zhaoyang?

This was a problem, indeed. Zhao Shengtian spread his hands out on the table and smiled wryly.

Mr and Mrs Li said with righteous conviction, "You should discuss this with your family. Your mother is a housewife, she has both the time and the responsibility: Doesn't your family understand Wuhan custom?

Maybe I should just take a rope and drag my mother over? Zhao Shengtian said, "Don't worry. Of course I'll go over and discuss it with them." He had changed his daughter's diapers three times already. The soup on the stove was boiled mushy. He noticed the sun setting in the west—if the diapers don't dry in time, what will we use tomorrow?

Mr and Mrs Li were afraid that Zhao Shengtian had a weak sense of responsibility, that he didn't feel pressured enough. Just as they were leaving they said, once again, that they had given

their daughter and granddaughter to him! "We won't tolerate
any mistakes!" they said. Zhao Shengtian knit his brows, but
remembering his manners, said, "Thank you! Thank you for
trusting me."

Zhao Shengtian's parents also came to see the granddaughter.

Li Xiaolan turned right over, away from their voices, leaving
every difficult problem behind her to Zhao Shengtian.

"Please go home," Zhao Shengtian said to his parents.

"You little bastard, can't anybody come to see you?" the old
lady said, pushing her son aside.

The two seniors picked up their granddaughter, cooing over
her, turning the whole scene into some kind of comedy.

"Tsktsktsk. Old man. You think my granddaughter looks like
the Seventh Immortal Goddess?"

"It's amazing! She's a god come to live among the mortals."

"What can I say about this child—the pain of parenthood is
even sweet-tasting."

"This dog-bastard boy of mine really is fortunate. Good!
Shengtian, you don't even pour your parents a cup of tea."

Zhao Shengtian poured them each a cup of tea, saying,
"Leave after you drink it, I've a lot to do."

The old lady said, "You stubborn little bastard. Still sulking."

She took out three hundred yuan and stuffed them in the
baby's clothes. Laughing, she said, "I must be sick not to be
able to take care of my granddaughter. Show some pity for your
old parents. This counts as buying things for mother and baby to
improve their health during nursing."

Li Xiaolan suddenly turned over and got out of bed. Taking
the money out of the baby's clothes, she threw it at her mother-
in-law's chest.

"Don't dirty my daughter. We don't need money," she said with an icy expression, then returned to bed, turning her back to everyone.

Momentarily, the two old people felt awkward. Zhao Shengtian took them by the hands and escorted them out.

The old lady mumbled as she went, "What did I do to get such a senseless daughter as this?"

Zhao's father said, "Shengtian, if you're still my son, you better take your wife in hand. Son, you were such a cocky young guy before—when did you ever lose a fight?"

Putting his hand together, Zhao Shengtian implored his parents, "Don't you two add to my troubles, OK? Now please!"

Li Xiaolan's unit sent a representative to come to see her.

The workers' union at Zhao Shengtian's factory also sent someone.

Friends and relatives came to wish them well.

Li Xiaolan was always sitting up in bed, Zhaoyang always lying in her crib. The two of them could say whatever they wanted and cry whenever they wanted, and no one would blame them. Zhao Shengtian, however, had repeatedly to make seats, pour water, wash glasses, make tea, pour more water, offer candied fruits to guests, and clean up after the guests left. Hey—he's a daddy now.

11

Zhaoyang cried all night. Zhao Shengtian and Li Xiaolan took turns holding and coaxing her. Holding, rocking, humming bedtime songs—but none worked.

Zhaoyang cried so that her face and lips turned all purple. As

soon as she cried she'd spit out all the milk in her stomach; it got
so that she was coughing up yellowish liquid. When baby daughter cried, mama cried along with her. Holding the baby to her
bosom, Li Xiaolan lost night after night of sleep. Tears
streamed down her cheeks as she pressed the little head close a-
gainst her.

Zhao Shengtian was so flustered he didn't know what to do.
An old lady neighbour of theirs suggested they go out and paste a
hundred "Heavenly Emperor" signs all around. She said
Zhaoyang was a "hundred-day-loud" baby. This kind of child
wouldn't stop wailing until a hundred days had passed. Only
pasting up "Heavenly Emperor" signs could have any effect.
When had they ever believed the old lady's feudal superstitions?
But they had no choice—they'd rather believe in it.

Inside the factory dormitory and dining hall, on the telephone
poles along the roadside, everywhere, in black characters on red
paper, were the markings of Zhao Shengtian's inexperienced
pen: "Emperor of Heaven and Earth, there's a crying child in
our home; for every person that reads this, our baby will sleep
until dawn." He even captured something of the style of contemporary songs. Later he added two more characters at the
end—"Thank you!"

But Zhaoyang still cried.

At last they made a painful decision: take her to the hospital!

The mother of barely a month put on a hat and, wrapping up
her baby in a scarf, went to the hospital. Zhao Shengtian didn't
want Li Xiaolan to go outside and breathe the autumn wind, but
she wouldn't listen—her pitiful little weeks old baby was going
outside, so what was there for her to fear?

The prognosis at the hospital was that baby had a calcium deficiency.

The hospital gave them some calcium powder and the baby a shot of vitamin D3.

On those beautiful days where the sun exudes brilliance and charm, all you see is a street full of happy children. Who knows they were actually so difficult to raise!

On Zhaoyang's fourth day they discovered she had some goosebump sores; on the seventh day, when they looked in her belly button, they found it filled with pus; on the fifteenth day her buttocks were waterlogged; on the twentieth day red spots appeared all over her face, which was diagnosed as baby eczema. Of the maladies common for month-old babies included in the pages of *Complete Child Development*, Zhaoyang got them all. Zhao Shengtian time and time again ran over to the factory dispensary, asking the doctor to examine his daughter. When smiles and good words were all used up, it was Zhao Shengtian's spirit that moved the doctor. Boisterous Zhao Shengtian was not so loud anymore, the doctor commented.

There was no way to be boisterous now—if you're loud like that, no one's going to help you. And living in the great mass of people, you can't ever ask anyone for help. This is the dialectic of life. Sooner or later, no matter who, the unfeeling dialectic will find you.

Had Zhao Shengtian and Li Xiaolan planned to have this child? No!

If you accept your child; will society then accept it? No!

There was still a whole set of procedures to undertake; otherwise your child was considered a "black person."

After Li Xiaolan got pregnant, a female member of the standing committee from her unit told her she must apply for a "birth quota". Li Xiaolan, however, was half-crazy with the early stages of pregnancy and had lost her appetite—how could she attend to filling out some form? The female member of the standing committee gave Zhao Shengtian a call, saying, "Your wife doesn't listen to reason. Our unit doesn't have the authority to permit babies to be born. If you don't apply for a birth quota you'll have to abort the foetus."

Zhao Shengtian said, "Now don't go mentioning anything about abortions—I'll come and apply myself."

Zhao Shengtian wrote the application and handed it in to the unit. Carrying a letter of introduction, he then went from the unit to the Sub-district Family Planning Office. After reviewing his situation, the Family Planning Office gave him a mimeographed sheet of paper, on which was printed the birth quota and the bright red seal. Zhao Shengtian only now recognized that the Sub-district Office was a government organization, possessing the power to determine life and death. In the past he had actually thought that it was nothing more than a bunch of gossiping old ladies.

Once he had the quota he went to the Municipal Family Planning Standing Committee. They collected the quota form and gave him a card. Pink with gold letters, the card read, "Wishing your whole family happiness and good health for mother and daughter." There was also a large "Happiness" character and a serial number, 004578.

In compliance with the directions on the card he then went to the Women and Children Health Protection Institute, paid five yuan, and received a little red booklet, titled "Wuhan Health Manual for Pregnant Mothers." Written in black characters on the cover was a reminder to the user: take care not to lose this booklet; you must carry it every time you are examined. The person on duty even gave Zhao Shengtian an oral admonishment, telling him: "When you have the baby, you must carry this with you; the examination after forty-two days requires possession of this book, as does reporting for residence permits."

Zhao Shengtian and Li Xiaolan put all of these little books together with the grain and cooking-oil tickets, so to make finding them each month easier. Even before the child was born, Zhao Shengtian had already been round Wuhan several times.

Now that she was born, it was time to obtain a series of permits for his daughter, to obtain for her every right afforded by law.

Zhao Shengtian went to get his daughter's residence permit. On the first try the office worker looked over the health manual and card, etc, then said, "I'm sick of these piles of things, I only want the birth certificate." The second day Zhao Shengtian brought the birth certificate but the office person had changed. This one had different ideas. "Everybody has a birth certificate. I want to inspect the birth card given by the administration office."

Li Xiaolan told Zhao Shengtian he was stupid: "Just bring all the identifications."

On the third go, Zhao Shengtian arrived carrying a bag filled with all their identifications. Just as the office worker was about to fill out the residence permit, he stopped writing and asked, "Have you a Single Child Certificate?"

"No."

"Come back after you've got it."

Zhao Shengtian blew his top. "What do you mean? No one said anything about a Single Child Certificate! So where do I get

it? All I know is: my daughter is a resident citizen so she should
get a residence permit! She's entitled to one!"

The office worker sneered; laughing sarcastically, he took up
a Wuhan evening paper and began reading. Zhao Shengtian
went to grab him, but was restrained by an older office worker,
who warned him, "We also have to act according to regulations,
you know. Don't act rashly, young man; this is a police station!"

Zhao Shengtian had no choice but to swallow his anger. He
went off to handle the business of the Single Child Certificate.
Later he took care of the General Medical Treatment Certificate. Returning to handle the residence permit, he then carried
the residence permit to the granary to take care of cereal and oil
subsidies.

It took him forever to find the place that handled General
Medical Treatment Certificates. They rested at noon, not re-
suming work until two o'clock, so Zhao Shengtian strolled
around a store to pass the time. After a bit, he sat down to rest
on the long customers' bench, and fell asleep. When someone
patted him awake, he asked, "Is it two o'clock yet?"

The person said, "It's nine o'clock. We want to close up."
The person was quite humorous, going on to say, "Sorry to disturb your nice sleep."

Zhao Shengtian had indeed slept a big sleep and felt unusually
fresh and vigorous. His mood similarly took a turn for the better. He couldn't just wake up and leave. He chatted a bit with
the person.

"Thanks. I owe you an apology. Do you know what I've
lacked most this month?"

"Money."

"Nope. Money is something I lack every month. This month what I lack most is sleep. Do you want to guess the reason?"

"Your wife had a baby?"

"Buddy, you are incredible!"

"My wife just made it to one month."

They both laughed heartily. They happily shook hands, then said goodbye.

After getting all his daughter's permits, Zhao Shengtian couldn't go another step further. Roughly calculating, he figured he had walked nearly hundred thousand kilometres. My goodness, my little Zhaoyang, just so that you can be legally born, just so that every month you can have some cooking oil, nine catties of grain, and one kilogram of pork, Daddy has walked half way around the earth!

The first month was such an exceedingly difficult month. With mother completely weak, and baby so fragile and foreign, Zhao Shengtian nearly suffered a breakdown. With Li Xiaolan unable to even get out of bed, her entire body aching and sore, he had to get up early everyday and do the housework. Then she ran out of milk. Though the young couple argued continually, they were still able to experience a kind of joy, a joy that overrode all other hardships. The joy was Zhaoyang's amazing progress. After ten days she began staring at the coloured bell. At fifteen days, she laughed. At sixteen days she began to make noises. At eighteen days she reached out her little hands and grabbed mama's clothing. After twenty days she began to shed tears. At twenty-five days she tried to raise up her head and neck. On the twenty-seventh day, she clearly cried out, "Muma." At twenty-eight days she ceased to be afraid of her bath water, happily moving her hands and feet about as if swimming.

Zhaoyang was drawing ever closer to her parents, pressing ever onward towards the outside world. Her weight was already
eleven pounds—the little thing was so fascinating! With her,
you really saw returns on your investment—it was worth it!

12

It seemed as if the couple was a match made in heaven. One was
very capable, one was not so capable. One ran things inside,
one handled outside affairs. When Zhao Shengtian and Li
Xiaolan first got married, they had no idea how things would
turn out; now, already, everything was clear. Li Xiaolan, who
in the beginning was so good at flitting about and chitter-chat-
tering, now neither flitted nor chattered, concentrating solely
on staying home and taking care of her child. All external affairs fell into Zhao Shengtian's hands. It is said that divorce
rates among arrangements such as these are the lowest.

They decided to hire a nanny. This, of course, was Zhao
Shengtian's job.

The nanny market in modern China is a vast, unpredictable
market—Zhao Shengtian remembered reading about this topic in
some magazine, but unfortunately had forgotten the article's
content. He had thought the article irrelevant to his life—who
knew that after only a short time he would personally set foot in
this marketplace?

Zhao Shengtian went to the Nanny Introduction Agency at the
Residential Committee. After he had paid the introduction fee,
attendant then asked him to describe his personal situation.
Zhao Shengtian then proceeded to tell him that his wife's baby
was nearly a month old, that both he and his wife worked. He
hadn't finished speaking when he was cut off by one of the at-

tendants. She was a hoary, single-toothed old lady holding a six-month-old baby.

"You both work, and the child-care centre only takes three-year-olds."

"That's right."

"Are both sets of parents gone?"

"No. Both living."

"Still alive and not taking care of their grandchildren?"

"Their health is poor."

"Oh! And my health is good?"

Zhao Shengtian balked at her angry question.

"Other people's children know how to show filial obedience to their parents, how is it that I raised a beast?"

Zhao Shengtian tried to calm her down. Chuckling, he said, "I want to hire a clean, healthy, normal-looking girl that speaks Mandarin. Age doesn't matter."

"But what about your parents not taking care of their grand-children? Since when are old lives more important than young ones?"

"You're right."

The Residential Committee director came in, and seeing the situation, patted the old woman: "You're making people dizzy again with all your long-winded sermons; stubborn old woman, you never correct your shortcomings."

Before long, Zhao Shengtian met a young girl. She was slender, with regular features, her face made up lightly. She nodded towards Zhao Shengtian and smiled slightly, showing the manners of a city girl.

"Might I ask what the monthly salary is?"

The minute she opens her mouth, it's money. Zhao

Shengtian's impression of her was immediately ruined.

"You see my family's situation—you say how much."

"Well ... the child is small and hard to handle; add to that the fact that it's a heavy responsibility for a single woman to bear. Then again, I'm afraid a young couple like yourself doesn't bring home very much money. OK. Let's say, fifty yuan."

Bye-bye. Zhao Shengtian stood up and left. Fifty yuan plus food, clothing and utilities was synonymous with Zhao Shengtian losing his job.

"Don't run off!" she said. "Forty-five yuan."

"Do you think I'm a private entrepreneur or something? I'm a worker."

"OK. We're all young, let's just say I'm doing you a favour. Forty."

This figure was the same as Li Xiaolan losing her job. This household-of-three's economic situation didn't allow anyone to lose their job.

Zhao Shengtian sent an urgent appeal for help to some roguish buddies of his. Very shortly, news arrived. Zhao Shengtian hurried off to his friend's house in Hankou to see a girl who he was told was "really not bad".

Things were even more interesting this time around. Zhao Shengtian didn't suit the girl's fancy. There was no single bedroom for the nanny, no Sunday vacation and she couldn't use the washing machine; she absolutely would not consider an arrangement such as this. She said, "Every one of us nannies from Anhui Province are good people; our work leaves you completely satisfied, and so, our requirements are a little higher." Zhao Shengtian's friends said, "Girl, why don't you just do them this favour; their factory will allocate them another room before long." The girl said, "OK—after you get the room I'll come back. Sure, I can pity them a little—but who'll pity me?"

"Forget it!" Zhao Shengtian said.

Altogether he saw seven girls. They came from all over, their ages ranging from seventeen to twenty. Zhao Shengtian, however, failed to hire any of them.

Some of them Zhao Shengtian simply didn't like. Out of common courtesy, he would strike up a conversation with them, but they wouldn't give him even a little face. Some of them, after listening to his introduction, said things like, "The introduction agency must have made a mistake, for no way am I taking care of a child." Thereupon, they would walk away without so much as turning their heads.

Zhao Shengtian rushed about for several days, to no avail. When he returned home after the last attempt, Li Xiaolan was busy making dinner in the corridor.

"Did you hire anyone?"

"Fucking hire this!" Zhao Shengtian grabbed Li Xiaolan's wok, scoop, bowls and spoons, throwing them down the stairs.

"Zhao Shengtian, you're crazy! What are you doing?!"

Zhao Shengtian still hadn't vented his anger, though, and continued stomping about, spitting froth as he shouted.

"Bunch of little whores! What's so great about those nannies? All they know about is money, money, money—they suck!"

"Forget it, Xiao Zhao. Don't scare Zhaoyang."

After lunch, Fourth Sister-in-law came over. She offered some advice to the young couple. "Explain to me what the matter is. Hopefully I'll be able to think of something for you. How much are you willing to pay a nanny per month? Is this money from the family or is it your own? Zhaoyang's milk powder makes the expense even greater, so that a single salary isn't e-nough to sustain her. What do you two plan to do?"

"Fourth Sister-in-law, the family wouldn't give us the money to hire a nanny unless we had a boy—this you know clearly. But we came up with an idea. Give it a listen." Holding Zhaoyang to her bosom, Li Xiaolan carefully went over the options, meticulously considering the vast number of intricate family expenditures. Not even a shadow of the mischievous little girl remained. Having a child had thoroughly changed her.

"We plan to give the nanny twenty-five to thirty yuan a month. We'll give each month's salary on time, absolutely without delay. Zhaoyang's nutrition mustn't lack in the slightest and the adults' food should include meat every day. If we solely depended on our present salaries, it would never be enough, so we've sold a few things. The nice mattress, the wind chimes, the expensive floor lamp—all these things are just useless, decorative pieces. Fourth Sister-in-law, don't go around saying all this and don't laugh at us. We also got rid of some of my jewellery. It's really helped us to think clearly about some things. If you don't have money, don't act as if you're wealthy—what's the point of being showy?"

She took out two thousand yuan of savings for Fourth Sister-in-law to see.

Fourth Sister-in-law sighed several times, her eyes red with tears. "Zhaoyang can be proud of you. You really are acting like parents."

Not long thereafter, Fourth Sister-in-law brought an eighteen-year-old girl, the daughter of a distant relative in her mother's village. She could be considered a cousin. Her name was Xiaoju.

As soon as she entered the room Xiaoju was drawn to Zhaoyang.

"What a sweet fat little thing, just like bread dough—what a cutie!"

Zhao Shengtian and Li Xiaolan exchanged satisfied glances. Finally they had found a nanny who spoke of children when she opened her mouth.

Xiaoju cradled Zhaoyang in her arms, one hand supporting the buttocks, the other supporting the back, her manner sure and confident. Fourth Sister-in-law said that she had brought up children from the time she was small, big brother's, second brother's, cousin's—she had taken care of no less than five children, and never had a single mishap.

Xiaoju said, "That's right, I really like little kids, not working in the fields."

Fourth Sister-in-law asked: "What do you think?"

Zhao Shengtian said, "All right!"

Fourth Sister-in-law mentioned that it was a long way home for Xiaoju, that it would probably take two or three days what with changing trains and all. Li Xiaolan understood immediately, taking eighty yuan and stuffing it in Fourth Sister-in-law's pocket. Fourth Sister-in-law protested, "What are you doing? We're one family here."

"We keep clear accounts with our own brothers; how could we let our Fourth Sister-in-law pay? The cost of the trip, plus food and drink, isn't cheap, after all."

"Everything's expensive these days." Fourth Sister-in-law clapped her hands together. "Well, good. I'm so glad I finally did something for you two."

Xiaoju wasn't familiar with the gas stove, didn't know how to burn the honeycomb coal brickets, and had never seen an electric rice cooker. She saw no difference between wiping the floor with a mop and sweeping it with a broom. Neither did she know how to handle the milk boiler. The temperature inside the milk thermos fluctuated. She wasn't accustomed to the concept of feeding the baby milk every few hours. She didn't recognize the Roman numerals on the quartz clock.

Zhao Shengtian put up a folding cot for Xiaoju, and made her a folding screen. Both these different things were put up in the evening and put away during the day. Li Xiaolan told Xiaoju to shower and wash her hair. She had bought her shampoo, soap, towel, toothbrush and toothpaste, a pair of flip-flops, and a pair of underwear. In addition, she gave her a set of slightly used clothes. For these she had to spend another load of money. Fortunately, however, she was mentally prepared; anyone who hired a nanny knew that when a nanny arrived at your home, she came completely empty-handed.

After not even a month, the family of two had become a family of four. Everybody had to get reacquainted with their surroundings.

13

Zhaoyang turned one month old. This was a happy occasion. In Wuhan it was popular to celebrate month-old babies. Zhao Shengtian and Li Xiaolan didn't give their daughter a one-month celebration, they just took her to the park to play for a while, taking a roll of pictures of her.

Later, the parents on both sides of the family had opinions on the matter, saying that they hadn't shown respect to grandpa and grandma's generation. But the young couple acted as if they hadn't heard, completely ignoring these trifles. They had learned to live by doing things their way.

Naturally, after reaching one month, the child changed.

Xiaoju shook the cradle bell, making Zhaoyang titter. Zhao Shengtian looked at his watch.

"A new record. Zhaoyang laughed for two minutes."

Li Xiaolan said, "Tomorrow it will be three."

Zhaoyang's cries also became louder and fiercer. Her two little feet kicked off the covers several times. Her strong sense of curiosity already had some clues to work with. Someone had given her a "Mickey Mouse" to play with. She stared at the big black nose, crying out, "Ah, ah." After he got home from work, Zhao Shengtian would call out "Zhaoyang"; she immediately understood him, turning her head around, laughing. Li Xiaolan said, "Daddy is going to work." Zhaoyang glanced over at Zhao Shengtian, looked at the room, as if she really wanted to say something.

Daughter had begun to communicate with her parents. Her parents were no longer merely mired in a pile of dirty diapers; their daughter now truly stirred their imaginations, even their dreams.

Most on Zhao Shengtian's mind was making money. With such a beautiful daughter, there was to be no more messing about. No way could he allow his daughter to experience hardship and suffering. Whatever other people's kids had, his kid would have too.

Zhao Shengtian pondered several scenarios. He could work without leaving his unit and be a private entrepreneur on the side. But do what? Open a restaurant? Nope. With the central government's proclamation restricting use of public funds for eating and drinking, restauranteuring had become a bleak profession. If he opened a hair salon, without skills he'd get no respect from his partners. He didn't know how to fix bicycles. To open a business you need a stylish facade, capital and some business experience. He wasn't a bachelor anymore; he couldn't afford to fail. Another idea came—maybe he should go to the coast? Those opportunities, however, only happened by chance; if he blindly went there, he'd never find any gold. Zhao Shengtian, Zhao Shengtian—you're twenty-six years old—what are you going to do? You have no knowledge and no professional skill to recommend yourself. You really are a scatterbrained idiot!

As soon as Zhao Shengtian told Li Xiaolan what he had thought, she woke him up in a hurry.

"It's all bullshit," she said. "You are simply not cut out for business. Scheming, business—no scheming, no business. You just don't think that way."

Zhao Shengtian had an inspiration while picking up his paycheck, when he noticed an inspection engineer's salary listed on the salary sheet. The inspection engineer's basic salary was one hundred and eighty yuan. It was said that he frequently did planning and work for outside units. From the clothes his wife and daughter wore and their manner, they appeared rather well off. This was the only proper road, one that received others' respect. Though people feared those like older brother Zhao Shengcai, they didn't respect him. Never has anyone ever truly respected a business person.

Zhao Shengtian decided to enroll at an adult school. He was going to study! He was going to learn a cutting edge profession.

When he graduated in three years he would be exactly thirty years old. Three-year-old Zhaoyang would be just beginning to understand things. In the daycare centre she would be able to say daddy was an engineer—no one would look down on her. His salary would rise according to an engineer's grade, as opposed to the slow changes in rank among workers. He was pretty clever. He was confident of success.

On Saturday some of his buddies called to invite him to go out on Sunday. The plan was to include mahjong in the day and dancing in the evening. At noon they would eat at the Laohuibin Restaurant. Qiaoqiao was treating. Qiaoqiao had recently won an award in a nationwide pop-song competition.

"I can't go. No time. Congratulate Qiaoqiao for me."

"Everybody thinks it would do you good. You've had it rough for so long, now. I'm afraid your wife's been too hard on you."

"Never mind Xiaolan. It's my own choice."

"So you're just going to brush us off."

Zhao Shengtian hesitated a bit, saying, "No—what are you talking about."

He wasn't so much brushing them off—leaving them was an even more appropriate term. Goodbye, you bunch of brothers. Wearing your fashionable clothes and haristyles, in and out of dance halls and tea houses, talking big, burning hot with friendship. Brothers who esteem the words "personal loyalty" above all others, friendships that would last forever—alas, it is goodbye. Zhao Shengtian held the receiver and looked at it for some time, unable to put it down. They would never call again.

On Sunday, Zhao Shengtian went to walk around in the bookstore.

Just as Zhao Shengtian was walking in the bookstore, full of lofty sentiments and aspirations, there was an accident back home.

Before she left the building, Li Xiaolan had clearly seen Zhaoyang lying peacefully on the bed, Xiaoju standing over her, changing her diapers. Very shortly thereafter, when she returned from hanging up a quilt cover, she found Zhaoyang's face all covered with blood in a most frightening manner. Xiaoju was in a state of shock, wiping Zhaoyang's face repeatedly, becoming more frenzied as she smeared it worse with every wipe.

"Zhaoyang! My Zhaoyang!" Li Xiaolan suddenly cried out, then began wailing. Her two hands shaking wildly, she stood there, not knowing what to do for her daughter on the bed.

"Xiaoju, what did you do to her?"

"I didn't."

"Quickly—tell the truth, Xiaoju!"

Li Xiaolan grabbed Xiaoju and shook her roughly. Xiaoju also began wailing.

"I didn't, I really didn't!"

"How could it be? God!"

Li Xiaolan clutched her gold watch, half-kneeling before Xiaoju.

"I beg you, Xiaoju, tell the truth. I don't blame you. This watch is worth more than three hundred yuan. Just tell me and I'll give it to you!"

"I don't want it. I didn't do it."

Zhao Shengtian came in, finding all the three girls wailing. Li Xiaolan saw him, then rushed at him and began hitting him.

"My child, did you see our child? Where have you been?"

The instant he saw Zhaoyang, Zhao Shengtian's two knees went weak. But he was the man, after all, so he didn't faint away.

"Quick! To the hospital!"

Wrapping up his daughter, he bolted out the door. Li Xiaolan recovered her senses, grabbed some diapers and a blanket and ran after him.

The blood appeared to be flowing from out of the nose and lips, but no one knew why. As he ran, Zhao Shengtian urged himself on: Faster! Faster! Daughter, you'd better not have anything wrong! We've already lived so well together—we can't go on without you! No! No!

Li Xiaolan was sobbing, her face hidden by a head of loose hair. Xiaoju eventually caught up as well, white as a ghost, saying over and over, "I didn't, I didn't."

The pedestrians on the road were stupefied. One after another, cars urgently slammed on their brakes. A traffic cop tacitly allowed them to run down the middle of the street, disregarding red and green lights.

A motorcycle flew over, screeching to a halt by Zhao Shengtian's side.

"Quick, get on!" the driver said.

A burst of applause came from the sidewalk.

Once they arrived at the hospital, things were extremely tense.

After an hour, Zhaoyang was on a drip, and slowly she went to sleep. Zhao Shengtian and Li Xiaolan, one on each side, watched over their daughter.

"Have you been off playing somewhere? I would never forgive you if anything bad had really happened to Zhaoyang today."

"I wasn't off playing."

Zhao Shengtian stared at the liquid inside the medicine bottle as it dripped downward.

"Hello, are you listening to me?" Li Xiaolan said.

"No. I was thinking of that motorcycle driver. He was wearing a helmet, so I didn't even see his face clearly—what a pity!"

Li Xiaolan suddenly felt that her husband had changed. He was completely different from the person who got into a fight the day of their wedding.

"You're right, it's too bad," she said. Zhao Shengtian's transformation, however, wasn't the least bit disappointing.

14

Completely lacking in medical knowledge, the young couple was told as plainly as possible by the doctor that the baby's bleeding was due to a rupture in a small blood vessel in the lining of her nasal passage. The baby didn't have any major illness. It was caused by the day's cold, dry weather, and because the baby was eating milk powder, a "big-fire food" (according to Chinese medicine). In addition, you wrapped her fragile little body too thickly.

There was no special medicine prescribed for the treatment. Two vials of medicine to start with. The child needed milk powder that was closer to mother's milk, fresh fruit drinks, vegetable drinks, honey, and appropriate clothing.

What brand of milk on the market was closest to mother's milk?

The doctor recommended one kind: "The Nestle Company's 'Nani' baby milk powder. The name in Chinese was 'Neng En'. My grandchild eats it, the results have been very good."

The couple thanked the doctor.

Zhao Shengtian and Li Xiaolan found "Neng En" at the food counter in Wuchang's biggest South Central Business Building. There were 450 grams per container, which was beautifully decorated. On the explanation was written: "Nani" baby milk powder provides baby with each kind of vitamin and mineral necessary for optimum development. Its quality guaranteed by the Nestle Company, "Nani" is known and unanimously trusted by mothers all around the world.

As one of the mothers in the world, Li Xiaolan wasn't familiar with "Neng En", but she trusted it.

"Xiao Zhao, let's buy it."

"Twenty-seven yuan eighty cents a bottle. Only nine *liang* of powder per bottle, though. According to this feeding and suckling chart Zhaoyang will probably eat it up in a week."

"Twenty-seven yuan eighty cents every week, plus fruit drink, honey, etc. Isn't that a bit too expensive?"

"Yeah. Milk powder is only milk powder, not gold. Those foreign devils are just stealing our money."

"Mmn. We don't need to get suckered."

Zhaoyang was given the local brand of milk powder most trusted by Wuhan residents, "Yangtze River". Because when she ate it her nose bled a little, they changed to "Baby" milk powder. But "Baby" milk powder wasn't clean; every time they boiled it a whole lot of flotsam rose to the top. They changed again, this time feeding her "Heilongjiang Excellent Quality" milk powder. But Zhaoyang refused to eat "Heilongjiang". Everybody racked their brains but couldn't explain it. In the end, Li Xiaolan tried a couple of mouthfuls, and found that it tasted strongly of rubber. Thereupon they changed yet again to a milk powder produced in Shashi. Zhaoyang actually ate 120mg in one sitting, but didn't have a bowel movement the next day. Even after using ointment, her anus remained dry and cracked. When after three days the baby's little anus was still parched, Li Xiaolan said, "Xiao Zhao, maybe we should try 'Neng En' after all?"

"OK, we'll give it a try."

Zhao Shengtian went to buy a container. That light blue bottle had an enchanting effect.

Surely unaware of the money issue, Zhaoyang loved "Neng En", drinking completely normally. Zhao Shengtian and Li Xiaolan also experienced the sweet taste of "Neng En", as the time spent getting up at midnight was now greatly reduced. Just add boiling water and it was ready. Shake it a little and it dissolved completely. After the child finished her milk the adults could go back to sleep—they could even continue with the same dreams. Xiaoju couldn't stop praising "Neng En". She didn't have to worry about the milk boiling over or lighting the gas store. It was simple, clean and safe; once you try it, you're hooked. The only fault they found with it was that one container of "Neng En" was only enough to last Zhaoyang for three days, not the one week that Zhao Shengtian initially estimated. They decided to use "Neng En" milk powder.

When the salesperson heard the customers say that they wanted ten containers of "Neng En", his expression immediately became modest and courteous. Warmly and eagerly he introduced the product to them. "When drinking this kind of high-quality milk powder, most people like to use it together with high-quality Tang drink." He picked up a bottle of the Tang powder imported from the United States (not a Chinese-American joint venture), and put it with the ten containers of "Neng En" milk powder.

"Here is the trademark, have a look. Specially chosen by the United States Space and Aeronautics Bureau..."

Zhao Shengtian said, "Beverage of the space age, affording e-poch-making enjoyment."

"Precisely! Want to buy it, sir?"

The counter was already surrounded by a host of rednecks, everyone intently watching the "sir". This was the first time Zhao Shengtian had ever been formally, respectfully addressed as a "sir" by people in a public place. Li Xiaolan was very proud of him. "We'll buy it." she said.

Another twenty-seven yuan. Altogether it came to 305 yuan fifty cents, Zhaoyang's major monthly expense.

Li Xiaolan's parents didn't approve of their daughter going about things in this manner. They thought it unnecessary to blindly worship things foreign, and neither was it necessary to be so extravagant. Vanity is the very worst quality of youth; they had seen this at the marriage; that they didn't point it out was only to preserve the mood of the new marriage. After having a child and still behaving this way—that wouldn't do.

Li Xiaolan thanked her parents for their adult advice. But because they didn't mention it during the marriage period, it had become invalid. Then and now were different, not the same matter at all.

"Lanlan!" Her mother said in a stern voice, "you're already a mother, we're discussing serious matters here—yet you still act frivolously!"

"God! I'm not serious? Maybe you didn't notice that from the time I had Zhaoyang I haven't bought any clothes or gone to the beauty parlour. But I have the authority to buy milk powder for my daughter. I love her. I'd rather be chopped-up and eaten than have anything to do with you!"

Zhao Shengtian hurriedly appeared on the scene to break up the fight. Unfolding his life story before his in-laws, he described how he had been born during a famine year. Harbouring lofty aspirations, his father named him Shengtian (victorious over heaven). But had he defeated heaven? Not even close. A calcium deficiency left him with a chicken breast and bow legs; he was three years old before he learned to walk. His grades at school were poor, and because he was malnourished, he kept falling asleep in class. Little Zhaoyang, however, after eating "Neng En" for a month, lacked neither calcium nor zinc. She was able to sit up after three months. She would even intentionally turn her face upward to set the adults laughing—her mental development was fantastic!

Xiaoju made Zhaoyang perform sitting on the bed, then raising and lowering her head. Zhaoyang watched as the adults chuckled up a storm.

The old pair admitted that Zhaoyang was being raised pretty well. They resolutely maintained, however, that eating imported milk powder wasn't the correct direction for child-rearing in China. Later though, when Zhao Shengtian escorted them down the stairs to leave, they managed to persuade him to accept one hundred and fifty yuan, saying nothing other than enjoining him not to tell Li Xiaolan. This was because they felt that Zhao Shengtian understood things a lot better than Li Xiaolan.

The Zhao family was also in an uproar over "Neng En". The older and second sisters, who seldom visited, came together, using seeing Zhaoyang as their excuse to have a look at the foreign milk powder.

At the game table, the old lady sighed emotively to her mahjong cronies,

"Back then I raised babies too, didn't spent a cent. Depended solely on these two milk bags of mine. All six babies grew up to tall and strong as horses. Things are strange today; they don't eat mother's milk anymore, they drink cow's milk, even foreign cow's milk—it really amazes me! You can't take a fashionable girl for a wife; they're clever, and they'll ruin your home. That bastard son of mine is as good as sold."

Also much discussed among Zhao Shengtian and Li Xiaolan's co-workers, "Neng En" became a piece of news talked about everywhere. There were even some people who called in to question the origin of the couple's funds.

"There're too many people noticing us. Xiao Zhao, are you afraid?"

"You afraid?" Zhao Shengtian replied.

"No."

"Exactly. What's there to be afraid of. It's only our daughter drinking a little 'Neng En'."

"Society is so complex."

"Learned a lesson, maybe?"

Whatever milk powder Zhaoyang liked to eat they would buy for her; never would they choose a milk powder because of where it came from, and never would they care about what other people said. On this point Zhao Shengtian and Li Xiaolan were in complete agreement.

Yes, from the time they were small they had eaten porridge and still grown to be adults. All their parents wanted was for their sons and daughters to become adults; their responsibility was thus fulfilled. But Zhao Shengtian and Li Xiaolan didn't just want their daughter to survive, they wanted her to have the finest quality body and finest quality mind possible, so that in the future, in an age characterized by fierce competition, she would be a strong player. With the arrival of Zhaoyang's generation, the Chinese nation could no longer afford to suffer from calcium, iron and mineral deficiencies; with strong bodies they would go on to create and invent, make their motherland wealthy and powerful. So many years, so many generations— we've been poor for too long, we should live well for a change!

15

"Comrade, please get a cassette for me."

Li Xiaolan thought that her voice sounded positively melodious.

It was the first time in several months that she had dressed up and gone strolling around in a store; she really felt like a person again. No husband by her side, no child, no nanny—this was how free and easy she used to feel. Everywhere in the store were large mirrors. Li Xiaolan saw in them that, once again, she was petite and slender. She was ecstatic, and when that happened she usually felt like buying a little something. Zhaoyang had begun to notice music. Listening to the radio the day before yesterday, she slowly twisted and turned to the music... wasn't it "Swan Lake"?

Li Xiaolan knocked on the counter. "Comrade, I'd like to buy a cassette."

"What are you rapping on the counter for? Speak up then, whose tape do you want."

"Xian Xinghai's 'Swan Lake'."

"Oh my god!" the salesgirl arched up high her eye-brows. "'Swan Lake' is by Tchaikovsky. Xian Xinghai did 'Yellow River', how'd you manage to mix them up?"

Gathered around the cassette counter were several stylish young boys and girls. Totally unrestrainedly they began hooting with laughter. Li Xiaolan had nowhere to hide her face.

She simply didn't pay attention to her own words, she just let them out. This was the current fad, saying who sang this and that song. In the past, Li Xiaolan would never had admitted defeat; coming out on top was her speciality. She would say, "That's right, I don't understand shit, but at least I'm not some graduate from the conservatory. Don't laugh too much, or you'll lose your tooth and can't find a husband." Being courageous enough to admit you don't understand shit, this was the carefree manner of today's youth. This time, however, Li Xiaolan couldn't act carefree, and she wasn't sure why.

Depressed, Li Xiaolan hurried home. All she wanted to do at this moment was to return to her daughter's side. She exhorted Xiaoju not to tell Zhao Shengtian she had gone to the store today. Zhao Shengtian would definitely wonder why she had come back empty-handed.

Xiaoju obeyed Li Xiaolan's words, but Zhao Shengtian nonetheless noticed something strange in his wife's manner.

"What's wrong with you today?"

"Not feeling well."

"Not feeling well where?"

"Everywhere."

"It's got to be because your nursing period didn't go well. It's just our lack of experience to blame. I hear that any sickness must be cured during the nursing period. It looks as if we'll need to have another baby." Zhao Shengtian chuckled at his own words. Li Xiaolan didn't laugh. She didn't think it was the least bit funny.

Zhao Shengtian also told her a piece of good news. He had enrolled in an adult university, and not only did the factory not mind, but moreover offered to pay his tuition, on the condition that, after graduation, he didn't request a transfer.

Indeed this was not bad news. Zhao Shengtian had made such rapid progress—he was going to be a university student. When they were dating, Li Xiaolan's biggest regret about Zhao Shengtian was that he didn't have a university diploma. Now that they were married, diplomas were no longer fashionable. All of a sudden, however, Zhao Shengtian had woken up. Li Xiaolan forced a laugh, saying, "Woken up? Congratulations."

"So what is eating you, huh?"

Li Xiaolan couldn't hold it in any longer.

"You want to know what's eating me? You have good news every day. You got a bonus. You met your target. The product has broken into some country's market. Your ball team won. You're a university student. But me—I also have good news every day. Zhaoyang isn't eating her hand anymore. Xiaoju found a one yuan bill when she went to get more soy sauce. Zhaoyang only wet three diapers—I've held her for five pisses now. She's gone from two bowel movements to one bowel movement a day. Soft, yellow, tubeshaped, with an even thicker smell. It's such good news—your daughter has begun to take adult's shits already."

Zhao Shengtian sighed deeply. "So, after all, you're sick of Zhaoyang."

"Nonsense. I'm not sick of her!"

Tears of hurt came flowing down Li Xiaolan's face. She opened her two hands to show Zhao Shengtian. Her hands didn't possess the least bit of feminine beauty. Cold sores, cracks, scars made by the cutting knife, and small holes pricked by safety pins overlapped, covering her hands.

"I use this pair of hands to serve you two, day in and day out. What right have you to keep me locked-up here at home, month after month? It's like I'm deaf or dumb—I know nothing about what goes on outside. I've lost contact with all of my friends. I haven't even seen a movie—why!"

Li Xiaolan ran out the door. She feared her wailing might frighten her daughter.

Zhao Shengtian chased her out the door. Taking hold of his wife's arm, he walked with her slowly down the road. Apart from silently accompanying her, there was nothing he could say. Li Xiaolan had already said what he himself wanted to say. His hands were also frozen and broken from housework and washing diapers; maybe Li Xiaolan hadn't considered it, but he had, long ago—the two of them had almost no sex life anymore. He also wanted to cry.

Who understood them?

Who was going to give a thought for them?

Who was going to notice the silent, roadside tears of this young husband and wife?

Hers was precisely the age at which one dresses up, puts on make-up, makes friends, advances in their studies, learns about the world—but it was also childbearing age. When even their parents weren't willing to give them an ounce of help, what was there left for them to do? It was a dead end, a constant irony. All she could do was have a good cry.

Zhao Shengtian suggested that she wrap up Zhaoyang and go
to the children's park everyday to get some sun, walk around a
little, breathe in some fresh air.

The *Complete Guide to Child Development* said that five-
month-old babies should get at least two hours everyday of activity outside to improve the resistance of their respiratory tract.

"There are many adults over in the children's park for you to
chat with. Xiaoju can make something simple for you to take.
Anyway, it's all food, right? As time goes on, things will get
gradually better."

Even when Zhao Shengtian had only just begun to attend university classes, he already showed himself to possess considerable knowledge. No matter how unhappy the wife, it was difficult to get angry at this kind of man.

16

As expected, Li Xiaolan encountered a whole new world at the
children's park.

Here, everywhere were children, old people, and young
women holding babies and toddlers. Li Xiaolan felt a certain
closeness to them, particularly to the latter group. Only here did
she truly feel as if she was among her own kind. The very moment she stepped into the park she had a premonition that something special was going to happen.

She met a woman carrying a year-old boy, a worker from the
Hanyang Cigarette Factory. With her tight pants and short jacket she was quite stylishly dressed. She especially talked about
how she had "fixed" her mother-in-law and sister-in-law. She
called her mother-in-law "the old cunt", and her sister-in-law a
"horny little cunt". "If that old cunt dares not to look after my

child, I'll take her grandchild and throw it in the water fountain right in front of her face. Of course it's all for show, you know."

At first, Li Xiaolan thought she was pretty funny, but when the girl began repeating herself, it lost its flavour. Moreover, her loud, brazen swearing had attracted the gazes of several others, causing Li Xiaolan to feel a bit embarrassed. When the woman began calling her own son a "little bastard", Li Xiaolan felt nauseated as if she were pregnant again.

"I have to go back now," Li Xiaolan said.

"But why—it's still fucking early, isn't it?"

"Yeah, but I've got an appointment."

Li Xiaolan hurriedly walked off. She didn't go home, however. Over by the artificial mountain, they met each other once again. Li Xiaolan pretended not to see her. The girl blinked her eyes at her in disbelief, then left.

Zhou Linna had a sweet face that people found attractive. She said to Li Xiaolan, "Wow, your baby is so beautiful!"

"Your baby is, too."

"How big is it?"

"Five months."

"We're half a year. So ours is big sister."

They took turns holding each other's babies, talking all about the lessons gleaned from their experiences raising children.

When again they saw each other, the topics turned more serious and personal. Zhou Linna was a single mother, who grew up spoiled and pampered in her mother's home. Her hobby music, her parents had previously given her violin lessons. Three months after she got married, however, her father-in-law died and her mother-in-law had a stroke. Seven months later, her husband died in a car accident. Shortly thereafter she was married to her husband's young brother.

"Jiaojiao was born four months after her father died. At that time I had already been married one month." Zhou Linna held her daughter tightly, her tears glistening.

In addition to working, Zhou Linna also had to take care of her mother-in-law and a baby, sewing, mending, washing, starching, and fixing three meals a day. A bank worker, her job didn't allow her to arrive late or retire early; neither could she afford to be distracted or careless at work.

Li Xiaolan couldn't refrain from shedding a tear of sympathy. There were still such unfortunate people in the world. Compared to Zhou Linna, what were her own problems? Zhou Linna wiped away the tears, saying that actually she lived pretty well, was by now used to it. Relations with her mother-in-law were also quite good; from her bed, her mother-in-law would watch her grandchild. Even now Zhou Linna would occasionally play the violin, her audience composed of one elder and one youngster. The audience was extraordinarily warm.

"Linna, you are really amazing!"

Li Xiaolan and Zhou Linna met Wang Yu together. A teacher at Hubei University, she was five years older than the other two. Her first child had been stillborn, the child she now held was her second. It was five months old, born on the same day as Zhaoyang. His name was Cuishu.

Wearing no make-up, Wang Yu was the very picture of simplicity and good taste. Her dress was tasteful cut so that it hugged her body. Slim and graceful, she appeared a refined young married woman.

Li Xiaolan and Zhou Linna adored Wang Yu's elegant manners; Wang Yu liked their vigour and frankness. Wang Yu and her husband were on bad terms, skating on the brink of divorce.

"But if you're divorcing, why do you still want a child?"

"It was just as I was preparing for the divorce that I began to want a child. I must have someone dear to me; looking after him will make me happy, give me strength."

Wang Yu warned Li Xiaolan and Zhou Linna that women must be strong and have self-respect. They should study more and have marketable skills. Otherwise, men would look down on you, from the deepest part of their being. Her husband was an assistant professor, young and full of promise. The first several years of their marriage they didn't want children; during those years, Wang Yu went all out to support him in his work. Now, he looked down on Wang Yu, instead seeing eye-to-eye with one of his female graduate students. They planned as soon as possible to travel together to the United States.

"A lover?! Why don't you sue him?"

"Why should I sue him? This development is actually most welcome. I can't respect this kind of man—my only fear is that I won't be able to get rid of him."

Here was another woman, living under the very same sky, so full of her own ideas and opinions, so full of ambition. Making friends gave Li Xiaolan new experiences, new reasons to sigh. All along, she had actually been the most fortunate person among them. Her life had been so smooth.

Li Xiaolan next told the stories of "Neng En" milk powder, Zhao Shengtian's scuffle as a new bridegroom, and the tale of her buying a cassette. Zhou Linna and Wang Yu burst out laughing as they listened. They both thought that Li Xiaolan was a lucky person.

"It's true," Li Xiaolan said. "These past few days I've thought that, too. Wang Yu has had four nannies so far, and I'm still with Xiaoju."

In the mild and radiant morning, the three of them sat in a row on the bench, playing and joking with their children. Sometimes they would just sit still and bask in the sun.

As a young mother, Li Xiaolan was like a satellite; having entered her orbit, she now lived normally and happily. From Wang Yu, she learned how to make rice wine and spicy pickled Sichuan vegetables. She also learned how to make sweet and sour hairtail fish, West Lake sweet fish and Hubei homestyle fish.

"You're not a good woman if you don't know how to make some dishes," Wang Yu said.

From Zhou Linna, Li Xiaolan learned that *Swan Lake* was a four-act ballet. The Russian composer Tchaikovsky used a symphony orchestra to tell the story of how Odette (turned into a white swan) and Prince Siegfried's mutual love defeated the evil sorcerer. She also learned about many other world-famous pieces. The three young wives agreed to become godparents for each other's children. Jiaojiao was older sister, Cuishu was second brother and Zhaoyang was third sister. They hoped that, hereafter, they could help and support one another, that each child would enjoy a promising future.

The final month of maternity leave flew by.

In this month, Li Xiaolan's burdens became more and more numerous. First was that Zhao Shengtian had begun to study hard, reading and doing homework daily. Second was that Zhao Shengtian's mother had gone to the hospital for an inflamed gall bladder and there was no one to look after her. Li Xiaolan made

Zhao Shengtian take some food over to her.

"After all she is your mother. Even if she doesn't understand proper manners, we can't act the same. There'll be a day we're old, too."

Zhao Shengtian was completely surprised.

"I thought you didn't care if she died," he joked with her.

Li Xiaolan, however, was earnest.

"I used to wish that, but not now. Actually, if she would help us to watch the child, I wouldn't let her get tired—I would still want to keep a nanny. I'd only let her watch her a little. That vigorous little life would be a welcome addition to any old person's retirement years. It's a pity she doesn't understand. All she knows is how to shuffle mahjong tiles and blindly favour boys over girls; she isn't a fortunate person."

Zhao Shengtian was left agape with astonishment at his wife's fervour and self-assurance.

This was nothing. Compared to Zhou Linna and Wang Yu, she was way off. Never before had she been so acutely aware of her personal childishness and ignorance. She was a bad housewife, inexperienced in life's hardships, unaware of how difficult life really was, poorly versed in the many commonsense principles of daily living. Despite several years working in the library she hadn't even read a single book through. Boy, did she regret that! From here on in she would do her best to bring up her daughter, treat her husband properly, and effectively manage this household of hers. She would strive to read and learn more.

One day for sure she would go to the cassette counter at the store and win back her pride, buying Beethoven's "Heroic Symphony", Bizet's "Carmen", Berlioz' "Roman Carnival", Bach's "Air on a G String" and "The Merry Widow". Little girl, do you know whose work that is? Lehar! And who wrote the "March of the Volunteers"? Nie Er. It's none other than our present national anthem. You mixed-up little girl—you're not fit to even work at this counter!

Yes, one day. On that day, Zhaoyang would say, "Mama, you really understand a lot of things."

"Zhaoyang, what will you be like when you grow up?"

"I'll be just like my mama."

"But Mama isn't stylish or pretty."

"Mama is much more than pretty; you have a special style, a bellyful of knowledge and an air of self-reliance."

A bellyful of knowledge and air of self-reliance—those were Wang Yu's words and style. It was also the new goal after which Li Xiaolan strived.

Li Xiaolan went back to work. Her first day back at work she became quite a piece of gossip in the library. She had got rid of her previously thick make-up and now went totally without jewellery. Her head of straight hair was gracefully tied back with a regular rubber band. She bumped into Ye Ye as soon as she went inside, and, covering a smile, said, "Hi, Ye Ye." Not hearing the usual address of "Little whore", Ye Ye was simply overwhelmed by the unexpected favour.

Everyone said, "Wow, Li Xiaolan, you really have changed!"

"Really?" she said, then replied to herself, "It's true. I have changed."

17

In the blink of an eye, little Zhaoyang reached her first year.

Zhao Shengtian and Li Xiaolan, in their new residence, celebrated their daughter's birthday. The guests were Zhou Linna and her daughter, Wang Yu and her son, Gao Shan and his son, and Liu Wuchang and his daughter. Gao Shan and Liu Wuchang were friends Zhao Shengtian had made when he had bundled up Zhaoyang and taken her over to the Health Protection Station to get immunized. The one-year-old child altogether received ten shots. Nine times the three pairs of fathers and their children had bumped heads. Often during the conversations they had as they waited in line, the three fathers found themselves in complete agreement. If this wasn't fate, what was?

The new friends went to look at each room, and all agreed that the little home was simple and refined. When Li Xiaolan heard the word "simple", she couldn't help feeling a bit hurt inside. None of them had participated in Zhao Shengtian and Li Xiaolan's raucous wedding, and thus had nothing to compare the present digs to. Li Xiaolan, however, had a basis for comparison. All the extravagant things were sold off. Still, simple was good also. These were their true colours—after all—they're just an average family.

The five, roughly one-year-old little devils, all decked out in their prettiest clothes, speaking their own language, teeter-tottered all over the place. The adults had the hardest time getting them to sit still around a small table to take their picture. Later they took away the tables and chairs and put a big cake in the middle of the carpet, thus making it convenient for the toddlers, as yet only able to crawl, to grab a mouthful.

The rug was bought specially by Zhao Shengtian and Li Xiaolan for this gathering; they even had it sent out to be sanitized with ultraviolet rays. Just as they expected, the little guys intentionally threw the cake on the floor, then picked it up again and ate it. The large cake was specially ordered from Wuchang's most famous, hundred-year-old shop, Cao Xiangtai.

The adults sang "Happy birthday to you"; the birthday stars, however, were unimpressed. Zhaoyang didn't possess in the least the grace and elegance of a host, smearing cream on each of the other little guests as she ate. This frightened some children to tears. Some, though, chuckled, saying, "Want more." It wasn't clear who started it all, but soon the little things all began crying out, "Eat. Cake. Eat. Cake."

Zhaoyang called out the clearest and loudest, her plump, little white hand waving all about, two little legs running hither and thither. So many "little friends" snatching and grabbing together at the food provided for quite an amusing scene. How crazy and loud you'd have to be before you could adequately express Zhaoyang's happy manner!

Zhao Shengtian stood in the midst of all the guests; Li Xiaolan, in her apron, rested against the kitchen doorway. They glanced several times at one another. The incomparably happy scene truly stirred in them a surge of emotion, causing them to sigh with the deepest of feelings.

Raising a child is so hard! Li Xiaolan's hips and back were still sore and aching; Zhao Shengtian's exhaustion still hadn't abated. Both of them were dark and thin. Child, until now, they haven't had a full night's sleep. So many teardrops and beads of sweat have been shed for you! So many times we've been suffered economic crisis, just so you could have milk powder—at the most difficult moment, we had only thirty-five cents left in our hands.

But raising a child is also so interesting! After eight months and seven days, you suddenly, completely clearly and sweetly, called out "daddy"; that made Zhao Shengtian, who had never cried before, instantly start gushing tears. Your daddy got into a fight the very day he married, your mama cursed all over the place in her bridal gown—such an unruly, ignorant, and totally romantic couple of young people. Then you silently changed them into solid, serious adults. They never knew love before you, and now they were full of love and generosity for other children, old people, everyone. And it's all because of you, child.

So full of energy, the little devils played until the cake was nothing but a bunch of crumbs—and then still refused to slow down. Standing in the middle of the rug, Gao Shan's son took his third piss. Zhou Linna's daughter took a shit, then sat right down in it. Though the children were unwilling, the adults eventually took charge and expertly concluded the birthday feast. Everyone thought it had been a fully satisfying and happy birthday party. Gao Shan's son turned one next month. He invited everyone to be guests in his home, saying that it was bound to be another exciting affair.

"Don't forget the date."

"Couldn't if I tried," Zhao Shengtian replied.

Having seen the guests off, Zhao Shengtian and Li Xiaolan discussed what to give Gao Shan's son as a birthday present, what clothing Zhaoyang should wear that day, and how Xiang would have to help them with the date, reminding them when it came time. Xiang was the young nanny they hired after Xiaoju left. Xiang replied, "OK."

Xiang and Li Xiaolan cleaned up the mess. Zhao Shengtian got ready to do his homework. Zhaoyang crawled onto a gift box and fell asleep. Husband and wife took their daughter and gently moved her over to the bed.

Li Xiaolan said, "Today was really tiring, but also really special."

Zhao Shengtian nodded his head in agreement. Brushing aside a strand of hair touching his daughter's eyelid, he laughed, and went off to do his homework.

Translated by Scudder Smith

To and Fro

FOR many a man, real life starts only after an affair with another woman. Kang Weiye happened to be one such man.

Like many others who got married through matchmakers, Kang Weiye and Duan Lina had been each given a brief introduction to the other through a go-between before they met. Duan Lina had a number of things in her favor, said the go-between. The same age as Kang Weiye, she was a Communist Party member, had a job at the Academy of Social Sciences, was progressive in thought, devoted to work, healthy, good-looking and 1.66 meters in height. Her father was an army officer at the division level in the Wuhan Military Zone. On hearing this, Kang felt dwarfed. He said instantly to Dr Li, the go-between, "Forget it. I'm no match for her."

Despite his reluctance, Dr Li set a date for him to meet with the girl. In the eyes of Dr Li, Kang was by no means inferior. Only a girl like Lina could be a good match for him. Dr Li, a woman who had seen much of the world, predicted: "Little Kang, this world is bound to change. A smart fellow like you will not be stuck in this workshop forever. You have a bright future."

2

One day in May 1976, at 3 o'clock in the afternoon, Kang
Weiye and Duan Lina had their first date, at the Flower Pavilion in Zhongshan Park in Hankou. Kang was punctual while
Lina, taking Dr Li's advice, hid herself far away from the pavilion, observing an anxious Kang.

Though Kang had been given a pretty thorough description of
Lina, he was, however, greatly surprised upon seeing the girl in
person. May was the season of flowers and trees with butterflies
and bees flitting here and there. The young, healthy and shape-
ly girl with white teeth and red lips seemed to Kang to have a
halo around her. Kang had never ever thought that Lina could
be such an amazing girl. He dared not look her in the eye.

Lina seemed at ease. "Hi, Comrade Kang," she greeted him,
promptly proffering her hand towards Kang. Kang barely
touched her fingers. Anyway, it was a handshake and they got
acquainted. After Dr Li left, Kang gradually became more of
himself. They found themselves two stone stools around a stone
table. Since the stool Lina was to sit on was not very clean,
Kang took out a newspaper from his pocket and put it down for
her to sit on, for he had noticed that she had on a pair of brand-
new army pants. It would be a pity to get them dirty.

They sat almost nose to nose across the stark little table. The
moist, warm spring breeze fondled their faces, while flying
catkins and fluff from Chinese parasol trees kept sticking to
their eyelashes. They had to forcefully blink from time to time
as though both suffered from sore eyes. Lina sat straight with
her knees close together. There was a slight air of aloofness
about her. She wore a loose dark blue jacket with a white blouse

collar over the jacket lapels. A pair of thick, short braids, tightly tied with rubber bands at the ends, were so neat that they seemed to have been cut with a hay cutter. From head to toe there was nothing fanciful about her—whether it was her plastic barrettes, the laced handkerchief, or the red wool-covered rubber bands. She held herself in a detached, serious manner. She was a girl of thoughts, of theory, with a strong sense of social responsibility. One glance at her could tell that she had once been a bright student. Sitting before such a girl, Kang felt all the more that the gap between them was too wide. He began to suspect that Dr Li might have not told her all about him.

Lina had a glib tongue. When expounding some revolutionary theory, she could keep talking on and on without stopping. Kang was an eloquent speaker too. But in awe of this girl, he became slow and clumsy. Sometimes, he even stuttered. The topics they covered were all about the fate of the Party and the country. It had nothing at all to do with love. They were like two statesmen rather than a young couple wooing each other. Gradually Kang lost interest and started to plan his retreat.

3

Kang Weiye wrote again and again on a sheet of letter paper: "Please do not write anymore to me." But he could not muster the courage to put the letter through the slot of a letterbox. Kang argued with himself, "She has far more advantages than you, what reason do you have to jilt her? A non-Party member, a shipper in a frozen meat warehouse with a meager monthly income of eighteen yuan, wanting to jilt a pretty girl, a Party member, with a salary of twenty-four yuan? Isn't this a deliberate insult?"

Duan Lina led Kang Weiye home to meet her parents, brothers and sisters. Similarly, Kang took her to his home too. He and his parents lived in a factory dormitory which had been converted from a large Russian-style office. The office was partitioned into two rooms which were filled with books. There was a public toilet and a common kitchen.

Lina's home was located in a large compound with high-ranking army officers living in it. A sentry was posted at its entrance. The compound was like a park with luxuriant trees, surrounding some villas. The garden fence of each house was covered with ivy, creeping plants, hanging gourds, beans and so on. Lush and sturdy Chinese greens stretched their leaves through gaps in the fences. Flat asphalt pathways led to the gate of each villa. Kang was uncomfortably struck by the world of difference between this compound and ordinary residences outside.

Lina's father was in army uniform, had a paunch, and stood with his hands behind his back. He merely nodded when Kang was introduced to him. Then he went to the sunny garden and sat there listening to the radio while dozing off. Lina's brothers and sisters did not engage in social niceties, but were all confidently nonchalant. They kept on with their snobbish talk in standard army language rather than local dialect, about top brass from local military zones to the Central Military Commission, boasting and joking. Lina's mother greeted him briefly and asked the maid to prepare a meal for the guest.

The visit led to a heated quarrel between Kang and Lina. Kang's strong resentment seemed, to Lina, rather naive and ridiculous. She argued, "According to your logic, Chairman Mao should not have resided in Beijing's Zhongnanhai—instead should have gone back to live in his native village in Hunan?"

"Duan Lina," Kang piped up, "I never thought you were so sly!"

"Am I sly or is it your peasant mentality? Your narrow mind and sheer ignorance?"

Kang smashed a cup on the ground and said, "Please think back a little—how many days have you all been living in the city? Have you washed off all the dust and soil on your bodies? And you dare speak of my peasant mentality!"

Lina turned ashen. "Only a shameless man would spit out such shameless words!"

This quarrel pushed their relations close to the brink. But people around them did not want to see them break up. Dr Li shuttled to and fro, persuading the young man and woman to make up. Finally, Kang apologized to Lina, but only for smashing the cup.

When they were in a happy mood many days later, Kang bantered, "In fact you did not want to say goodbye to me, did you? Actually it's you who ran after me, right?"

"Get away!" Lina seemed to admit it.

Kang asked, "Why? I am neither a Party member nor a government functionary. What is it that made you like me the first time we met?"

Kang did not get the soul-stirring response he expected. Lina told him frankly: In the first place, according to Dr Li, Kang was a nice person, well educated, bright and with a promising future. Secondly, he was tall and robust and also from a revolutionary family. Thirdly, he had spread a piece of newspaper on the stone stool for her to sit, the first time when they met. This showed that he knew how to look after others. Fourthly, he was a man of scruples and never casually mixed with girls. Fifthly, one of her classmates, He Hanru, had told her that Kang had been praised by the Minister of Water Conservation when still in primary school. Lina added, sounding a little discouraged, "For a tall girl like me it is difficult to find a man fifteen centimeters taller and at the same time with many good points. You are the only one who measures up. As for Party membership and a good job, I don't see much difficulty in resolving those things."

Lina gave five reasons clearly and readily, which made Kang feel both disappointed as well as impressed.

Sure enough, before long, Kang joined the Party and became the director of the general office of the factory. On the job, he gained more experience, and was afterwards transferred to the local government supply bureau and appointed a section chief. Kang was on top of the world, and the two years passed quickly. Within so short a time, Kang became another person. Success in his career is a man's best nourishment. Recognition by society is a man's best tonic. Fame and gain are simply fuel for a man's vitality. Now there remained no trace of listlessness about him. He looked full of vigor. He was always smartly dressed. When speaking, his voice was resonant and full of confidence. He could be called a handsome, elegant young man.

One Saturday evening that winter, Lina invited Kang home to keep her company since her parents were out of town. After dinner, it began to snow. The dancing snowflakes fell heavily but quietly. They watched the falling snow through the window in a cozy, warm room while chatting about it. Lina kept saying it was too warm inside. Her cheeks were rosy, her eyes shining. She shed her jacket first. After a while, she took off her pullover. Finally she only had a pink blouse on. Wave upon wave of a young woman's warmth, so mysterious and enticing, assaulted Kang. Kang grew hot all over. A strong urge kept pumping within him. His eyes were locked on her. They teased, flirted with each other—half earnest, half fooling around—then finally, in a fluster, made love.

Afterwards, it suddenly dawned on Lina that they had done something improper. Deeply ashamed, she buried her head in her pillow and wept. "What a lousy thing I have done," Kang thought. "This was sheer stupidity! The consequences could be unthinkable. It is me who should cry!"

4

Kang broke down crying that night after his first time with a woman, a night filled with lovely snowflakes.

He had murmured soft words to her in hoping to console her, tucked the quilt for her and then fled like a thief to the guest room. He gulped down a big glass of water and fell on to the bed, unable to hold back the tears that streamed down his face...

Early the next morning, Kang left, leaving a simple note for Lina. Heading into the wind and snow, he walked for the best part of the day from Wuchang, crossed the Yangtze and Hanshui River bridges to Hankou, his mind turbulent as the snow swirling around him.

He kept putting off dates with Lina by making all kinds of excuses. Inwardly he was gripped with mixed feelings of shame, guilt and regret. One day, two months later, Lina barged into his place. They had a talk of historic significance.

Lina had obviously lost weight, and looked even more serious, almost cold and harsh. She got right to the point, asking Kang to give a verdict on their relationship. Kang thought for quite a long time and said that it was not that serious. "What's there to explain? Both of us are still young. It is high time we worked hard for the Party and the people. It is also high time we reaped in our achievements. Personal things should come second."

Lina listened carefully and then said, "Do you mean you are going to reject me?"

"Not at all!" Kang butted in. "Please, don't think that way."

"Are you speaking your mind?"

"Of course."

Lina mused for a while, her eyes gleaming murderously. "Comrade Kang Weiye," she said, "you've forced me into this. We've been courting for more than two years. Your status has changed completely. Certainly it is owing to your own efforts, but there was help from my family too. A man must have a heart. If you ditched me two months ago, I wouldn't have said a word. But now our relationship is no longer an ordinary one. You have changed the nature of it. From an innocent girl you have turned me into a woman. You ought to shoulder your responsibility. Listen, Lina is no frivolous person. Once I'm yours, I'm yours forever. I hope you will think it over carefully and give me a definite answer within three days. If you have convincing reasons, I can forgive you. Otherwise, I'll go and talk to the person in charge of your office."

"You are threatening me," said Kang. "What's the point of talking to the office? Do you think they would listen to a one-sided complaint from you?"

"Then you force me to do this. All right, just look at this." She produced a panty from her army satchel. It was dotted with

blood stains and yellowish patches. Hard evidence! Kang in-
haled deeply and said, "OK, I'll give you an answer in three
days."

Three months later, Kang and Lina got married with a grand
wedding ceremony. Three years later, their daughter Dini was
born. That year Kang turned thirty.

5

For years, Kang behaved himself and worked hard. When his
day came to an end, he returned home. Once home, he kept
busy with household chores. Lina at first kept having miscar-
riages. Losing blood many times made her rather weak. Then
when she gave birth to her daughter, she had a massive hemor-
rhage. Now she was a bag of bones. His daughter was small, his
wife feeble. He was busy with work yet his income was meager.
He pedaled a bike to work every morning as the sun rose and returned from work as the sun set. Life was hard for him. But he
braced himself to tackle any difficulty that came his way. Think
of the Red Army in the Long March, and of his own days farm-
ing in the country, he used to say to himself. He struggled tena-
ciously. He was earnest in doing anything no matter how small it
was. He believed that as long as they worked hard, they would
move step by step towards their ideal life.

As Kang had expected, Lina treasured this little family of
theirs. She was able to ceaselessly bring home things from her
parents, from appliances to fruit and vegetables, and always
with a good reason. Whatever their neighbors had, they had
too. At least they had a decent life in the eyes of their relatives
and friends. It was a life not lacking in material comforts. Naturally Lina wore the pants at home. Kang did not mind at all.

He could not care less about such trifles as shopping and cooking. It was Kang's parents who grew impatient with Lina's
growing tyranny and their son's chickenheartedness.

In 1980, a year after their marriage, Lina brought home a
document one day from her father. It was a speech made by
Deng Xiaoping at a politburo meeting. She was engrossed in it,
even reading it in the toilet, a red and blue pencil in her hand.
Afterwards, she announced a piece of shocking news, "It seems
my father is finished. All veterans will have to step down. A
great number of youngsters with academic degrees will be promoted. Weiye, from now on, you must get ready to do something solid and impressive so as to create a good impression on
your management."

Kang said jokingly, "Is it that serious? Do I have such a good
chance?"

Lina knit her brows and scolded, "Don't you sense something?
You don't have any sense of politics. It would be too late for regrets when the time comes."

"All right," said Kang, "what you predict must be correct."
But inwardly he found it ridiculous.

Unfortunately, as it turned out, what Lina predicted was correct and what Kang thought turned out ridiculous. At the 12th
National Conference of the Chinese Communist Party in 1982,
the Central Advisory Committee of the Party was founded with
Deng Xiaoping as its head. All its members were aged veterans.
Since Deng took the lead, the veterans had nothing to complain
about. The system of "once a leader, always a leader" was abol-
ished. After that, a million army men were demobilized. Lina's
father's army career came to an end.

Kang meanwhile did not do as well as expected and was

dropped from the list of candidates for office director. Lina, who had lately been in a very bad mood, meant to settle accounts with her husband. "Now look at you. Do you still think it is not serious enough?"

Kang was speechless. Lina began a tirade, calling him daft and muddleheaded. She warned that he must wake up and mend his ways or his future would be ruined.

Not able to bear it, Kang retorted, "You might have a point—but must you be so harsh? The majority in the streets are just ordinary people. So what? After all I am a section chief at least!"

Lina sniggered. "There you go again. You just won't listen to me. Wake up, why don't you! Nowadays, the old ones get retired, while the younger ones get promoted. A man in his thirties, a mere section chief—to hell with you! Just you wait and see!"

Again, facts showed up that what Lina said was right and Kang was the fool. The higher you climbed up in the civil service, the more you had to work for and worry about people and, at the same time, the better the treatment. When Lina's father had been in power, he had a car to travel around in, a good canteen to dine in. There were free tickets for the cinema and theater. If he fell ill, he was given the best possible medical treatment and medicine. At home there were several telephones with or without extensions. He could just pick one up and talk to anyone free of charge even if they happened to be living on the other side of the world. When cooking gas ran out, privates waiting on him would bring him a new canister of gas. Even the maid had been provided by the army. All these could not be calculated in terms of money. Put it this way: Lina never had to worry

about her clothes, food, living and traveling expenses when she
was under that roof. It was people like Lina who glared at others but never vice versa. No one would say "no" to them. Kang,
after marrying into this family, enjoyed all those privileges and,
without realizing it, had gotten used to it. He never realized he
was privileged too, not in the least. But life was changing.
Gradually he found the medicine in the drawer beginning to pe-
ter out. Lina no longer brought home fresh meat. When his
daughter, Dini, had her birthday party or felt unwell, no car
was sent to pick her up...

They often had to squeeze into packed buses, to stand in a
queue in a hospital and pay for medical treatment. Many a time
they were cold-shouldered. Even at the food market, they had
many unhappy experiences. Though they asked for lean meat,
they were forced to take a fatty chunk despite their protests.
"Take it or leave it" was the reply. Another headache was the
nanny. They had to find one themselves of course. The first one
was unsuitable. The second suffered from liver disease. The
third ate and drank behind their backs and liked to get away
with small things. If she thought the New Year's gift for her was
not good enough, she would stage a strike. All these things
greatly annoyed Kang. Lina simply couldn't take it—she became
very edgy and often picked quarrels with others. Kang tried to
pacify her. But as soon as he opened his mouth, she would
throw a tantrum and put all the blame on her husband for being
mediocre. "If you had listened to me," she said, "and used your
brains, you would at least have been made a department chief.
Our family wouldn't be in such a fix. You are totally good-for-
nothing!"

Kang was burning with rage too. But on second thought, he

decided not to fight it out. Generally speaking, she was right. Only the strongest would survive in this world. But what was there so blame-worthy about him? He asked himself if he had done anything wrong. The answer was no. Whether at work or at home, he had done all he could.

The turning point for the Kangs began when Kang decided to give up his job in the civil service and go into business. There were many reasons for him to make such a big decision. But the most important one was that he could no longer stand their present stagnating life. In for a penny, in for a pound—he would show them! Should he fail, he would throw himself out of a high-rise window. After all, he had only one child. She would be well looked after by both paternal and maternal grandparents. Lina had all along been keen on the state economic reform. Many of her friends did business and had hit the jackpot. Sometimes she could not help talking to Kang about them. Now when Kang put his foot down, she became hesitant. A woman with her background did not like the idea of going into business—better to be an official. After all, Kang would lose his "iron ricebowl," a secure job, once he resigned. His bureau would no longer take care of his health care, retirement pension, benefits for his child nor compensation in case of death. Who could give them guarantees that ill fortune would not befall them in the future? This was a difficult decision to make. Lina could not push her husband to take such a risk.

But this time it was Kang himself who made the decision. He had been to Beijing on business and happened to meet with He Hanru in the Palace Hotel. Hanru had been Lina's classmate in middle school, and his classmate in primary school. During the chaotic years of the "Cultural Revolution," they had worked the land together in the countryside. For a period of time, they had been bosom buddies. Afterwards, Hanru had been assigned to work in a small workshop under the neighborhood committee just because his father had been a capitalist. But he had worked there only a couple of months and then fled to Xinjiang to join one of his relatives there. Before he set off, Kang had thrown a farewell party for a tearful Hanru and collected donations for his ticket. Now in this grand hotel, Hanru was transformed beyond recognition. He had his hair creamed and neatly combed back. White shirt, smart suit, perfumed all over with a mobile phone in hand. He invited Kang to a late afternoon tea—a spread of dimsum. "The most popular food for you Chinese today is Cantonese cuisine," he said. "Don't stare at me like that. I am a citizen of the Marshall Islands now."

Kang's eyes grew wider. He would never have thought the world had changed so fast. He Hanru had become a foreigner! This citizen of the Marshall Islands worked for an American company based in China. According to his business card, he was a general manager. He said his annual income was two hundred thousand American dollars. "I've brought China several large hydropower stations already," he said, sounding like a big shot.

"My official congratulations—to hell with you, Hanru!" Kang said.

They punched each other and broke into hearty laughter.

Hanru took another room in the hotel for Kang and they had a good talk that night. They reminisced about the old days and discussed the future. Kang accepted Hanru's offer to start a branch company in Wuhan. That's what is called "seize the opportunity, join the tide of reform," Kang said to himself.

The day Kang resigned, he and his wife sat up in bed without a wink of sleep the whole night. Like an arrow poised on a bow, for Kang there was no turning back. He was feeling particularly decisive and determined. The rearing of the child, the household chores and so on had to be left to Lina. To go into business was like going on to a battlefield, he said, and he would have no time for the family. The sufferings of the past few years that Lina had gone through made her very supportive of her husband's decision, though the fact was she had cherished hopes that as long as Kang worked on without tripping up in the office, there had been hope for his promotion—and a comfortable and steady life would have then been assured. One important reason Kang had made such a decision was that he thoroughly understood Lina's mind. She was touched. Her knitted brows smoothed, her voice becoming soft, Lina had never been so compliant. She nodded and told him not to worry about the home front since Dini was quite big now. Besides she was adored by her grandparents on both sides. Lina herself would take care of her schooling.

Though it was midnight, Lina made a long-distance call to He Hanru in Beijing: "So I'll give Kang Weiye to you now. You may cheat anyone but never him! You know my father's temper. If you should fool his son-in-law, he might shoot you."

Lina, as though talking to a child, encouraged Kang, "Go ahead! With your education, with your brains and talent, with your connections from work over so many years and the connections of both families, you are bound to do better than those uncultured self-employed individuals who have no connections. Even if you should fail, we still have nothing to lose. I am working for the government. A family needs only one to be employed by the government. Don't you agree?"

"Sure. As always you are right." This time Kang's praise was genuine. Moved, he held her hand and kept on chatting. Finally Lina said, pointing to his heart, "Kang, after you have made a pile, you must never ever have any affairs with women. If you do, I'll end our lives together."

"What are you talking about?" Kang retorted. "Such an insult! What do you take me for? A womanizer? Don't you know me after ten years of life together?"

"Make a vow then," said Lina.

"I swear if I take another woman, I will perish."

Lina instantly covered his mouth. Both of them found it ridiculous. After daybreak, Kang, like an eagle long confined deep in a mountain, flew into the boundless blue sky, leaving his dusty bike, that he had pedaled to work with every day, lying in a corner of the corridor.

6

All that had happened in the past became the past. Kang Weiye's revolutionary decision enabled him to start a new career. Office work grew distant, odds and ends at home faded out, as did Lina. Kang started out a "good-for-nothing" and turned into a man rolling in money.

Lina's purse began to bulge. They had their rooms installed with a two-in-one air-conditioner, and bought an automatic washing machine. Their small TV set was replaced with a large one, their old refrigerator with a new one. When shopping for meat, no one would glare at her. As long as she had a bulging purse, she could get the choicest cuts of meat. She would never be worried about medicine. Doctors would not give her good imported medicine on a health care program, but she could always find what she needed in the pharmacies. As this little family was turning rich, Kang was going through certain changes himself though that Lina was not so keen about. Take his hair-do for example. In the past, Kang had spent fifty cents in a small barbershop run by the neighborhood committee. All he had required was to have his hair cut short. Now he preferred to go to the Shanghai Beauty Salon for a haircut. He asked for cologne and conditioning mousse especially for men. He had not cared much about his clothes in the past, wearing whatever Lina had bought him. But now he had suits, causal wear, and favored designer labels. Lina could no longer buy any clothes for him. For years, when introducing her to others, he would say, "This is my *airen* (beloved)." Now he called her his "*Taitai* (Madam/wife)." Lina did not like terms like "Miss" or "Madam." They reminded her of the old society. It was decadent, she thought. So she had protested, "I am a member of the Chinese Communist Party, a cadre. Don't call me '*Taitai*!' If you don't like the word '*airen*,' then just call me 'Comrade Lina.' How nice to be called 'comrade!'" Kang stopped calling her "Madam," but didn't call her "comrade." Lina was so serious about Kang's changing mentality, she consulted some psychiatrists in the Academy. Her colleagues knew Kang well and told her Kang's changes were natural and normal. It would be abnormal, they said, if a businessman acted like a government official. Lina thought it over and observed the outside world. Finally she had to accept it. All things have both advantages and disadvantages. One could not butter one's bread on both sides—Lina certainly knew better than that. And Kang knew well how to behave himself. For example, he had female secretaries for several years, but there had been nothing unusual between them. After all Kang Weiye was Kang Weiye, one of

the generations raised by Mao Zedong. No ordinary businessmen
could match him.

What was most important was that he brought home more and
more money. This made Lina buoyant and proud. She began to
gain weight, to like wearing smart clothes. Time to time, she
would buy some gifts for her parents. She would ask the taxi
driver to drive the taxi right up to her parents' door. When decorating and refurnishing one's home became the vogue, she had
to keep up. Kang not only agreed with her ideas but also instantly gave her a fat stack of bank notes. She went to great trouble
to turn their apartment into rooms resembling a hotel. The ceiling of the sitting room was dotted with colorful lights. It was
full of a festive atmosphere every day. Soon she became the center of admiration. Everybody would say to her, "Fortune is
smiling on you. Your husband is so nice, so capable, bringing
you all the money you need." "Bah!" she would say, but with a
small smile betraying her. "All you know is the facade. How
can you call him capable? What money has he earned? It is not
easy to do business these days. What fortune do I have? A businessman rarely stays at home. Things big or small all fall on my
shoulders. What a life!"

As life was easy and comfortable, time for Lina seemed to slip
away quickly. Several years passed. As for Kang Weiye, time
had not slipped away unheeded during the past few years. When
he had talked to He Hanru in the Palace Hotel that year, then
he had not believed that it was so difficult to do business. But he
immediately experienced all the hardships he could not have
imagined. It was like learning how to swim when he had been a
boy. He seemed wholly submerged in darkness and unable to
stay in one spot. His hands were unable to find anything to

grasp on to. He could not beat a retreat now, nor could he give up or run away. The only way to hold on to life was to struggle. Nothing else would work. Since entering business, he had been undergoing tremendous changes every day, every hour, every minute. How could Lina, her mind sown with the seeds of orthodoxy, understand all this? How could she accept it?

At the beginning, Kang did not realize that he would slip out of Lina's grip—after all they had lived together for more than a decade. Whenever he returned home from a business trip, he was enthusiastic and warm. No matter how busy, he would put on the clothes he had bought from Hong Kong or the United States to show them to Lina and tell her the interesting things he had seen abroad. At first, Lina nodded in admiration. But soon she became silent. Gradually there was an indifference in her silence. Her indifference then turned into disdain, and then disgust. The look on her face suddenly made Kang realize that he was like a worm wrapping himself up with his own silk thread. He had to be careful. He bought a wardrobe and a single bed and put them in his office suite. Whenever he bought some clothes, he would leave part of them in his suite. At the same time, he began a "peaceful evolutionary" approach to change Lina, trying to reform her, from her ideas to her lifestyle. Now and then he would buy her lipstick, bottles of perfume, or pairs of stockings. As well, he taught her how to use them. He did all this for Lina. He knew her too well. The generation of his age had been brought up in poverty and had gotten used to a poor life. What was more, they had taken pride in living in poverty. Kang hoped that Lina would soon catch up with the changing times. They had been man and wife for years now. They had gone through hard times together when in their prime. They had a lovely daughter, Kang Dini. Kang believed that they had been successful so far and should never split. Forty-year-old Kang did not want to see any fire in his backyard, since the victim would be no one but their daughter. At the thought of his darling daughter, he was willing to give up anything. It was true that he was somewhat afraid of his wife. From the day their paths crossed over ten years ago, Lina had always had the upper hand on him. He didn't know why, but each time he grew an inch, she managed to shoot up a foot.

Lina did not appear to be swayed or corrupted by his money. She ate what she had to eat, wore what she had to wear, not letting slip any chances to enjoy a better life thanks to Kang's money—but she somehow remained her old self.

Early spring 1992. He Hanru, together with his project manager Pearl Lin, came to Wuhan to discuss an important deal with Kang Weiye. They wanted Kang to persuade the management of a large hydropower station under construction to purchase some US-made components and parts for which Hanru was the agent. If they could make the deal, Kang and Hanru would be able to get a commission of ten per cent of the price, that is, 140,000 US dollars. Hanru was responsible for providing business information and Pearl Lin was in charge of the project and gave assistance from the head office in Beijing, while Kang was to head a team of specialists for the negotiation and import of those components and parts. It was no easy job rounding up a team of experts to convince some high-ranking officials. Therefore, Hanru said, once the job was done, he would get 40,000 dollars and Kang 100,000 dollars as remuneration. He would remit the money from the United States and deposit it in Kang's Hong Kong bank account. Having discussed everything, Pearl Lin handed Kang 5,000 dollars for expenses. Americans believed that only money could get things done. In the early '90s, one dollar was worth ten or more Chinese yuan in the black market. Hanru stuffed the fat stack of hard currency into Kang's pocket. Yet he did not ask for a receipt. Kang knew this was a trustworthy friend. He also knew that he had won himself respect and trust with dozens of years of honesty and integrity.

As soon as they left, Kang went into action. He invited people to meals, to play tennis. He talked to one person one day and another the next. To wait for an international call or fax, he had his meals delivered to work and slept on that single bed in his office. His mobile phone kept ringing. His secretary was on call at all times and arranged for Kang to fly to Beijing or anywhere else at any minute.

Lina pressed him to tell her, "What business are you busy with? How come you are so busy?"

Kang replied, "Nothing special. One must seize the opportunity in doing business. Once the ball is rolling, we have to go all out."

Lina would not let him go so easily, "I hear that Hanru brought a girl with him when he came. Was that so?"

Kang said, "Oh please! Don't put your nose into others' personal affairs."

Believing that "to condone evil is to encourage the evil-doer," Lina warned Kang, "You must be careful of yourself. He who gets too close to vermilion becomes red; he who gets too close to ink becomes black." She had been sharp-tongued all her life, so Kang did not take her words to heart. Despite his busy work, he bought himself a Rolex watch, a Montague leather belt and a pair of English air-cushion leather shoes. He did not care much about the brand of the shoes so long as they were truly imported and fit his feet—and the price well over a thousand yuan, since anything under could only be "shoddy and old-fashioned." But he had been keen on the brand of the watch. A Rolex was a masterpiece of craft, so elegant, so delicate—so perfect. It would last for ages and could be handed down from generation to generation. It was worth buying. In fact, he had intended to buy one long before. This time, it was the result of encouragement from Hanru. Hanru had his theory: If you want to make the greatest deal in the world, you have to have the best gear in the world.

Noticing those articles, Lina asked, "How much have you made? To squander money like that!" She visited a few stores and learned that it had cost Kang altogether 80,000 yuan for the watch, the leather belt and the shoes. She was shocked.

Thinking of Hanru having affairs with women, thinking of Kang's indifference towards her warnings, thinking of the changes in Kang's appearance, speech and demeanor, Lina suddenly realized that he must be trying to pull the wool over her eyes and corrupt her with money. He had already gone very far. If she did not stop him he was bound to go astray one day. The fate of this family would be unthinkable. The more she thought, the more frightened she grew. She firmly resolved to pull him back on track. Everything must be restored to normal. It was true that money was evil. She must be very vigilant about it and would not let money seal off her mouth and numb her mind.

7

After careful and painstaking preparation Lina got set to confront her husband. One day, she called Kang and asked him to come home under the pretext of illness. As soon as Kang entered the apartment, she locked the door and sat down, looking very sternly and pointedly at him. Kang explained to her why he had bought the watch, the belt and the shoes as well as his thinking on such expenses. Then he begged her to let him go, saying he had an urgent matter to deal with. But Lina's reply was a firm "No!"

"Oh please, I truly have something very important to do."

"I think," said Lina, "there is nothing more important than the future of this family of ours. Let's get to the point!" With that, she switched on all the lights in the sitting room as though it was a formal business negotiation. She herself was thoroughly exposed in the blinding lights.

Helpless, Kang took a seat. This was the first time he had had a serious look at her in the past four years since he had gone into business. He had been so busy that Lina had all but become familiar background scenery. He had seemed unaware of her existence—with her everyday clothes, roughly combed hair-do, careless slippers, never anything different. But today it was all different. In the bright light, Kang took a good look and got a shock. Lina was wearing a silk blouse with a colorful, abstract pattern and a cream skirt, black leather pumps and black pantyhose. On her neck was a gold necklace from which dangled a shining heart-shaped pendant. Her chest was no longer full and the skin of her neck was flabby for she had become plump and thin, plump and thin several times. The glittering jewelry did not suit and the necklace on her was a mockery. A woman without curves should not wear a silk blouse. Besides, the blouse was a mass-produced one without style, with the two shoulder pads

so high that her arms appeared artificial. Even less should she
have tucked the lower part of the blouse into the skirt, it only
revealed her round stomach. She was so badly dressed yet
feigned aloofness and elegance. Suddenly Kang remembered the
first time he had met her in the park. White shirt, green army
pants and black velvet shoes, she had been a picture of neatness
and cleanness. With serene features and a cool expression, she
had been pretty and lovely. How could she turn out like this in
the blink of an eye? It had been fifteen years after all. Nothing
particular had happened to torture her in those fifteen years.
How then could a woman develop into such a terrible state?

Lina, meanwhile was giving him a good dressing-down and finally said: "I'm not perfect either. I paid no attention to your
business in the past. From now on, I'll be with you at all your
business meetings. After all we are in the same boat. I've decided to be the chief accountant of your company. Please make all
the necessary arrangements for me."

Kang was so stunned he did not know what to say for a long
while. With Lina having turned so foolish, it seemed he had no
choice but to fight it out today. "The chief accountant is appointed by the head office," he said. "Besides, you know nothing about accounting."

Lina retorted, "I can learn. You know I am quick to pick up
things. I'll talk to Hanru in Beijing myself."

"Talk to Hanru first then." Kang took his mobile phone and
dialed. When it went through, Kang put the phone by Lina.
Hanru, like a little elf hidden in the phone, spoke up: "Hello?
Hello?" Lina jumped up and moved to one end of the sofa. She
stared at the phone and glared at Kang. Then she turned to the
phone again, her face all red. She wanted to turn it off but had

no idea how to do it. Kang had barely switched it off when Lina exploded: "Kang Weiye! Don't push me into a corner! I'll do what I say."

Kang raised his voice too: "Let me tell you this, you are not to go to my company unless I quit the company. The head office would never allow a couple to run a company."

"Why do you refuse to let me work in the company?"

"Why do you insist?"

"You have a guilty conscience, you are afraid, you loathe me. Right?"

She had uttered the very words he had been holding back. So Kang took over and said, "Yes, I loathe you! I loathe being blackmailed!"

"All right," she instantly stood up, erect, clenching her fists, her head held high. She looked like a woman soldier, minus the uniform, ready to fight. "How wonderful! You have let the cat out of bag at last. So you loathe me, eh? Do you remember how humble you were carrying frozen pork and running around? Remember how I helped you step by step? Remember how grateful you were to me? How much meat did I bring you from my family, and how many vegetables did you eat from my family's garden? Remember those things humbled you yet satisfied your vanity? Remember your words, 'Without you, I would not be here today? You are my parents.' Kang Weiye, tell me, do you remember all these things?"

Kang's face turned ashen, and he yelled, "Shut up! Don't force me to say anything hurtful. Open the door quick! Let me go! I am leaving this nasty place."

"Just a moment. You have not answered my question yet. Do you remember or not? Ashamed of yourself, huh? Still want to save face?"

"Duan Lina!" Kang lost control of himself and let loose the most vicious words: "You have simply gone too far! What is there to be ashamed of? I am a man working hard to earn a lot of money to support my wife and child. What is there to be ashamed of? It is you who should be ashamed. You ought to know blackmail is the worst, the dirtiest trick in the world. You resorted to blackmail to get me to marry you. Remember that ridiculous panty of yours? But you will never achieve your ends again. Go and complain to my American boss! Better look at yourself in a mirror first, so you'll know how low you have sunk!"

Lina shouted at the top of her lungs: "Bullshit! You bastard..." But her voice grew weak and she fainted to the ground. Her face had turned deathly pale, blood oozing from her nose.

Lina thus lost her first battle.

Lina was hospitalized for a month. When she was discharged, she was still very weak. Their ten-year-old daughter felt the tension between her parents. Fear was written all over her little face. In front of her father, she would try to please him by saying good things about her mother. In front of her mother, she would do vice versa. Kang, seeing her daughter's feigned smile, felt a pain in his heart. He often came back home to see her. Relations between Kang and Lina became no more than watching TV with their daughter sitting in between. It was a stalemate. But stealthily each tried to get an upper hand on the other. Lina racked her brains every minute trying to find a way to subdue her husband. But Kang had already given her up. To him, she was his daughter's mother. As an up-and-coming man, he had a bright future before him.

8

It was at this juncture that Pearl Lin came into his life. She was a typical southern girl, small and slim in build, with a slightly golden complexion, deep-set eyes, high cheekbones, full red lips, dark and long eyebrows, reminding one of sexy, aggressive types like Sophia Loren. Beauty in the traditional sense was no match for this type of girl, though if China were still isolated, a girl of this type would have been no beauty at all. Luckily, she lived in an era when China was open to the outside world and reform was in full swing. She was born in Guangzhou and brought up in Beijing. She had majored in English at university and could speak Cantonese, the Beijing dialect and was fluent in English with a good accent. These three languages were the basic requirements for a good job in business. Upon graduation, Pearl did not go to the place assigned to her by the university. Instead, she was employed as a secretary by a wholly British-owned enterprise. During the trial period, her monthly salary was 6,000 yuan. When she became a full staff member, she was given an annual salary of 96,000 yuan. After two years, she shifted to an American firm with an annual income of 120,000 yuan. When Kang met her the first time, she was already an experienced, smart businesswoman. She kept up with international fashion trends as far as clothes were concerned. The perfume she used was Chanel. The colors of her clothes were rather out of the ordinary-crab-gray, aquamarine, almond-yellow, dark purple, cherry-red. Ordinary girls did not wear dresses in such colors. Pearl knew her advantages. First, she had a face with sharp features, a body with noticeable curves. Secondly, her skin was most refined, elastic and tanned, a shade all the rich in the world pursue—but whereas rich people had to spend tons of money going to beaches to sun themselves in order to get this tan, Pearl had been born with it. She wore suits no one in the street dared to wear. Her waist-long hair was full and wavy, held together with a delicate clasp at the back of her head, to reveal her full forehead. When walking in the street, she was full of self-confidence and pride, her eyes straight ahead. She was a typical modern girl working in a foreign firm in the city.

Pearl was no stranger to Kang for she had come with He Han-ru once to Wuhan, but that had merely been for business and she had not made much of an impression on Kang. It was like watching the sun rise from the balcony of Kang's home. At first, the sun was remote, something alien. Because of the distance, it looked very clear but without feeling. The sun gradually pierced the clouds and rose inch by inch into the sky, until he could feel its warmth and the glint of its light. The light grew stronger and stronger and its dazzling light blinded his eyes. Bathed in the sun, he began to melt. He could not help it, could not escape. Perhaps this was the fate people talked about, he said to himself.

Shortly after that summer, Pearl was sent to Wuhan by the head office to see how things fared under Kang Weiye. Since she was closely connected with the deal, Kang himself drove a car to pick her up at the airport. It was pouring in Wuhan that day. Thinking the weather in Beijing was no good either and the plane might be delayed, he called Pearl before going to the airport. Her reply was very brief: "The plane will take off as scheduled. I'm now boarding the plane." Kang raced his car towards Nanhu Airport in Wuchang. The flight usually took one hour and forty minutes from Beijing to Wuchang. But you could never be sure how long it would take from Wuhan to Wuchang by car because of traffic jams or waiting for a train to pass. He had broken into a sweat by the time he got to the airport. But Pearl did not arrive as planned. Kang waited in the airport for three hours like an ant on a hot pan. He kept dialing his phone and repeatedly went to the information desk. He was told both by the loudspeaker and the information desk that the plane was delayed due to the weather. Hanru was in the United States, and the people in the head office could only tell him that Miss Pearl Lin was flying to Wuchang. No one could help him and he could only wait patiently. So their first encounter was not smooth, and somewhat dramatic. They had only met once before and their exchange of words had been brief. This time when they caught sight of each other in the distance, they began to smile despite the people milling around them. Pearl took off her little silk scarf from her neck and waved it energetically at Kang. Pearl's good looks and unique style of dress attracted the eyes of several men besides Kang. He pretended to be nonchalant but at heart was very pleased. As a man, he had never had such a feeling. It was refreshing and stimulating. But on second thought, he began to shake himself out of it. What was Pearl to him? What was the point of lapsing into such a dream? Instantly, the feeling turned sour. It was difficult to describe with words. And he looked solemn again. He shook hands with her as a manager of the branch company and uttered the standard words, "Your presence is most welcome." Pearl replied quickly, "Thank you for coming to meet me, Manager Kang." Noticing Pearl becoming businesslike, Kang blamed himself for overdoing it. So he cracked a joke, "Got hijacked?"

Sure enough, Pearl became relaxed. Smiling, she said, "Pity

no one hijacked the plane." She had come by Air China, which was widely reputed for its safety. "The flight was actually punctual but the plane could not land because the runway was slippery after a downpour. So it flew back to Beijing. When the plane got back to Beijing, the passengers were not allowed to leave the plane. So I was unable to get in touch with you. I was quite desperate. It was hopeless and I had to steer my thoughts in another direction: Does it indicate that I would run into a little trouble at first when assisting you, then things turn out smooth later? Or maybe the flight trouble I had may cancel out later setbacks on the work front? Manager Kang, do you believe in such stuff? I have some religious leanings. I'm the kind of employee who does what I am told. At heart I do hope everything goes well for me and thus I may win a nod from my boss. So sometimes I do pray to God for blessings."

While listening, Kang could not help feeling surprised: What a sharp girl! My estimation of her was all wrong. We were talking about the delay of the flight, yet she smoothly diverted the topic to work. She is here to inspect my work, yet she only said it is to assist me. She was trying to flatter me first, thinking I might be unhappy about her coming. So she hinted that she was aware of the problems and hoped I would not give her a hard time. She was only doing her job. What is smart about her is that she came to the point in a natural way as soon as she arrived. A difficult situation was handled in an easy way. Kang had to change his attitude towards her. He had mixed feelings of admiration, respect, vigilance and relief. To work with such a bright woman, all you had to do was hint at something and she would understand it all.

So Kang came to the point too. "You are really smart, Miss

Lin! I also believe that your troubles have been suspended out by this trip. With me here, everything should go smoothly from now on. I can assure you."

Pearl shot him an understanding glance. The sound of her young, healthy, resonant voice flew about merrily in the car much like that of a bird's song. "Manager Kang, you are a nice guy. Manager Kang, could you now do me a favor? I'm hungry. I could not touch the food on the flight." Pearl certainly knew how to measure her words. She said what she wanted and stopped at the right moment. Now she acted like a spoilt child to please a man, but no further either.

"Say, what do you fancy eating?" said Kang, his heart singing.

"The faster the better!" she said. "Any restaurant will do as long as it's clean. I don't have to change, to put on any makeup. There's no need for formality, endless toasts, or fancy dishes. Just a soup, a couple of dishes, a bit of rice, a plate of fruit. Manager Kang, you have no objections, I hope?"

"Several of my deputies and some department chiefs are waiting at a restaurant to give you a welcome dinner."

Pearl sat back, looking disappointed, and said in dismay, "Again! I understand. Doing business, eh! OK, thank you, Manager Kang."

With one hand on the steering wheel, he flicked open his mobile phone and told his subordinates that the plane was delayed and there was no need to wait. Then he found a restaurant in Wuchang that satisfied Pearl's wishes. Of course it was no ordinary restaurant. An ordinary restaurant served no fruit. It was not simply two or three dishes on the table as Pearl had asked. Kang asked for a deluxe room with audio and video facilities.

The table was covered with a tablecloth. Pearl was most pleased and kept thanking Kang and God. When the food was brought to her, she said, "Manager Kang, I've changed my mind. Shall we have a little drink?"

Of course, Kang agreed. As a man made of flesh and blood, Kang could not resist a beautiful young girl's charms. "You know more about foreign wines, I'll leave it to you," he said.

"Why foreign wine?" she retorted. "Do you think I'm a girl fond of things ostentatious? Or do you think I've become a foreigner's slave just because I'm working in a foreign firm?" She ordered two glasses of Dynasty Dry. Kang loved Dynasty. How could she know this was his favorite, he wondered? Was it a coincidence or had she done some homework before coming here? No matter what it was, he felt closer to her. With the soft music of some pop songs in the background, they clinked wine glasses and toasted each other for successful partnership, for a good start of a genuine meeting of minds, for health, for friendship, for this wonderful evening brought about by the delay of the flight. Cheers!

It was indeed a wonderful evening. It was beyond all of Kang's expectations—Pearl was extraordinarily astute, quick-witted and her face shone when she spoke. He had barely uttered a word to her when she had come with Hanru. On the surface, Kang had shown respect to her but had thought to himself that she was but a decorative vase for Hanru. But now after this short episode, Kang looked at her in a new light. She made his heart thump. Kang did not dare to think any further. A wonderful evening, an evening worth remembering—he stopped at that.

Pearl Lin stayed in Wuhan for three days. They were three

hard-working days for both Pearl and Kang. They hit it off well. Pearl was strict, earnest and devoted to work. She even made a number of good suggestions. She had bought a return ticket and her schedule had all been fixed. Kang could not go and see her off at the airport since he happened to have a business appointment which could not be changed at such short notice. Kang said goodbye to her in the lobby of her hotel. When shaking hands, their fingers gripped with an extra tightness, and it was slightly longer than a usual handshake. However, nothing showed on their faces.

That night, Kang realized that he was actually worrying about her trip home. After much hesitation, he picked up the phone. Pearl cried out in delight at the other end: "Manager Kang!"

"How was the trip?" he asked.

"Very smooth" was the reply.

Kang rang off. After all, he had no guts to go further.

9

It was the end of the year when Pearl Lin came to Wuhan again. The Chinese New Year was on the threshold. Traditionally, people visited one another on this occasion, so Kang planned to take this opportunity to single out a few key people in the hope that he would have more orders in the new year. He Hanru called from the United States: "I would like to ask Pearl to give you a hand. She knows what to buy. Perhaps you need such a consultant at times. Women have a genius for bribery."

It seemed nice of them to send him a consultant—yet obviously she would be here to supervise his work, to keep an eye on him. It was okay for her to do some shopping, but to take presents to prospective clients would be his job alone. He kept in touch with them himself, and naturally it was just he who could do such transactions. He was not so daft as to let someone else to put their fingers in the pie.

Before he even touched the subject, Pearl said of her own initiative, "Manager Kang, I must make it clear now. All I'll do is go shopping with you and when you go out on business, I'll curl up in the hotel room and watch TV."

"That's fine," said Kang, relieved. What a clever girl, he said to himself. How could a man not like her?

Kang was a man of world, after all. He was able to pretend that he had no personal feelings for her. This time when she came, Kang had asked a deputy manager to meet her at the airport. He had called a meeting of key persons in the company and stressed that they should "be on guard internally but relaxed externally" towards Pearl Lin. No one should mention anything concerning their business to her. He knew none of them could match Pearl.

Kang invited Pearl to a welcome dinner in a restaurant at a four-star hotel. A table was laid out with a dozen men and women from the company sitting around. All the men were in suits and all the women in skirts. As soon as Pearl got to the hotel, she spent more than an hour in her room. When she came out, she was in an orange-colored cashmere overcoat. As she entered the dinner room, she took off her overcoat and revealed her black evening dress, a diamond necklace and a pair of diamond earrings. Her deep-set eyes resembled pools of limpid water sparkling with stars. Beneath them were her rosy lips, tempting and seductive.

Pearl's appearance and demeanor stunned all present. Obviously there was a world of difference between them and their guest. After a few cups of wine, they were busy eating, drinking and chatting, ignoring Pearl. Waitresses kept coming in and out just to have a look at Pearl. Some stood in a corner staring at her. Pearl felt awkward and embarrassed. At this critical moment, Kang came to her rescue. He said Pearl looked a bit tired and she might go to her room to rest if she wished. Holding her temple, she expressed her gratitude and apologized for leaving first. After that she hurried back to her own room. Kang stayed back and enjoyed the dinner together with his subordinates. Afterwards, he asked his driver to drive him home. Another spate of emotion thus dissipated.

On Kang Weiye's horizons, Pearl Lin was not like a star rising steadily upwards. There were always clouds and mist, obscuring her from time to time. Kang had all the excuses under heaven not to see her, yet so many reasons and events brought them together. A middle-aged man, Kang had seen a lot of the world, however, he was rather ignorant about love. He had no idea that one should not hesitate about love. Pearl, a girl of the times, had had so many boyfriends that she had lost count of the number of them. Her principle towards love was very simple: date him if he is worthy of love, ditch him if he is not. So it was not difficult to deal with her. Just tell her: "I love you" or "I don't love you," as simple as that. But Kang's hesitation kept Pearl in suspense. She found it refreshing and exciting. In her eyes, Kang was a cut above others. He was so unfathomable, so steady and so good at controlling his feelings. It was very rare to meet a man of this caliber. Such a man would not easily fall in love. But once he fell for someone, he would be head over heels in love with her. Kang's hesitation aroused this modern young woman who nurtured hidden dreams of romance.

Kang was like a piece of dough, becoming more resilient with the kneading. This had never happened to him before. For the past few years, he had been running around doing business. He had been to many places and spent many an evening in a nightclub or a pub. He did meet a couple of pretty young women who had tried to hit on him. But he was able to resist such temptations. Now what had come over him? He just could not forget her. Was this love? He wondered.

Even if it was love, he concluded, he should avoid it. It was all too complicated. On the one side, he was a man in his forties and had a wife; on the other, she was a young woman just beginning to flower, modern and fashionable. What consequences would lie in wait for him? Oh, better to just forget it!

To reinforce his decision, he amended his plans to go on a business trip with Pearl alone. Instead he chose to have a veteran secretary, Old Plum, accompany them despite the risk that she might talk. Right before they set off for the trip, Pearl discovered that Old Plum would go with them. Old Plum was wearing a gaudy gauze scarf, her face made up with shoddy cosmetics. Pearl almost fainted. She withdrew from the door of the car and said she would like to have a word with Kang in private. But Kang's secretary said, "Miss Lin, we've got to catch the train. You will have lots of time to talk to him on the train because we've booked a deluxe compartment."

Not looking at the secretary, Pearl said, "If we fail to catch this train, there will always be another. It is not me but headquarters in the United States which needs to talk to him."

Pearl woke He Hanru up from his slumber in the United States around midnight and wanted him to talk to Kang Weiye. Hanru said over the phone, very annoyed, "Weiye! Pearl is the only one who knows up this deal of ours. People will be very envious if they learn you could make a hundred thousand bucks out of this deal."

"I know. I will be very careful arranging everything. But I never go on a business trip with a woman alone."

That sent Hanru into peals of laughter. "Are you telling me that you sleep only with one woman, eh?" he asked as a joke.

Pulling a long face, Pearl got on the train. She was polite towards Old Plum and spoke very little to Kang. Kang did not seem to mind at all. Sipping a cup of tea Old Plum had poured for him, he sat in the corridor outside the compartment, watching the scenery go by outside the window and cooking up his plans of how to deliver the presents. Pearl was lying down on her berth and had opened a magazine to read. She stared at the page but never turned it over. Old Plum thought she was the most needed person now and became very energetic. One moment, she went out and said to Kang, "Manager Kang, don't pull a long face like that on Miss Lin. Find an excuse to make her feel better. There is no need to offend an up-and-coming star at the head office." The next moment, she tried to pacify Pearl. She started by praising Pearl's good looks and then shifted the topic to Kang. She said that Manager Kang was upright, straightforward, easy-going and kindhearted. How clever Pearl was! She rolled over and called her "Sister" in a warm voice and said her bad mood had nothing to do with Kang. She was upset because of some mild criticism from headquarters. She would take the initiative and speak to him in a moment. Seeing the outcome of her work, Old Plum was delighted. With a little prompting from Pearl, she rattled away about Kang. She told Pearl that Kang had become prominent at a very young age. The

Minister of Water Conservation thought highly of him. Because
of his talent, he was praised highly by the Municipal Party Committee. He had joined the Party and was appointed a department
chief when still very young. Later he had the farsightedness to
give up his official post and plunge into the sea of business.
Kang was also a family man. He knew how to love his wife,
how to raise his daughter. And he never casually mixed with
girls. She also mentioned that his wife's parents were high-ranking army officers, and how sharp and smart his wife was. As she
spoke, Pearl kept nodding her head. From time to time, she uttered a sound of amazement or sighed with her hand over her
mouth, which made Old Plum even more excited and talkative.

Then Kang appeared at the door and said, "Old Plum, go to
the dining car and book a table. Bring back a snack for you and
Pearl." As soon as she left, Kang said to Pearl in a serious tone,
"A clever person like you shouldn't be so nosy."

"With that Old Plum of yours, did I need query? It is you who
brought her along. A clever man like you should never do a
thing like that. You've lifted a rock only to drop it on your own
toes."

Pearl had not only dropped all formality in addressing him,
but was also nonchalantly kicking her feet in mid-air while lying
on her berth. Her feet were delicate and crimson toenails could
be seen through her stockings. A beautiful anklet dangled above
one foot.

Kang glanced at her feet and instantly withdrew his eyes.
"What a devilish girl you are!" he said. "Let's see if I can't kick
you off this train!"

"Come and try, come and try!" said Pearl.

At this, their eyes locked. Pearl leapt up and kissed him on the cheek and promptly returned to the berth. She stretched her hand toward Kang. Kang took her hand and put it on his lips. Then he went to the corridor. Just as he sat down, Old Plum walked unsteadily back.

Within such a short time, their gloominess had gone. The sun had risen. The few months of a tug-of-war had played the role of yeast in a brewery, allowing the wine of emotion to grow even more pungent and stronger. However, with Old Plum around, they could not dare to lose self-control and gulp it heartily down. All they could do was have a sip on the sly sometimes. Then there was a long time relishing it. This was the best catalyst for love, taking no risks yet promoting the development of their relationship.

Both Kang and Pearl had enough experience with love to know the benefits at times of self-restraint. They did not send Old Plum back, instead the three of them traveled to Yichang, Chongqing, Shanghai and Beijing. On the way, Pearl did all she could to win Old Plum over, making her feel that Pearl was a very nice, agreeable young woman willing to dote on her. Pearl had turned the tables, and got what she had wanted, so that she became even more charming, her eyes more aglow. Kang, with such a beauty beside him, was in good mettle. As it turned out the trip gleaned far greater results than he had expected.

10

The day came at last. It was a fine spring morning when Kang flew to Beijing for his date. It was the first time he had felt such longing and excitement, a flurry of sweetness. A man over forty seemed to have metamorphosed into a boy of eighteen. Unable to control himself, he seemed full of impetuosity and kept smiling to himself. He told himself with a feeling of repentance: this is as it should be and should have come earlier. The thing he had missed or lost before had been recovered by him at last.

As soon as he mounted the ramp leading to the entrance of the aircraft, he left all worldly things on the ground: his savings deposit, company, business, family, close relations, fax, telephone, appointments, negotiations, opportunities, and the notice of good tidings of a hundred thousand US dollars deposited into his Hong Kong bank account by He Hanru at any moment... The deal had been a success. When the news had come to him not long before, he became besides himself with joy. A deal without a cent of capital up front, a deal netting him a million Chinese yuan! What a god-given gift! Now he had shed all those earthly burdens which his life had completely been centered on. To hell with them, just this once! The earth was still circling around, wasn't it? He was no long a manager, no longer a son, a husband or a father. He was but a lover! As he lowered his head and entered the cabin, he felt as if he were entering a time tunnel. He would go through this one-hour-forty-minute time tunnel. At the other end of the tunnel was a place called Beijing. To him, the name of Beijing was tantamount to the Garden of Eden.

Pearl was waiting at the arrival gate in the airport. Kang, whose eyes were filled with love, could not make out what Pearl was wearing. All he saw was a grain of gold gleaming in a pile of sand. Pearl threw him a kiss which made Kang feel as if he had entered straight into the Eden.

A standard suite on the top floor of the Great Wall Sheraton Hotel was awaiting them. Kang had booked it through an international travel agency on the Internet.

There was not a soul in the long corridor. The floor carpet was thick and soft. The whole world seemed to whirl around Kang Weiye. The door was opened and then closed. Before it was shut, Pearl hung the "Please do not disturb" sign on the outside knob. The instant the door clicked softly shut, Pearl kicked off her shoes and threw off her bag. She stretched out her arms and threw herself into Kang's embrace. When she could speak, the first sentence she uttered was, "I love you! I love you, love you!" Her face glowed, her eyes moistened, she had gone insane. With her hot hands, she fondled Kang whose bones were still smarting with regret and hidden pain. For this moment, Kang felt, he could not thank her enough. He held her petite body and kissed her without cease. He was unable to speak. At last he murmured, "I'm dying for you!"

Repressed feelings which had built up inside him for over a decade, now burst out. It was like a surging tide that drowned Pearl. Like a fish in water, Pearl frolicked along wave upon wave of surging tide. One wave behind pushed the wave in front. Before one wave eased out, another wave began to rise. Kang could not believe that this man with such virility was but himself. Finally Pearl hid herself in the bathroom, saying, "I used to know our company had a renowned entrepreneur, but now I know he is also a famous madman!"

"OK, I accept your criticism," said Kang, rather ashamedly. "Now come out, will you?"

Pearl came out and put her hands on his shoulders and said meaningfully, "It is my turn now." She took his hand and introduced Kang into a world of love that was totally new to him.

Then after getting dressed up, they went to dine in a small restaurant of the hotel. The expensive service charge and simple

food put off many a customer. However, this was exactly what
Kang and Pearl needed. In the first place, they did not have to
go out and change settings. Secondly, they just signed for the
payment which was more elegant than paying in cash. Signing
went well with love. Pearl chose a little table beside a French
window. Nearby was a tall Brazil-nut tree. Soft music seemed to
be wafting out from those green leaves and lingering over the
leaping flames of the candles. They sat facing each other with
only the light of candles encircling them. Laid on the table were
a few plates of dishes decorated with beautifully sculpted carrot
flowers and lacy lettuce leaves. Two wineglasses were half-filled
with red wine. When it was time to end the meal, Pearl waved a
finger and a waitress came over immediately and began to clear
the table. Then there came a crystal plate of fruit: red strawber-
ries and watermelon, purple grapes, yellow honeymelon and
green kiwi fruit. In a five-star hotel, fruit of all seasons were
available. They talked animatedly, their lips constantly moving.
Each feasted their eyes on the other. It was all so tranquil.
Struggles in life belonged to others. Not a stir of wind would disturb the peace enjoyed by Kang and Pearl.

"Pearl," said Kang, "do you know how I treasure this moment
of ours? How wonderful life is!"

Pearl replied in English, "Yes." Her voice was totally different from usual. It went perfectly with the music, wine, green
leaves, candlelight and out-of-season fruit. It was so soft, so
sexy. On hearing such a voice, Kang felt his heart begin to
pump. "Say it again," urged Kang.

"Yes."

"I never knew a woman could have another voice."

"As long as she has true love."

"Come, let's go to our room!" Kang said.

The room had been cleaned, readied for the night. A corner of the snow-white quilt had been folded down. A fragrant red rose laid beside the pillow. Pearl said that she would like to play a game with him and covered his eyes with a handkerchief and led him into the bathroom. Music started in the room. It was a saxophone solo. The pitch was not particularly low but sounded remote. Whirling and descending, the notes seemed to fall from heaven.

"Do you like the saxophone?" asked Pearl.

"Sure," was the answer. Kang dared not pursue this topic further. From the dinner in the little restaurant to this saxophone, he was so ignorant that he felt he was an utter country bumpkin. He was somewhat ashamed of himself.

Pearl seemed to have read his mind and said, "You don't have to be bashful. Just relax, relax. I love you. Love everything about you. Forget anything troublesome, just be with me." While speaking, she began to peel off Kang's clothes. Without realizing it, Kang tried to fend her hands off but soon gave up. He smiled shyly. Pearl said, "How can you all of a sudden become so coy like a virgin boy?"

Kang removed the cover from his eyes and saw a naked Pearl lying in the bath filled with clean water. Rose petals were floating on the surface of the water. Pearl played with her own body with those petals. Her fingernails and toenails were also painted red. Her seductiveness made Kang's heart miss a beat. What did a married man know? He had never imagined such a picture let alone now see it with his own eyes.

After this Kang became very gentle. They caressed each other in the bath, had meals in the most elegant way, strolled the streets at midnight, side by side, without a word. In the room, they went about barefoot in only shirts or blouses, listening to music, drinking foreign wine. Sometimes, Pearl had her hair put up in a bun on top of her head, sometimes she just let it down. When the afternoon sun slanted through the thin curtain into the room, Kang let Pearl turn around in slow motion so that he could enjoy watching her slim figure in silhouette or in the slanting light. Nothing could be more beautiful than her body. He remembered his sadness over his first date at the age of fifteen, and thought of that girl named Dai Xiaolei. Dai's beautiful curves had left an indelible impression in his mind. He could not help telling Pearl the story of Dai and himself. He had never before told anyone this secret buried deep in his heart. Now he revealed this wound to Pearl, who, in return, healed his wound with the language of her body. Again, he said to himself, with mixed feelings of grief and joy, "This is right." He had at last found what he had let slip and lost in the past.

A week passed. It was time to part. As if they would never see each other again, they broke down in tears. Tightly they embraced each other. Pearl had long since prepared a gift for him—a necklace made of a purple silk braid dangling with a heart-shaped jade pendant. She put it on his neck and buttoned up his shirt. "Just for good luck. I hope it will help turn trouble into fortune." Her meaning was, of course: "Don't talk about marriage. No responsibilities, no promises. Just treasure our love." The more understanding Pearl was, the more moved Kang felt. He knew, as custom, it was he who should give her a present. But he had forgotten. Now he had accepted a present from her and it would be inappropriate for him to give her a gift in turn. He felt he owed too much to her. All he could say was,

"Pearl, I am sorry. Indeed, I've let you down."

Pearl did not know what to say and just covered his mouth with her hand. Pearl was so grief-stricken that she was unable to see him off at the airport. She took a few tranquilizers and lay down in bed. Kang sat beside her, caressing her arm, forehead and cheeks and let her drift into sleep. After she fell asleep, he gazed at her for a while and then left a note beside her pillow. He wrote: "Darling, I will love you forever."

11

As soon as he arrived in Wuhan, Kang went to the office. It took him three days to sort out all the urgent matters. At the end of the third day, Duan Lina came.

Kang said, "I was about to leave for home."

Lina said, "I'd like to have a word with you."

Kang said, "Shall we talk it over at home?"

Looking sideways, Lina said, "I think it's better to talk here."

Sensing that all the staff were watching them, he made an effort to be polite: "All right." Kang led her to his office and asked the secretary not to let anyone enter. Having had an affair in Beijing, he felt a sense of guilt. He opened a bottle of mineral water. While gulping down the water, he took a close glance at Lina. Since their last quarrel, Lina had worn an expression of grief and hatred whenever they met alone. She wore the same expression again today.

"What is it? Is there anything we can't talk about at home?" asked Kang.

Lina said, "Dini will be home soon from school. She has to concentrate on her homework. We should not disturb her. Is it not convenient here?"

"Of course there's no problem. How's Dini?"

Lina proudly replied, "She's doing very well. She ranks the third in her class, the fifth in her form. Last Thursday, a notice was put up by the school that Dini had won first place in a municipal essay competition."

"Excellent!" said Kang. "Is her health good? How about her appetite?"

"Thank you!" said Lina. "Thank you for still remembering the child. She's well and grows so fast. She badly needs nutrition."

Kang said, "I'm really too busy and have not taken enough care of her. You've done a tiring job looking after her. I'm very sorry and feel guilty. But I will try to do my best in the future."

"Very well. So you've admitted it at last. You know it is a hard job to look after a schoolgirl nowadays."

Kang said, "I've said I am sorry. What else do you want me to say?"

"Please lower your voice," said Lina. "I'm not here to fight with you. I'm afraid of you. I know you are very busy and you are the breadwinner of this family. I dare not disturb you. What I want to tell you is that your daughter has grown up and is still growing fast. The workload on her is heavy. She needs good nutrition. This is the first point. Secondly, she's a pretty girl and has begun to pay attention to her appearance. In her class, she is the most shabbily dressed girl. This hurts her self-respect. A daughter of our family must not forget to carry on the good tradition of being economical and hardworking. But times have changed. She should have some decent clothes to wear. Nowadays, good shoes and clothes are so expensive. Thirdly, next season she will be a junior-middle-school student. Perhaps you don't know, but she has to pass the examination with flying colors in order to get into a municipal key school. Only then will she be able to go to university. Dini is, of course, sure to pass the exam. But in case she cannot not bring her talents to full play in the examination and loses one or two marks, you will have to pay a big sum to the school to enroll her. Tens of thousands yuan maybe. We must be prepared."

Kang understood now. She had prepared herself well for the second assault. A good girl raised during the era of Mao Zedong, she had all along regarded money as dirt. In appearance, she still stood by her values—but no longer regarded money as dirt.

Lina had come to the painful realization that her time was past, a woman in her forties, still working for the government. It was the time for people like Kang. But she had to stick with him for the rest of her life. Besides Kang, who else could she turn to? She thought she knew her husband. He was basically a good person and did have feelings for her. What was most important was that he had no interest in other women. A man who had no interest in other women would always go home. For the time being, he had become complacent because of his success in business. Once he was broke, he would return to his old self. Lina had found a new weapon: squeeze all the money out of him.

Kang's guilty conscience and fear had all vanished. Tapping his huge desk with a pencil, he said mockingly, "Make it brief, you need money. How much do you want?"

"Only eight thousand a month."

She called eight thousand a month "only!" How ruthless!

Kang did not know what to say for a moment. He closed his eyes, rubbed his eyebrows. A smiling Pearl appeared before his eyes. The jade pendant on his chest began to quiver. On the lower floor of the five-storey building where he rented his office, was a large department store. The previous day when he had seen a friend off, he happened to pass the jewelry counter. He had shown his pendant to the counter manager and was told that it was worth at least ten thousand yuan. He had thought it was something worth several hundred yuan at most, just an ordinary ornament girls were usually fond of. In fact, even if it was worth only a few yuan, it would not lessen her feelings toward him. But he had never expected Pearl to be a girl with such strong feelings. People deeply in love did not mind the amount of money. But the amount of money sometimes did indicate one's feelings. Money was something vulgar indeed, but after all money was also a scientific unit of evaluation. Nowadays, many people believed that a beautiful young girl having an affair with a businessman was only after his money. If his affair with Pearl was made public, people would think the same. But they were wrong. Pearl was truly in love with him. How could a girl pursuing a rich man quietly give him a gift worth ten thousand yuan?

Kang's hands dropped from his eyebrows and said, "Okay, three thousand a month. As for Dini's examination, we'll see when the time comes."

"You've fallen into an occupational hazard—you are bargaining with your own family!"

"If you don't like it, just forget it then." With that, he rose to leave.

"Stop!" she yelled behind him. "Did you go to Beijing on

business?"

Kang replied without bothering to turn round, "You are not to meddle with my work."

"Dini won a big award and wanted to give you a call. Was that so wrong? But you had your mobile phone switched off the whole time. No one in your company knew which hotel you were staying at. Is that normal? Where on earth have you been this last week? What on earth did you do?"

"If you need money, I'll give it to you. But don't try to put your fingers in my business. It has nothing to do with you, nothing at all!"

With a sweep of her hand, Lina knocked a set of tea cups and a vase with some geraniums inside off the tea table.

"This is not to happen again," said Kang. "In the future, if I see you in the office, you'll kiss that month's three thousand bucks goodbye."

"How dare you!" cried Lina. "Kang Weiye, I'm warning you, if you are having an affair behind my back, I will destroy you without giving you a proper burial."

Kang pulled open the door and left.

Kang got home and saw his daughter with her head buried in a pile of books. He sat down beside her and asked a few questions. He congratulated her on winning the competition and promised to buy her a walkman. Dini was so delighted that she hugged him and kissed his cheek. But suddenly she realized that her mom was not home. This was something strange. "Where's Mom?" she asked. "She left me a note saying she had gone to your office."

"She'll be back soon," replied the father.

"Dad, I owe my award to Mom. She helped me prepare for the competition and, what's more, she had guessed the topic for the composition right. I had written up the composition beforehand, so of course I would win the award. Invite her to dinner on my behalf. How's that?"

As they were talking, Lina arrived. She was calm and nice, not a trace of her ferocity but a moment before could be detected. Naturally Kang would not reveal anything either. In reality, they were locked in a fight—where the prize was their daughter. "Okay, I'll do as Dini says," said Kang.

Amidst cheers, Kang drove his wife and daughter to a restaurant Lina chose. She said that it was a well-decorated restaurant, reputed for its good cooking and inexpensive food. The restaurant was quite crowded, filled with the pungent smell of smoke and drink. Kang found it somehow repulsive but Lina seemed to like it. Mother and daughter ordered a whole tableful of food, eating, drinking, talking and laughing heartily. For his daughter's sake, Kang feigned smiles, bearing the veiled barbs of innuendo from Lina.

12

Kang missed Pearl badly and called her once or twice every day. He suffered for a fortnight before flying to Beijing again on a Saturday afternoon.

Long separations and short rendezvous made them relish their love more, and the shadow of Lina only made it even more piquant. As it turned out, Kang was unable to control himself. Once a week, he either flew to Beijing or Pearl flew to Wuhan. Hidden in hotel rooms, they did and said all kinds of silly things. They were simply inseparable.

At this juncture, a call from He Hanru pushed their love a step further. Hanru had changed his mind and decided to give Kang forty thousand US dollars and keep a hundred thousand for himself. He had no guilty conscience at all and retorted self-righteously to Kang's protest over the phone: "Didn't we talk it over beforehand? It was me who got the deal and let you also make some money since you are my good pal. How could I get the smaller share? It is only right and proper that I get the bigger amount. Luckily I signed a memo with the Americans. You may come and check. Besides, though we had no contract, we do have a witness. You can go and ask Pearl."

Kang hung up and immediately dialed through to Pearl. Pearl told him that Hanru had already called and promised to immediately go through all formalities for her to go to university in the United States, on top of a birthday present of ten thousand dollars. The dollars and a bouquet were already on her desk. They had been brought to her by a friend of Hanru's. "Looks like you are faced with a hard nut, too," Kang probed tentatively.

"It's not hard at all," said Pearl. "Even if it happened to someone else, I would argue it out. One must have a heart. I'll talk it over with the general manager and you just wait for good news."

To Kang, Pearl's attitude was more important. Her sense of justice and honesty moved him. He looked at her from a new angle. Who would have thought that petite Pearl would be capable of such great courage and awe-inspiring self-sacrifice, so difficult to find in today's commodified society and business world. What he had before was the perfect lover, what he had now was a best friend. A man needed a lover, but perhaps more so a friend. Pearl was both a lover and a friend. What a wonderful world! At a time like this, he found her a treasure. Her reassurance was complete, rare and important.

Pearl brought no good news to him. Americans only trusted things in writing and could not care less about dispute between two Chinese "fighting over the spoils." Pearl was enraged by this insult to Kang. She insisted the Americans should apologize but they refused. Over that, she resigned. After hanging up the phone, Kang drove to the airport and flew to Beijing. He picked Pearl up from an apartment she shared with another young woman and went straight to the Great Wall Sheraton Hotel.

As soon as they entered the room, Pearl broke down in his arms, making Kang's heart ache. He caressed her hair with deep feeling, patted her on the back and kissed away her tears. They embraced so tightly that the sound of their clothes rubbing together could be heard. It was a long hug, a hug between two hearts. It was an embrace to protect each other while all around them was a wilderness full of raging beasts. A room in a large hotel was like a hidden corner in a huge mansion. In a place like this, one's mood was of great importance. If you were in a good mood, you would find the room cheerful, if you were in low spirits, you would find it gloomy and it would make your mood worse. Kang and Pearl, deeply hurt, clung to each other in this unfamiliar environment. Each looked over the other's shoulder and saw only a stark wall. There was no warmth, let alone a feeling of home. All this deepened their sense of growing dependence on each other and made them yearn for a place of their own. Both Kang and Pearl were extremely intelligent, so they knew quite clearly the obstacles in their way. An age difference of fifteen years in itself was not something extraordinary. But it was a special time and China had changed too fast. Eight or ten

years was like one generation. Kang had gone through the ordeal of the "Cultural Revolution" and of "being re-educated" in
the countryside. To Pearl, that was only a backdrop against
which she was born. What she had experienced was having to
study hard in order to go to university, to search up and down all
over Beijing to rent an apartment, to bargain with a foreign em-
ployer for an annual remuneration of a hundred thousand yuan.
Being not of the same generation, they had nothing in common,
as far as life experience was concerned, to keep them going over
the course of time. Despite their mutual passionate love for each
other, they dared not think about the outcome of their affair.
So neither would touch the topic of their future.

It was a love hanging in mid-air, a love existing in airplanes,
over telephones, in hotel rooms. It was just like a dream. Kang
poured out to Pearl all his bitterness and remorse about his marriage with Duan Lina. With her head tilted, a hand cupping her
chin, she listened and was touched. Her eyes turned moist from
time to time. She took a box of tissues from the bathroom and
wiped her tears and nose time and again. As Kang recounted his
story, a pile of white tissues built up between them, like a little
hill of bitterness and remorse.

Moved, Pearl said, "You are a healthy man full of love for
life. Yet you have endured such a woman for over a decade.
You have never had another woman. Oh my! If you are not a
saint, then your wife must have a mental illness. Shall I introduce you to a psychiatrist? You can take her to see this top-notch
doctor from Germany."

Kang said, "Don't be silly. If she learns about your existence,
no doctor would be able to solve the problem. Now let's hear
your story, OK?"

Pearl was frank. She admitted her biggest worry was not un-
employment, not being broke, not even being unable to go
abroad to study. What troubled her most was she had fallen in
love with a man whom she should not have. She had enough
money to get along for a while. With her abilities, it would not
be difficult to find a job. As for going abroad, it depended on
opportunity. If you had a good life in China, you might not
need to go abroad. But love was the most difficult thing to manage. She had gone out with several guys of her own age. But she
found them all too weak, weak in life experience, in intelligence, in courage and even weak physically. She spent some
time with an Australian, but they did not get along. When you
cracked a joke, he would not laugh—instead, he asked you to
explain in detail what was so funny. Jokes came down to a kind
of humor and mutual understanding—once explained, there was
nothing that funny. Both of them became bored. For a period
of time, Pearl thought He Hanru might be a good choice. Hanru
knew how to look after and please ladies. But they were not able
to get very far. As time wore on it became a kind of touch-and-
go relationship. Love, she found, was unattainable. She did not
lay much stock in marriage. Marriage was not her life goal. In
this life of hers, she might get married, might not. Her ideal
was to meet a man she truly loved, who loved her too—a life
and death kind of love. When she had first met Kang, she had
sensed something might happen between them, but she did not
want to get involved with a married man—it was too troublesome. She would have to deal with a group of people who were
irrelevant to her. It would be pure folly, a waste of time. But
there was no way out. Kang's attraction was too great to resist.
She had tried her best to control herself. But inevitably she en-

countered something called "love." She had to surrender—but what would follow after the surrender? God knows!

She spoke like a naughty girl, her eyes darting about, her gestures graceful. Her lovely red fingernails were eye-catching. When her story came to an end, she leaned her head on his shoulder and kissed the back of his ears, the most sensitive part of him. Kang held her hand and told her, "It's easy. You are mine. I won't allow you to leave me. I will marry you. We shall never part."

As a matter of course, a new real life began to unfold itself before them. Kang decided to take Pearl to Wuhan. They decided that for the time being she should not get a job. Instead she would return to Guangzhou, her hometown, and have a proper rest. Kang would find an apartment in Wuhan. Afterwards, they would have a little world of their own. Pearl would stay in this little world of theirs resting, giving Kang advice on his business and waiting for his divorce. After that, everything would get on to a normal track. Pearl would no longer hide herself. She would join Kang and plunge into business side by side with Kang. Together they would struggle for eight or ten years. Then they, husband and wife, would travel all over the world.

"Shame on you," Pearl said, "already talking about 'husband and wife!'"

"What are we if not husband and wife?" Kang retorted. "Is there any couple in love more deeply than us?"

Once their goal was set, there was nothing to worry about. They began to tease each other and decided to have a party to celebrate. Having put on their makeup and smart clothes, they went out. A handsome man and a beautiful girl. A perfect pair!

Pearl returned to Guangzhou while Kang went immediately into action. He found an apartment in a residential area called the Dream Lake Plaza, which was located by East Lake. The buildings here were all three or five storeys high. It was a lot cheaper and safer than a villa, and draw less attention. Those buildings were surrounded by endless fields, yet only twenty minutes away from the city center by car. The place perfectly served Kang's purposes. Quietly he bought an apartment with two sitting rooms and two bedrooms. A friend helped him to get the apartment decorated and furnished. It cost him almost four hundred thousand yuan. On the deed was Pearl's name and her ID number. He wanted to give the apartment to Pearl as a gift. He would make Pearl trust that he was a capable, generous man with good taste. He would make Pearl feel that she was right to choose Kang as her man. The money for the apartment was neither too much nor too little. He did hesitate for a second when paying the money—but it was soon done. Money, he thought, was something you could not take with you when leaving this world. As a man with some money, he ought to spend it on the woman he loved. Besides, she was so much in love with him. The present she had given him that first time was worth ten thousand yuan. How could he be outdone by a woman? But what was most important was that they were truly in love with each other. It was not a casual affair. Pearl was not the type who only targeted millionaires. And he himself was not a womanizer who kept a woman on the sly. They were bound to get married one day. In fact, once married, the apartment would become their common property. It was a matter of time. In the final analysis, Kang lost nothing. It had been preying on his mind for some time and finally he concluded that he was considerate in thinking and smart in action.

Kang believed that his divorce would also be smartly wound up. He thought Lina no longer had any love for him. All she wanted was his money. She had a strong sense of self-respect and often threatened him with divorce. When talking about her woman colleagues' reluctance to getting divorced, she used to show her disdain openly. Her view was: as soon as her husband mentions the word "divorce," she would immediately shut the door and leave. Except for her clothes, she would take nothing with her.

When a confident Kang said "divorce" to her, he did not expect that she would stand up and just walk away, then shut herself up in her room, screaming, "No way!"

13

The divorce thus ran aground. Lina's "No way!" was a telling blow to Kang Weiye. It threw him for a loop at first, but he would not be bullied. He banged open the door, fetched some of his clothes and announced that he would from now on live in the office. "Piss off!" was her reply. Anyhow Kang achieved a little at this first stage, since living separately would make it public.

What happened ran counter to what Kang had expected. It was he, not Lina, who had to pack and leave. But the worse would come later. On the second day after Kang moved into his office, several leaders from Lina's office paid him a visit hoping to persuade Kang to change his mind. Kang was busy but he could not send away these men responsible for an administrative office. Kang used to be an administrative worker himself and knew very well that to say "busy" to a visitor was tantamount to humiliating him, despising him. So Kang was very polite with them. With a big smile, he asked his secretary to pour cups of tea and prepare some fruit for the visitors. They said, "Sorry to disturb you. Hope we are not disturbing you."

"Not at all, not at all," replied Kang. "You are rare visitors. On usual days, it is not easy to get you to visit us. Please, don't stand on ceremony. Have some fruit."

They said, "Duan Lina is a good comrade."

Kang said, "Yes, that's for sure."

"You are a good comrade, too."

Kang began to shake his head and sighed.

"What's important is that you two have all along cared for each other. We all know that you've not even exchanged rough words in more than ten years of marriage. Now you are doing well in business and life is getting better. Your daughter is so big. We must say you are doing very well.

"It is natural for a middle-aged couple to have a dangerous spell of what they call 'indifferent feelings.' It will soon be over. When one gets on in age, one needs a good companion. The best companion is your wife or husband. There are many such examples.

"Comrade Duan Lina loves you with all her heart. Your raising the question of divorce and the open separation have hurt her self-respect. But still she is ready to forgive you. For the sake of her child, her family, she would endure anything. Please think it over."

When they finished their long-winded persuasion, it was time for lunch. Kang said, "I'm most grateful to you for coming and for caring about us. I will think it over carefully. But now I'd like to ask you to join me for a simple lunch."

So they stayed and had lunch with Kang. At the table, they relayed that Lina had said that she wanted a reply from him within three days.

Three days passed quickly and Kang ignored Lina. Every day, he was busy with his business, with his new apartment and with calling Pearl. "Is everything OK?" Pearl asked. "Fine! Everything is fine!" he said in a cheerful voice. "Darling, I'll soon come to bring you here."

In fact, Kang was unable to see Pearl very soon for Lina started a "people's war." She mobilized all the people she could. She went to see Kang's parents. So his parents came to see him about it. Kang said, "You've disliked her all along, haven't you?"

"That's something different," they said. "You've been together for so many years. Your child is now a junior-middle school student. Why do you want to divorce her? Tell us the truth."

"The truth is there's no love between us," Kang argued. "In fact, we have been separated for a long time."

"Why raise the issue now? Is there someone else?"

Kang knew it would be hard to deal with his parents. They would not give up if he did not tell them the truth. Once they learned the truth, they might help him. At least, they would not bother him like this again. Besides, he could not hide Pearl forever. She must inevitably meet them. So Kang told them about Pearl. It was very brief, nothing of the extent of their crazy relationship or his plans for the future. But they showed no intention of taking his side. On the contrary, they said sternly, "It's impossible! For the sake of your daughter, you shouldn't act like this. It's true that Lina is no match for you. It's true you've suffered a lot. But that is not the reason why you and this woman want the divorce. We know too little about her to jump to the conclusion that she is after your money. But at the very least she

is too young. You would be unable to satisfy her needs either financially, physically or psychologically. You are not of the
same generation and your thinking and your words can't con-
nect. You are drinking poison to quench a thirst."

Kang had brought a lot of trouble on to himself. Although his
parents were not the nosy type, in this case they wouldn't let
him go, and stopped at nothing trying to trace the whereabouts
of this Pearl. Lina's parents were worse still, calling him again
and again asking him to go to Wuchang to see them. Kang made
excuses that he was too busy to go. So one day, they came to his
company and stopped him in the corridor. Lina's father, still in
army uniform, slapped him in the face before saying anything.
Kang was not prepared for this and staggered. This was very
embarrassing with all his subordinates watching behind him.
Seeing their boss in such a fix, they swarmed up trying to push
the old couple out. With his eyes open wide, the old man craned
his neck and yelled, "I'm being polite only hitting this boy. If I
had a gun in my hand right now I'd shoot the bastard!"

These words had the junior executives bristling with rage—
they loosened ties, rolled up sleeves and pointed threateningly at
the old man, shouting: "Where has this old skunk come from?
An old man like you should just piss off! Too daft to understand? In broad daylight, you try to throw your weight around in
our office, eh? You're off your rocker! You slapped our General Manager, you must apologize. How dare you threaten to use
guns! Are you looking to die? I bet you know nothing about the
law!"

With his arms akimbo, the old man laughed. "Listen, you
young brats! This country was won by me. The people I killed
were just like you lot, raking in money from the public without

scruples!"

Lina's mother grabbed one of the young executives by his fingers, trying to pull him away. The younger staff all piped up: "Want a fight? You've come here to fight, is that it?"

Kang was pushed out of the crowd. He asked his secretary to bring him a thermos bottle. Then he kicked the bottle against the wall. The loud explosion made everyone jump. He shouted: "Go to your offices right now, all of you! Keep your mouths shut no matter what the old couple say. They are getting on in age. Whatever they say can be forgiven. If they want to stay here, treat them as my distinguished guests. If they do anything unconstitutional, call the police. I'm sorry. I've got to go and attend to some business."

With that he left, leaving the old couple behind. Later Lina's brother called to threaten him: "Kang Weiye, what you did to my parents is intolerable. You better watch out whenever you step out your door!" Kang's telephone set had a record function and his underlings immediately took the tape and went to a local police station. The policeman told him, "Manager Kang, don't worry. I assure you we'll take care of him."

The police went into action. Young and old went into action. Lina also mobilized everyone she could to join in the fray—besides leading members of the Academy, Kang's old superior, a department chief, also came to persuade him. Lina herself came to Kang's office and opened all his drawers, rummaging through all his correspondences hoping to find some evidence. Luckily, Kang and Pearl never wrote letters—they used the telephone. Stealthily Lina tried to buy off Old Plum with a gold ring. But Old Plum gave it to Kang and reported that Lina had asked her if Kang had another woman. "I did not say a word," Old Plum

said in a low, conspiratorial voice. "I said you don't have another woman. I said you are not that kind of man."

Kang Weiye became the focus of the talk in his own company.
Everyone's eyes were shining with excitement, like searchlights
shooting beams in his wake. All this made a fool of Kang, who
felt bitter and frustrated. All he wanted was a divorce, as simple
as that. One might get married, one might also get a divorce. It
was very normal—millions of people in the world got divorced.
He was not the first. Why had things turned into such a mess
falling on no one else's head but his?

Every time Pearl called, she would ask when she could join
him. "Pretty soon, darling," he always gave the same answer.
He did not want to let Pearl know about all the chaos at his end.
He would rather keep it all to himself instead of pouring out all
his bitterness to a woman. Pearl seemed very understanding.
She never pressed him but talked about their love and how she
missed him. The more she missed and loved him, the more pressure he felt. He must hurry and resolve his old marriage or he
would truly let Pearl down.

The stalemate lasted for three months, sometime fierce,
sometimes at a lull. Lina hid herself behind a screen and tried to
make Kang succumb through a protracted strategy of guerrilla
warfare. Some friends advised him, "You are being taken in.
It's a divorce between you and Lina, not anyone else. Talk to
Lina directly and ignore all the rest. Ask her to name a price.
Obviously she refuses to divorce just for the sake of the money.
No pain, no gain. Give her a lump sum of money."

Kang and Lina met after three months.

Three months of battle had made both look thinner. A woman
suffers through much more than a man. The hair at Lina's tem-

ples had turned gray. But she was full of energy. She crossed her legs, with her head slightly up, her arms folded in front of her chest. "Money?" she said with a snicker, her eyes shining. "Kang Weiye, do you really believe that money can move mountains? Please calculate, how much do you think can buy back my youth? How much was my love worth? How much do you pay to mend a broken family? What's the cost of my daughter losing her father?"

Kang did not want to go on discussing such rhetorical issues. So he said, "For the benefit of Dini, it's better that we get a divorce through mutual agreement. If you really don't want to cooperate, things will not go as you wish once the case is taken to court."

Lina said, "OK, since you've made up your mind, I'll not be an obstacle. But you must satisfy one of two conditions. You can have a choice. One, bring that woman to me and let me have a look at her. That being the case, I won't take a cent from you. Or two, give me a lump sum of five million. I'll leave it to you to make a decision."

Kang was speechless, shrugging his shoulders. Here he faced an extraordinary woman. "Put you in a fix?" Lina said, smiling wryly towards Kang. "I can change the condition. But I find it difficult to say it aloud. Come over, and I'll whisper it into your ear. Don't look at me. All right?"

A dubious Kang came closer to her. Lina approached him too. Then all of a sudden, she bit his ear. The pain made Kang scream and jump. Her lips were red with Kang's blood. Still smiling, she said in a low voice, "This is just a warning. Kang Weiye, if I find there's a woman, I will kill her."

14

Kang's love affair clouded over. He was not what he used to be despite his efforts to present a normal facade. At the airport, Pearl felt that something was amiss. "What's come over you?" she asked. "Nothing in particular," replied Kang. After several months' separation, they had been longing for this moment. They had imagined many a time the exciting moment of reunion and the words they wanted to say to each other—but no one could have known it would be like this.

Pearl grew anxious and asked again, "What's happened to you?"

"Nothing," Kang said fretfully. He did not want to tell anyone that he had been bitten by Lina, not even Pearl. He did not want to scare Pearl.

But Pearl read his mind. "Is it the divorce?"

Kang said, "Yes."

Pearl kissed him on the cheek and said, "This is not something unexpected. It doesn't matter with me as long as I'm here with you. Nothing can get in the way of our happiness and joy!"

Kang said, "You are right." With one hand on the steering wheel, he stretched the other hand to stroke her face. Pearl was too young, he said to himself. How could she understand that both happiness and joy were fragile. They could easily be affected even by a stir of wind, not to say a bloody threat from Duan Lina.

When they got to Dream Lake, Kang would not let Pearl get out of the car right away. He turned off the engine, and looked around like an alert hunting dog. When he was sure that no one was tailing them, he let Pearl get out. As soon as they got out of the car, Kang pulled her by the hand towards the building. Pearl said, "I'd like to have a good look at the surroundings." Kang ignored her. Upset, Pearl pouted and forcefully pulled back her hand. Luckily they soon got into their new apartment. This dwelling had not come easily—built not from straw and wood, but from their tears, their hopes and dreams. It was their past and future, their deepest feelings and highest peak. In this world this was a little world totally belonging to themselves. Kang opened the door and the keys clinked against one another with a crisp metallic sound. In the quiet corridor, the echoing sound aroused indescribable feelings. Pearl held Kang at the waist, burying her head in his back.

The new apartment was now before their eyes. The quality wooden floor, the French windows, the lower part of the walls covered with cloth, and a green tree in a big pot. Pearl in a photo was smiling towards them. In the closet hung silk pajamas. On the table was a plate of fruit. A lamp on the tea table beside the sofa shone with warmth. Kang proffered a silk-covered box to Pearl. She opened it to find the present to her—the deed and a ring of keys. "Oh!" she let out an exclamation of delight and fell on to the ground, pretending to have fainted.

A beautiful woman took a hot bath in the bathroom, her singing enlivening the whole apartment; the fragrance leaking out of the bathroom enveloped the man—this was a real home! Kang tapped himself twice on the face, feeling proud of what he had achieved, as well as happy. Despite the dark clouds over him, he got what he had wanted. It could be said that, all in all, he was quite a lucky man.

Pearl emerged. But she had been transformed into a gorgeous bride in a white gauze wedding dress with smooth lines. Her hair

was in a bun on top of her head. Her eyes were radiant with
love. She catwalked towards Kang and made an unemotional
pose. A saxophone rendition of "Homecoming" happened to be
playing. Kang gave her warm applause.

"Let's go, bridegroom," said Pearl.

"Where to?" he asked. But instantly he realized that Pearl
wanted to go out to eat. So he hurriedly said, "We are home
now. There's no need to go to a restaurant. I've bought a lot of
food. Shall we go to the kitchen?"

"Go to the kitchen? To cook?" Pearl asked with her eyes wide
open. Little by little, the gleam in them faded, disappointment
written all over her face. There came the sound of Kang's voice
as if from far away: "We can't go to any restaurant. Too many
people in this town know me. We must under no circumstances
be seen in public at present." His explanation could not abate
Pearl's change of feelings. She could no longer hold herself up
and her legs gave way. She fell on to the ground despite her expensive wedding dress.

"Won't it be fun to cook for ourselves today?" said Kang.

"What fun? That would portend forever firewood, rice, cooking oil and salt. How did you become so petty bourgeois?"

Kang was as shocked as Pearl. How could she say such nasty
words after all he had done and given her despite so many difficulties? Should he put up with it or give her a piece of his mind?
He did not know what to do for a moment.

Pearl spoke up: "I'm sorry, Weiye. In the past we did not
talk about such trifles in life. Since we are now living together,
I must tell you frankly that I don't know how to cook and I hate
cooking. I dread cooking smoke which would do great damage
to my skin, hair and health. Besides, it is too time-consuming to

do Chinese cooking. My meals are simple: a boiled egg, a sausage sandwich will do. If we want to have something fancy, we can always go to a restaurant. Since I was small, I have seen my mother toiling in the kitchen. Her body and our home reeked with cooking smells. I swore never to follow my mother's footsteps in this life of mine. Don't you understand what I mean, Weiye?"

"I see," said Kang. He understood now. He had to admit what Pearl said had a point. But he had grown up for forty years with piping hot rice and dishes at every meal. He simply loved them. His mother's work in the kitchen brought joy to the whole family. To him, the picture of his working mother was the ideal image of a woman. Kang would never accept eggs and bread every day.

Kang said, "All right. You take a rest first. I'll go cook the meal."

"Why? Why must you cook?" asked Pearl. "I don't like a man cooking in the kitchen. In fact today is our wedding day. You ought to put on your best suit and take me to the best restaurant. I don't mind being seen in public. I couldn't care less about what others think of me. You've been secretive the whole time since I saw you at the airport. Almost like a thief! This is not your old self. People would only grow suspicious of me, saying I am a prostitute or a concubine hidden here. But I am not afraid. What are you afraid of? This is because I love you so!"

Pearl leapt up in agitation and went up to Kang. She looked him in the eye, waiting for his response. Naturally Kang did not want a fight. But he would do everything he could to stop her from going out and attracting attention. People of her age had no way of understanding the minds of people like Duan Lina, and therefore, had no idea what Lina was capable of and the possible dangers. Kang realized the other side of Pearl. It was not that she was too young to understand—she was just that type of person, with that perspective. Without saying a word, he stretched out his arms and held her to his chest.

Not to embarrass Pearl further, Kang emerged in a short while from the kitchen, no cooking smells on his body. To keep his image, he did not put on an apron. This dinner of historic significance was as simple as a few eggs boiled in salty water and a plate of sliced cucumber. Pearl had long since shed her wedding dress and was in loose casual wear. She made an effort to keep her spirits up and sat at the table. This was the least tasty dinner they had eaten since they had fallen in love.

Kang and Pearl's new life began. It was so different from what they had imagined. And it swerved so sharply. They had thought that once they had their own little world of freedom, their love would last forever. They had thought that once they lived together, their love would deepen. They used to have so much to say to each other and have to part without being able to tell each other all that was on their minds. Now they had all the time in the world, but where had all those words gone? Inwardly, they were anxious, searching for words. Sometimes they thought they had found a topic. Once out of their mouths though, they were not the words he or she had meant to say. Pearl insisted on eating bread, but Kang found bread not substantial enough. They could not indeed light on the feelings of a husband and a wife. A husband and a wife were not like a pair of lovers in courtship. The life of a husband and a wife should be realistic and everyday, but they just couldn't seem to find that common ground. They did not see eye to eye on many specific things. On such occasions, both of them felt caught in a dilemma. When one detected the other's sense of dilemma, both felt uneasy. They became more polite and discreet towards each other.

15

Kang now had to do business, be on guard against Lina, and look after his elderly parents and his daughter. On top of all these, there was Pearl with whom he had to be very careful. From the beginning of their new life, he found it day by day more and more difficult to juggle all of these things. One day, he detected a gray hair on his head. He pulled it out. Then he found another and another. Finally he gave up, gazing at himself in the mirror. He suddenly realized that there was no use pulling out all those gray hairs.

Life was hard for Pearl too. Kang usually did not come home during the day. In the evenings, he had social engagements. When he returned to Dream Lake, he was either exhausted or drunk. The two-day weekend does not exist for businessmen. Once in business, you are deprived of a good rest. He had to fix times to see his daughter, taking her to McDonalds or to drive toy cars in the park. Besides, Kang still refused to go out together with Pearl. He had fallen into a new habit of looking around from time to time as though he was in the shadow of constant danger. He had to wait until he and Lina were divorced, only then would he be able to be a man and take Pearl out.

Pearl could no longer ignore how things were going with Kang's divorce. She pressed Kang to tell the truth. When she learned the truth, she found it laughable. Lina's refusal to a di-

vorce simply placed Kang in a trap. An argument broke out between them. "Can't you go to court?" she said.

"No way. If that happens, my daughter would have to appear
in court too."

"So what?"

"She is too young to go to court."

This was beyond Pearl's comprehension. "A court is a place
where people give reasons. What's wrong with that?"

"Of course it's no good for a child. In court, Lina would spew
out the most vicious words. I won't allow my daughter to hear
them. It will destroy the rest of her life."

"But you have not done anything yet. How can you be so sure
of your assumptions?"

"You don't have kids. It is impossible for you to understand
this point."

"Suppose I'm a kid. If my parents have no love for each other, I would not object if they wanted a divorce. As a matter of
fact, the father I have at present is my stepfather. We get along
very well."

"Just think, how many girls are as modern as you? My daughter is more traditional."

"And just what do you mean by that?"

"I didn't mean to slight you."

"I didn't say you're slighting me. You've spoken your mind."

"Oh please, Pearl! The pressure on me is already very great."

"So you think I'm quite relaxed, eh? Am I making a big fuss
about nothing?"

Kang could hardly control himself. "Didn't you say you
wouldn't care about your social status? Didn't you say you would
wait for me forever? Do as you said. Don't bother about this

headache of mine. Sooner or later, I will get it settled."

Pearl could no longer control herself either. "Are you kidding? Do you mean that my concern over this situation stems from worries about my status? Let me tell you this, I am still who I am. I'm not anxious, I'm not pressing you for the divorce. What I'm saying is that your way of thinking is utterly wrong!"

"That's what you think. But it's me who knows if the shoe on my foot fits. No one else could know better than me."

"Of course! Who else would know every last bit of dirt on the long, unending years of your married life?"

"What do you mean?" Kang demanded, agitated.

Pearl got even more furious: "I mean fucking nothing!"

Both of them turned white. They stared at each other like strangers. Strings of tears fell down Pearl's cheeks. Kang left the room, banging the door shut. He drove around the East Lake. It was the small hours of the morning when he finally returned. Stealthily he opened the door. Pearl threw herself into his arms. Both broke down in tears.

The following day, Kang got a call from Pearl in his office. "Weiye, perhaps it is better for me to leave for a while. What do you say?" she said with a wry chuckle.

At this, Kang cried, "Pearl!" He found there was a lump in his throat. He moved away from the receiver. When he gained self-control again and tried to speak, he only heard beeps. He knew Pearl had made up her mind.

It was time to part. Pearl's only request was that she wanted to take Kang to dinner before leaving. Kang could not refuse her. He had to brave it out even if it was a sea of fire.

That day Pearl was in black, only her white blouse collar

showing over the black lapels. She wore a pair of wide-rimmed
sunglasses. Her nails were painted crimson, the color of blood,
moving against the backdrop of her black dress, making Kang's
heart shiver. They left an indelible impression on his mind. This
was exactly what Pearl had wanted. She insisted on driving, saying that she had never driven in Wuhan. She spoke little. To liv-
en up the atmosphere, Kang kept bringing things up: the lawless
buses, the hateful cyclists, the ridiculous wordings on advertise-
ments—all which had nothing to do with what was actually preying on his mind. Pearl drove up to the Asian Hotel in Hankou.
As they entered the lobby, Pearl lightly held Kang's arm. They
went up to the revolving restaurant at the top. Four violinists in
black formal wear were playing Mozart's quartet. Classical music was quickly becoming the latest fashion. Pearl was familiar
with Mozart for she often went to concerts in Beijing. But Kang
was unable to recognize it. Lento, allegro or minuet, to him, it
was all just music. On their table sat a red rose which was beginning to wither. Pearl picked it up with her fingers and showed it
to the head waiter. The man came up and apologetically
changed it for a yellow one: "A yellow one?"

Kang said, "It'll do." Pearl nodded. Again they ordered Dynasty Dry. It was a buffet.

"How do you find the food here?" Kang asked.

"Very good. What do you think?"

"As long as you find it good, it's fine with me."

"Weiye."

"Pearl."

Their hands on the table touched for a moment. Kang said,
"This is probably silly. But I've got to ask, will you come back
again?"

"That's not a silly question."

"Give me a call as soon as you get to Beijing."

"Of course I will."

The dinner lasted until the restaurant's closing. The candle on their table had almost burned down. A waitress came up and asked if they needed another candle. "No need," they said in chorus. Instantly they shot each other a glance. A helpless sense of loss showed in their eyes.

Pearl left, like a golden crane, without a trace after her flight. Kang had expected such an ending—that was how she handled things. Later on, Kang heard that she had gone to Australia. Someone else said that she had gone to the United States. Anyway, she was most likely out of the country. On hearing this, for a moment, Kang was assailed by an indescribable emotion. Was it sadness or relief? After all, they had been so much in love. But it was like a dream, where upon waking, everything was gone. A lifetime regret. Before Pearl had left Wuhan, she had sold the apartment, lock, stock and barrel. As a matter of course, she had pocketed the money. This more or less made Kang's heart turn cold. Though, when asked, he had told her, "Do as you wish. I've already given it to you."

Kang returned to his usual, busy life.

Translated by Wang Mingjie

The Heart More Than the Flesh

ON the plateau over four thousand meters above sea level lived a Tibetan young woman. Leaning against the low doorframe, she was spinning sheep's wool. She gripped the handle of a nameless wooden implement and turned it around and around, twisting the jumbled mass into skeins of crude woolen yarn.

The first day I saw her she stood spinning. Way beyond her loomed the vast blue sky. Treeless mountains jutted up in the distance, with only some slowly roaming yaks visible on the ridges. In front of the door a lazy dog lay on a mound of earth basking in the sun. On the second day the young woman was still spinning. Everything around her was just as it had been the day before. On the third day she was also there spinning. All was as before—as if here you could touch the infinity of time—a century whizzing by, no different than a single day.

On the fourth day I walked over to her. She lifted her heavy eyelids and looked at me. Then she smiled shyly. I took over the shiny handle, and she showed me how to spin the wool. I practiced till my arms ached too much to move anymore. As I lifted my eyes towards the sky I saw the sun—still in the same spot, not having moved at all. My heart was filled with a boundless sense of sorrow.

I spoke with her through gestures. She showed me all the woolen fabrics she had woven over the past twelve years—rucksacks, blankets, tapestries, cushions, and shawls. I liked one of the shawls and wanted to buy it. The shawl revealed a Tibetan Buddhist legend through a medley of colors: an awesome-looking deity wearing a fiendish mask was brutally stomping on an unknown defeated enemy.

The young woman hesitated for a moment. To weave such an exquisite shawl she had put in two years of painstaking work. If I must have it, she would charge me a very high price. She said she would accept nothing short of twenty yuan.

I took the single one-hundred-yuan bill out from my coat pocket and with it bought this unique talismanlike shawl from the young woman, who had spent two years of her young life to weave it, up on the highest plateau of the world. The young woman would remain on the plateau forever, but I would go on to many different places wearing the shawl she had woven.

From my friends I received not a few sneers. Lan Ye said, "Will you dare wear it outside?" I said, "Of course I will."

Li Xiaofei and Wu Shuang naturally thought I was a bit mad. But Mou Linsen, a professional artist after all, had a fairly high opinion of the shawl—though he couldn't understand why I had paid one hundred yuan for a thing of such limited value. He stroked my head, and said, "I hate to see young girls play rich ladies. Do you want to splash money around to show you have a kinder heart than most other people? It's not your turn to do that yet!"

Mou Linsen gave me another one-hundred-yuan bill, and de-

clared that from now on I must use the money only to buy food.
I tried to explain but nobody wanted to listen. I couldn't make
them see what I had felt when I stood facing the young woman
on the plateau. All I could do was to get excited and scream: "I
like it, I like it! Why don't you guys mind your own business?"

From then on I would stubbornly wear the shawl wherever I
went. Lan Ye kept smirking at me. What did she know, anyway!

I was still among my friends, but my heart was no longer with
them.

Sometime in the afternoon I got up with some difficulty from
a lethargic sleep. After rubbing my eyes for a long time, I shuf-
fled to the window in a feverish daze. From there, I looked out
into the crystal blue sky and then at the Potala. I wrapped the
much disputed shawl tight around my head, so that only my pale
face showed: in the area surrounding each of my cheekbones
there was an unhealthy scarlet spot, my lips were a dark purple,
and I wore Tibetan silver earrings studded with turquoise. Like a
witch, I started to appear at the same window each afternoon,
and passed the idle hours of my youth looking out.

I had stopped liking my job in the restaurant, wearing a
cheongsam which didn't suit me, greeting all the burping diners
at the door with a polite smile. What a slimy lot were some of
the men who came to the restaurant to eat! How could they deserve to be smiled at by a pure young girl! I loved art, I loved to
paint—but everybody sneered at me when I told this to them.
There was a wide gap between me and my parents. They didn't
want me to go traveling with my friends, and they couldn't understand me. They were too old! I had no chance to fight in a

war, no chance to purify my soul through toil in the countryside, no chance to study at university, not even a job to do. I
had gotten stuck in a lusterless moment of history.

The hotel I stayed in was next to a spacious training ground.
At three o'clock every afternoon a team of young horsemen
came there to train. Every day, unmovingly I would watch them
from the window, until they got used to my being there. Of all
of them, a rider of a golden horse was the most expert. When
he spurred his horse on in my direction, he would glance up at
me several times. I liked to watch the young men riding horses.
I admired them—but in midst of this sense of admiration often
rose in my heart a nameless desolation that knew no bounds.

Now I was waiting for them to come again. Mou Linsen was
by this time in Ngari; Wu Shuang was gone far away to northern
Tibet. As for Li Xiaofei and Lan Ye, they still remained in
Xigaze. Only I was left behind in Lhasa. Yes, I was alone...

Before we entered Tibet we promised to stick together no
matter what happened. But as soon as we arrived in Xigaze we
split up. The three men wanted to go to three different places.
After they got soused to the gills, they began calling each other
names to display their prowess. None of them would yield to another.

I said, "What's the difference between one place and another?"

The men took no heed of me. Only Lan Ye, trying to sound
intellectual, told me calmly and articulately, "It is certainly not
the same."

I said, "Oh, yeah?"

With that I began to laugh mockingly and loudly, which made

Lan Ye's face puff up.

Lan Ye was a petite girl from Anhui. She had acted in Huang-
mei operas for a local theatrical troupe. After she got acquainted
with Wu Shuang, who was then touring Anhui, she went off to
Beijing with him to seek her fortune. The girl had a very slender
waist and a bewitching face. A born beauty. She had entered Tibet on Wu Shuang's adoring arm, but now she was in Li
Xiaofei's lap. Li Xiaofei had been my boyfriend, appearing every night in the restaurant where I had worked as a waitress. I
hadn't expected that once he saw Lan Ye, he would never be
able to take his eyes off her.

Li Xiaofei announced brazenly, "Why can't I enjoy such a
beautiful woman!"

Midst the rising music in the dance hall, Li Xiaofei had arro-
gantly stretched out his hand to Lan Ye. Lan Ye hesitated for a
second, then she determinedly left Wu Shuang and sailed directly into Li Xiaofei's arms. Before the music ended, Li Xiaofei
and Lan Ye were already locked together. Lan Ye reapproached
Wu Shuang to fetch her handbag, and Wu Shuang stared eerily
at her. Lan Ye smilingly said to him, "I'm sorry."

Wu Shuang only nodded his head.

I was at once angry and mortified! Before Li Xiaofei had a
chance to say anything, I decided that I would take the initiative
by deserting him before he did me. I walked up to Mou Linsen.
He patted his lap and I sat obediently onto it. I knew Mou Linsen liked me, but I knew even more clearly that he liked lots of
other girls as well, though none of them could occupy his heart
for long. He was a modernist painter. He regarded himself a
celebrity and acted accordingly. He often caused women to suffer. For a long time I had maintained a cautious distance from

him, but at a moment of a certain day I suddenly became his
girlfriend. I placed myself atop Mou Linsen's knees. He looked
at me briefly, and then pulled me to his chest as if a tacit agreement existed between us. Wu Shuang struck the table and shouted: "Bravo!"

Li Xiaofei was somewhat dumbfounded. My prompt reaction
to what he had done must have taken him by surprise, or perhaps he hadn't intended to establish a permanent relationship
with Lan Ye at all. Now Lan Ye tickled Li Xiaofei's armpit to
make him giggle. I for my part clutched Mou Linsen's shoulders
and let my hot tears trickle down his back. What—oh what indeed—was all this about? In all the thirty-one years from the
founding of New China to the beginning of the 80s, we hadn't
been able to see so much as a man and a woman kiss each other
in a movie in this country! Fourteen years had barely passed
since then, but we have some people who seem to have suddenly
scaled the entire expanse from the whole of socialist society to i-
dentify uncritically with the cynical hedonism of the youth culture of the capitalist world. Relationships between people were
so free and naked, the world had become boring. But I had to
act this way. Only in this way could I avoid being ill-used by Li
Xiaofei.

Now I was very ill. I believed this was because I had displeased the gods, but my friends were all highly skeptical.

When we had first arrived in Tibet one of Mou Linsen's
friends had taken us to watch a "celestial funeral." We waited
near the funeral grounds on the top of a hill. When the leading
vulture landed and quickly tore off and devoured a large chunk
of the now lifeless flesh, I couldn't help screaming with horror.

The vulture turned his head around and looked fixedly at me. The cold dignity in his eyes made me shudder. A gossamer sensation of fear rose in my heart, and I fell completely silent.

In a matter of just minutes the corpse was gone, rising to the skies so neatly, so thoroughly. Except for the bones that remained after the vultures left, the landscape was also very clean with only the fragrant *sang* curling up into the air. *Sang* is scented smoke. Cypress twigs and pine leaves were piled up and lit, and barley-cakes were roasted on top. Amid the aromatic plumes of smoke, the minister of the funeral took away the deceased man's skull, which would be used as a brick in erecting a wall. After the wall was completed, people could lean on it and rest when they wanted to. It was all so natural and open-minded. I was ashamed of myself for having screamed. Conviction comes with sudden enlightenment sometimes. Now I really believe that the celestial funeral was a necessary part of the cycle of life. People live and die. They repeat the stories passed down from their ancestors. Attempts at escape are but futile. Now if we choose to look at it this way, isn't life a series of cycles? Those vultures were sacred birds, indeed. If they hadn't been sent down from heaven, how should one explain their timely arrival at the celestial funeral ground?

The night after I had screamed I ran a fever, and I sweated a great deal during the several nights that followed. After each bout of sweating I would wake up because of the icy, wet pajamas which clung to my body. During these first moments of waking, I always smelled the distinctive aroma of *sang*. Slowly I began to understand the cause of my illness.

I proposed to my friends that we buy a *hada* (a piece of white silk usually presented as a gift) to take to the Jokhang Temple and pray to Buddha. They were all amused at this. Mou Linsen simply lost his temper with me, saying that I must take antibiotics three times a day. I followed his instructions for two days, only to find that my temperature had risen higher and I had begun to cough.

How may we convince our fellow beings, whose vision is confined by their limited experience, that things do exist which haven't been yet proved? If, when humans still hadn't invented electricity, I had pointed to lightning in the sky and said that someday it would be used as electric lamplights to illuminate the world, I knew nobody would have believed me.

Mou Linsen said, "Enough already? what do you know?!"

I lay on a not so clean bed in a hospital ward. My temperature was still running high, and I nearly doubled over whenever I coughed. In an alpine region like this, the doctor said, running a high fever and coughing were dangerous symptoms.

Wu Shuang asked, "What shall we do?"

Mou Linsen said, "Leave her some extra money."

Wu Shuang wondered, "Shouldn't one of us stay to look after her?"

Mou Linsen answered, without looking at me, "A woman might run a fever or cough a good many times during her whole life, but we on this earth have only one Tibet, which is losing its unique primordial mystery every minute of the day!"

I said, "Mou Linsen, in this world there is also only one Kang Zhu."

Mou Linsen, the man who was supposed to be in the throes of love with me, chortled. He said in a cynical and callous tone, "I can find fragrant grass everywhere."

Wu Shuang said, "Take it easy, Kang Zhu. He just likes to

joke around. You *are* joking, Mou, aren't you?"

Mou said, "Who's joking? Damn it, if we keep hesitating, do we still deserve to be called men?!"

Wu Shuang had a slight build and a sallow complexion. He had just been abandoned by Lan Ye, so he was not quite confident of himself as a man. He stamped his feet saying, "All right, I'm going!"

Wu Shuang was going off to Nagqu. It was said that Nagqu was the world's highest town above sea level. He expected to run into one or two hurricanes and hailstorms on the great desert there, but he thought that by getting closer to the sun he might receive more ultraviolet rays and thus darken his pallid face.

Wu Shuang had once been the "campus poet." Although poetry began to falter thereafter, some last bits of affection for women were still alive in his heart. At parting, he felt my burning forehead with a hand and said, "Excuse me for leaving you."

"I'll be all right," I said.

I brushed Mou Linsen's hand aside. To him I repeated the same words.

Things did turn out to be all right. What if something had really happened, with Ngari and Nagqu both so distant and out of the way? As for Li Xiaofei and Lan Ye, they were so much in love, they seemed oblivious to everything else in the world.

Alone in Lhasa!

Empty-handed I sauntered aimlessly through the city. Apart from the languor caused by the lingering fever, I was feeling pretty good, and I actually missed nobody.

I was alone in Lhasa. Although girls like myself would very likely be scoffed at if we voiced our sufferings to people, only I knew our suffering. We didn't have much life experience, we had more than enough to eat and drink, but we suffered nonetheless. My stay in Lhasa marked the beginning of a new phase in which I would think on my own. It was time for me to see the world with my own eyes.

Each day in the early morning sun I ambled off towards the Lhasa River. August was a summer month here, but it was rather chilly in the mornings and evenings. I still had my extraordinary shawl wrapped around my shoulders—it exuded a strong odor of mutton. Along the river I strolled, stopping every now and then. The local Han people all looked at me suspiciously. The bed of the river was like a vast prairie. Gazing into its waters you could feel perfectly relaxed and tranquil.

After lunch I took a nap. In the late afternoon I watched the horsemen train. At sunset I wobbled out of the restaurant and headed down to Parkor Street. Only when evening set in and the traders and tourists quickly thinned out, did the Jokhang Temple resume its magnificent form as an ancient holy place of worship. I walked slowly down the street as if in a trance, laying down a pebble when I saw a Mani Stone Mound for religious worship, completing a circle when I came across scripture-chanting, and feeding a newly freed sheep with some barley-cakes. I was praying to the gods on behalf of my sick body, and I was also praying for my dull, unenlightened mind.

Quite often, I was too tired to walk further. When that happened I would sit down in the public square and look at the Tibetan dogs romping all over the streets. Here were the slender and graceful flowers popularly known as "Lord Zhang." There in front of the temple were the huge gray slabs, shiny like a smooth mirror from the constant rubbings of pious pilgrims' bodies. The very sight struck a sensitive chord in my heart. Think of those Buddhist worshippers who prostrate themselves fully: have they not been beneficiaries of modern civilization at all? Of course they have. When a person believes in something or does something, he always has some reason. I was beginning to understand people. In the future I would not foolishly laugh at this or that anymore.

I also enjoyed looking at Tangkars. Tangkars resemble the colored silk fabrics used by the Han. Ours were largely produced in Suzhou and Hangzhou in the southeast of the country, and they conveyed a sort of quiet elegance—a lake surrounded by green hills, a bridge over a clear, winding stream, and so on. The Tangkar's bold colors and rich, exquisite patterns represented glorious golden rays and rosy-hued clouds encircling Buddha. The features of Buddha were incomparably full of grace, simply resembling a good-hearted granny. Traders hung Tangkars all over the enclosing walls of Jokhang Temple, so the local residents and tourists saw Buddha's bright, broad smile from a great distance. Sitting on the edge of the raised flower bed in the square, I watched the amiable Buddha raptly for a lingering moment. A feeling of warmth and forgiveness flowed through my heart.

No less delightful was the sight of elderly Tibetan women clad in heavy blue robes pissing on the street. They squatted there with the poise of dancers. The loose-fitting robe aptly concealed everything from view—only a slight trace of liquid would wind its way out from beneath it. They didn't even try to avoid meeting people's eyes with their own. When they looked at you just as you did them, you would find that the look in their eyes was of innocence and serenity. This was how real masters of their own country looked and behaved. You might be convinced that this was just a city, but that's solely your business. For them, the city was still just as much mountains and prairies and pastureland as ever. May they be blessed!

I never tired of looking at the robust Kamba men! As an old Tibetan phrase put it: Amdo's horses, Kamba's men. The famous Kamba men were one of the finest men on earth! They were of a towering height, with broad shoulders, slim waist and sturdy long legs. Each threw his chest out and held his head high. Their faces were distinctly outlined as if carved with a knife or sharpened with an ax. Their complexion was dark and shone with the luster of silk. The Kamba men were beautifully attired, too: their robes were all embroidered with silk, their boots reached up to their knees, their tall hats with fur trim were adorned with a red tassel, and a Tibetan knife studded with a gem hung down from their sides. They had a valiant, swinging stride. One day a young Han woman, who had also come into Tibet as a tourist, was sitting beside me. She looked at the Kamba men passing by, and said excitedly, "I love them, I surely do! I want to marry them! What about you?"

I gave into a peal of laughter. I answered, "I'm not so sure. I've been told they never wash their feet."

Over the past twenty-odd years of my growing up, I had always been instructed by others. Parents, teachers, TV programs and films kept prattling on about what was beautiful and what was ugly, what was right and what was wrong, and what was true and what was false. In actual life, however, many such standards don't work. I was fed up with being told about this and that. I only wanted to see things with my own eyes. I would travel from one place to another, open my eyes wide, and look

at as much of the world as I could. Through what I perceived for
myself, I thought I would know what I should do and how. I
would be answerable for whatever I obtained, be it happiness or
unhappiness. From now on I would stop blaming either gods or
men.

I heard a knock on the door.

I turned around to face the door, rather dazed, not knowing
whether the knock was really for me. I had no friends in Lhasa.
My friends were away visiting different interesting places. Nobody had knocked on my door once in the past ten days.

Then another knock—it was my door for sure.

I remained standing by the window and said, "Come in,
please."

Gyamco the horseman thus walked into my life in Lhasa.

He was none other than the one who had been riding on the
magnificent golden horse during the training sessions. For the
past ten days we had been looking silently at each other.

Gyamco had the blood of a real Kamba man in him, but now
he was wearing a Han-style athletic shirt. Horsewhip in hand,
steaming and sweaty, he stood at the door saying, "Hi, my
name is Gyamco."

I said, "Hi, I'm Kang Zhu."

Gyamco smiled. It seemed as if he was about to say something, but then he checked himself.

I waited for him to explain his purpose in coming. I didn't
withdraw from the windowsill I had been leaning on. I was feeling sick and dizzy. I shivered with cold. I wrapped the shawl
more tightly around my shoulders, and looked at Gyamco
through my rather heavy eyelids.

After some hesitation, Gyamco made a deep bow to greet me more formally, "I'm very sorry to disturb you. *Zhaxideleg*!"

Zhaxideleg was a Tibetan greeting of good-will.

Then he made as if to close the door and leave.

I said, "Gyamco, what did you want to talk to me about?"

Gyamco replied, "*Mei sheme zhengjing shi*" (nothing important really). So the man could speak standard Chinese quite fluently!

He said, "You don't look very well. Altitude sickness?"

I said, "I'm afraid not."

Gyamco said, "Are you ill? Are you alone? Nobody around to look after you? All right, let me rush you to the hospital!"

Gyamco was ready to act at once, but I hastily stopped him. "There is no need to go to a hospital. I have medicine. This kind of illness is not for doctors to cure. I think I have done something wrong to make the gods angry."

"You think so?" Gyamco was obviously pleased to hear this. "You really think so? Do you believe in Buddha, too?"

I said, "Not yet, but this is really how I feel."

Gyamco said, "Then your illness will be cured."

I said, "How?"

Gyamco said, "By praying to Buddha."

I couldn't help smiling.

Gyamco said, "Pray with all your heart and Buddha will look after you. Tomorrow I will take you to the temple."

"That sounds fine." Then I added, "Tell me, why did you come up here, Gyamco?"

Gyamco said, "I'll explain, but you must promise me you won't do anything about it."

I said, "Why?"

"Because you're ill," Gyamco said. "I didn't know that before I came up."

These kind words made my heart ache. I suddenly thought of Mou Linsen and the others who had left me alone in Lhasa. Tears poured down my cheeks like rain. It came out that Gyamco had made a bet with his teammates. They had said Gyamco would be the winner if he could bring me down to the training ground from my restaurant room. If the reverse happened, then he would lose the bet! The stake was beer. This was a typical prank between boys. Deeply grateful to Gyamco for his kindness, I would gladly have deferred to such a small and harmless wish. But Gyamco insisted that I really shouldn't go because of the unbearable heat outdoors. He seriously pointed out that a person must always keep his or her word—since I had promised him not to go down, he expected me to stay upstairs no matter what.

Gyamco asked, "Will you promise?"

I said, "I will."

I hadn't expected that the other young horsemen would make so much of their triumph! They cheered at Gyamco and whistled loudly. And it turned out that what Gyamco had staked for the bet was not just one or two bottles of beer but one whole case for each! Now he returned with the cases on his shoulder and distributed them among his friends. They in turn popped the bottles open right in front of him, and gulped the liquid down like crazy. Several even mischievously waved their bottles towards me as if to thank me.

I was amused at all this, but I was also rather upset for Gyamco's sake. At a crucial moment like this, what need did I have to stick to such a silly promise? I left the window and walked into the toilet, where I put on some lipstick in order to make myself look better. Then I flew straight down the stairs.

I suddenly appeared on the training ground. One of the horses there, a purplish roan, raised its head skywards and neighed. The horsemen were simply dumbstruck. They looked incredulously at me and stopped drinking their beer. I walked up to them and bowed my head, saying: "*Zhaxideleg.* "

They hastily returned the salute, some murmuring "*Zhaxideleg*" and others crying "*Ni hao*" (hello). A wave of confusion swept through the entire crowd.

I walked through them and then stood still before Gyamco. The poor man greeted me with both surprise and joy! I raised my face towards him and asked, "Would you give me a riding lesson?"

Gyamco burst out roaring: "Hah!"

He lifted me up at once and placed me on the back of his bay horse. He held the reins in his hand, and called for beer with an energetic wave of his arm.

The training ground was bubbling with excitement again. The other men were overjoyed for the bet they had lost. Boxes of beer now piled up in approximity to Gyamco whom almost everyone wanted to give a punch of admiration. Gyamco looked around him and then declared: "Come on, pals, let's drink the beer together."

His teammates asked in unison: "What about Kang Zhu?"

I said, "Of course, I'll treat you to drinks, too."

The boys chorused: "Great! Great!"

Then Gyamco helped me off his horse. He tore off the cap of bottle after bottle with his teeth. I toasted the horsemen one by one. They were all Tibetans, and each had an amazing capacity for drink. After they gulped the stuff down, they toasted me in turn. They raised their bottles level with their eyebrows and began singing a drink-toasting song. They made as if to go on singing forever unless I agreed to their request. What a devastating trick this was! I was left with no choice but to go ahead and put myself through the ordeal. The young horsemen began to dance Gorzhuang, singing and drinking! I was deeply moved and joined in the festivity myself. Formerly I had used to indulge in disco or cheek-to-cheek dancing, and had never taken a fancy to that prudish stuff called "social dancing." Now I discovered a new way of dancing which I really loved: Gorzhuang. For the sake of our joy and our friendship, to express an inner pleasure which words could never define, we swung up our arms and kicked out our legs, we hopped and bounced energetically— we used no artificial lights, special floor, costumes or hi-fi e-quipment—and we had great natural rhythm and voice. For most of us Han people, dancing was awkward, almost play-acting. Here dancing was not an activity—dancing was pure joy! I lost myself in joy, as I danced with staggering steps under the influence of a low fever and alcohol. Gyamco stayed close by, fearing that something might unexpectedly happen to me.

But I managed without mishap.

So at last, Gyamco triumphantly taught me how to ride a horse. This was something I had always dreamed of doing since early childhood. I admired those who could manage a horse with thorough confidence and grace. But when I got on horseback myself, I found that even a saddle provided no comfort at all. Although it was padded with a piece of leather the thing still hurt a great deal. And the stirrups were not easy to get accustomed to either. Soon after the horse began trotting, a big hole appeared on one of my silk socks which were rubbing against the brass stirrups. The horse's back was much broader than I had imagined, so I had to split my legs wide apart, leaving no strength in them to hold the horse securely in between. Before the animal could go much further and the men could stop cheering, I blacked out and fell down head first.

Horseman Gyamco thus stepped into the period of my life in Lhasa, and sure enough he was a Kamba man alright.

Gyamco said, "I must help cure your illness."

Gyamco took me to the Jokhang Temple with five bottles of yak butter in his hands, and asked me to pour a small spoon of yak butter into each and every perpetually lit altar lamp that I could reach.

I said, "Are you joking, Gyamco? There are as many altar lamps in the temple as there are stars in the night sky."

Gyamco appeared somewhat displeased. He asked sulkily, "You think this is a joke?"

I said, "What is it then?"

Gyamco said, "You know you have offended the gods, but saying fine words alone is no remedy for this. You should show your repentance through action."

I thought it over and agreed.

So I added yak butter to the lamps in the temple one by one.

After this was done I just wanted to sit down and rest, but Gyamco said we should first make a vow to Buddha.

I was taken under the biggest statue of the Buddha in the temple and made to kneel before it. I didn't know how to make a vow, so Gyamco urged me to repeat the prayers after him.

Gyamco murmured in a whisper, "I am Kang Zhu."

I echoed, "I am Kang Zhu."

"I am Han."

"I am Han."

"I have through carelessness offended the gods."

"I have through carelessness offended the gods."

"I beg my Tibetan friend Gyamco to pray for me. May I be forgiven and the punishment for my wrongdoing kindly withdrawn."

I couldn't help laughing at this, but under Gyamco's grave stare I repeated his words just the same: "I beg my Tibetan friend Gyamco to pray for me. May I be forgiven and the punishment for my wrongdoing kindly withdrawn."

Gyamco went on: "Gyamco will chant the six-syllable mantra and prostrate and kowtow continually at the entrance of the Jokhang Temple from sunset today till sunrise tomorrow."

I was astonished to hear this!

Prostrating oneself fully was no different from doing push-ups in the eyes of us Han people. You had to lie down on your stomach and kowtow, get back on your feet, lie down and kowtow again, get back on your feet again, and so on and so forth. Meanwhile, you must chant the mantra too. If this was only repeated a couple of times it wouldn't be much. But how could one do this the whole night through!

I exclaimed: "Gyamco!"

Gyamco looked puzzled. "What's the matter again? Just follow me and finish praying."

I said, "How could you promise to do such a thing for a whole night without asking me first? I'm not going to let you do it!"

Gyamco said, "Then shall I do it for two nights?"

I was annoyed and shouted at him: "Gyamco!"

Gyamco said, "How come you're so stubborn? Prostrating and kowtowing for one whole night is the least we must do. Once my dad's stomach was upset. To help him I did that for three days and nights. If only you have piety and perseverance, what is a night of bowing? Fine words will get you nowhere. If you really want to reach for Buddha and be saved, how can you spare yourself in your plea for mercy?"

During the last part of his speech he switched back to his native tongue to express his feelings more fully. Then he realized that I didn't know Tibetan at all, so he tried to translate his words into awkward Chinese.

At last I said, "All right, do it then."

I lay prone on the rush hassock and murmured to the all-knowing Buddha, "Gyamco will chant the six-syllable mantra and prostrate and kowtow continually at the entrance of the Jokhang Temple from sunset today till sunrise tomorrow."

A huge round and bright, cold moon came up. Dogs scampered all over the place, fanatically, in the moonlight. It was night in Lhasa.

Summer nights in Lhasa are very cold. I nestled on the vestibule of the temple, wearing Gyamco's long sheepskin coat, covering my head with my woolen shawl, with only my eyes showing.

Not far off was Gyamco the great horserider—Gyamco the valiant Kamba man and true friend beyond compare. Over and over, he lay face down and touched his head on the ground earnestly yet with a quiet dignity, murmuring "*an-ma-ni-ba-mi-hong.*" Although I was only an arm's length away, he couldn't

quite see me. I had no way to catch his unseeing eyes, so I had
to content myself with the fine luster off his deep-colored
cheeks. The crimson doors to the temple were now closed.
Tranquillity reigned. The square only a short distance away was
paved with cement, a modern building material. In 1990 the sacred fire of the 11th Asian Games was kindled here. Only the
shiny gray slabstones seemed to be moving like animated objects
in concert with Gyamco's towering form. To be truthful, I
couldn't appreciate the magical powers of religion, though I
wished I could. As I saw it, all that was currently passing before
my eyes was worldly, practical and ordinary. By what means,
then, did this young Tibetan man achieve his communion with
the gods?

I wasn't sleepy at all. I fixed my gaze on Gyamco, then
looked away towards the square. I looked at one of the windows
in which a light suddenly came on and then died out. I looked at
the whole of Lhasa during its night. I compared myself with
Gyamco and came to believe that he was a truly blissful man. He
had faith, so could always find himself a place for dispelling ill-
nesses and cares of all kinds. Such a place would never come
within my reach. I believed Tibet to be a piece of hallowed
earth, but people like me had no way to enter that realm. For
example, I could never prostrate myself and pray all night for a
friend taken ill. And, whereas I would always remember this
wonderful night in Lhasa, it would be because of my true friend
Gyamco, not because of the gods we had come to worship. Later in my life when I brought up this Lhasa story—the gods forgive me—I would only mention it as an entertaining tale, with a
cigarette held between two fingers. As for the likes of Mou Linsen, I hated them yet couldn't walk out on them; I was disap-

pointed and hurt that they could be so unsympathetic and irresponsible, but I admired their bold and uninhibited ways. Under their influence, I would soon learn to turn a cold heart to friendship, love and responsibility, and head off to any place I liked with no regard for anybody.

My heart feels desolate when I think of all this. Oh Gyamco, your friendship was misplaced on an ungrateful woman.

To my surprise, my fever was totally gone by the time I got up from my bed to watch the horsemen train the next afternoon.

I invited Gyamco to a meal in return for the great kindness he had shown me.

He was both confused and dissatisfied about all this. Throughout the dinner he looked restrained and cheerless. In the middle of it he pulled off his shoes, and this caused a foul smell to rise. I pretended not to mind, but I couldn't swallow one more bite of the food. The other customers in the restaurant cast sidelong glances at us, and Gyamco obviously sensed the tension.

He asked, "Why are they looking at us?"

I said, "Who knows? Don't worry about it."

He said angrily, "How can I go on eating?"

I said, "Well, you just go on eating with your mouth."

He said, "If you really want me to eat, you should get some buttered tea for me."

I called to one of the waitresses, "Bring some buttered tea please."

The waitress said, "I'm sorry, but we don't serve buttered tea."

Gyamco said, "In that case, let's go to a teahouse, then."

We left the restaurant. Gyamco took me through a narrow

lane and soon we found a teahouse. The wooden benches in the
house were greasy black, and the top of the table was covered
completely with flies, but there was hot buttered tea!

However, I couldn't bring myself to drink this tea. I wasn't
used to the taste of it, and more importantly I wouldn't drink
from a bowl which had just been ridden with flies.

Gyamco cheered up a little, and he asked, "Tell me why those
foreigners and Han people looked so curiously at us."

I said, "OK, I'll tell you, but you mustn't get angry with
me."

Gyamco said, "I won't. With such fine tea to drink, how
could I get angry?"

I told him that those people had looked at him because his
running shoes had an odor.

He suddenly understood, saying, "Oh, that! Why couldn't I
take my shoes off if I didn't feel comfortable in them?"

I chuckled.

Gyamco sighed, "People in this world are getting more and
more bossy."

He declared flatly, "But I love to take off my shoes, and I
will go on doing it in the future. No one can stop me."

I agreed with him on that. So long as we remained harmless
socially, nobody should prevent us from doing what we liked. A
small bit of odor does no real harm. Yet not without some regret
I thought, "If Gyamco didn't have this habit, that would be
nice."

From a very long dream I switched back into partial wakeful-
ness. For a minute or so I couldn't even tell what time it was and
where I was.

Mou Linsen, with a denser growth of beard on his face than when he had left Lhasa days before, was sunk deep in my sofa browsing through a book.

I slowly sat up with the quilts still piled around my back, and looked all around me, trying to make the distinction between dream and reality.

Mou Linsen said, "Hello, Kang Zhu."

I said, "Hello."

Then I realized that here was Mou Linsen who had just returned from Ngari. I heard myself saying, "Why, Mou Linsen, it's really you!"

Mou Linsen appeared to be somewhat moved. He tossed the book to the floor and walked straight over to me. I extended my arms in a sudden burst of feeling, too. We made to hug each other like lovers, but when we scrutinized each other at closer quarters, this mutual attempt at intimacy suddenly crumbled. We both saw that between us there would be no hugging any more. With swift inspiration, I made a show of reaching towards my shawl. Mou Linsen for his part only patted my head lightly. Both of us were somewhat distressed and disappointed, but made a show of looking indifferent nonetheless.

Mou Linsen said, "It seems we were right to leave you in Lhasa. The doctors sure knew better than the rest of us, anyway. With the flush in your cheeks, you look terrific!"

His words thoroughly sobered me up. I jumped off my bed and, not finding my shoes, dashed barefoot to the window.

Gyamco was looking up at my window.

I waved energetically to him, loudly declaring, "There's no fever today, I'm just fine now!"

Gyamco grinned back triumphantly. He cracked a whip in the

air and went tearing off into the distance with his teammates, raising a storm of noisy elation.

Behind me, Mou Linsen clapped his hands in glum and icy appreciation, saying, "That's great, carrying on with a Kamba man like that."

"Don't talk nonsense," I said. "Don't you talk about Gyamco in that trashy way you and I used to!"

Mou Linsen said, "Well, well, it looks like true love."

I said, "To cure my illness, Gyamco kowtowed and prayed in front of the Jokhang Temple for a whole night. What right do you have to ridicule him?"

Mou Linsen said, "Kowtowing all night? What a strong man!"

I interrupted him, "Mou Linsen, I'm serious. If you go on scoffing at Gyamco, don't blame me for getting angry!"

Mu Linsen had never seen such a serious expression on my face. Never. Before, in his eyes, I had been no more than another modern, happy-go-lucky type of girl who ran after any celebrity.

He looked me up and down for a while, then said, "You do seem to have improved a lot during these few days."

I got confused under his gaze. I said, "OK, OK, tell me something about Ngari. Is it really a no-man's land up there?"

Mou Linsen instantly resumed his contempt for me, saying, "Why should I talk about Ngari with a woman? All women know is that love-dovey, you-be-good-to-me, I'll-be-good-to-you stuff."

Mou Linsen lit a cigarette and waited silently for my counter-attack. As a speaker I was no match for him. He never treated me as his equal. On the strength of his gender, age, experience and knowledge about the world, he always patronized me from those commanding heights.

Without bothering to take up the challenge, I bent down to look for my shoes. They were well under the bed. Mou Linsen must have come close to my bedside while I was asleep. I wondered whether, once or twice in his life at least, he had watched a sleeping young woman with some real love. I couldn't understand this society of men. We didn't have a chance to see love films such as *Waterloo Bridge* till after the country's opening and reform. We couldn't stop our tears during the two hours we sat in the cinema, but as soon as we were on the streets, it was as if it were another world. We never got to go through a time when flowers of this kind blossomed. We went from feudal stories of crying women forced into bridal chairs almost straight into cynical hedonism. Men shook off all the responsibilities and conscience they used to have towards women. They tried shirk any responsibility, kept changing their minds about what they liked or wanted, and never bothered to carry out a promise they themselves had made. They thought I was young and didn't understand things, whereas I thought it beneath me to argue with them. The one simple, effective way to deal with them was to break with them and find someone new. I could always find a new boyfriend—there were enough fish in the sea. So if Li Xiaofei left, there was still Mou Linsen, and if Mou Linsen left, wasn't there Wu Shuang? If Li Xiaofei could not hurt me, how possibly then could Mou Linsen?

I pulled out the shoes from under the bed and put them on. Then I slipped out into the corridor, shouting, "Wu Shuang, Wu Shuang!"

Wu Shuang immediately appeared out of his room. As expected, he had a very tanned face now—where skin had peeled off, dark and light patches showed, like he had developed lupus during his stay in Nagqu.

Wu Shuang said, "Has your illness gone?"

"Yes," I said.

Wu Shuang said, "I've been worried about you all these days, even feeling very guilty. Maybe we shouldn't have left you alone in Lhasa—that was most inhumane. While in Nagqu I tried to call you, but they couldn't put me through."

Mou Linsen quoted from a folksong, ironically, "To a distant maiden I would write, but there's no postman to carry my words of love her way."

"No," Wu Shuang said a bit embarrassed, "I never thought of writing to her."

I got Wu Shuang to sit down beside me, and pressed him to tell me things about Nagqu.

Mou Linsen stubbed out his cigarette in the ashtray, and said mockingly, "Well, it seems there's something in that popular saying after all."

Wu Shuang asked, "Which one?"

Mou Linsen said, "In dealing with a woman, one should always bestow small favors on her and never show her real, great benevolence."

Wu Shuang said, "Are you saying I'm giving small favors?"

I acted as if I didn't hear their words, and continued questioning Wu Shuang about his travels in Nagqu. Then Li Xiaofei and Lan Ye pulled their door open and stepped out together in the diminishing light of dusk.

Lan Ye said pre-emptively, "Hello, dear, we didn't know you were ill. But you look perfectly fine now."

I said sarcastically, "But you don't look enough so, my sweet.

The shadows under your eyes show that you might have indulged yourself too much. Are you engaged yet?"

Li Xiaofei ran to Lan Ye's rescue. "I haven't seen you for quite some time. Can we hug each other just this once?"

I said, "No problem!"

I clasped Li Xiaofei tightly and wouldn't let go of him. Not daring to look into my eyes, he only muttered anxiously, "Don't be foolish, let me go."

But I didn't let him go, until he said with a whine, "Have some mercy on me, your ladyship!"

Everyone burst out laughing. I shoved Li Xiaofei towards Lan Ye. He stepped on her feet, and she bounced off to one side in an alarm more exaggerated than real. The rest of us laughed again.

All of this was deadly boring! I lit a cigarette for myself and puffed at it several times. Then I walked over to the window. There wasn't a single soul left on the training ground.

Mou Linsen approached the window too. He stood behind me for a moment, then put his arms around my shoulders and said, "Come on, let's go out to eat."

We dined at a local restaurant called Star of the Plateau. A friend of Mou Linsen's soon joined us there. He had brought us five airline tickets for ten o'clock the next morning. I didn't like this guy who had provided us with such efficient help, and flatly refused to chat with him during the meal. This greatly befuddled him. On our way, Wu Shuang had proposed that we invite Gyamco to eat with us. Mou Linsen had vetoed the idea, saying that only the five of us should go tonight so we could enjoy our long-awaited Han food among ourselves. He had emphasized that we could invite Gyamco some other day and treat him to the best Tibetan food in Lhasa. I had thought Mou Linsen was telling the truth. But as soon as we were seated around the table after we arrived there, his friend turned up with our tickets. So they had already fixed everything up long before dinner.

Mou Linsen did not give Gyamco a second thought. Nor did Wu Shuang. The moment he saw so much delicious food he forgot everything else. There was even less need to mention Li Xiaofei and Lan Ye—they were a totally licentious, disgusting, mercenary, snobbish, honey-mouthed and dagger-hearted, foul-smelling couple! The very thought that for a time I had actually had a relationship with Li Xiaofei made my flesh creep.

They had left an ailing girl to her own resources here in Lhasa, and enjoyed themselves elsewhere, as much as if nothing had happened. Now they comforted themselves by thinking that I was totally recovered, completely disregarding the fact that someone had helped me generously during their absence; that in helping me he had actually helped them all. Suppose something had happened to me, or that I had still been ill, then the entire company wouldn't be enjoying such a satisfactory meal tonight!

Chewing on these thoughts, my mood changed from bad to worse.

Mou Linsen ordered almost all the Han-style dishes on the menu. Then everyone fell on the food like hungry wolves, clamoring that ours was after all the best food.

After the first round of food and drinks, Mou Linsen asked Lan Ye to sing songs for our friend who had secured the airline tickets for us. Lan Ye said, "But I'm afraid I can't sing very well."

Li Xiaofei said, "You're a professional. If you can't sing

well, who can?"

Mou Linsen said, "Come on Lan Ye, don't keep us waiting."

Lan Ye smiled politely. "Since you all insist, I'll have to make a fool of myself and sing."

Wu Shuang whispered in my ear, "Her show of nervousness exposes her lack of grace—she may be pretty but she's not very appealing."

I didn't utter a word. I was still drowning in the depths of despair, ashamed and depressed—that we as a group could be so heartless in our treatment of a friend such as Gyamco.

Amid the flashing lights from the automated musical fountain, Lan Ye sashayed her way onto the karaoke platform. Seeing it was her moment of crowning glory, she puffed her chest out, swayed her hips, and glanced flirtatiously this way and that way, fully revealing herself as a cheap, third-rate actress. Only Li Xiaofei was overcome and not disgusted by her superficial charms—Mou Linsen, Wu Shuang and I all shifted our eyes from the display.

The first number Lan Ye presented was "A Loving Couple Returning Home Together." It was her favorite song, which could also best express how she felt at this particular moment. When she began with, "Two birds perch on the tree together; green hills and winding streams show their smiling faces," she sounded breathtakingly melodious and enticing. All the customers in the dining-hall gasped in admiration and then burst into thunderous applause.

Mou Linsen, Wu Shuang and Mou Linsen's friend, each with a cigarette between his fingers and a glass of draft beer in his hand, were chatting volubly about Ngari and Nagqu: "Ngari might well be the last piece of land on earth still unpolluted by modern civilization." "Ngari boasts the highest mountains and the remotest sources of water." "The high altitude and the strenuous climate of Nagqu were beyond what one could imagine." "Nagqu's grasslands, yaks, tin houses and blizzards were ever so unforgettable!"

I kept on smoking cigarettes. With my coarse, showy woolen shawl draped over my shoulders, with the lipstick on my lips gone, and crouching moodily in my chair, I smoked one cigarette after another. In those days of seclusion I had forgotten all about tobacco. Gyamco didn't even know I could smoke. Now that I was back among my peers, I craved it again. I waited intently. How desperately I wished they would speak about Gyamco. If only they would let me tell stories about him! But they didn't.

Mou Linsen snatched away the tenth cigarette I was smoking. He said, "What the hell do you think you're doing, Kang Zhu? You're behaving like a hoodlum."

I said, "So what? So be it..."

Wu Shuang said, "Kang Zhu, behave a little, OK?"

I turned to face Wu Shuang and said, "Not OK!"

"Why should I behave if you guys don't?" I added.

Neither Mou Linsen nor Wu Shuang answered my question.

I demanded, "Give me the cigarette."

I thought Mou Linsen wouldn't grant my request, but he did. He tossed the cigarette and his lighter over to me, then went on talking about his trip to Ngari.

Nobody tried to stop me from smoking, so I couldn't stop. I puffed away on my cigarette amid Lan Ye's sounds of singing, until my lips became chapped. There was a bitter taste through my whole body, from the heart to the lungs to the stomach to

the mouth. I thought about how I might bid farewell to Gyamco. The airline tickets had come, and tomorrow I would have to
go. But now I was squandering these remaining hours here in a
karaoke bar. Repeatedly I urged myself to stand up and walk
out, to go to Gyamco's home and tell him that I had to leave
soon, that I did appreciate everything he had done for me as a
true friend. Yet time trickled by and I couldn't get up. I didn't
go to Gyamco's home, and in fact didn't dare to, because I
didn't want to complicate matters, or to turn a simple matter into something like a melodramatic scene in a movie. When I rose
to my feet, if Mou Linsen or any of them would have gone with
me to Gyamco's, everything would have been fine! But they
didn't.

When we returned to our rooms it was past midnight. Although Mou Linsen escorted me all along the way, my spirits
sank still further.

Sitting on my bed with my hands cupped around my knees, I
silently turned things over in my mind.

Lan Ye had not come back to our room to sleep any of the
previous nights, but she made an exception tonight. She looked
cheerful and bright, humming lilting tunes as she undressed and
took a shower. She flitted all around the room wearing a feminine embroidered silk nightgown and sorted through her belong-
ings to pack them. She spread out all her newly bought Tibetan
jewels on her bed, tried them on one by one, and posed in front
of me after each new one, asking: "How does this one look? Do
you like it?"

At first I just said it looked very nice, then I stopped respond-
ing to her. But the thick-skinned woman kept asking: "Does it

look nice? Does this?"

I said, "Could you please just leave me alone?"

Lan Ye bit into her lower lip and giggled. "So what's on your mind then?"

Lan Ye continued, "To be frank, Mou Linsen is much more of a man than Li Xiaofei—he has both fame and fortune. Anyway, we're merely having fun together—who can tell who'll be with who in the future?"

I said, "Oh, give me a break!"

Lan Ye said, "So this must be over Gyamco then. Even less reason for heartbreak. Kamba men may be especially handsome to be sure, but it's said they beat their wives, eat barley flour, drink buttered tea, and live in tents... How could we Han people endure such a life?"

I stared daggers at Lan Ye, but this didn't stop her from prattling on. She said, "Have you ever sneaked into that Kamba man's tent? If you want to, I can accompany you there and afterwards keep my mouth shut about it all."

I took a big mouthful of water and held it in my mouth, and at the same time beckoned Lan Ye to draw closer to me. When she reached me with a puzzled look on her face, I spat this water all over her face. She fled in panic, her bewitching face and her seductive nightgown soaked through.

When Mou Linsen, Wu Shuang and Li Xiaofei rushed into the room, I was wailing as loudly as Lan Ye was.

It was half past six in the morning, though the sky hadn't lit up yet. Here in Lhasa, the sun would not rise till after nine. Mou Linsen constantly knocked at the door to nag me. Lan Ye, who had gone back into Li Xiaofei's bed the night before, was now still nestled in his arms. Together they sat on the steps in front of the hotel, and she seemed to be basking in his stream of soothing words.

Provided that we set off at half past six we would surely be able to arrive at the Gonggar Airport before eight. There was still enough time left. But again and again Mou Linsen and Wu Shuang urged the rest of us to hurry and get in the jeep. They appeared as if they were dying to return home, so much so that they behaved like they were honoring a pledge to be punctual. After what had happened between me and Lan Ye they must have become more aware than ever of what I had been so unhappy about. They obviously did not want to think about Gyamco. Whereas Mou Linsen knew all of this in his heart, he deliberately made a show of knowing nothing at all. He looked at Gyamco in the way he had done Tibet's mountains, lakes, temples, grasslands and vast blue sky. We were tourists, we'd paid our way—see all the sights to satisfy our curiosity, then move on. How could he or they behave so unfeelingly!

Through the window I saw them get into the jeep, but I lay back onto my bed and didn't stir an inch.

Wu Shuang came upstairs to call me again. I shammed sleep and didn't respond to him. He was so anxious that he was wringing his hands unconsciously. He said, "Do get up, Kang Zhu. Please. I'm willing to apologize to you for all four of us. I know we behaved rather shamefully."

Mou Linsen barged into the room and said, "Come on, Wu Shuang, what are you gabbing with her about?!"

Mou Linsen dragged me up from the bed, rushed me downstairs and squeezed me into the jeep, saying in a self-righteous tone, "You women got no bloody brains but a lot of gall! You even dare fool around and risk missing the plane."

But of course it turned out that Mou Linsen had been only too fussy about being on time for the plane. Everything went smoothly on our way, and the jeep raced forward like a shot arrow. Well within an hour we arrived at the airport. By the time we climbed out of the jeep, the sky had barely turned pale blue.

The airport lounge was packed with people of all races, Han, Tibetan, and other Chinese national minorities, and foreigners. The myriad of human odors blended together to assail our nostrils. The Tibetans seated themselves on the ground in circles, some drinking buttered tea, others eating barley-cakes, still others producing roasted legs of mutton from the folds of their clothes and savoring them. We quickly withdrew, and crowded back into the enclosed space in front of the lounge. There we stood or sat down on our baggage. It was very cold outdoors, and we were each wearing clothes of all lengths, which made us look like clowns. Everyone talked, smoked or tried to get some warmth by hugging themselves and stamping their feet on the ground. They looked relaxed, indifferent and carefree—all we needed to do now was to get on the plane and go home.

I wrapped my famous shawl tightly around my shoulders, and walked off to one side with a lit cigarette in my hand.

It was bit by bit getting lighter. I was leaving Tibet in less than no time. This afternoon, Gyamco would look up at my window as usual but find that I was no longer there. I hadn't even said goodbye to him before leaving. His teammates' faces would be gloomy? I could see them.

Wu Shuang walked over and said, "Kang Zhu."

I turned around to look at him.

Wu Shuang said, "Kang Zhu, I've just found a public phone

booth over there. Shall I go there with you to make a call?"

I looked away from Wu Shuang, my eyes brimming over with tears. I nodded my agreement.

After the two of us got out of their sight, Wu Shuang said solemnly, "Listen here, Kang Zhu. It was Mou Linsen who thought of calling Gyamco, not me."

He went on, "To be honest with you, I really think it will do just to make a phone call to him. We've had no time to meet with him, and we've had no need to. It will be much better to keep him in your memory than politely invite him to dinner out of politeness. It's not like you and Gyamco have gone so far as to fall in love?"

Wu Shuang was waiting earnestly for an answer.

I said, "Not quite. I'm just so ashamed of ourselves! Are we not just faithless, and ungrateful?!"

Wu Shuang agreed, "Yes, that's so. How did we ever become this way—unable to carry out a responsibility or make a commitment, not in a position to fend for ourselves nor to rely on others. But that's the way we are."

I said, "Don't say anymore—let's just make a call now."

I dialed to the Sports Commission and got Gyamco on the phone without much difficulty. I said, "I'm leaving. I'm sorry I don't have time to see you before I go. I got the plane ticket last night."

I continued, "Gyamco, I just want to let you know I'm very, very grateful to you!"

Gyamco cut me short by asking, "Where are you now?"

I said, "At Gonggar Airport."

Gyamco asked, "What time are you leaving?"

I said, "Ten."

Gyamco said, "Wait a moment then."

He immediately hung up.

I called the same number once again, but Gyamco was already gone.

I sat on my baggage and lit another cigarette. I blew the light plumes of smoke towards the mountains and grasslands in the distance. Mou Linsen walked over to take the cigarette from my lips and raise a cup of hot milk to them. I obediently took the cup and drank from it.

Mou Linsen ran his fingers through my hair, saying, "I knew you were a good girl."

I tilted my head to look at Mou Linsen, thinking hard over the words uttered by Wu Shuang: "We neither can carry out a responsibility nor make a commitment, fend for ourselves nor rely on others."

Mou Linsen looked back at me. After a long while he found his voice again: "I'm sorry, Kang Zhu."

With that he turned and walked away. I accepted his apology in total silence.

With the blue sky and white clouds brightening up, prayer flags had begun to flutter in the wind and dust to rise. The streets and roads were again bustling with human activity. Vehicles came and went. The Tibetan men and women walked by slowly, rattling prayer-wheels in their hands. They possessed a singleness of mind, being at peace with the world, as though their bodies were on this world but their hearts were not. They made their way to the Potala Palace, Jokhang Temple, Sera Monastery, Zhaibang Monastery, and many other holy sites. Step by step, they have a long long way to go on a long long

road, through spring, fall, winter, summer, then what...?
Thinking of all this, wave upon wave of sorrow churned up from
deep in my heart. Couldn't it just be that we all must have faith
before we can keep to promises, before we can entrust ourselves
to any of our fellow beings?

Lan Ye looked at her watch again, and said loudly to Mou
Linsen, "It's time we checked in and got our boarding passes."

Li Xiaofei stopped Lan Ye. He said to Mou Linsen and Wu
Shuang, "That Gyamco, or what's-his-name, must be quite an
interesting person. I'd like to see him just once."

I suddenly stood up, giving them all a start. I felt as if I was
hearing the distant sound of a horse galloping towards us. I
craned my neck in order to see better, and everyone else, in surprise, did the same. We didn't see anything, however, so we
had to sit down again.

Mou Linsen said, "Fuck!"

I asked them to go and get their boarding passes first, and
then wait in the lounge. The three men didn't agree. What kept
them waiting out here was curiosity, rather than any genuine
feeling of guilt. The premonition that I had had of Gyamco racing down on a horse shocked them in a profound way.

Mou Linsen said, "Darting on horseback between the city's
restaurants, bars and cars to see someone off at the airport—
now, that's really something!"

Li Xiaofei wouldn't buy the story—he assured Mou Linsen
that Gyamco most probably would get here by taxi.

Wu Shuang said that he would rather see Gyamco race down
on horseback. "Wouldn't that be miraculous indeed!"

In the middle of everybody's speculation, a magnificent gold-
en steed emerged on the grassland, cut across the highway and

raced towards the airport! I jumped up and waved my arms desperately: "Gyamco! Gyamco!"

Gyamco didn't stop his horse until it came right in front of us. His ruddy face and the sturdy front legs of his steed flashed before my eyes, as I was lifted up from the earth's surface. Gyamco grabbed me onto the saddle as if he were picking up a lamb. He sat behind me with one of his big hands securely clasping my waist. Then he cracked his whip and galloped back towards the grassland. During this split second, I heard Mou Linsen, Wu Shuang, Li Xiaofei and Lan Ye cry out in dismay: "Hey! Hey!"

I was flying and flying, over a vast expanse of green grassland!

Gyamco said, "I promised to see you off, and now I'm here to do it. I promised also that I would let you have a good taste of horse-riding."

I was at a loss for words.

One side of the grassland was an immense, gentle slope. Above the slope was Tibet's perfectly clear, blue sky. Under the sky stood several trees. All through the trees hung prayer flags. The wind blew past my cheeks, rattling the big earrings I was wearing. What with the horse jolting, I felt my blood boiling all through my body. A flying horse was not easy for me to ride— my ankles hurt very much as they constantly rubbed against the stirrups, and my thighs and buttocks felt as if they were being bumped against or dismembered. But in my heart I was only too happy! Wasn't it true that deep within every woman there lay dormant a dream where she was carried off by a handsome young man riding a fine horse? It was so ancient, so unrealistic a dream that we youth of the 1990s had completely forgotten it. Now, all of a sudden, Gyamco was here to fulfill this dream for us. Not only for me, but for us. My companions were standing on tiptoe looking towards the grassland and waving their arms. Many other passengers also crowded into the square—they pointed towards us and clapped their hands enthusiastically.

Tears streamed down my face and trickled down into the earth. I knew such a thing could happen to a woman only once in her whole lifetime! Gyamco was bestowing on me as a woman the most classic of honors.

Then he brought me back to the airport. He gently placed me back among my companions and said loudly to all of us: "*Zhaxideleg*!"

With that he turned his horse around and sped off into the distance. Cars almost piled up on the highway, as they screeched to a stop, with smoke filling the air.

After we got the boarding passes, we joined the queue waiting to go through the security check. My legs trembled so much that I could hardly walk. Mou Linsen and Wu Shuang had to prop me up from both sides.

As we went through security, the woman officer asked, "What's wrong with her?!"

Mou Linsen answered, "She has just re-emerged from a fairy tale."

The moment before we actually boarded the plane, Lan Ye made up with me. She sat down beside me and said, "If I were you I would choose not to leave Tibet."

I smiled quietly towards Lan Ye.

It was not for me to stay on in any one place. I had lots of other places to go. I wanted to see a great many things with my own eyes. I didn't have a permanent job, I couldn't support my-

self economically, and I was no good at solving difficult problems. I could no more carry out a responsibility or commit myself on any issue than the rest of them could. What did Lan Ye
know, after all!

The plane was soaring into the sky. I had asked to be given a
seat by the window. Now I pressed my face against the window
and looked out on Tibet's mountains and hills, grasslands, red-
walled temples, and a highway buried in a deep valley. To one
side of the highway I saw that same grassland and slope of hill.
On the hilltop, a handsome young man on horseback stood there
motionless. That was Gyamco!

Oh, my horseman Gyamco!

I kept gazing at him till thick white clouds blanketed the
earth's surface.

At that moment some poetic lines, which I had come across
during my stay in Lhasa, quietly revealed themselves:

Ah, this grassland—a boundless ocean, a starry sky!
Ah, this grassland—a herdsman's song, a lover!
Till the end of time, to the ends of the world,
My love is bottomless, boundless.
I've long dreamed of dying at the height of my heart's passion,
... But why is my dream but a dream, oh, why?

30 September 1994, Wuhan
Translated by Wang Weidong

图书在版编目（CIP）数据

不谈爱情/池莉著；王明杰等译．－北京：外文出版社，2004
（熊猫丛书）
ISBN 7-119-03663-7

Ⅰ．不…　Ⅱ．①池…②王…　Ⅲ．①中篇小说－作品集－中国－当代－英
文②短篇小说－作品集－中国－当代－英文　Ⅳ．I247.7

中国版本图书馆 CIP 数据核字（2004）第 025605 号

外文出版社网址：
　http://www.flp.com.cn
外文出版社电子信箱：
　info@flp.com.cn
　sales@flp.com.cn

熊猫丛书

不谈爱情

作　　者　池　莉
译　　者　王明杰等
责任编辑　陈海燕　李　芳
封面设计　唐少文
印刷监制　张国祥
出版发行　外文出版社
社　　址　北京市百万庄大街 24 号　　　邮政编码　100037
电　　话　（010）68320579（总编室）
　　　　　（010）68329514/68327211（推广发行部）
印　　刷　北京市密云春雷印刷厂
经　　销　新华书店/外文书店
开　　本　大 32 开
印　　数　0001—5000 册　　　　　　印　张　11.375
版　　次　2005 年第 1 版第 1 次印刷
装　　别　平
书　　号　ISBN 7-119-03663-7
　　　　　10－E－3607P
定　　价　16.00 元